THE TRIDENT AND THE PEARL

THE FISHER KING: BOOK ONE

SARAH K. L. WILSON

orbit-books.co.uk

ORBIT

First published in Great Britain in 2026 by Orbit

1 3 5 7 9 10 8 6 4 2

Copyright © 2026 by Sarah K. L. Wilson

Maps by Tim Paul

The moral right of the author has been asserted.

All characters and events in this publication, other than those clearly in the public domain, are fictitious and any resemblance to real persons, living or dead, is purely coincidental.

All rights reserved.
No part of this publication may be reproduced, stored in a retrieval system, or transmitted, in any form or by any means, without the prior permission in writing of the publisher, nor be otherwise circulated in any form of binding or cover other than that in which it is published and without a similar condition including this condition being imposed on the subsequent purchaser.

A CIP catalogue record for this book
is available from the British Library.

ISBN 978-0-356-52860-1

Printed and bound in Great Britain by Clays Ltd, Elcograf, S.p.A.

Papers used by Orbit are from well-managed forests
and other responsible sources.

Orbit
An imprint of
Little, Brown Book Group
Carmelite House
50 Victoria Embankment
London, EC4Y 0DZ

The authorised representative
in the EEA is
Hachette Ireland
8 Castlecourt Centre
Dublin 15, D15 XTP3, Ireland
(email: info@hbgi.ie)

An Hachette UK Company
www.hachette.co.uk

orbit-books.co.uk

THE TRIDENT AND THE PEARL

WHAT WOULD YOU HAVE OF ME, MORTAL QUEEN?

They aren't spoken words. They're the crash of the sea and the beating of the waves. They're the howl of souls caught up in the shaking power of the storm. And yet they make my heart race. I fight against a chattering jaw—my body's natural flinching from so great a glory washing against my mind. My will must be greater.

"Spare my people," I beg succinctly. "Still this storm."

WHAT BARGAIN WOULD YOU MAKE FOR THIS BOON?

I had thought I was not one to plead. How naive of me.

"What would you take, Lord?" I ask, choked. I dare not withhold anything.

YOUR FUTURE.

I swallow, looking again at the empty patch of ocean where my husband has disappeared. The grief swelling in my throat tells me he asks for too little, for already my future is lost to me. But if I am bargaining for lives, then I am bargaining for Lieve's life, too, if he is not yet lost. If there's even a chance he could survive this, then I must fight for it.

"Yes," I say so quickly that the word blurs into the storm. "All of it."

For those ruled by devouring gods

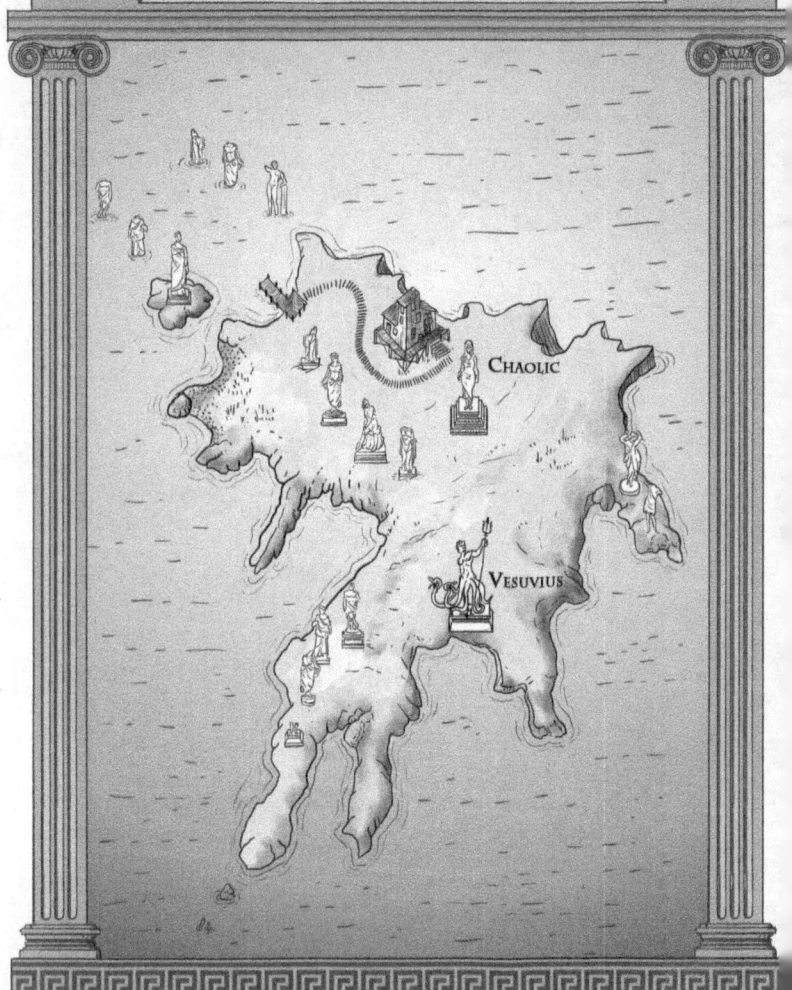

Chapter One

I was born into the embrace of the sea on a moonless night in the month of the Ragged Tides. My mother did not bleed out her life into the sea with my arrival, nor was my father visited by a terrible curse.

In fact, neither one of my parents passed away until the summer of the Year of the Peacock brought yellow fever to our fair shores. By then, I was a woman grown, and when I took up the Pearl Crown and settled the mantle of woven seed pearls over my shoulders, I did not need to have either cinched to accommodate me.

I was not forced into an arranged marriage to a man the age of my father, nor obliged to dance attendance on an emperor who might make demands on my kingdom if he couldn't make demands on my person. Instead, I married my childhood friend Lieve, a man of smiles and teasing jokes

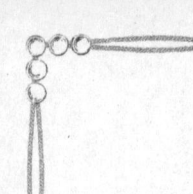

who filled our short marriage with laughter.

One might think I wasn't to be at the heart of a fairy tale at all. One would be wrong, as I was. And the discovery of how very wrong I was nearly became the end of me.

But I am getting ahead of myself.

This tale starts with the sea and with a storm.

If you've spent any time at the sea, you know its smell, but if you've spent time traveling *many* seas, then you know that the smell of the sea is different in every port. Here on the five Crocus Isles, the sea smells of brine and spices and a little of the honey-sweet crocuses that grow on all five islands.

"Coralys." Lieve's voice is rough, but it has to be to pierce through the howl of the wind.

My eyes snap to him. He sets the back of his knuckles against my cheek in a moment of public intimacy he'd never normally allow. He is always tightly controlled, my Lieve. Always a ship smartly rigged.

His brown eyes soften for a half a breath, he almost smiles, and then he brushes a kiss across my lips.

"I will be back shortly," he says, and I think this time that some of the roughness is emotion.

I tangle my fingers in his, unable to find words. If I beg him to be careful, it will only instill the idea that I doubt him. If I make him promise to come back to me, it will put weight on his shoulders that does not need to be there. If I tell him what an honor it has been to be his wife, it will feel like I am already reading his eulogy.

Or mine.

The Trident and the Pearl

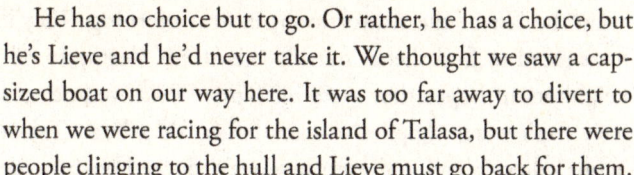

He has no choice but to go. Or rather, he has a choice, but he's Lieve and he'd never take it. We thought we saw a capsized boat on our way here. It was too far away to divert to when we were racing for the island of Talasa, but there were people clinging to the hull and Lieve must go back for them.

So, I muster a smile—seas and skies, where do I even find it?—and it seems to be enough.

Our fingers tighten. "I will be here," I say—my normal response when he leaves me, but today it feels like some kind of declaration. Some kind of challenge to the wind and seas that lash our islands with increasing furor.

I will be here, I tell them. I will not be moved. Keep trying all you want, you will not budge me.

"Your Serene Majesty." Turbote shifts from foot to foot just one step above me. His white beard is so wet it looks like the foam collecting in tufts on the edge of the sea. "Please. We must hurry. You dare not wait!"

Our fingers untangle and Lieve's strength slips away from me. He tosses a last warm look over his shoulder and then hurries down the steps. I'm memorizing him without meaning to, tracing his muscular shoulders and tight, lean frame. He's purpose come to life, leaning forward as he jogs back to the boat.

I wrench myself up another stair and away from him.

I try not to look back, but I do. Twice.

We sent away the last of the ships yesterday after the harbormaster brought me a fish with a coin in its mouth—a terrible omen of devastation for my people—and we sent

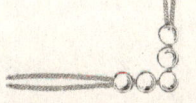

away the last of the seaworthy boats this morning. They'll have raced to find shelter outside this storm, fleeing to our neighbors in hopes they were hit lighter than we and still have fresh water supplies or piers left to tie a boat. Talasa is our tallest island and even here we'd docked against the temple steps halfway up the holy hill. The pier is deep below the waves.

Now, all we have remaining are boats so unseaworthy that they cannot be trusted to set out into the surf with our precious people for anything other than the shortest of journeys. They're all that's left to take Lieve out to search for those we saw stranded.

One more glance over my shoulder. I've lost sight of Lieve in a wall of blowing water. I try to tell myself I'll see him again, but my inner voice is a liar.

The storm has not relented in three days—not only that, it grows more angry as the hours pass, swelling up over our islands, battering every bit of our lives until they crumble and fail or sink beneath the furious waves. The line of dockside fish markets is nothing but matchsticks. The pottery market lost the roofs off every shop. My own palace is knee-deep in brackish water, the imported rugs ruined, the riches buried in the green brine of the sea.

We are already climbing the hundred stone steps faster than I imagined was possible. Turbote's wet robes slap his legs in an arrhythmic beat. He's panicked. He's *been* panicked since we left the main island on Lieve's wreck of a boat and came here to the island of Okeanos's Temple. The boat

doesn't carry many people. A mercy, perhaps. Instead of my entire council of bickering advisors, I am accompanied only by Turbote, my most annoying counselor and the priest of Okeanos.

Our ancestors carved the temple from stone, following the natural ebb and flow of the white rock bones of our islands. The steps swirl up like waves tousled by a benevolent breeze to where the temple rises—enormous in scale in a way that bids the worshipper to wonder if the gods had actually met man here once, and if this place had been carved to suit their size rather than ours.

At the center of the temple is a single statue of Okeanos, carved of white marble. If the god truly lives and if he looks like this, then I am impressed. The image is two men tall and boasts intricately carved tangles of long hair fanned out to one side as if he was caught by the sculptor in the middle of twisting, trident in one hand, a set of five chains in the other. His blank marble eyes house a fury impossible to portray in stone, and yet it is there.

I, who once told Turbote to his face that the gods were nothing but a beautiful dream, am here to plead with him. I, who refused on the first day of this cataclysm to so much as offer a single prayer, have come now on my knees. I know this for what it is. Futile. Desperate. The last thrashing of a dying whale trapped on the shore.

But I can no more stop thrashing than the whale can.

"We'll plead with any god who will listen when we get to the top," Turbote gasps. "Let me do the talking—pray by

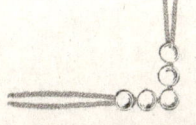

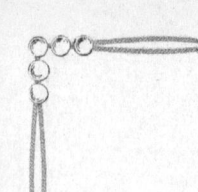

all means, but any bargain should be made by me. I am the priest."

We spill out into the temple—two tiny figures at the highest point of the Crocus Isles standing under the last sign of our strength and will. Above us stone waves crash. Below us real ones swell ever higher, lashed by rain.

We told the council that I would go and pray, but Turbote and I both know what that means. Nothing comes from nothing. If any of the gods deigns to bargain with me, then I'm going to be asked for something. Yet my riches are already lost to the sea, my people scattered to the winds, my power evaporated with them. So, it's my life they'll have or nothing.

Turbote is praying loudly to any god who will hear, but mostly to Okeanos. He presses my head down hard so that my chin hits the white rock and I taste blood in my mouth, half expecting to feel the knife of his blade cut my throat. He's dousing me with holy ocean water. In his enthusiasm I'm half drowned.

"Pray," he begs from above me. "Add your words to mine! Please, Your Serene Majesty."

"Gods of the sea and storm," I shout out over the blast of the wind, and as if in answer the wind blows twice as hard, whipping my long black hair behind me until it snaps like a banner. "Show yourselves!"

And for a long moment there is no response.

Not that I thought there would be.

Everything is still. Everything waits with me. Water

trickles down my neck, down my spine, making me shiver, and there is no god who comes to claim my life. And no god who comes to save us. I draw in a deep breath, about to let out my resignation with a sigh, when I freeze.

A whirl of wind kicks up, spinning so hard around the temple that I hear a crack, and then one of the decorative waves behind me falls and shatters. Turbote screams and falls back, but I do not. Because worse—so much worse than the destruction of the temple or the wrath of the gods—I've lost sight of the little dot bobbing on the waves.

I swallow, stand, and take a step forward as if I could fly out like a pelican and swallow up my beloved from the waters and carry him to safety.

But of course, I can't. I'm mortal still.

WHAT WOULD YOU HAVE OF ME, MORTAL QUEEN?

They aren't spoken words. They're the crash of the sea and the beating of the waves. They're the howl of souls caught up in the shaking power of the storm. And yet they make my heart race. I fight against a chattering jaw—my body's natural flinching from so great a glory washing against my mind. My will must be greater.

"Spare my people," I beg succinctly. "Still this storm."

WHAT BARGAIN WOULD YOU MAKE FOR THIS BOON?

I had thought I was not one to plead. How naive of me.

"What would you take, Lord?" I ask, choked. I dare not withhold anything.

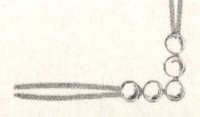

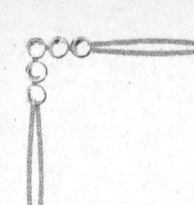

YOUR FUTURE.

I swallow, looking again at the empty patch of ocean where my husband has disappeared. The grief swelling in my throat tells me he asks for too little, for already my future is lost to me. But if I am bargaining for lives, then I am bargaining for Lieve's life, too, if he is not yet lost. If there's even a chance he could survive this, then I must fight for it.

"Yes," I say so quickly that the word blurs into the storm. "All of it."

I think I hear a laugh, but I am not certain, for the wind shakes us again, ripping at us so hard that a piece of my dress tears away and is a tenth league out over the sea before I notice it has broken free.

I can barely breathe, my air is snatched before I can draw it in, and then suddenly the wind stops. The waves still. I hear water pouring, and it takes a heartbeat for me to realize that it's running from the stone down the slope of the hill in rivulets.

Out over the still sea—unnaturally bright and peaceful to my eye—my green islands rise up out of the water like a half-drowned child rescued and hauled into a boat. They are torn and ragged, but they gleam like lost gems recovered. My islands. Restored to me. My heart leaps.

Can it...would the gods truly bless me so? It feels like grasping at air. Impossible to hold. I can no longer deny that they exist. I must not deny their blessing, too.

AND NOW THE PRICE.

The storm has passed, and yet the voice in my mind is as howling as a turbulent wind.

"The price," I agree, but my eyes ache from looking, searching. I don't dare blink. I'm scanning every bit of water I can see. He only disappeared for a moment. He might be out there in that calm water. He must be.

YOU WILL MARRY THE FIRST PERSON TO SET HIS FOOT UPON THE PIER. YOU WILL BE HIS BRIDE. HIS STATION WILL BE YOUR STATION. HIS CROWN YOUR CROWN. HIS PEOPLE YOUR PEOPLE.

I blink, confused. "I am already married, Lord."

ARE YOU CERTAIN?

I am certain now. And it guts me like a fish brought to market.

I wail my pain and fury into a still, perfect sky.

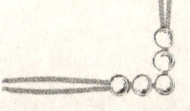

Chapter Two

By the time the waters begin to recede, the sun is sinking in the sky, and though the rains have stopped, the clouds are heavy, and I am born all over again on another moonless night.

"We'll sit here, then, until morning," Turbote says, shuffling his bones to the floor beside me and kicking his legs out over the edge of the stone steps like a child. He seems smaller than he did an hour ago.

The temple is built into the crown of the mountain so that the land sweeps out from it like a skirt, the frothing ocean its lace. From the temple, all is seen, just as all is seen by the gods. I grit my teeth at that similarity. They might see, but they only care if it benefits them.

There's a lightness to Turbote's tone that seems like it's coming from a faraway land. "A fire would have been nice,"

he says, not seeming to care that I have no part in this conversation. "It would have lit the way for any boats, but no matter. Everything is far too wet to burn. Eventually people will make their way back. The fleet from Andalappo will be close and they may be the first to set foot on the dock. Their prince would make a fine choice for you, though that's likely too much to hope for. We'll see their lights from here if they make landfall."

Now that the winds have calmed, there are lights dancing in the distance across the span of many waters. He's right. There are boats and ships out there. Soon, my people will return from the safe harbors and dry land they hoped to find in Andalappo. The swell was so strong here that three of our islands were completely submerged, and the other two nearly so, but Andalappo is a string of island mountains. When the sons and daughters of the Crocus Isles return, they will be safe.

It's the birdsong that breaks me.

The Crocus Isles are thick with emerald-fronded plants, broad leafed and bountiful. Below us, in the last scraps of light, I see them waving gently as if all is well, though it is not well at all. And then the birds begin to sing, telling one another that they've survived this terrible storm. That it is past. That they are whole. If they hadn't gone and sung, I could have held the tears in, but the fool things won't let up with all their cruel joy.

I sink down beside Turbote.

"We can send someone down to demand their captain

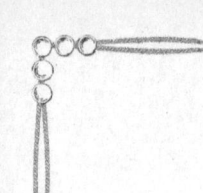

disembarks first," he says, sounding happy. "Or any noble they have aboard. That should suit well enough. As long as it isn't Gheric Rodehands. That miserable traitor."

"Opposing monarchy doesn't make a man a traitor. He loves the isles, too." We are both so tired of this ongoing argument that Turbote doesn't even bother to answer back.

"I wouldn't worry if I were you, Your Serene Majesty. The council will take it all in hand right away."

"Worry about what?" I am long past worry. I can't even see it on my horizon anymore. What is left to worry about? The worst has happened, and it can't be taken back.

"Who you'll be forced to marry, of course." Turbote sounds put out.

I snort gently. I will marry a gull if I must. I care not at all.

"We'll make the best of it!" Turbote can't disguise his satisfaction anymore. It would make me bitter, except I know it's only relief to have survived. "We're good at making the best of things."

"The council will see to the rescue of survivors, the rebuilding of the isles, and the restoration of order," I say calmly. "My heir is Cousin Delarte. He was on the *Merrymaker* when it set out two days ago. If all has gone well, they'll return with the rest. He'll need a strong council to help him reign."

"My queen?" Turbote sounds rattled. I regret stealing his temporary joy. "Coralys? You heard the gods speak. You bartered with them. You must marry! If you break your pact

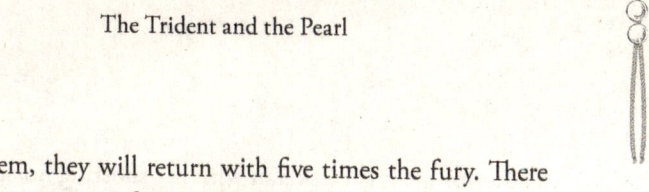

with them, they will return with five times the fury. There will be no survivors from such wrath."

I turn to him and make my voice firm, thankful he won't see my face in the falling darkness.

"Counselor Turbote, tomorrow we will recover and bury our dead. And I will marry the first man to set his foot on our pier here on Talasa, whoever it is. And I will go away and be his wife and my crown will pass to Delarte. You heard the god. His station will be mine. And his people my own."

"But, my queen—"

"Enough. The gods have spoken. And so have I."

And with that I close my eyes, lean against the too-large pillar, and let my sorrows carry me through the long, aching hours of the night. I am certain that Turbote argues against my will, but I cannot tell you what he says, for I am not listening.

In my mind, I hear a sad song singing, one usually sung to children to list out the gods, though why we end it in sorrow, I could never divine.

Take your breath for Aurelius,
Drink your drop for Okeanos,
Plant your seed for Glorian,
Give your kiss for El'Dorian,
Sing your song for Ordanus,
Strike your hammer for Alexandros,
Walk your trail for Pagetto,
Dig your grave for Treseano,

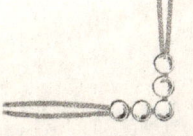

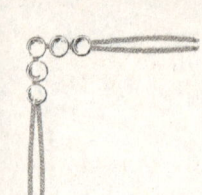

But for me it is Heskatan with her snorting horses,
And Markanos will guide me through battle's courses,
And your love will fade, my dear, as my death takes me
And in the Nightwaters, all ten gods I'll see.

Perhaps my Lieve sees the ten gods now, though his war was not with men but against an angry sea. Perhaps he'll have seen which god bargained with me—Okeanos, most likely, as this is his temple.

When dawn creeps in, my bones ache from sitting on cold stone all night. To my surprise, Turbote is not with me.

I walk through Talasa like one in a dream, a lump in my throat for every scattered line of wood or stone I see where once there had been a dwelling, a rough exhale for walls toppled and wells filled with brackish seawater. In the top of one tree is a dead goat. They'll have to climb to bring him down again.

I feel as though I am a ghost walking through my own land. My eyes skim over roofless houses and matchstick remains, unable to settle on just one loss under the bulk of so many.

I reach the docks—dry now and accessible—in time to find Turbote weeping.

Washed into shore at his feet are Lieve and Rasale and pieces of the wreckage of their boat. I barely recognize my beloved husband without the gleam of life in his eye. His fists grip a line so tightly that we must leave it in his hands. He did not surrender to the sea; it tore his life from him.

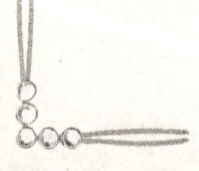

Rasale, Lieve's crewmate, looks more peaceful. Perhaps he did not mind the last embrace of the waves. I linger over them, tasting bitter dregs in my mouth. Had I been just a few moments faster in my prayers, perhaps they would yet live. There is no sign of Carmante, who sailed with them. He did not make the journey back.

I do not need to look at my husband's lifeless body to know he is gone. I have felt his absence keenly all night. I do not have to hold his empty corpse. I do not have to look once more into glassy eyes. I do not have to lay him out on the door we find blown off a dockside shed, or arrange his limbs, or tear fronds from those plants that survived to garland him.

I do not have to. But I do.

Which is how I miss seeing the first boat return.

I *do* see Turbote, though. He is opposite me, where he has been doing for Rasale what I have done to honor Lieve. It's when he freezes in horror that I know what has happened.

"Your Serene Majesty," he chokes out.

Anyone can step on a dock. And with every boat and ship we had filled with people fleeing the storm and the floods, is it any wonder that in the distance I see craft upon craft bearing down upon us like migrating butterflies in a swarm?

But fastest among them, quickest to return to the fold, is not the fleet of rescuers promised by Andalappo. It's not the rest of the council. Not a merchant boat's ruddy-cheeked sailor or a huddling family clinging to one another.

Instead, a lone sailor in a tiny boat with a single sail—the

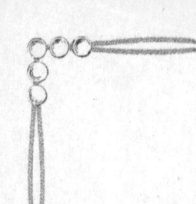

name scrawled across the prow illegible in the peeling paint—ties his boat to the other end of the long pier.

I have never seen Turbote run. I'm not sure I've seen *any* man of his age run. He tears down the pier screaming, waving his arms. The part of me who is watching all this thinks it's almost funny. The part of me gently holding my dead husband's hand thinks nothing will ever be funny.

Turbote makes it almost halfway. It's a valiant attempt. But he does not succeed.

The survivors close to the pier, surprised to see Turbote sprinting, follow him, but even through the small crowd I see the moment the man—a fisherman, I'd guess, based on the nets hanging along the side of the boat—stumbles onto the pier. He's either badly beaten or much the worse for drink. He can't walk a straight line, and he falls into a quickly retreating Turbote as if embracing a long-lost relative.

Turbote shakes him off, and I get one glimpse of the man. His skin is sunburned. His hair an indistinct color slightly bleached by the sun and pulled back into a gnarled knot. He's bearded. His clothing is ragged and hangs over his body in a way that makes it hard to tell his height or width. But he's a man. And I suppose that means he'll be my wedded husband soon enough.

Turbote is speaking loudly and with hands waving—likely explaining the situation to this man. He pays Turbote about as much mind as I usually do.

Our eyes meet from across the distance, and his narrow as they watch me in a distinctly predatory manner.

I do not like that I look away first or that I feel suddenly both hot and cold all at once. I see my future in those twinkling lights as surely as if I've read it in the stars.

I have too many duties to speak with him now. Or at least that's what I tell myself, but I know the truth: I must set my husband to rest before I meet the next man I'll marry. I owe him that much respect, at least.

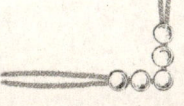

Chapter Three

The morning and afternoon pass in a blur of arrivals: relief, hope—for other people—and then the hour of solemn burials at sea for those dead we've collected, including Lieve. I know there will be many days like this to come for the Crocus Isles. But the rest will be without me.

By now, the council is all here, the island is flooded with people, the weeping is shot all through with joyful reunions and glad surprises. Under the bright sun and over the azure waves—mocking things when they were so harsh and cruel yesterday—the rescue fleet from Andalappo arrives. They carry supplies for my weary citizens: clean water, fresh food, canvas and rope, promises and well wishes.

The last ship to throw anchor and send in boats is the *Merrymaker*, which holds Delarte. My cousin is twenty-six summers and favored in looks, but soft from drink and good

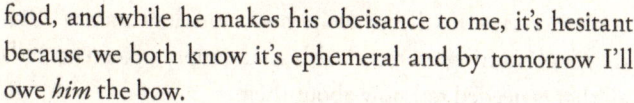

food, and while he makes his obeisance to me, it's hesitant because we both know it's ephemeral and by tomorrow I'll owe *him* the bow.

"You're all here," I say, looking up at my counselors and Delarte hovering a little away and speaking in hasty whispers. "Which should be more than enough for you to conduct a wedding and wish your monarch well on her new life."

"You don't have to do this, cousin," Delarte says.

It's performative, but that's fine because everyone knows it's his piece in this little drama. He's delivered it well. It even sounds heartfelt, and maybe it is, but it doesn't matter because it's a throwaway line. It's the ones that come after that matter.

"We do," I say calmly, gravely.

There's doubt in Delarte's eye. I'm sure there's doubt in mine. But I received my boon, and now I will pay the price.

Turbote is grim. "I heard the voice of the gods. This is the payment they take for their mercy. Our queen is right to offer herself as the price."

"You should have managed it, Turbote," one of my counselors says in a tetchy tone. "It's a simple thing to order a man to stay in his boat. If it had been a member of our nobility, there'd be no talk about a change of rule. We could have said she was staying with her people and that the noble was of her station. Things would go on as they always have. Instead, you've let it all fall apart!"

Turbote wrings his hands.

"You don't have to do this, Your Serene Majesty," another

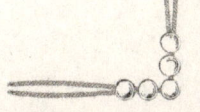

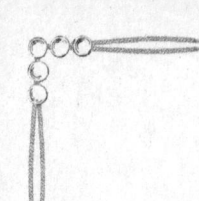

counselor says. I will not recite my counselors' names. That they had nothing more valuable than empty objections tells all that is needed to know about them.

"If I do not fulfill my vow, I will have broken trust with the gods," I tell them quietly. "And if I break trust with them, then they will break trust with me. Do you already forget how many of our own we have lost? How severe the storm was? How very narrow our escape became?"

They're silent.

"Still..." Delarte lets the word hang in the air. "To step away from the Crown..."

"Is the only option left," I tell him, and this time I put steel in my voice. "A commoner stepped onto the docks. A commoner's wife I will be. That means I will no longer be queen. It is the price the gods demand and I will pay it."

"They ask for too much," Delarte mutters. As if me giving up my crown and marrying a stranger are the true tragedies here. As if it is not Lieve and the others being sent back into the sea.

It is agreed that the wedding will take place the next morning. Morning is the time of weddings and the tide pool will be warm and ready for the ceremony. For one last night, I will be queen. Delarte is happy, for he looks benevolent as a result of this decision, and the council feels they have done all they can, which sets their hearts at peace.

"I'll stay here," I say, looking down the pier to where a pair of guards has been set by the council to watch the fisherman I'm to wed tomorrow. He sits, leaning against the bitts,

huddled over himself as if he is still ill or injured. I wonder if he'll be a problem. "If it's good enough for him, then it's good enough for me. I'll be his wife in the morning."

Turbote scoffs. "We set the guard so he wouldn't slip away."

"You didn't set a guard on me."

Turbote looks side to side as if he's uncomfortable, and then to my utter surprise he steps forward and wraps me in an embrace. I'm so stunned that I freeze, arms straight and stiff.

"What is this?"

"Coralys." His voice breaks. "Like a daughter you've been to me. Willful and brave. Fair and just. No one would think you would run from your duty. Not even now."

And I know I should feel something. Surprise would be appropriate. Affection would be permissible. But I see an old man touched by the voice of the gods who thinks now that his queen is the center of some great epic tale. I disentangle myself from his arms and say kindly, "You've been a good counselor, Turbote. Do not ruin it by softening now."

He laughs, dashing tears from his eyes. "You've saved us all. Who would think the gods themselves would barter with you? You're honored, Your Serene Majesty."

"Live a long life, Turbote. Make Delarte as miserable as you've made me."

He laughs again as if that was a joke, but then he's on his way and I'm grateful to see his back. I look down the pier to where the fisherman sits with his head tipped back. Hardly

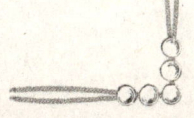

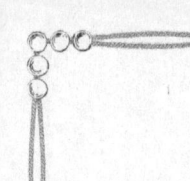

an auspicious beginning to a marriage—one forced by the hands of guards and man, the other forced by the threat of the gods.

I make my way down the dock, watching him as the distance grows shorter. I have not had a good look at him yet. I do not know if I am wedding a youth tomorrow or a man as old as Turbote.

Even as I draw close, it's hard to tell. He's hunched over himself as if in pain, one arm wrapped around his middle, his head bowed. He has a wild beard that hangs in hunks like rushes and spreads out to the sides like the tail of a thrush. It is not an attractive thing, but to be frank I've never met a man good at judging what's attractive in a beard. Mayhap the fisherman thinks he looks very well indeed with a face like a thrush's tail.

"I don't think we need guards," I say mildly when I reach him. He has not bothered to stand at my arrival—or even look up. The guards don't move, so I fix them with my steady gaze. "Leave me one lantern."

They look at each other. I don't know their names, though I know the names of all my own palace guards, so these are part of the regulars. They're worn and tired, uniforms salt-stained and rumpled.

I'm surprised by how offended is the part inside me that can feel their hesitance. But no one forced to marry a piece of flotsam after a storm can brag that she's too good to be ignored by the guards. I'm still laughing at myself when I put a hand out to be given a lantern.

"There's food at the palace, they tell me."

I've hit the right note. They exchange another glance, offer a pair of reticent salutes, and give me one of the lanterns. Their footsteps echo down the pier. Voices drift in muffled tones and the sounds of people preparing for night echo over the water. The waves batter the sides of the various craft tied up along the pier, and the shushing lull of them calms me enough to sink down to the decking and place the lantern between myself and this mysterious heap of beard and cloth.

"Do you believe in fate, lady?" he asks me, and I'm so startled by his voice that I nearly tip over the lantern.

"No," I say a little sadly.

I wish I could lay all this at the feet of some unknown divine storyteller, cruel and immovable. It would be a comfort.

"Do you believe, then, that your choices shape the course your life sails? That you are arbiter in the place of fate?"

He mocks me. And he does it with such a voice. His appearance may be shabby, but the gods have given him a voice that seems to have the power of the great swells of the sea behind it. I think if he were dressed well, giving orders, there'd be no hesitation in those he commanded. *He* wouldn't have to tempt the guards away with food. I smile slightly at the comparison.

"Who should I blame but myself?" I put to him.

He makes a sound that at first I take to be a fit of some kind and I look around helplessly. I am not practiced in healing arts. I make to rise, but his hand snaps out and grabs my wrist, and I freeze.

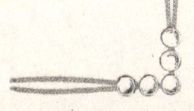

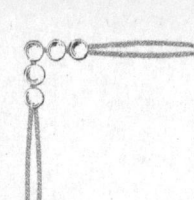

There's a lot of power there. Too much to make me feel safe. Not an old man, then. The hairs on his arm are dark. His forearm is well shaped and darkened by the sun. He holds my wrist in a firm grasp, but not so tightly that it hurts. I am surprised at the gentleness of his touch. It takes a breath before I realize that the sound I hear is him laughing.

"You don't blame the gods, then? For this fate of yours? To marry me, a poor fisherman?" His expression is hidden by the long hair that falls around his face.

"Is that what you are?" I ask curiously. But his words strike a chord in me. I do blame the gods. Not for the marriage. I care not about that. I blame them for the death of my Lieve. For the deaths of the rest. For being able to stop it but toying with me first instead.

The fisherman's hold on my wrist tightens, and for one terrible moment I have a strange feeling that he is not what he seems at all, but rather some monster of the deep come up to claim my soul.

"A fisherman?" he says, seeming pleased with the title. His words break my reverie and he loosens his hold on me. "Among many things, I am certainly that."

"And will you take me willingly to wife tomorrow?"

"Isn't that what they've kept me here for?"

I open my mouth and then shut it with a click when he looks up at me for the first time. His eyes are bright and sharp. Those are not the eyes of a fool. They are dangerous eyes.

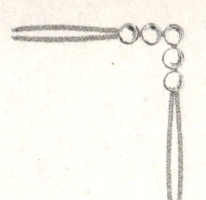

And they are also beautiful, like the sea just before a storm. They draw me into an intimacy I do not want.

I swallow hard. I know nothing of this man but his dress and conveyance. He could be anyone. Not a ghazul or a kraken, obviously, but perhaps a criminal. Perhaps a man who enjoys the torture of the innocent. Perhaps a pirate or reprobate or drunk.

And I will be his wife.

It will not be like my marriage to Lieve, where I was queen as well as wife, equal—superior, even—by birth and blood. Nor will it be the sweet partnership between us where trust was so strong.

I am about to learn a very different kind of marriage now—the binding of disparate souls, the tying of divergent fates.

"You know that you've been held here to marry me," I say coolly, refusing to break our shared gaze. I will not bend first. "They would have told you."

"A bargain with the gods." His eyes flash in the lantern light. Against my will, my breath catches. "As if a mortal can bargain with the immortal for anything and come out the winner."

"And yet, I did," I tell him. And I'm not sure if my voice is cold because he is toying with me, or because the idea that the gods were playing with me last night is taking root and growing in my heart. "Tell me, fisherman, why else but because you are to wed me tomorrow are you kept here on my pier unmolested?"

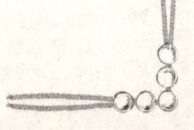

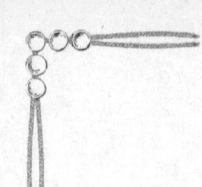

"Your pier?" He finds that amusing.

"Until I marry you," I say firmly. "Until I marry you and abandon this life of mine, I am Coralys, Her Serene Majesty, queen of the Crocus Isles, seventh of her line. My ancestors built this pier—and the others of the five islands. They carved our palaces and courthouses, shiphouses and temples from this rock. They set in pools and springs, fountains and terraced gardens. We are a haven of bounty and spices and peace between men."

He smiles as if he is charmed by a tale. "Is this so, Coralys? You are so very favored as all that?"

"Yes." I am annoyed now.

His voice softens. "Is it true that your husband died in the storm? Or is that one more exaggeration I should lay at this man Turbote's feet?"

I feel the blood drain from my face, annoyance shattered with the strict reminder that grief is my companion this night.

"It is true."

I cannot decipher the emotions rippling across his face, but he is very grave when he speaks.

"Your people lived—mostly—but your kingdom is drowned. Where will the terraced gardens be today? Washed away. Your beloved fountains filled with debris and brackish water. Your silks ruined, your rugs trashed, your riches washed out into the greedy mouth of the howling sea. I name you Queen of the Drowned, for that is what you are."

"What is that to you?" I ask softly.

His answer is so faint that I barely catch it. "What indeed?"

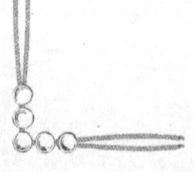

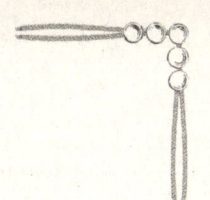

He drops his hand suddenly, as if stung, and I feel cold.

Carefully, I retreat to put a post at my back and close my eyes.

"Are you going to run?" I ask him.

"There's nowhere to flee." His words sound bleak and one corner of his mouth hitches in a way that makes me wince in sympathy.

"Is marriage to me so grim as that?"

But he does not answer and I do not care if he runs. It will only mean that I am bound to follow, and I think that maybe chasing him would be preferable to him chasing me, so I close my eyes and I lean back against the pier.

This journey is too important to abandon now. Because I have made a choice as I spoke to him. I have decided I will climb up out of the mortal mirk and find the gods, and I will have my revenge on them for withholding their mercy like it was a game and plucking my husband's life like fruit from a tree. And the thought of this new purpose swells in my breast in a way that sits very nicely alongside my grief and drives all doubt from my mind.

The fisherman is whistling something tuneless that sounds like the wind in the rocks of the shore more than the song of a man. It suits my mood perfectly. Neither one thing nor the other, just like me tonight. I drift in and out of cold, comfortless sleep, and I clench my fists and wish I could pray for revenge, but with the gods as my enemies I refuse to pray at all. Instead, I simply hope and I cling to the haunting sound of that whistle until dawn.

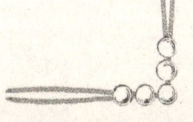

Chapter Four

Any island kingdom will have great reverence for the sea. It is from the sea that we gather food and riches and by the whims of the sea that we live. We are blessed or cursed by the waves, and the tide steals or gifts as it wills.

And so, on the Crocus Isles, anything we do of significance, we do in the sea.

We start our lives born into its salt, no matter what the cost is to arrange it. I've seen pregnant women in the middle of a gale laboring against a standing rock, bidding their child come before the winds sweep them away, friends and neighbors encircling them, wet and wind-whipped, holding thick ropes so that they will not be washed away, and once the infant arrives it may find refuge in a floating tar-painted basket. My own birth was to calm seas, and yet even I taste my name in the brine, for each mother speaks the child's

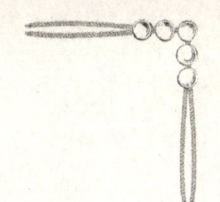

name as the babe is dipped beneath the waters so that the ocean may know them and understand we belong to it. We are the people of the sea.

And when we die, we are released to the sea once more, our names released with us, in thanks for the gift of our lives upon the waves, just as I gave Lieve to the sea yesterday.

When the time came for me to ascend to the crown, I was raised to the throne within the waters, the Pearl Crown set on my head as it had been set on each head before mine. The crowd gathered there with me, their clothing wet and heavy, the swell of the tide rocking them back and forth and knocking all the small, clustered boats against one another with hollow wooden thunks. Our wind that day was strong, and flower petals—torn from their stems by snatching winds—drifted down around me and my subjects. The Crocus Throne is what we call the natural bench that rises just up out of the surf, great towering rocks soaring upward on either side. It's formed in such a way that you can sit on it, and when you sit, the waves will crash hard all around you in a swell of white foam and violent power. And so, I was baptized a second time when I sat as monarch.

The people of the Crocus Isles also marry in the sea, both parties going down into what started as a natural tide pool but was carved by our ancestors into a perpetual greenish-blue pool with a mosaic floor. It represents the birth of both parties into a new life and it tells the sea we are now one.

I walked into the pool with Lieve on our wedding day. I remember yet his abashed joy as we entered it together,

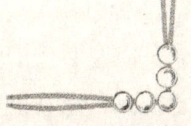

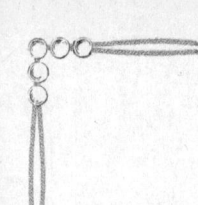

hands clasped tightly. Weddings, just like those other events, are conducted naked. Naked we are born into the sea, naked we return to it, and naked we marry to embrace our new lives together without secrets.

That seems ironic today. I know nothing about the man I am marrying and naked flesh will not change that. It will only be a stark reminder of what I have lost and what I am losing.

My grim council arrives at dawn with Delarte in tow. My cousin has been drinking and he offers me a wobbling smile and a bow that isn't mocking only because of the misery in his eyes. Mayhap he sees his future here in me—ruler but a decade and now desolate, soon to be stripped of even her royal clothing. I smile at him. It's nice to see that someone understands the full weight of today's events.

We make our way silently from the pier to the tide pool. I hear the fisherman making that terrible coughing choke that I think is one of his laughs. Perhaps Delarte and I are not the only ones who see the grim humor in this.

"I've always thought the marriage pool was beautiful," Turbote says stoutly when we arrive.

So have I. Although today, it's just a worn mosaic of the face of the God of the Sea flooded over by bluish-green water. I am too heavy with grief to see the beauty of it.

The fisherman leans over to look and again his face twists with grim humor. The line of his neck is very masculine and I wonder idly if the jaw under all that beard is equally defined and firm.

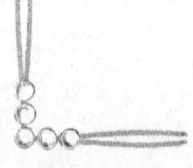

I shoot him a sidelong glance, but I say nothing.

The council arranges themselves around the pool in the required places and with great ceremony they draw out and affix the ceremonial blindfolds. It's a mercy I'm grateful for. As much as my mind and heart are elsewhere, it would still make me blush for my cousin and council to see me stripped naked before them. The fisherman is a different matter. He hasn't known me all my life, questioning my rulings or bowing before my throne. I am nothing more than an inconvenient stranger to him.

I begin to strip off my raiments. I am still wearing some finery that I hadn't thought to discard in the madness of the last few days. A pearl belt that Lieve gave me is particularly hard to part with. I place it directly into Delarte's hands and he flinches from behind his blindfold.

"Yours now," I murmur.

One of the counselors, Maevelys, blindly helps me to unweave my hair from the circlet of pearls around my head—the Pearl Crown, that is to be Delarte's today as well. Maevelys stands with it in her hands afterward, her back straight and her eyes blindfolded.

"I always found this a strange tradition," the fisherman says as he shrugs off a pair of leather sandals. "But fear not, Queen Coralys. You were made for this day."

"This day?" I ask him, not bothering to hide my disbelief. "I was made for this day when I remove my crown and wed a stranger only one dawn after I buried the husband I loved?"

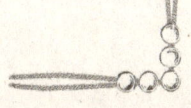

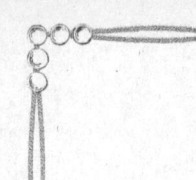

"This day exactly," he says, and he sounds very old suddenly.

I look sharply at him. In full sun and up close, his eyes are very green. They've changed from last night. Now they are the sea at noon, bright and beguiling. His beard remains scraggly, his hair sun-bleached in streaks but mostly a brown that nearly matches his brown skin. I do not think he is old. His shoulders are broad, though he hunches them forward, and his bare arms are attractively muscled. When they move and flex, they have a vitality to them that draws my eye. But he doesn't seem young, either.

He's slow to undress. I'm down to my skin and feeling the cut of the morning breeze while he is still removing his belt and pouch.

I stand with a straight back and crossed arms. I miss Lieve. I wish he were here. It's a silly thought, for were he here there would be no wedding at all.

It is only when my intended grunts in a way familiar to me—the sound of one of my guards taking a hit on the practice field or my husband when he cut his thumb with a scaling knife—that I realize something is wrong.

I turn sharply and bite back my gasp. Naked men are not unfamiliar to me. I knew Lieve's strong male body as I know my own. This man is close in size to Lieve, I think. Although still his height is hard to gauge. And no wonder.

The fisherman is a mass of bruises, one layered over another across his broad chest and sleek abdomen. He stands hunched around his middle, one arm drawn in as if

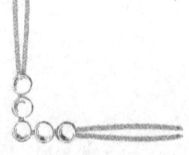

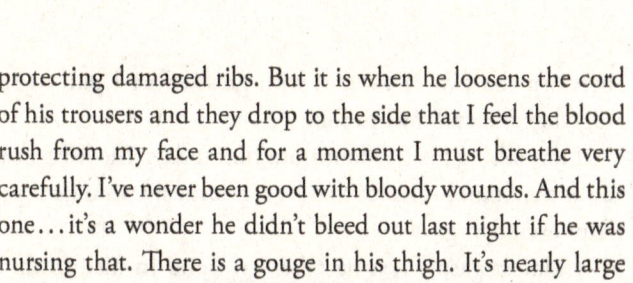

protecting damaged ribs. But it is when he loosens the cord of his trousers and they drop to the side that I feel the blood rush from my face and for a moment I must breathe very carefully. I've never been good with bloody wounds. And this one... it's a wonder he didn't bleed out last night if he was nursing that. There is a gouge in his thigh. It's nearly large enough to put my balled-up fist within the ragged flesh. And that seems impossible, for is not the femoral artery there?

"A healer," I gasp. "We need a healer."

There's a ripple of wordless murmurs from the blindfolded assembly. They must not be peeking, or they'd see as easily as I do what a mess the poor man is.

"No need." He grunts and waves a hand in denial as if he does not note that my hands are trembling, suddenly reaching out as if I might steady him.

I try not to dwell on the details of the fisherman's injury, for every glance makes me feel more ill. The wound is gory and open. It has barely missed destroying his manhood, gouging into the meat high up his thigh. Either he was impaled on wreckage quite brutally or someone has stabbed him several times with a spear.

The council whispers together and I hear Turbote loudly quelling them and the words, "The sooner it's over with, the better."

Finally, the fisherman meets my eye, and to my surprise there is no pain, no shame, no misery at all in his eyes. There is only steadiness. I know my eyes are wide with shock, but he shakes his head minutely as if bidding me keep this secret

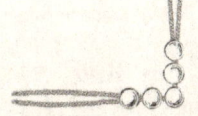

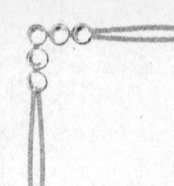

between the two of us, and with great effort I pull myself together and seal my lips shut.

I am taking his freedom from him today. The least I can do is maintain his secret that he is grievously wounded, perhaps even dying.

I almost gasp when he takes my hand in his, brushing his thumb over my knuckles. I find I am gripping his hand back, longing for a little of that equanimity.

"This day was made for us, Lady of the Sea. Are you ready for it?"

Such an odd pronouncement. "Lady of the Sea" is officially one of my titles. Or it will be until I step into the water.

With a regal lift of my head, I squeeze the hand not cradling his ribs—noting the thick calluses of a life at sea—and I look to my council.

"Let it begin." My voice doesn't even shake. I am doing very well.

"Are you truly certain—?" one of the counselors begins to say, but I cut off any other objections.

"We will be wed this day. I will fulfill my bargain with the gods."

And then they will get a lot more than they bargained for.

There are no more hollow objections.

We make our way down the steps and into the water together. I see now why the fisherman looked drunk. His legs barely support him. I'm not sure he'll live the week out. I may be a widow twice in a seven-day stretch. He doesn't lean on me, though.

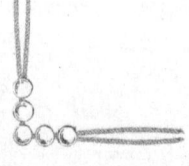

He flinches when the salt water meets his injury, and I wince in sympathy. His blood clouds the pool around us, swirling in garish patterns of red and coral against the pale bluish green. Little flashes of my first wedding rise to my mind unbidden. The warmth in Lieve's brown eyes as we entered the waves contrasts in my mind's eye to these piercing green ones that look as stormy as the sea has been these past few days.

The water slips up past our waists and I recall the beauty of Lieve's vitality contrasted to this battered wreckage of a man who is claiming me. He takes my other hand in his and I feel a pang. These hands are warm in an unfamiliar way and laced with mysteries I do not know.

We stand together, clasping both hands, and I know it is an effort for him to do this much because his body sways as he hunches over his wound. He has locked his gaze steadfastly to mine.

"From the sea we are given, to the sea we return," Maevelys intones. "And in marriage we die to our old lives and live now anew in a life together. You are dead now to the old Coralys and the old..." She pauses awkwardly, suddenly realizing that we've been using this poor man as a playing piece in this game without knowing so much as his name. "My apologies, good sir, but what is your name?"

"Oke," he says, and it comes out half a grunt of pain.

"And the old Oke," Maevelys says with a frown. It is a common name, one of the most common on our shores, and I'm certain it makes my marriage to him all the more

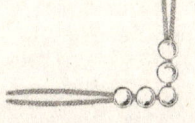

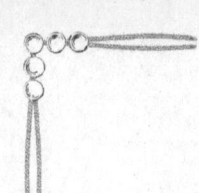

debasing. "And you will rise from this pool bound as one in the eyes of the gods and the fates—your two ropes entwined into one line with room for none other. Do you agree to this?"

"Aye," Oke says over my "Yes."

"Then speak your oaths," Turbote says unhappily as the wind picks up and swirls around us.

I speak first. I know the words. I've presided over weddings myself, and yet these vows feel too intimate right now, said to a stranger with no one watching me but him.

"I come to you as Coralys of the Crocus Isles, my titles and family in my past. I give myself freely to you to be your wife." I almost choke over that part. It feels like a betrayal of Lieve to say these words to another. "I give my oath that I will deny you nothing—not my wealth nor my name, not my affections nor my comforts, not my body nor my fate, nor the children of our union. In all things I tie myself to you no matter the storms that come or pass. I vow faithfulness and honor to you all the days of our lives."

His eyes flicker not a mite. And then he speaks.

"Water to water, life to life, I give myself to you. Bound by the water of life in your veins to the water of life in mine, tangled up as a man tangles with a woman, heart of my heart, as two waters meet and mingle, we will be one. Where your future flows, there will mine flow with it. As you ebb and recede, so I retreat. As you flow and rise, surely I go with you. Wherever your soul lingers, there will mine be, and if it slips into the Nightwaters, even there will I join you. Never

will I leave you. Never will I forsake you. And if I fail in my vow, then may the waters be leached from me, and my mouth be salted, and may I be buried in the sand far from the rush of the sea."

And then he kisses a knuckle, lifts it reverently above us, and bows his head, breaking our eye contact for the first time, and just as I'm breathing a sigh of relief, he takes a tentative step forward and presses a very bold kiss to my brow, leaving me with a face full of beard and the sense that I am somehow honored in a way I do not understand.

Then the fisherman pulls me under the water with him, dropping so that we are both dunked fully beneath the surface of the pool, and for a moment we are staring at each other wide-eyed in water that laps in and out of the ocean into this pool, green bubbles floating up all around us. He says something I cannot make out and then he finds his feet just as I do and pulls me up with him out of the water.

Trickles of water run off me in rivulets. My hair is plastered to my body, and I'm gasping like a fresh-caught fish. That wasn't part of the ceremony.

"Before the authorities of the Crocus Isles and before the eyes of the gods you are wed," Turbote announces. "Hear, O sea, our queen is wed. Hear, O ocean, these two are now one, bound by vow and water, made one in the justice of the waves. May the gods take note that our former queen has fulfilled her vow that we all might be spared."

"What was that vow he spoke?" someone is whispering to Maevelys. "Is that one of the ancient ones?"

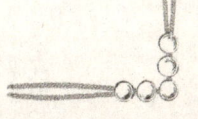

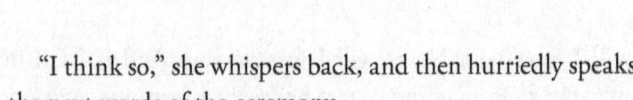

"I think so," she whispers back, and then hurriedly speaks the next words of the ceremony.

"As the husband shelters his beloved, so the wife is sheltered by him, and as a sign of this she will leave this place wearing nothing but what he gives to her."

It's only as she's speaking that I recall what that means. The fisherman has come wearing nothing but the most basic, bloodstained clothes. Now I know why they are stained. I climb the steps with him, and I realize with a blow that feels like a hammer to my chest that I am no longer queen. I knew, of course, and yet I did not feel it until now. I'm so stunned that I only realize I've been standing there dripping naked with my lips parted in surprise when the fisherman—Oke—holds his tunic out to me.

"It's long enough to almost be a chiton," he says with a rueful smile, and then when I'm still too stunned to speak, he straightens with a tight, strangled sound and tries to put the tunic over my head. His whole torso flexes, and it is easy to see every muscle tighten as he has not a shred of extra fat on his frame and possesses a body very neatly put together. But despite what looks like a strong effort, he winces as he tries to bring his arms high enough for the task. He must be stiff from hunching over his wound all night in the cold on a hard dock. I stop staring and recover my senses enough to take the tunic from him.

"Thank you," I say woodenly as I put it on. He is right. While the garment hung loose around his hips, it reaches nearly to my knees, though there is no belt and I must knot

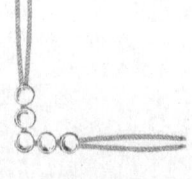

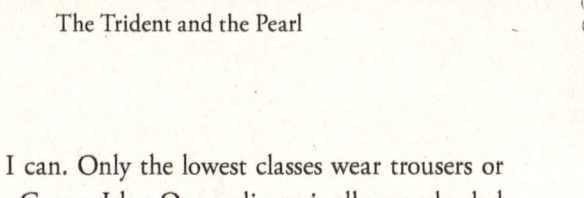

it as best as I can. Only the lowest classes wear trousers or tunics on the Crocus Isles. Our audience is all properly clad in ankle-length chitons. Despite my new husband's words, I will look exactly as I am in this outfit—bereft.

He kicks his sandals to me and I thank him again. Once his trousers are tied back on, I speak: "It is done."

And by my words, my council realizes we're dressed and they remove the ceremonial blindfolds. But it's not to my side that they move to congratulate or say goodbye. They do not even meet my eye as they crowd around Delarte and speak in hushed tones with him about the crown and belt he holds. I am born anew by means of my wedding, the old queen dead and gone.

"This isn't your home now," Oke says practically, stepping between me and them. His grim smile does not comfort me. "I think I'd better take you to mine."

Still, no one seems to notice when he leads me back to the pier and back to his battered fishing boat and settles himself painfully in the stern where he can work the tiller.

"Do you know how to manage the sail?" is all he says to me.

"Yes," I say, for there is no child of the Crocus Isles who does not learn to sail.

"It's your responsibility, then," he says, and he leans back and sets his eyes on the course with a pained look on his face as we weave between boats and ships out into the surf and the relentless sun.

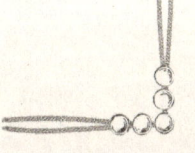

Chapter Five

I am personally offended by the wind today. It is gentle and caressing as if it wants to seduce me into believing it is my friend after all it's done to me. But I know the truth. I know that at the behest of the gods it gutted my nation and swept away my heart and my future.

My new husband steers the boat. His head bobs in a way that worries me. He looks as if he might lose consciousness at any moment. It's only his white-knuckled grip on the tiller that tells me he's still with me.

I search the boat for a waterskin or food or anything I might use to sustain him, but to my horror there are no supplies. I clench my jaw. Fool of a woman. I should have examined the craft myself before we set out. I should have ensured we were supplied. I allowed myself to grow distracted by emotion, and now look where I am. Alone with a

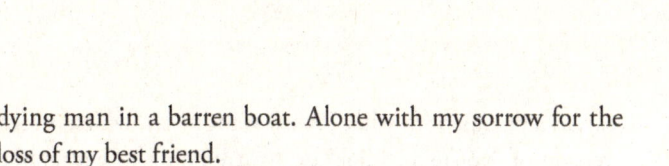

dying man in a barren boat. Alone with my sorrow for the loss of my best friend.

"You seem distressed." Oke's words are mild.

I meet his eye and once more a strange heat washes over me. I do not like this feeling of being seen to the bones. Lieve never looked at me like this. It makes me more naked than I was in that marriage pool. But I am Coralys of the Crocus Isles. I do not look away.

"We are not prepared for any length of voyage," I say carefully. "We have not so much as a skin of water aboard."

He nods gravely, but his eyes are glassy and I wonder how much he's even paying attention.

"You are an observant woman."

I make a sound that is half scoff and half snort. "Don't try to distract me with flattery. We must turn around and get supplies before we go to wherever your home lies. We aren't too far out yet. It will be an easy thing, if humiliating, to go back and beg some water and food from the dockmaster."

I glance across the tufted waves to my emerald jewel islands. Already my mind is thinking of them as a foreign place, no longer my home.

"My home is very near," Oke says, amused. There's a smile dancing around the curve of his mouth and I realize with surprise that it has a nice shape. Were it not hidden by his dreadful beard I might even name it comely. "Do not fear, wife. I agreed to see to your care when I put my clothing on your back and I will do it."

I draw in a long breath. "I want very much to trust you," I

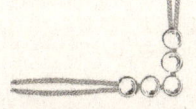

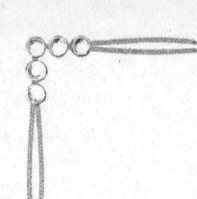

say, as a precursor to what I *really* want to say, which is some version of "you're an idiot" or "you're going to get us both killed," but I don't get that far.

Instead, his eyes widen and the glassiness fades for a moment into a focus so intent it pins me in place as he says, "You want to trust me? After all that has befallen you?" Each word feels weighted, almost hopeful. I fear a wrong answer will set me down an irrevocable path.

"Yes?" I say.

He nods and swallows as if he's making a huge decision.

"That might be best," he says to himself. "That might be best, yes." And then his gaze shoots to mine again and his timid smile is almost boyish when he says, "I'd like to trust you, too. I would like to tell you everything. But you need time to heal and mourn."

"There are some things you don't need to tell me," I say a bit dryly. "First being that you need someone to see to your wound."

He forestalls me by raising two fingers together between us. It half looks like a warning and half like a reverent ward against a devil.

"It is a godwound," he says, gaze still fixed on me. It's as if he's tied a line to my soul and I cannot look away.

"What is a 'godwound'?"

He ignores my question. "You're not to try healing it. To do so will not work and it could make everything worse. Godwounds are never-healing."

"I may not know what a godwound is, but I know

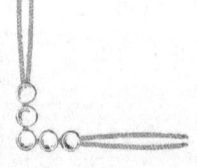

nonsense when I hear it. I will heal it if I get the proper supplies and the opportunity."

He opens his mouth, shuts it, frowns as if studying a difficult puzzle. "I have not indulged in marriage before. It seems such a fraught thing."

I draw back a little, offended. "Fraught? Or practical?"

He glances up at me almost shyly, a small half smile on his lips. The expression seems incongruous when set against his rough beard.

"Binding two disparate souls? You find this practical?"

I don't want to tell him that my marriage to him is nothing but grim practicality. To the degree that my last marriage was for friendship and affection, so this one is for convenience. If he feels some measure of wry humor in our circumstance, well, he's entitled to coping with an unwanted bond in his own way.

He moves to reach for a coiled rope that has slipped out of place and is tangled. I reach past him and coil it for him, frowning when I look up and see satisfaction in his eyes.

He shifts suddenly as a wave hits our prow a little more forcefully than the rest, and my hand stretches out to support him before I realize what I'm doing. All my mind can see is that terrible injury to his thigh. I wince in harmony with him as he takes up a cross-legged position on the hard bench. That can't be comfortable. The wound needs stitches at the very least. How has he not yet bled out?

"Is your wound magical, then? An act of a god?" I ask.

He makes a gesture of acquiescence. What kind of fisherman tangles with those powerful enough to inflict such damage?

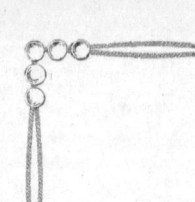

"How did you come by the wound?" I press.

"I have enemies. One surprised me. In the dark. When I thought I was in a safe place."

An injury made by an enemy who has the power of a god? This is a disaster. I can barely get my next words out. "Which god has wounded you? Or was it one of their god-touched servants?"

Oke lets go of the tiller and leans forward.

"What are you doing?" I ask.

"If we are to trust, then one of us must trust first." His earnestness is almost innocent. It stands in stark contrast to his physical power and dangerous secrets. He has a strange way about him, a stillness like the calm beneath the surface of the sea. It colors his every flicker of expression, his every movement, shading them with a depth and purposefulness that speaks of consideration and suggests more premeditation than I've seen in any other man.

Perhaps he is not as old as I judged him to be. Perhaps it is only this strange depth that makes him seem so. Now that I'm sharing such a tiny boat with him and watching him sway to its every movement, he seems younger than me. His torso moves easily with the boat, and it is tanned, lean muscle and taut, firm skin under all that bruising. The only lines around his eyes are the lines of sun on the skin, not of age. He is not an unattractive man.

Regardless, more than any husband, distracting or not, I need an ally.

He clears his throat. I blanch a little as I realize his wound

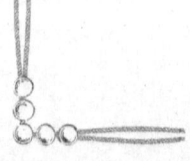

has soaked through his trousers again. I don't care what he says, he's going to need that tended. Or he'll die and leave me in this hulk alone.

"The truth is," he says suddenly, looking furtively around as if he might be overheard. "What is coming next may be too unsettling—even for you, who has been a queen and dealt in power for all your life. I do not want you to recoil from me when you see it. I would like you to be an ally."

"As you've said, *husband*, I am..." I stumble here. "I *was* a queen. I am certain that with time I will learn your profession. I respect your work upon the water." I spread my hands as if to indicate that all this is his. Flattery? Perhaps, but I do not want to offend him from the very start. "But I can assure you there is very little you will have seen in the rest of the world that I will not already know. And whoever your enemies might be, they are mine now, too, and I will not flinch from them."

His mouth quirks into a half smile. Not offended, then, but not believing me, either. "You'll learn my profession?"

I smile a little queasily. "If you wish it."

"I do." He sounds very sincere in the fervent way of the young, whom life has yet to beat into a more measured approach. "But not right away. And we will not discuss my... dangerous entanglements... immediately, either. I know grief. I know it most intimately." The sympathy in his eyes makes a lump form in my throat. "I would not burden you yet. Not until you've had time to make your peace with your loss and your new station."

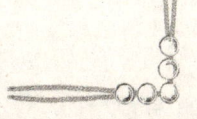

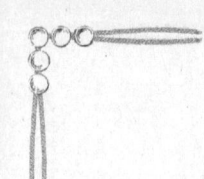

That is surprisingly kind. But I am not yet ready to speak of my loss; it fogs my mind and blots out all other sentiment. I try to change the subject.

"Did you say you've never been married?" I ask gently. "Have you never, then, been in love?"

He frowns. "That is my tale to tell. And love does not factor in. Instead, I'll speak to you of my home, which is not far from here."

We've set a course due west of the Crocus Isles. I frown, trying to bring up sea charts in my mind. What is nearby? There is the Isle of Glass, which some say had been made so during a terrible cataclysm—but that is nothing but a smooth green stump of glass that rises only far enough out of the water to be a hazard for ships and a landing place at low tide for passing birds. I can think of nowhere else nearby.

"There is little close in this direction," I say warily.

His smile grows anxious. "It doesn't have to be close. It is a small place—small and secret and all my own, and I never let anyone else within it. I only bring you there now because you are my wife. Do you understand?"

I nod, but I do not understand. What kind of life does he live that he receives no visitors?

He shifts uncomfortably. "I feel compelled to warn you, for I know how stories work. They're powerful things. Sometimes there's nothing you can do about how they sweep you away, and I am afraid we are both caught up in one. I do not want to see us dashed upon their fateful rocks."

He's speaking nonsense again. Perhaps Turbote was right.

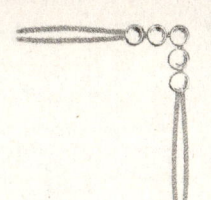

Perhaps we should have taken measures to ensure we picked who would step onto that dock.

I raise an eyebrow. "Is there a tale, then, of a fisherman and a queen who sail to his island? For if there is one, I have not heard it."

"I merely wish to warn you, Drowned Queen," he says, watching me carefully. "So that you do not misjudge what comes next."

I don't need anyone else deciding for me how I will react to a thing. I can react on my own without prompting. I've been doing it for twenty-nine years. Grief has not robbed me of autonomy.

I return to the point, very intentionally not looking at our wretched craft, distinct lack of supplies, and tattered clothing. The sun is already beating on my head so hard I think it might drive me mad, but all these warnings have me wary. What could be troubling enough that he must warn me? I can only think of one thing that could earn him both a wound of the gods and secrets he cannot share. He might be the chosen hero of one of them—though the idea of that is as laughable as a queen marrying a fisherman.

Even so, I have to ask. "Are you god-blessed as well as a catcher of fish?"

"I am the Fisher King," he says coolly, avoiding my question. "I see everything from the view of the sea, from the eye of the whale, from the end of the tentacle."

"I cannot imagine," I say dryly. "And so, you are the Fisher King. Is this the same thing as the Drowned Queen?"

"Precisely so."

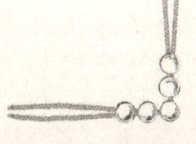

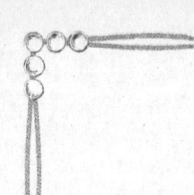

I have not yet decided if I am amused or annoyed. He is not taking my questions seriously.

"And what do you fish, Fisher King? Do you go after great schools of tuna and cod?"

He laughs, and if I must admit something, I'll admit I love his laugh. It ripples like water now that it is no longer rusty and broken.

"I fish for possibilities."

"And is marriage to me one of those possibilities?"

He leans forward so far now that we are nose to nose. I feel the brush of his against mine. It's an unsettling level of intimacy I'm not certain I'm prepared for. It mimics too much the closeness I shared with Lieve. And it does not help that whatever he reeked of before has been blown away and he smells now only of the sea and of a strong young man—a man who has married me and likely would have plans to bring me to his bed were he not so grievously wounded.

"It is the greatest of possibilities, Lady of the Sea, but I do not need to lay hold of what is already mine." He draws back, watching my breath catch, and runs a hand over his beard. I've seen Turbote do that when about to engage in a tricky negotiation. "I crave your complicity, wife. I have... plans."

"Plans?" I am careful in how I pitch my voice. It is neither no nor yes just yet.

"There are some who have wronged me," he says carefully. "Precisely who, and precisely how, I do not fully know, and I dare not lay bare to you yet. First, we trust this much, then more later. Yes?"

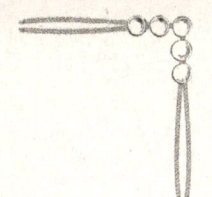

"Yes," I agree, and I swallow and match his trust with my own. "I have been wronged, too."

"Have you?"

"And I, too, want my revenge," I say, clenching my jaw. I want it with all the aching longing of my mourning heart.

"And will you tell me who has wronged you?" He is very grave, and I am pleased that he takes my concerns as seriously as his own.

I give him a long look. "When you tell me the names of your enemies, I shall reveal my own. Suffice it to say, they are powerful indeed."

"And how will you take this revenge?" His voice has taken a wary edge. Perhaps he fears being caught up in a plot of murder.

"However I can," I say grimly, but it is sorrow that fills full my voice. "A life, or a soul, or the tiniest scrap of flesh—what I can take, I will, and I will use every violence at my disposal. Will you help me?"

He runs a hand through his hair and curls his body around his wound before looking at me with a worried frown. "I will help you see clearly. I will keep you from harm if I can. As for vengeance, that we must speak more on later, I think. When you have had time to consider if this is truly the course you must take. But know this, Coralys of a drowned crown and a storm-tossed fate, you are my wife and I will shed any blood I must for your sake, ruin any creature, destroy any bastion. I will shirk no great task that must be done for your good."

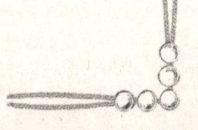

Chapter Six

I think he's probably crazy and definitely dangerous, but as long as he's willing to go along with my plans for vengeance, then I really don't care. I will find the god responsible for the death of my husband and I will make that god suffer to the full measure that I have suffered. Even if it seems impossible.

Oke cannot prevent it. In his current state, he can't overpower me, and I'm not certain he will live the seven-day out in either case.

He settles back on his seat looking almost content. The wind whips up, tossing the sea in choppy frenetic waves, and I snug his tunic around me for what little protection it offers.

"Home then, I think," Oke says. He scrubs his fingers through his beard as if considering something, lifts that hand, and makes a twisting motion as if he is turning a large bowl.

My vision warps like I've gone underwater. I grip the gunwale tightly and try not to panic. Two blinks and my sight is clear again and I'm looking at the waves just as I was looking at them before.

A trick of the imagination, then. Nothing to get worked up about. I have been under a great deal of pressure. And if the sea looks brighter, sharper, wilder, it's only because my heart is racing from a little burst of surprise, not because anything has changed.

I glance back at Oke, keeping a smooth smile on my face so he doesn't notice my little...episode. He's standing now, one hand still on the tiller. He's loosened his hair and it whips behind him in the wind like a sail. I'd think he was enjoying himself if it weren't for the steady drip of red on the floor and how he hunches over one side.

With care, I turn instead to the bow. I find my hands shake every time I think again of the wound I saw. There is something passing strange in how he might bear it but not die of it. Perhaps he is a hero of the gods—set above we usual mortals—or something more powerful and unnatural still. But no, I am only shaken up and imagining things.

Turning to face forward is not the relief I thought it would be, for an island rises before us that was not there before. And it is not the green glass nub I'd expected, though I could almost swear this is where that is located. No, the isle rises up like a fortress from the sea, white stone walls pocked with birds' nests and green plants.

Carved into the white rock, and then marching out into

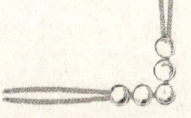

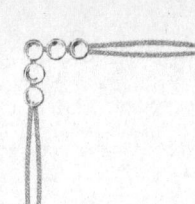

the water like a welcome party, are a series of stone statues colossal in size. Wind and waves have worn them so that their proud, human features have rounded and softened, but I get the terrible sense that they were once flinty and that that very sharpness remains in spirit and watches me. They vary in fashion of clothing and weapons as if marching through the generations from ages past until now.

"You have an army," I say mildly.

"These are no friends of mine," Oke objects absently as we sail past one of the statues. It's only visible from the nose up—the pounding waves smash just under the vacant stone eyes. It's missing an ear.

My eyes flick from face to face—some half-hidden by surf, others fully exposed. They are all watching me. Or they seem to be. But we are sailing toward a small bay nestled into the island that cradles a jetty. Perhaps these stone monstrosities were erected to purposely make visitors' skin crawl. It seems a strange choice, but I can hardly blame the man bleeding in the boat for it. These statues are hundreds of years old, judging by their weathering.

And I should know about them. An island like this? Just off the coast of the Crocus Isles? It should have featured in my lessons as a child. I should have been taken to tour it and charged with guarding it and been given the heavy responsibility of keeping the statues from falling into greater disrepair.

I glance at Oke and he almost smiles. "You get used to their judging looks. Or at least, you promise them you'll someday make them proud instead."

"How long have you lived here?" I ask, keeping my tone light and trying not to shiver.

He waves a hand as if it isn't important. "For as long as I've been the Fisher King."

My heart is racing.

"And are there truly no other people here?"

He laughs softly. "Just the guardians, the birds, the souls of the dead, and me."

My skin crawls with his words.

Well, I tell myself, you wanted vengeance on the gods. You might need to face a certain amount of strangeness to manage that. But it will be worth it to avenge the man who stole sugar buns for you when you were a child, stole your kisses thereafter, and made your throne so strong and sure that you never had need to doubt until the gods unleashed their cataclysm upon you.

I set my jaw, face forward, and concentrate on the task at hand.

"Mind the sail," Oke orders me in the crisp tone I'm used to aboard ship. And before I realize I've jumped to obey, my hands are already at work, trimming sail and preparing to dock as he steers us into the jetty.

I'm busy for a few moments in the kind of way that makes worry impossible, and by the time my tasks are done and I can look up again, we're pulling up alongside the dock—a feature as much in need of maintenance as everything surrounding Oke—and the whole bay is laid out around me in a glory of frothy waves, white gleaming sand, dancing tree limbs, and blank staring stone faces.

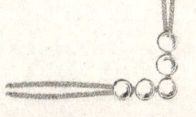

I'm so overwhelmed by the side-by-side glory and strangeness of this place that we're almost fully docked before I realize there is someone waiting for us on the very end of the jetty and that my husband is frozen like one of the warrior statues as he stares at our welcomer.

The man is young—twenty summers, perhaps—and lithe of build. He lounges against one of the uprights of the jetty, standing on tiptoes on the final board of the structure, looking as at home as a cat walking on the top of a narrow wall. At his hip dangles a spatha sporting a guard studded with sapphires, and at his throat hangs a huge uncut moonstone on a golden chain. He winks at me as we grow close enough to see details, and his pointed chin and bouncing black curls combine to give him the look of mischief come to life... and to visit.

"Who is this?" I ask in an undertone, trying to tug down the rough tunic I'm wearing to cover my knees. It's not working.

In contrast, the stranger is dressed in a short exomis of carmine silk, draped to reveal one creamy muscled shoulder. He's knotted it almost indolently around his hips in a way that highlights what it's meant to conceal. He's well muscled despite his lithe figure, and clearly wealthy despite his slothful pose. That exomis is stitched with thread of gold and his wide belt is of fine-grained leather, sewn with seed pearls. Even at my finest, I would have struggled to find riches to match the ones this young man festoons about his person with seeming carelessness.

"A cousin of mine," Oke says shortly. He seems displeased.

We draw up to the jetty and he begins to tie up without acknowledging the raised eyebrows of this "cousin" of his.

"No greeting? How terribly rude," the cousin says. "You won't ask me in?"

Oke gives him a speaking look. Blood or not, they are not friends.

"You may not set foot on my ground."

Where Oke's laughter is the murmur of the waves, this stranger laughs light as air. He looks very pointedly at his sandaled toes on the edge of the dock. They almost seem to hover over the wood, though of course that is impossible.

"Is that so? And yet I've found an inch that will allow me. And perhaps the lady will invite me in. Who are you, fair lady?"

I size him up. A layabout, I decide. Those lily-white hands bear no scars or calluses and that kind of attitude is not that of a leader of men. Royal, no doubt, in those clothes. But not a royal I know. And I know everyone along the coast of the mainland within a hundred leagues of here.

Perhaps Oke exaggerated when he called him cousin. But I have no explanation for how he is here with no boat, no attendants, and no guards.

"I am the fisherman's wife."

I've learned over the years that men who think they are important rarely agree to associate with those they consider under them. I already don't want to associate with this man. I'm happy to be as low as he'd like.

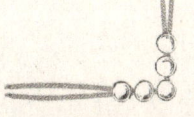

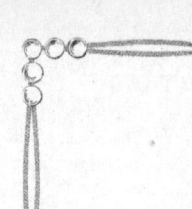

"Felicitations!" His eyes grow wider. "What wonderful news! I came to find out if my old friend had perished and instead I discover he has wed!"

"Perished?" Oke stills, watching the other man like he is a threat, and I realize this cousin must know about Oke's wound.

"A little bird told me some ill had befallen you," the cousin says lightly, brushing a gaze over Oke, who straightens as if to hide that he is wounded, though there is blood leaking through his trousers. "It seems it greatly exaggerated."

Oke grunts.

"Invite me in, lovely fisherman's wife, and we will drink to your good health."

I watch him blank-faced. Am I a child of five summers to fall for such a simple ruse?

"What was she, cousin?" the cousin presses, his smile turning cunning. Clearly, he is not one to pick up on the desires of others. We both want him gone. "A priestess? A princess, perhaps."

He is clearly trying to flatter me.

"A queen." Oke's voice is firm. The smile is gone. His tone remains light, but it feels barbed.

"Alive and married to a queen. What a funny turn of events."

I frown. He doesn't seem surprised, despite his words.

The cousin shifts slightly as if to highlight the sword at his hip, and something I can't quite translate flashes in his expression. "And you are well?"

He points to where Oke has dripped blood across the jetty.

"Quite well." My husband's voice is a sheathed sword sliding free.

I wonder what it costs him to stand up so straight. He offers a hand to help me disembark, and I take it. I don't need it, but also I don't dare shame him in front of this man. I do not understand what flows beneath the surface of their conversation.

"Then you'll come to Midsummer Eve, of course?" There's something in our visitor's voice. A hint of a challenge mixed with mockery. "To the Resurgence."

"What is the Resurgence?" I ask.

It occurs to me that there's another way to be a rich layabout that doesn't involve ruling a kingdom. One could have the favor of one of the ten gods. If this cousin were the champion of a god, he might know where they are. Or at least where one of them is. And he might be able to appear places without a conveyance. He might even be able to inflict godwounds. But which god has given his favor to this peacock? Not Heskatan or Markanos, known for battle. Not with that unblemished skin. Perhaps Ordanus, God of Art. They say he craves pretty things.

And what would that make his cousin?

Beside me, Oke stiffens just as my feet hit the pier.

Our visitor smiles. "Have you an unfulfilled dream, Queen Fisherwoman? Some vile little hope of the heart? Or perhaps you are too pure for that. Perhaps you love light and

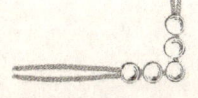

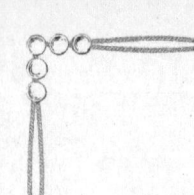

beauty and there's some injustice you'd like put right." He has blue eyes. They light up from within when he sees he's struck a chord. "If you come to the Resurgence, you can have anything you desire, Ragged Lady. You could ransom a god." He smirks. "Think on it. And if you decide to come, make the payment, and join us."

"The payment?"

He splays out his fingers for me. They're bedecked with gem-encrusted rings. Except for one that's missing.

"Cut off your finger, throw it into the sea, and say, 'I wager my soul for the will of my heart' and I'll bring you to where I am. Easy enough."

"I think you've said enough now, cousin," my husband says. "And even if you have not, you have utterly bored me. Fly off somewhere else."

And without another word, he sweeps an arm around me, turns, and sets an unrelenting pace up the jetty toward the heart of the island. I look back once and see our visitor standing there. He raises his hand like he's holding a bowl, and as my eyes are still widening, he twists his hand and disappears. An icy chill slices down into my belly. I have seen magic. And I have seen it done twice—I'm certain of that now.

Chapter Seven

Not only do you live alone and bring no one here, you also refuse visitors. Even relatives," I say as I walk with Oke. My mind is racing, grief set aside with this puzzle spread before me. Oke is a god-chosen hero. So, the question is, which god chose him? It feels obvious. But I do not want to race to conclusions.

He's given up his pretense of good health. He pauses as the dirt path widens to a boardwalk and he leans against the railing, teeth gritted and head bent down. The muscles of his wide shoulders flex and flex again, bunching tightly under his skin as if he is fighting an inner battle.

I wait, cautious. I was given a jungle cat once as a present from an ambassador of the Andalappo Isles. He was hurt in transit, though no one knew it, and when I opened the door of his cage to examine him, he shot out, claws first, and

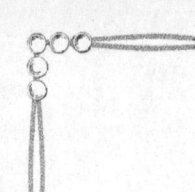

tore a great chunk from the head steward's leg. Oke's heaving back reminds me of the cat just after that attack.

Even here bleak statues line the path, their massive faces watching us, their graven eyes bearing witness to Oke's pain. I half expect one to come alive and step into our path. Perhaps this island is his solitary haunt now, but the statues speak to a long history of men in this place.

"Do not invite anyone to our island, I beg of you," Oke says after a moment, holding up his two fingers again in what might be a blessing or a spell of some kind. "You do not know what power you possess here."

"The power of hostess?" I say wryly. "Yes, it is a mighty load to bear. I know not how I'll manage it."

"Precisely," he agrees, huffing out his breath, running a hand through long hanks of hair, and then leading the way again. He's dripping blood all down the path. His meeting with his strange cousin has unsettled him.

"If I am to live here as your wife, I should know how closely my husband dances with death. If your wound is never-healing, will you die of it?"

"It is my fervent hope that I do not."

Men. They always think they can ignore anything they wish to avoid—right up to the moment it causes disaster. I make an annoyed sound in the back of my throat.

He turns to me and lifts a brow. "Do you want me dead, then, Coralys? Would you be a widow twice in as many days?"

"If you die tonight, or even tomorrow, what is to stop the

gods from claiming I have broken faith with them?" I allow myself to soften enough to let a little wry teasing creep into my voice. "Surely if it is my curse to marry, then it is also my curse to stay married."

He snorts a soft almost-laugh and for a fleeting moment we share a dark smile of shared gallows humor before he elaborates.

"The wound is carved by the hand of a god and linked to their power; it can only be dispelled by their will or by breaking the power of their curse."

I feel a little ill at the thought of that. He may be right that there's no cure for it, then. But he is no simple man to have offended a god so well as to earn this punishment. And while it might be easy to guess which god has sponsored a man who styles himself as the Fisher King, it is not so easy to guess which god has cursed him. Again, my mind starts to spin out a list. Is it Treseano, God of Death, who holds his wound? Or perhaps he offended the very god who gave him power—Okeanos, God of the Sea, who demanded this marriage.

"Which god wounded you?" I ask him boldly. "And what do you mean by a curse?"

We've been climbing. The boardwalk ascends a set of thirty stairs. At the top of them, I take his arm and wrap it over my shoulders. He smells of sweat and salt, but he leans on my shoulder with greedy relief. I have to bite back a wave of sadness. The last man to have his strong arm slung over my shoulders was Lieve.

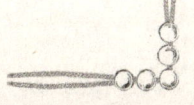

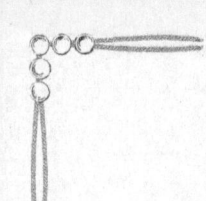

We stand still a moment, him catching his breath, me taking in this view of the island and the statues at varying heights all over it as I await his answer. Being here is like finding oneself in a city of the dead. Despite the ghoulish atmosphere, the foliage is verdant and lush and that bay is enticing. If the fishing is as good, a family could live here very well.

I try to see beyond the island, staring out into the wavering blue horizon. There's no sign of the Crocus Isles, though I'm certainly looking in the right direction. Not a tiny lump of land or even a wavering in the line of the sea. Out there somewhere, my people are picking up their lives again. And out there somewhere the gods who stripped them bare and stole their loved ones are living free and easy. I will not forget.

"The very wound is a curse," Oke says when he gets his breath back. "Power isn't free. You know this. Think of being queen. Your power is bought with a price. You command the people, yes, but also you are commanded by them. Not by them as individuals, mayhap, but by their needs, by their traditions, by their will. The monarch who bucks all three finds herself fish food in hours."

I nod. He's talking sense—though I notice he has not named the god who hurt him. My eyes narrow in suspicion.

"All power works this way. Think of the power of the talented blacksmith. For each piece he crafts, he exchanges a portion of his heart, of his imagination, of the breath of his life, of the strength and energy of his body. A smaller example, perhaps, but it is a thread that runs through all human endeavor.

"So it is with the power of the gods. Each action requires sacrifice. Each binding binds the binder. If one wanted to create a boat from the carcass of a whale, well and good, but perhaps one must live as a whale for as long as one has use of the boat—a sacrifice for a crafting. A pain for a boon. And each one is tuned to the god who wills it—the crafting of verdant things is stronger in the hands of Glorian, for instance, than it would be in the hands of Okeanos."

"Theoretically, obviously," I say when his words trail off, "for you are no god. But how do you know these things? Did your god teach you? Did your cousin?"

I am edging very close to announcing my suspicion outright. For who has not heard of humans favored by the gods as their champion heroes? Who has not heard of their works, both wondrous and terrifying? Though they are rare, the stories are not. I'd be a fool not to see that's what he is.

He grimaces. "My cousin? He's taught me a thing or two. And I'll not soon forget."

I feel a chill. "He's not complicit in your wounding, is he? Did he lead an angry god to you?"

Oke meets my eye, and I almost step back from the intensity of his gaze before I remember I'm helping him along the boardwalk.

"I do not yet know which god has wounded me. It may very well be my cousin who is to blame in the end. Trust I will discover the culprit and put an end to this."

Perhaps our ends align more than I guessed. Did he balk at a task from his patron? Or did he enrage his god's enemies

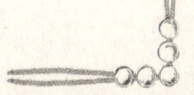

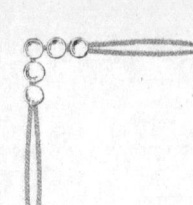

and draw attention to himself? It's hard to look at him without laughing at either suggestion. He looks like nothing more than the fisherman he claims to be. But the truth is clear as a coin in a fish's mouth. He is a god-touched hero. And he's drawn me into his world of power and wrath by bringing me here. I must learn the lay of things as quickly as I can.

I press on. "And these exchanges you speak of? They are permanent? Once a thing is sacrificed for and purchased, then it's kept forever?"

He scoffs and I find the bitter sound of it bracing but also a small comfort. I am deep in the currents of bitter sorrow and disillusionment myself, and both are welcome on the lips of another.

"Did you get to keep crown and kingdom forever?"

"No," I say wistfully. "I didn't get to keep my dear husband, either, if we're listing gifts snatched back by the gods. And I would have rather had him than ten crowns."

Oke grunts at that and I am not sure if it is meant to be agreement or compassion.

"He was the love of your life, then?"

It's a question he means to sound casual, but I answer it in the spirit it is given—with sincerity—though I choke a little on my words, wrenching as they are.

"He was my very best friend and a kind and loyal man. And I will miss him every day I'm granted."

I'm blinking back hot tears at even such a short admission and I'm grateful when he does not press me for more. What does he want? Should I bare my heart to him and show him

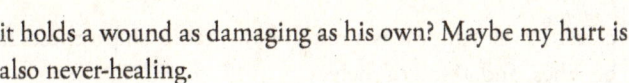

it holds a wound as damaging as his own? Maybe my hurt is also never-healing.

We turn a corner, and his home comes into sight. I hold back the sigh that wants to escape me. I don't know why I expected his home to be anything better than the boat or the tunic, but some silently optimistic fool in the back of my mind was clinging to the wild hope of a real house. What does it matter, really? I can mourn here, I suppose, as easily as anywhere else.

What greets my eye is a tiny fishing shack made of driftwood boards and flying a ragged flag above it made of sailcloth. The flag is stitched with a symbol of Okeanos—tentacles wrapped around a fishing spear—a good omen, I suppose, though whether that god would feel honored by a ragged banner I could not tell you. It is a clear sign that I have guessed correctly. He is the scion of the God of the Sea.

"All things come unraveled eventually," Oke says, and I don't know if he means these powerful acts made by sacrifice, or my life, or his home, or his relationship to his sponsor god. "Whether by time, or by neglect, or by purposeful breaking."

I force the door open with some effort. The hinge needs repairing, of course. I'm grateful that at least his home does not smell of mold or decay. It's open to one side with only sailcloth curtains to offer any shelter. They are currently tied back. A huge loft bed hangs from chains in one corner—large enough to sleep an entire family and heaped with ragged pillows. Closest to the door is a small makeshift kitchen: a hearth set with wood, a jumble of hanging pots and pans, and a bit of a hutch with a breadboard. On that side but

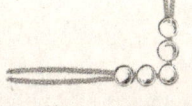

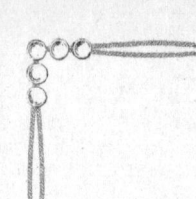

closer to the window is a rough-hewn table, ship's chests for benches, and a wall of shelves.

To my horror, someone has filled every inch of the shelves with priceless books. The weather will ruin them. All this wealth of knowledge in sea air and exposed to the elements. It's a crime.

I am blinking back tears and I cannot say why. I do not think it is for the books.

"Welcome home," Oke says wryly. He walks to the open side of the wall, leans against the post there, and looks out over the sea. He sounds almost emotional himself when he says, "I declare that what is mine belongs to you. It is yours."

What a formal way to make the offer. I look around the room, my eyes settling once more on the books.

"Thank you."

"You should read as many of those as you can." He's still looking out over the sea where the sun is sinking low over the water. Is it truly so late in the day? "And if you'll heed the will of your new husband, you'll give me the boon of not sawing off your own fingers and throwing them into the sea."

He turns to me and takes my hands in one of his, using the other to gently touch the tip of each finger.

I shiver at his touch and hope he does not notice. It is a small betrayal of the man I mourn to find the touch of another enticing, but what I long for is not passion, it is arms to hold me while I cry, someone to make the world safe again, someone to make it possible for me to be the Coralys I was just days ago.

His gaze flicks up from my fingers to me and my breath

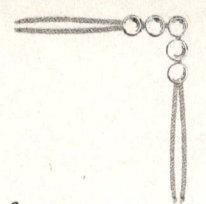

catches at what I see in his eyes. There's a flicker of something there. Interest. Desire. It is hard to be certain of the depth of the intent, but it is unmistakable.

"I have counted." Though his actions are needlessly intimate, his expression is grave.

His green eyes have shifted from what flickered before to something very alike to understanding and they make the backs of my legs feel weak for a moment. Is it a wonderful thing to be seen or a terrible one? I cannot tell you in this moment. I know only that he does see me somehow in a way I did not yet expect.

"There are ten fingers here. I would like it to remain so."

"I think I can manage that much," I say a little more tightly than I would like. My voice is not fully my own.

I steal a surreptitious look at his bleeding wound. With night approaching another bride might anticipate—or fear—the attentions of her new husband. Given how painful his wound seems, I have nothing to fear on that score. Though I am starting to suspect fear would not factor into things.

"How are you supplied here?" I ask.

"I have what I need." His tone is distracted. "And as for you, you'll find clothing in the chest nearest the door. Feel free to change out of that stained tunic. There is fresh water in a shell behind the house."

He nods with his head toward the side of the house I did not see when we approached.

"And bandages?" I ask, lifting my chin and forcing any other thoughts aside for the moment. "You may object to my

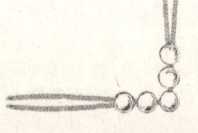

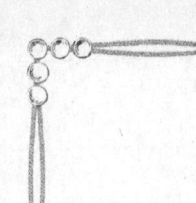

desire to help treat your wound, but I have steady hands and at least I can bandage it. It should not be rubbed and dirtied by your clothing. If you do not have it tended, you will surely die. And not even of magic. Of mere human neglect."

He drops my wrists as if they have burned him, and steps back and curls protectively over his wound like an injured animal. If he were not such a large, muscled man, I would say he looks wary of me, as if he is trying to protect something vulnerable from an enemy. I understand the vulnerability, but I am no enemy.

"Leave it be" is all he says, and with that he stalks—or tries to stalk, but there's a hitch in his step—across to the hanging bed.

He pulls himself up painfully and crawls to the far side of it, hunching around himself like a creature about to lick its wounds.

Fool of a man. If he'd accept my help, he might heal. As it is, I have no confidence that his wound won't fester. If he wants to die, let that be on his own head. This is the last time I will offer to tend it. I've never responded well to stubbornness, and I don't plan to start bending to it now.

I run a hand over my face. There's a lamp on the table and a tinderbox. I could light it.

But I'm hungry and there's no food. I'm tired from the day and worn with a combination of new experiences and jagged sorrow and I find I am suddenly too weary to contemplate anything but sleep.

There may be only one bed, but it's large enough for my

entire royal council. What kind of fisherman has a bed so large? It will certainly suffice for us both. Even if he spends all night in unrelieved physical agony and I spend all night in the emotional equivalent.

Reluctantly, I go outside in the dusky light, creep around the side of the cottage over jagged rocks and soft moss, and I find the place where a giant clam shell larger than any I've seen before catches water from a little runnel off the roof. The water smells fresh. I drink from the shell and then bathe my hands and face. I wish I could strip off the tunic here and wash myself entirely, but I am not yet so secure as to be willing to parade about the island naked.

I creep back into the cabin. Oke has not moved, but his breath hitches when I enter, so he is not asleep.

I open one of the chests in the fading light with hesitant hope. There is cloth within as he promised. I draw out the first few things I find. They are all men's things—his, if I had to guess. They are plainly made and large for me. I draw out a tunic made of sailcloth so thin from wear that it's soft. It will fall to my knees like the other one did. It's clean, however, and smells of some faint spice.

With a surreptitious look over my shoulder to be sure Oke's back is still turned, I strip out of his ruined tunic and begin to slip on the fresh one. The neck hangs open, falling over one shoulder.

Behind me, a sharp intake of breath makes me freeze and steal a look behind me. Am I wrong, or is Oke trembling a little, his back still to me? I think I am not wrong.

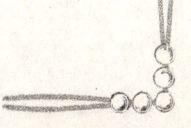

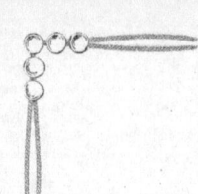

I shake my head as I drag the rest of the tunic over my form and roll the sleeves up to my elbows. He should have let me tend that wound.

But such thoughts are soon forgotten as I slip into the wide bed, far from my new husband. He does not greet me. We do not touch. But I feel the heat of his body radiating across the space to me as I curl on my own little sliver of bed with my back to him, like two curving maple seeds on the same key.

I bury my face in my hands, and I try to sleep, but what comes instead is a terrible loneliness that cannot be comforted, for there is no Lieve to nestle into. His warm arm will never drape over me again. His sleepy kisses will never again decorate my shoulders and neck, and without them I am bereft. I let myself sob soundlessly into my hands and I think my grief is private until my new husband sits up, making the bed sway, pads across the floor, and steps out into the night.

I sit up, too, worried I've angered him, and I wait, wait, wait, until through the open window I see the white sail of his fishing boat by the light of the moon. He's out on the water and I know he is not returning tonight. I sigh and fall back onto the ragged pillows.

It turns out that plotting revenge and pondering mysteries do not warm the bed the way a husband can. Not even a husband forced to wed a once-queen and wounded in a way beyond considering.

Chapter Eight

I wake to the sound of a crash, and I sit up to the sight of a turquoise sea and a perfectly clear azure sky through the open side of the cottage. A brisk breeze roughens the ocean and birds dive, screeching, over the water. Everything is too bright, too perfect, too white in the pale morning light. It is as if they conspire to mock the salt stains on my cheeks.

It feels like a hard tackle block in my throat to remember that I'm here because I've lost everything and that I can't even pore over the trade numbers or discuss the problems with the harbor break wall to distract me from the empty years yawning out before me.

The door shudders while I'm still suppressing grief, and framed within it, holding up a mother-of-pearl fish whose eyes are as round as my own, is a young man.

I swallow, blinking for a moment before I realize who it is.

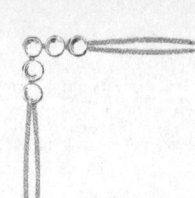

That chiseled jaw is exactly what I expected to see under the thrush-tail beard. And now that it is gone, the rest of his face makes for a very different sight. He has a strong nose, noble features, and steely green eyes. He's beautiful, if I am allowed to admit it.

He's untangled his hair and put it in a tidy knot. A cuirass of pearls is strung in ten separate strings so that they form a garment of their own that lies across his bare chest. Even more pearls hang in long strings knotted loosely around his hips in a wide sash. They clatter in the breeze coming in through the window. His feet are bare and his trousers made of sailcloth—plain and serviceable against the contrast of such extravagant wealth.

And he is... formidable. Powerful. Vital in a provoking way. He looks exactly like what he is—god touched. I have one moment of the strangest sensation that I ought to sink to my knees, that I'm seeing something so *other* and distant from humanity that I am compelled to bow, but then I suppress it sharply. I am Coralys of the Crocus Isles. I bow to no one but the gods.

It's the red stain of blood across the left side of his trousers that yanks me out of that strange sensation and reminds me that my husband is dangerous. Not just in the sense that he is feuding with powerful entities but in a new way. The kind of way that makes my cheeks flush hot and guilt taste bitter on my tongue.

My eyes snap to Oke's and his are hard as green jade, but his mouth twists with humor, and his expression is narrowing to something like appraisal.

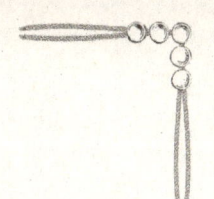

I straighten my shoulders. If he expected swooning or simpering, he should not have married a queen. Even a drowned one.

I draw myself up to my full height, keeping my expression stony even as he lifts his eyebrows. He can judge my reaction all he wants. I am not the one making a fool of myself in pearls. Besides, there's little he can do with all that appraisal when he's still dripping blood from the bite of his enemies.

With as much dignity as I can muster, I slide from the bed, ignoring how I am now the one dressed raggedly, and hold out a hand.

He looks at my hand silently as if he does not know what I'm asking for.

"Where's your filleting knife?" I ask, and he finally realizes I'm reaching for the fish and shoves it abruptly into my waiting hand.

"In the other chest," he says, wrenching his gaze away from mine and frowning.

"You could spend some of those pearls for pillows without holes in them. Or a proper boat," I tell him calmly as I lay out the fish on the table and open the other chest. The fish arcs upward. It's still fresh enough to be longing to live. I know the feeling. I press it in place with one palm and feel the slickness of its skin meet mine.

The sailor's chest is a tangle of mismatched things, all of which could be replaced by much better items by spending just one of those pearls. I am irrationally annoyed by this.

"Or you could spend them on an army to defeat these

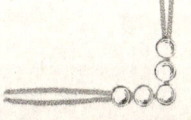

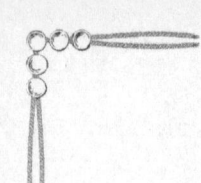

enemies you want ruined," I say as I rise successfully with knife in hand. I give him a wry look. I think we both know his enemies cannot be defeated by mortal men.

"The pearls aren't for spending. They're for keeping." His voice is thoughtful, as if he is working out a puzzle. "Here. Fill this. If you can."

I look up and he's thrusting something else at me. A brass thimble. It's patterned all around the outside with waves and swimming squid. How odd. I take it in my fish-slimed hand.

I frown at him. "Fill it with *what*?"

He shrugs, looking away with sudden shyness. His brows pull together.

"Riches."

I stare at the thimble. Oke's beard may be gone, but he is no less cryptic than he was before. And no less mad. I shake my head.

"Why don't you just put some of your pearls in it?" I suggest practically.

"Not that kind of riches."

"If you say so." I set the thimble on the table and go back to looking in the chest. I'm hungry. Maniacal tasks like filling thimbles with riches can wait until after I butcher, cook, and eat this fish.

"Thank you," he says quietly. "I must be fishing. I will return as soon as I may."

I'm still looking for a board to cut the fish on, and by the time I look up again he's gone.

I walk over to the door and watch him retreat down the

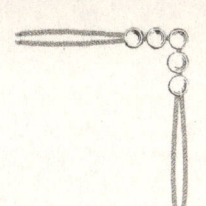

boardwalk. He's moving at speed despite his wounded leg, as if he's fleeing a fire, practically sprinting through the striped morning shadows of the judging statuary.

I bite my lip. I'd like to figure this man out. Oke may be an ally, he may even become a friend. But right now, he is a riddle, and unless he soon tells me who he serves and who he opposes, I must discover it for myself.

Besides, I cannot live my life overwhelmed with grief, and a puzzle will give me something else to fix my mind upon. Already I feel the rolling breakers of loss threatening to sweep me away again, as they did last night, and I know if I let them, I might not be able to claw my way back to the surface.

My lower lip is already shaking and tears are welling in my eyes, but I don't have time to dwell. I give his bookshelves a determined glare. They are incongruous in this vagabond place, and they are where I will start once I have filled my belly and made something of this hovel where I am to live. Surely there will be some clue to his allegiances there.

I work to light the small fire set in the hearth. I cook the fish. I'm not much of a cook. I had servants for that when I was queen. But I'm blessing my mother's soul today for deciding it was important for my education that I spend one year helping each branch of the palace servants for a week. Most of my time in the kitchens was spent chopping vegetables and washing dishes, but I *watched* a fish cooked and so I can cook one. To a degree.

What I can't do is anything else about the state of this house. There are supplies—a broom, needles and thread, a

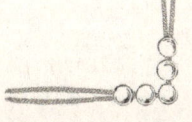

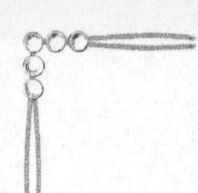

bucket and rags—but an examination shows me it's not dirty, merely shabby. Not in disrepair but rather extremely old.

That's fine. I'm not here to keep house or charm a husband. I'm simply biding my time until I'm ready to destroy a few gods. I wonder if they can be killed. There's tale after tale about it, and where would such tales spring from if not history? And yet I've never known someone before Oke who claimed to even meet a god, never mind hurt one. It seems an almost impossible task.

But "impossible" has never been a word that applied to me.

I'll take this little by little, like the old proverb. How do you eat a great whale? One mouthful at a time.

I need a weapon before anything else.

I would pray for one, but the irony of asking the gods for a weapon to destroy them is too much for even me.

I did not believe in gods before, but I made a bargain with them all the same and I heard their voices in the wind. They are out there and they are responsible for all my calamity. And I will feed them their own sorrows and return back to them tenfold the destruction they have wrought on me and mine.

In the end, I pick up that strange thimble as if it might be a clue and turn it round and round between my fingers as grief for my beloved takes a moment to wash over me. I let sorrow unmoor me for a few minutes before I stuff it back down and carry on. Like the tide, I expect it will rise often, and like the tide it will have to recede. I refuse to accept anything else.

Grimly, I wash the other tunics and the dishes, eat my fish, and finally go to the bookshelves.

These books have been shelved in no discernible order. A book on the campaigns of the Orange Fleet is shelved beside a book of epic poetry and that is beside a book of maps of the Crocus Isles. I want to pull that out, but I need to focus. There's no clear theme between the selections that might offer a clue, and there's nothing on theology, which would have been the most helpful in destroying the gods, but there are two books of myths that I pull out in hopes that one of them is based at least in part on truth.

As I draw out the second book, something small falls off the shelf, hits the ground, and then rolls under the bed.

I chase after it. It is another pearl. A black one with no setting. If Oke had only mentioned he had an enormous wealth in pearls, we could have properly outfitted his boat before we left my home.

I bring the pearl to the table with me along with the books of myths. I should put it back. Even if my husband has so many that he loses track of them and they fall out of the bookcase, still, stealing is stealing.

But revenge can be expensive, too.

"What is mine belongs to you," I murmur, quoting Oke's words from last night.

I set the pearl in the thimble. There. He has his first chunk of "riches." I stare at it, thinking of another black pearl. One that Lieve wanted to buy for me set in silver.

"It's too extravagant," I'd told him. "I don't need to wear wealth. Better to use it for the good of the isles."

On a whim, I get up, dig into the chest, and come out

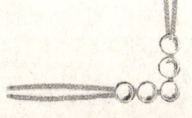

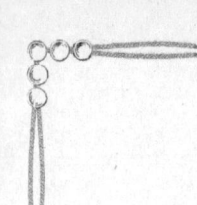

with a weatherworn belt of green leather that has a small pouch affixed. I saw it there before, but I had nothing of value to keep safe. Now I do. I jam the thimble and pearl into the pouch and look around, because I am loath to have a pouch on my belt that is only for the trivial, and when I see a chipped belt knife and a flint I add them in as well. Everyone should have a knife for practical tasks like cutting lines or lighting fires.

I snug the belt around my hips and go back to work. Opening the first book at random, I read it with furious intensity.

It tells the story of Kilinippa, a princess—it's always a princess—who had to do five impossible tasks to free her husband from the halls of the underworld and release him from the wrath of the gods. She must have loved the man very much. If suffering can win you a boon, she'd earned a lot more than one soul by the time she was done with these tasks.

Poor thing. She would have been better off born a merchant's daughter or married to a fishmonger. People of simple backgrounds are never dragged into these terrible stories. Their stories are hard enough—full of empty bellies, sick children, and death in childbirth, but at least no one makes them mix with gods and madness.

But these are the kinds of stories I need. Though this one tells nothing about how to *find* the underworld or any other god-inhabited place, it does indicate that one exists.

Someone has slipped a little piece of parchment between the last pages of the story. I pull it out and run my eyes idly

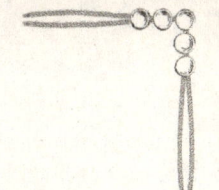

over a penned list upon the scrap. It reads like a task list a madman might make. Or like a selection of notes for a new myth.

Win a god's oath.
Wed the drowned queen.
Collect the dead to serve.
Fill a thimble with riches.
Heal the crown of the sea.
Turn the betrayer's heart.
Mend time with golden stitches.
Drink the ocean dry.
Spin moonlight into silver.
Split the seven seas in twain.

This list is eerily similar to something I've read before. Five of these tasks I recognize as Princess Kilinippa's. She spun moonlight into silver on a drop spindle she stole from the goddess Glorian. She used gold to buy back the home of her husband's ancestors lost to them by treachery, thereby "mending time with golden stitches." She made the one who betrayed her beg forgiveness before the king. For returning the spindle, Glorian agreed to give her children peace. And...yes, there it was...she drank a tavern called "the Ocean" dry by means of marching an entire town through it in one evening. Not all that impossible, it seemed, though I have the feeling that if by doing this she earned some kind of magic for herself, then it must not have been very potent

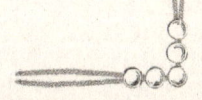

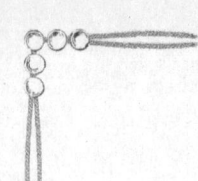

since she was clearly relying on creative misinterpretation to fulfill some of these tasks.

But the other things on the list...I feel like I've heard of them, too. I frown for a moment.

Plector!

It takes me some time and three more books from the shelves before I find the passage from the historian Herolithus on the deeds of Plector, an ancestor of mine. According to the text, Plector was tasked by the gods with five great tasks for the overturning of what was called a "curse upon the seas most terrible." Unfortunately, Herolithus seemed more intent on explaining the political turmoil of the islands and the various players there and less on the actual tasks, which he deemed fanciful and more of a ruse of Plector's to win the hearts of the people than any true deeds done for the gods. He did note one of the tasks involved marrying a "drowned queen." To fulfill so grim an order, Plector had sailed to a far-off land, drowned a queen there with his own hands, and then staged a mock wedding at the local temple. It was an act Herolithus assured the reader was very unlikely to be true and certainly only a tale told by bards who made their coin on "thrilling and horrifying the base populace."

But there it is. Written down. And my strange husband who holds magical power in his palm and claims to be wounded by the gods had called me "Drowned Queen." A coincidence? I doubt it.

He's also handed me that fool thimble.

I study the list again and my mouth goes dry. Mad or

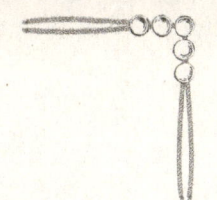

sane, this is clearly my new husband's list. Filling the thimble is fourth on the list. Wedding the queen is second. Does that mean he thinks he's fulfilled the other two? Has he won a god's oath? Has he collected the dead to serve him?

I snort at myself. I must be dazed with grief and loss to cast myself in such a ridiculous sailor's tale. But I am starting to believe it was not coincidence that brought Oke to my docks. I am starting to think that he names me "Drowned Queen" to make me so. That he saw what the gods had done to me and swooped in to take me on purpose.

I swallow against a dry throat and shoot a furtive glance to the door where he loomed just hours ago in all his pearl-encrusted glory.

If he is following some mad plan laid out in myths to gain himself an otherworldly power—well, that makes him worse than mad. It makes him worse than dangerous. It makes him a tool of indolent gods. I know full well what it is to involve yourself in the workings of gods...and what it will take from you. And I am alone here on this island with a man neck-deep in the business of gods.

A book falls from the shelf and I jump, letting out a shuddering breath. Now I am the one manufacturing stories and leaping to foolish conclusions. Shaking my head, I go back to the shelves and return the fallen book to its place along with the others I've taken out. There are plenty of stories here. I'll not be bored in days to come. But I do not think I'll find the means to my revenge here. Or a hint to my husband's loyalties.

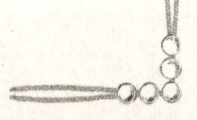

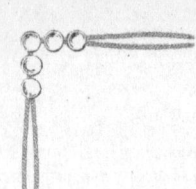

I trace a finger down the spines of the books a little sorrowfully, my mind back in my own library listening to Lieve read aloud to me. It feels like a lifetime ago.

My finger catches on one book that sticks out farther than the rest. I push it back to make it line up with the others, but it does not budge. Frowning, I draw it out.

The Twelve Furies of Vesuvius.

I have never heard of Vesuvius. I open the book. The first page is a woodcut of an angry-looking god holding a trident. He's bare-chested, and where he ought to have legs there are octopus tentacles. Beneath the woodcut are the words "Vesuvius, God of the Sea."

But that is not right. Okeanos is the God of the Sea. It was in his temple where I bargained for my people's lives.

The book is old. Too old, I would have thought, for this kind of binding. It is bound like a modern book with fine stitching and good-quality vellum, the leather tooled carefully across the exterior, though the edges of the pages crumble and the story within speaks of lands I've never known.

Perhaps it is a tale spun to tell of a time that never was. I am about to put it back on the shelf when I see what was keeping it thrust outward.

A lever.

I look around as if someone might be watching, but I've never been very good at banking my curiosity. I hardly wait a moment before I pull the lever. To my surprise, the bed hanging on chains rises into the ceiling, and the chains I thought were affixed to the floor pull up a trapdoor.

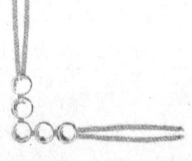

A trapdoor with steps leading downward.

Hidden lists. Hidden levers. Hidden steps.

I take a step toward the trapdoor, but I'm arrested by the sound of someone on the step outside the door.

I spin around, jam the lever back in place, cover it with the book, and I'm there panting and blessing the gods that the trapdoor shuts quietly when Okeanos slips into the house with a shy smile on his face.

"There's a bloom of jellyfish," he tells me as if my heart isn't racing. "Come and see."

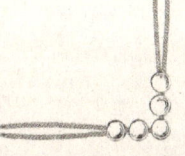

Chapter Nine

"They're beautiful," I admit as he guides the boat through the jellyfish bloom, sailing slowly, silently over the undulating masses of translucent bodies. They're layered one over another, as beautiful and transient as the days of life that layer in much the same fleeting way.

I hang over the gunwale, letting myself be mesmerized by what I see. The movement, the gentle rock of the boat, and the warmth of the sun on my back lull me enough that for a moment I can push everything back inside and drift. I am nothing but this moment. I am no one but the beholder of languid patterns and intricate flows. I am not a grieving queen but only a pair of eyes beholding in wonder.

"What did you do while I was gone?" Oke asks me in a gentle hush. He has a hand on the tiller, but he's stretched over the side of the small boat, too, his eyes tracing the

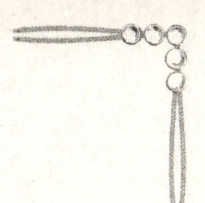

jellyfish. A crease in his brow tells me something troubles him.

"I read your books," I tell him idly, and it is a moment before I realize he has turned to me. His hair has spilled free of its knot and it catches on the breeze and blows around his face as if to hide emotions he does not wish to share with me. I push on boldly. "And I discovered my husband was making notes from the deeds of legends."

The hardening of his expression is enough proof that I have hit the mark.

"Ten impossible tasks," I challenge before turning my eyes back to the moving jellyfish.

I want to dive in with them and drift just like that until my legs and arms cease to be full of bones and edges. Until I am nothing but a ripple in the current of this life, here and then gone again. It has nothing to do with this conversation. It is an ever-present thing, never-healing like my new husband's wound.

I throw all caution to the wind. What does it matter?

"I saw your list, Oke, and I read the books. The tasks of Plector. The tasks of Kilinippa. You put them into one list. Ten is the number of the gods. The number of the holy. The number of the impossible."

"Impossible is not a thing that exists," Oke says fervently, edging toward me. He's let the tiller go and the boat float where it will. We have no sail up and there is not much current.

"That's what I've always said," I murmur.

His voice has a note of appeal in it when he says, "Nothing

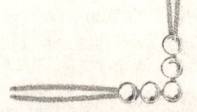

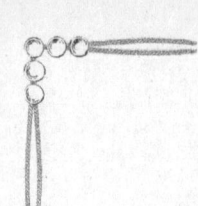

can be truly impossible when pitted against an unyielding will."

"And do you have such a will?" I ask him in a way meant to provoke. I am annoyed because making wild claims about strength of will is usually something *I* do while others look on wide-eyed. I mislike having my tactics turned on me.

He doesn't answer straightaway and I can tell he's startled by my tone, but then surprise fades to something warm in his eyes that I read as attraction. His lips part, and I realize I don't want to hear what he will say. I slip past him and take the boat's tiller in hand.

He watches me, amused, but he does not comment, simply settles into tying the loose end of a knot as if we two always work together. Eventually he says, "I have the will to do whatever I must. What is it to you, Drowned Queen?"

His easy manner only makes me more agitated. "And will you do those things you listed? Those wild tasks? Moonlight to silver? Gods' oaths?"

His brow furrows and his expression flickers from mood to mood as if he is trying to make a decision about something. We stand side by side under an azure sky above a writhing mass of one of nature's wonders. It would be almost a tranquil scene if we did not each have secrets hanging over us like storm clouds waiting to drop rain upon the water. Instead, our conversation feels portentous.

"What would you say if I admitted that out there, I have people I care about, too? A people tormented and hounded. A people who need someone to protect them," he says.

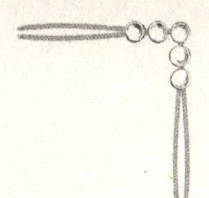

"I might be relieved," I say. I want him to tell me more. I want him to tell me everything.

"Relieved?"

"Who are we if we love nothing at all? I was a queen. I was a beloved wife. I was honored and powerful only yesterday and now I stand here barefoot in a threadbare borrowed tunic. My only comfort is that I saved my people. I may have lost all else, but they are safe."

"Exactly. That is exactly it, Coralys," he says. "You, of all people, understand what it is to give your comfort, your safety, your entire heart for the good of someone else. So, if I tell you I have... goals. Plans. That I am undertaking a great act of wonder, can you not agree there might be some purpose or even necessity to that?"

He seems to be holding his breath, but I will not answer him. Of course his motivations sound noble. That is not what I'm questioning.

"This is beyond the realm of good reason," I tell him frankly. "Surely there are other ways to help your people than to try to perform an act of power."

He makes a frustrated sound in the back of his throat, rubbing his shaven jaw as if he is annoyed there is no beard to pull. I get the distinct impression he is hiding something from me and struggling to answer without revealing it.

"Trust me when I say to you this is what is needful. What must be accomplished. And only I can achieve it."

"And where do I fit in these star-spanning dreams of yours?"

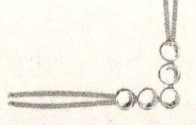

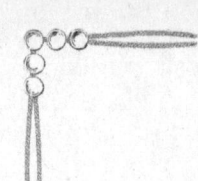

"You, Coralys," he says, reaching forward and slipping a stray strand of hair behind my ear, "are precisely in their center."

As if that is not wildly troubling. I lean back so that his hand must fall away.

"And do you have the backing of a god?" I ask with a bitter snap to my words because even now he is hiding the most important part. That he serves a god—and likely the one who ruined me. "Tell me, Oke, do the gods condone your unattainable mission? Do they applaud you for trying to achieve what the scholars call impossible?"

He shakes his head and I look up into his impossibly deep eyes. "There is no one striving to achieve this but me, Drowned Queen."

"Not even the god you serve?" I say, daring him to tell me the truth.

"And who would that be?" His refusal feels defiant.

And the way his jaw hardens and his lower lip divots with displeasure makes my breath catch. Anger suits him. I hope I look as well-dressed in it.

"You tell me," I say with the quiet of true anger.

When he will not answer honestly, I go back to staring at the jellyfish. He can keep his secrets, but then I will keep mine.

We watch the jellyfish for a long time, both lingering in silence. It is the kind of silence that acknowledges we are two ships sailing different courses, even if we are temporarily thrown together. He sighs as the stars are coming out.

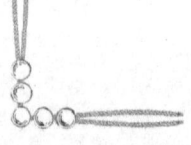

"You would not be so beautiful if you were not so furious with me, I think, Queen Coralys," he says mildly.

"Then I shall strive to remain so," I tell him, but his acknowledgment and compliment have served to soften me. "Better angry than sorrowing."

He nods. "Sorrow is the gift you give what cannot be or is not anymore. It is a gift to the past. Anger is the gift you give the future, a sacrifice offered to unrelenting gods in hopes they'll choke upon it and you can rebuild the world as you like it from their bones."

I look at him sidelong. "How long have you been waiting to share that thought with someone?"

He waves with two fingers, dismissing it as nothing. "Oh, not more than a decade."

I snort a laugh and it breaks the tension between us, and when he looks at me again, he has softened, too.

"Be as furious as you like. Burn me to cinders with your fiery gaze. But know this, Coralys. I hide nothing from you that I will not eventually expose when the moment is ripe."

Something about how he has worded that makes me have to swallow hard and I hardly notice when he takes the tiller back from me and steers us to land.

He leads me up from the shore and then we go and clean fish.

"Like this," he says gently, all traces of belligerence gone when he puts his big hands over mine and shows me how to slide the filleting knife through the fish more smoothly.

We pile the flesh of the fish up silently together, my

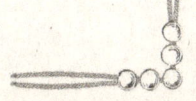

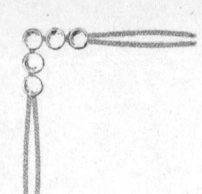

movements flowing into his as if I have worked alongside him all that decade he was thinking up his theory of sorrow and fury. We move from one task into the next in tandem.

"We work well together," he suggests with a beguiling quirk in the corner of his mouth when, after the fish are clean, we coil ropes side by side so smoothly that it is as if we can read one another through movement alone.

I remain silent, lest a single word betray the conflict churning in my heart. It is not enough that we can laugh at the same dark jokes. It is not enough that we seem made to be harnessed together like a pair of draft horses. None of it is enough if he will not speak the truth to me.

"I'll buy you new clothing when next I am near a market," he offers as we make our way home. And his cheek dimples when he says it. He's being charming. And accommodating. Generous, even. But none of that is enough to fully cool what burns like a hot ember in my chest.

I do not trust a man who keeps secrets from me. And were I able to trust, there would still be the yawning gape in my heart to contend with. Every kind thing he says, every compassionate gesture hurts because it is someone else who is supposed to be here saying these things to me, doing these things with me, and my real husband will never be here again.

We eat together and we retire together—both once more to our separate sides of the massive bed. I try with all my considerable will not to shudder my way into the sobs that try to catch hold of me. But when I inevitably cannot sleep

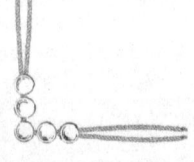

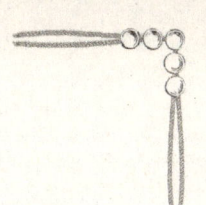

and he is shifting and suppressing groans once more in lieu of rest, I do not wait for him to go out in the boat alone like he did before. Instead, I am the one to abandon the bed and creep out into the night.

When I was a little girl, I used to find the call of the sea comforting. I imagined I could almost hear a voice in the tides whispering my name. My mother would leave my window open, laughing gently at her fanciful child, but despite her laughter I was convinced that the sea was my friend and as long as it was nearby I would be safe.

I cannot feel the same way anymore. As I stumble out of the cottage, choking on the tears already falling in a patter and splatting hot on my bare feet, all I can think is that the sea has taken from me everything I loved. I do not find comfort in the sound of it. Its crash and murmur is a cruel taunt.

It's bright enough in the spill of moonlight that I need no light to make my way out across the island. I do not follow one of the paths—not even the ones I haven't trod yet. I crave the risk of walking where I can barely see. I want to do something dangerous. I do not know if I do it as a defense to keep Oke from following me or if I half wish he *would* follow. I crave being told I am a fool. I want to have someone to yell and rail against. I want to fight. And there is only one other person on this heap of an island.

But by the time I find a steep, jutting cliff that ends in nothing but furious surf below me, I no longer want to be found. I want only to rage alone. And I do.

I glare at the surf and I hate it for being so vast and

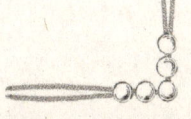

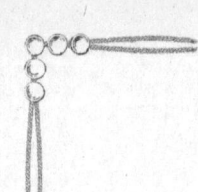

unfeeling, so impossible to make pay for what it stole from me. I weep bitter tears and let the sobs shake my body and I creep out to the very edge of the cliff to where the balls of my toes cross just over and curl around the lip of rock. My belly is tight with emotion, my eyes glazed over and breath sharp and painful.

And then a fear-roughened voice breaks over the roar of the ocean: "Coralys!"

I whip my head around, and I must still be glaring, because Oke flinches back. He's come close to me without me even realizing and I regret ever wishing he would follow me. Grief is a cup I must drain alone.

"What are you doing?" he asks, looking from me to the sea and back, and the look on his face is so horrified, so panicked, that I nearly choke on a dark laugh.

"I'm standing on the edge of a cliff," I say acerbically. "What are you doing?"

"I am watching you." He huffs a self-deprecating near-laugh as if he realizes his mistake, but his eyes—almost black in the moonlight—are on my face and I know he can see the tears gleaming and giving me away. He takes a half step forward, his voice uncertain. "You loved him very much. Your husband."

"I would gladly take his place and give him mine," I say fiercely.

"I had not met your husband," he says gravely, "but I am certain he would have made an easier wife than Queen Coralys."

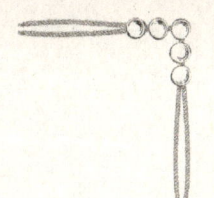

I choke on a laugh, and I'm not sure if it is humor or just a way not to cry more. "With such wit it is a wonder you do not have more friends."

His smile is a little wistful. "What was his name?"

I choke on it. "Lieve of House Carnelian."

He makes a sign of blessing for the dead. It's a thoughtful gesture, but I glare at him balefully for it. He has no right to honor my dead. I haven't given him permission for that.

"Lieve of House Carnelian," he repeats, and the way he says it, like an apology, breaks the resentment in me, leaving only a second spill of tears.

I turn my face away so he will not see them. I do not make a sound.

He steps out from among the tall rocks and into the moonlight, joining me on the lip of the cliff, waiting patiently for me to clarify. When I glance at him, I see him watching me out of the corner of his eye, though he faces forward.

I want desperately to push my grief back down into my chest.

"What would you have me tell you?" I ask bitterly. "That every time my eyelids close I see him go again beneath the water never to return? That I still feel the ghost of his touch in every breeze that brushes my skin? That I expected this morning to open my eyes to his smile and saw instead only a strange place and an empty bed beside me? That I miss his jokes? I would not give you the satisfaction."

My eyes well up and my vision swims enough that I take a cautious step back from the edge, and then to my utter

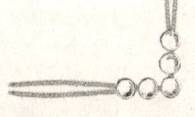

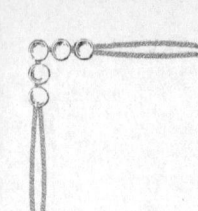

shock his arms wrap around me and I'm pulled against his solid chest in an impulsive embrace. The shock of it sends my mind reeling and for one wild moment I am simply enveloped in warmth.

"Of course you would not, you maddening queen," he murmurs gently. "Why would you allow yourself to be comforted when you can choose to be made of prickles? But I am not easily pierced by the teeth of your thorns."

He is warm and strong and certain as if he can ward off all trouble, as if he might even turn back the pages of time and mend my heart. And it is too much. It is far too much.

Tears spill hot and fast from my eyes and I'm clinging mindlessly to him without conscious thought, shuddering as waves of agony sweep over me and hollow me like the surf eroding the shore. I press my face into the crook of his shoulder and suck in long breaths. He's making soft shushing noises, and when he strokes a gentle circle with his widespread palm between my shoulders, I am overcome.

I wrench myself abruptly from his arms. We look at each other, both breathing heavily. His face is startled, lips parted, already looking as if he regrets his choice.

I do not give him time to express any such regret. Rather, I say, "We should return to the cottage. There may be all manner of dangers on this island."

"We are the only two living souls," he whispers.

But I do not answer his protest. I dry my eyes, swipe my cheeks with the backs of my hands, and lead him back to our shared bed.

"Grief is its own vast sea," Oke says in the darkness of the cottage as we settle back in to pretend to each other that we will sleep. I cannot see his face, but I hear the catch in his voice as he speaks. It is full of experience. "And none of us can cross it by the same path. Do not hurry your journey, Coralys. Certainly, I have no such requirement of you."

It's much harder not to cry when he is so kind. I wish he would stop and let me push all this away where I need not dwell on it at all.

But as I fall to sleep, in the confusion that comes as unconsciousness descends, I do not know if I am longing for the arms of Lieve to hold me or the arms of the one who has tried to comfort me.

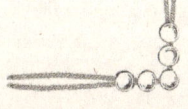

Chapter Ten

I do not need any light to descend the stone steps, for the room beneath is as open to the air on one side as it is with the cottage above, carved into the same cliffside. The builder was clever enough to create several long slits about as wide as my body in the side wall and fit them from floor to ceiling so that the stone room, while guarded from the elements, is well lit.

With Oke gone fishing again, now is my chance. He's hovered very close since the night he feared I would take my own life, and while I appreciate his company, my fingers itch to unveil the secret I knew was beneath us, waiting to be exposed.

I have imagined all manner of things over these past few days, and now that my chance is here, I am almost afraid to be disappointed by it. But from the moment my head dips below the cottage floor, it is hard to keep my mouth from falling open. In stark contrast to the room above, this cavernous space is rich beyond my experience. None of my palaces have boasted such intricate murals as the ones set into the mosaic floors. Stylized waves and stars are woven in swirling beauty from tiles no larger than my smallest fingertip and fitted to form the floor. I think they might be reminiscent of the Cryciene Period, but the method of shearing the tiles into such delicate shards was lost after the War of Eastern Tides and we never rediscovered it.

The builders chose pale blues and stark whites for their patterns, and mosaics crawl right up the walls to waist level, where they morph into smooth white stone and then elaborate wave-and-tide cornices. I think that the walls and cornices may have been carved directly from the stone when this room was set into the rock, and my mind can't help tallying workers, materials, and cost. I would estimate three years of effort and ten seasons of wealth for my nation would be soaked up in trying to replicate this. And it's all sitting here where no one can enjoy it.

There are riches on display, set on plinths and small pedestals. They're valuable, no doubt, but they're displayed like a collection rather than like useful tools—a draped shawl here, a burnished breastplate there, a small red stone vase, a carved sculpture no larger than my hand depicting a donkey of all things. They're vaguely familiar, as if I've read of these things before. Is that meant to be the daffodil blade of Corephus used to cut the snake venom from his brother's heel? I've never seen another attempt to create the relic of the tale. But a collection of items from legends will not help me now

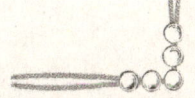

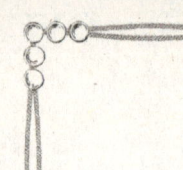

and I do not bother with them. I'm sure I'll have plenty of time later to peruse everything on this island if I wish it. All I have is time and the weight of it clogs my chest if I dwell on it too long.

I go first to the dominating feature of the room.

Placed in the very center—surrounded by enough space to admire it from every side and surely planned when the room was built, for the mosaic swirls out from it—is something I've only ever read about but never seen before, a marvel of modern engineering, a treasure so priceless it might turn back the tide of a war. A water clock.

It is hard not to gasp at that. I was offered plans for one once for a kingly sum. The seller had given me only a brief peek at them and that peek had been enough to tell me I had neither the expertise nor the resources in my kingdom to properly make use of them. Such an item is a master craft and the work of years to produce. I'd been sorry to turn it down, though, and I had thought long on the glimpse I'd had months after the seller's boat had left our shores.

The builder of this clock—to his great credit—has been restrained in the details, choosing white marble rather than gaudy golds.

In the center of the water clock is a marble figure that can only be one of the gods. He is depicted with a fishing spear slung across his back and throttling a sea monster in each hand. He looks noble—if a naked man can look noble when he has no face. Considering the intricate detail in every other aspect of the statue, from the froth on the waves twisting

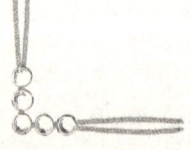

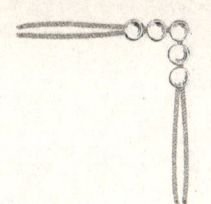

around his knees to the curls of his hair, it's an arresting thing to see the face is gouged away in great hunks as if someone took offense to it.

I look up to where a half circle is set above the figure's head. Rays reach out from the center. Three of them are golden. Seven more are black. That is not the current time—but neither are there only ten hours in the day.

How very odd.

As I'm thinking it, a bell rings and I catch my breath as water pours from the half-circle sun into the waiting mouth of one of the sea serpents, who then turns on a lever, falling from the statue's grip until its head is close to his feet, where it coughs the water into a narrow trough. From that trough, the water falls into the pool of green surrounding the statue and the sea serpent rights itself again.

My heart is pounding in my chest. I need no more proof that my husband's ties are incontrovertibly to Okeanos, the God of the Sea. I need not even his own admission.

I climb back up the steps in a hurry, suddenly afraid I might be caught, remove the broom, settle the bed back in place, and snatch the book that had disguised the hidden room from the shelf.

My breath is coming quickly. But what have I to fear? The worst has already happened: My heart has been shattered, my people decimated, my husband drowned. What could this new husband do in his wrath that could top that? Nothing. I dare him to try. Him and his sea god sponsor.

I snatch up *The Twelve Furies of Vesuvius*, reading

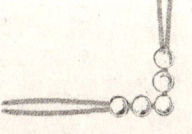

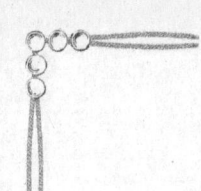

quickly while standing beside the empty place on the shelf. I will put it back the moment I hear a sound. My heart is pounding.

It is a strange book indeed. Its author—who does not name himself—seems to think he is writing something factual, though of course it cannot be so. He lays out the names of the gods first and my eyes skitter down the list, hardly paying attention, for I know these names by rote: Aurelius, God of the Air; Glorian, of Growing Things; Heskatan, of Horses; Pagetto, of Travelers; Treseano, of Death; El'Dorian, of Love; Alexandros, of the Hammer; but my mind stutters when I get to Lichenchus listed here as God of War, when I know well the name of that god is Markanos. And now here is listed Typani, Goddess of Art, who ought to be Ordanus. I frown at the book as we reach the God of the Sea—who ought to be Okeanos. Who has been *worshipped* as Okeanos for as long as my people have lived on the Crocus Isles. Instead, this whimsical writer has named Vesuvius, chaotic God of the Sea, Lord of Rage and Passion. I flip back through the book, frowning all the while. It is so very old that even in turning the pages the edges of the vellum crack and soft dust falls from the edge. The penned words—copied with care—are slightly faded, but even faded they speak boldly.

I linger over one passage.

> "And so Vesuvius slew his predecessor, Chaolic, and passed from creature to god. For those we call gods

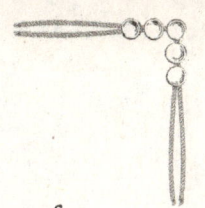

are not such, but only caretakers under the banner of heaven."

My already racing heart is caught by waves of hope and rushes faster still at this information. Can this be true?

"And, verily, the soul of Chaolic complained loudly upon her demotion and roared across the seas in many storms and threw her case before the Lord of Lords beyond the veil of the heavens, but the Lord of Lords heard not her plea, for it was written upon the bones of the earth that Vesuvius should take her place, and that the sea should boil, and the shores shrivel, and the people fear the sea for an age until another came and took his place after him. That other would be he who holds the souls of his dead close and walks with succor in his footsteps, blood and flowers line his path, and though his power is cleaved in two, so will he still bear the spear of judgment, and will he drag from the sea her riches and from the gods their prostrate obeisance."

I can hardly breathe. Here, at last, is the hope for which I have been looking. If the gods can be killed and their places taken, then I can truly hold Okeanos to account for all he has done. It is possible.

More than that, I have the key to his ruin right here on this island, in this house, in the form of his chosen hero. My husband. The Fisher King.

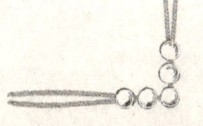

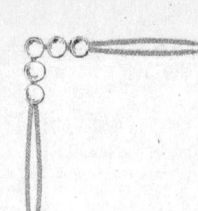

My fingers practically tingle with the excitement of it, but I must be deliberate, for I am only a mortal and no mortal stands more than the most slender of chances against the will of a god.

I am no longer content to remain in this cottage waiting.

I know where Oke will be even though I have been married to him such a short time. He will be fishing. And I must see him with my own eyes so that I may weigh whether I might turn this champion of a god into a weapon for my own hand.

I make my way under the watchful eye of the statues. They make the lonely haunt feel as though it is inhabited by ghosts.

The sea is calm again today, soft, pale blue and so smooth it reflects the tufted clouds above. It mocks me in its peace, and for a moment I glare at it and tremble, but the tears do not come.

Tears will not bring back my innocent husband or the people who depended on me. They will not make wrongs right or tear down hubris or dethrone heartlessness.

A small part of my mind reminds me that neither will revenge. But that, I choose to ignore. I will feast on revenge. I will sup on retribution. I will sate myself with vengeance until I am aching with overindulgence.

I wait as the sun sinks lower and lower, wreathing this island in an undeserved golden crown.

I expect to see his sail while still a long way off, but instead he appears so suddenly that my heart freezes in my chest and I have to force myself to breathe.

His little boat has materialized from nothing and is beside the dock as if it never left, but his emergence is seared across my vision and I can see very distinctly the shape of his upheld hand—shaped like a bowl, just like before—and I wonder what will happen if I try to make that shape with my hand, too. If one mortal—even a god's pet mortal—can perform such magic, surely another can as well.

He's already lowering his hand, and I'm surprised that he smiles peaceably when his eyes find me. He is not put out that I am down on the beach waiting for him, then.

I help him tie his boat to the dock, my hands trembling.

"You are waiting for me," he says as if testing the idea for merit.

"Yes."

He is beginning that winning smile of his again, but I cut him off.

"You are god touched," I tell him, throwing it in his face. "You serve the will of Okeanos, God of the Sea."

I give him time to deny it. But the sudden woodenness of his expression is enough proof that I have hit the mark.

"Each time I see you anew you level accusations at me," he says mildly, pushing past me to climb the steps back to our cottage, but he does not meet my eye.

"Is it an accusation if it is true?"

We climb together, fish in his hand and worry tucked deep in my heart. I do not want to fight him. But I demand that he relinquish his secrets.

"I am your wife," I say baldly, and he flinches. "I am

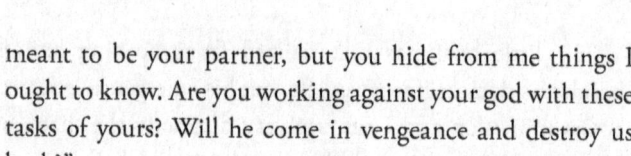

meant to be your partner, but you hide from me things I ought to know. Are you working against your god with these tasks of yours? Will he come in vengeance and destroy us both?"

I might even want that. If he comes in fury, he will be here. I cannot think of another way to access a god.

"You need not fear such," he says. "I would not willingly place you in danger. It's a rare woman who would give her future to save her people. I honor that."

"You honor me? Then be honest with me. Tell me who you serve."

His eyes are a driftwood fire—green and scorching.

"I do honor you, Queen Coralys," he says tightly. "And I have told you that I will reveal all to you when the time is right. Which is not now. I, too, have a people I am devoted to protecting, and I will trade myself for their futures day by day, piece by piece. Tell me this, if you do not like my answer, will you make it your goal to hinder me?"

I lift my chin and refuse to answer that. If he will not bare himself to me, then he cannot expect that trust from me, either. But if he will not let me in, mayhap he will let me out.

"Would you sail me away from here if I asked you to? Back to my home and people?"

"No." The word is barely audible, but I know men. I know it is not negotiable.

"Will you tell me why there is a treasure beneath your house?"

He looks at me sharply. "I do not touch that treasure, and I

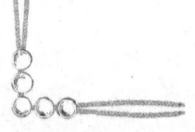

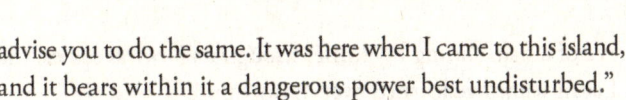

advise you to do the same. It was here when I came to this island, and it bears within it a dangerous power best undisturbed."

Ah. So he guards it for his master like a large dog sleeping on a bound chest.

"Who are you?" I demand, bold as the seagull, not bothering to disguise the frustration in my voice. Daring him to meet me in my boldness. Giving him this chance to be a true husband to me. "Tell me the truth."

"In time I will tell you all," he says, exasperated. "Every detail. But does not your dead husband deserve the honor of your sorrow? Do you not deserve the consideration of being given time to grieve your many losses? I would not begin our lives together by robbing you of what is rightfully yours. How can we stand together in my fight if you do not know I am your ally just as I require you to be mine? No, more than allies, friends."

Lieve was my friend. And he would not have hidden himself from me.

I look away, blinking furiously, and when I turn back he is already making his way painfully back up the boardwalk steps, leaving a trail of smeared blood in his path. He has distracted me from my purpose by touching my grief.

I dash my tears aside and stiffen my spine. This will not do. Grief is a terrible force, and if I let it govern me, I will be useless for all else. But I will not let him use it to maneuver me, either.

I follow him into the house and silently help him cook and prepare fish, and it's only when I'm looking into the black

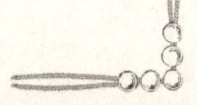

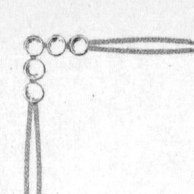

eye of a fish, sliding my knife through its flawless scales, that I turn what I've learned over in my mind.

Oke knows how to work magic. I've seen him do it twice. He must think he can use it to work his list of tasks for a people he loves. But he does not have the backing of a god in this, which means he is alone in his endeavors. And maybe he has not confessed his plans to me because he does not see me as a wife, or a friend, or an ally, but merely as a tool. Just as I see him.

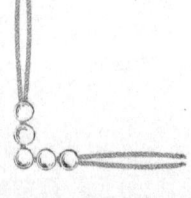

Chapter Eleven

It is almost as if Oke can sense my restlessness and sudden coldness to him in the same way that he senses the movements and shifts of the sea, for in the coming weeks he remains close to me, despite the way his wound hinders him. He will sail out through the curling waves to fish, or he will weave through the rocky trails around the island to check on set traps and tide pools, hobbling and hunched but never giving in to what must be agonizing pain, never leaving me long from his sight. I will be just settling into mending a net under the winking sun and then he'll suddenly be there, slipping quietly from around a rock, as certain and variable as the sea herself.

"Come," he says, one morning after rejecting my plea.

He leads me through the growing light of dawn on a very still day to mark the places where his nets are set around the

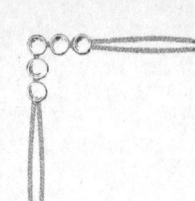

island. We find them through the dappled morning sun and shake flashing fish and many-legged sea creatures from their seaweed-bearded grasp.

"If you hunger, you'll know where to find them."

As if this makes up for keeping the truth from me. As if I can be put off like a child with a treat.

He smiles at each one before flinging most back.

"Don't you need to sell them?" I ask him, but if he is taking fish to market, he never tells me and he never seems to be gone long enough to sail to a harbor, though he brings home oil, wheat, wine, and once even lemons, stocking our small kitchen with them one after another.

If he meets with his god, I do not see it, and if he sends word by messenger bird, I catch no glimpse of it.

When he is gone, I work around the island under a bank of sadness, indulge in crying jags where none but the gulls and the statues can hear me, and when I am tired with weeping, I rage and throw things at the silent statues. I dwell often on my theories and the conclusions I have drawn, thinking them through first one way and then another until I am utterly certain in myself that I must find a way to destroy Okeanos. And that I must find a way to draw my reluctant husband into it with me. But though I try to plan it out, none of the plans I think through seem sufficient to turn his heart or trick him. I have never so deviously manipulated another person before. I have always simply ordered and it was done, but now I must do a thing new to me and I must do it perfectly the first time.

I sit and stare at small things—minnows ebbing and flowing in small schools where they can escape the sudden illumination of the sun, a tiny bird snatching up curling strands of grass, the clouds configuring themselves first one way, then another. And I mull on how I will convince my husband to confess all to me, and how I might in turn maneuver him into taking up arms with me against his master. There will be a way. And I will find it.

Two weeks after our confrontation, Oke offers me a chiton of fine linen—still shorter than I find dignified, but while it is appropriate for a wife of a fisherman in its simple cut, it is soft and the shoulders are clasped with a pair of bone fibula pins. These are well crafted and could easily belong to a merchant's wife. I raise my eyebrows at them and wonder if he has sold a pearl. If he has, I would have asked for sandals instead, as I have returned his to him and my feet are bare as I slip out over the rocks and memorize the paths to the tide pools. But I thank him prettily for his efforts and I catch his half-hidden smile that evening when I wear the chiton over our evening meal. And I try very hard not to feel guilty about how I will use him.

"I brought you an orange also," he tells me in the way he has that is both shy and strangely sweet.

He hands it to me, and I look at it. He's kept to what he said he would do and left me time to grieve without interruption, treating me with care as if he believes I am recovering from a long illness. But I cannot find it in my heart to be grateful. I am frustrated beyond words. For every day that he

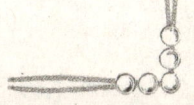

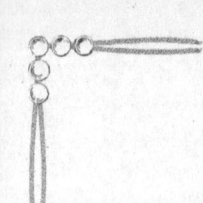

refuses to admit his true nature to me, I lose a day where I might have planned how to use it for his god's downfall.

"If this orange is an apology, I do not want your apology," I tell him frankly. "What I want is your trust. You have brought me here to your island—your home, not mine. You have dressed me in clothing you have chosen. Given me tasks that you selected. You know all my past and hold my future entirely in your hands and yet you will give me no truths in return. Not even an answer about your true nature."

He swallows and looks out to the sea—as he so often does. His emotions pass one after another over his face like squalls over the sea, but to my annoyance, he remains gracious as he always is, never short with me, unfailingly kind, and utterly unmoved.

"Are you done mourning, then, Coralys?" he asks me gravely. "Would you not want just a few more weeks before we consummate our marriage in full?"

I swallow, my cheeks going hot at the heated look suddenly weighting his gaze. I am not, in fact, ready for that. It would feel like a betrayal to Lieve. And how can he suggest it when his body is mangled and broken?

"Are you not at ease in my company?" he presses. "Do you not feel a kind of harmony as we work side by side in the many tasks that make up our life here? You watch me for signs of fever. For my godwound turning bad. For the wince I make whenever I lift something heavy. Do you think I do not see? That is friendship. We could be happy, I think, you and I."

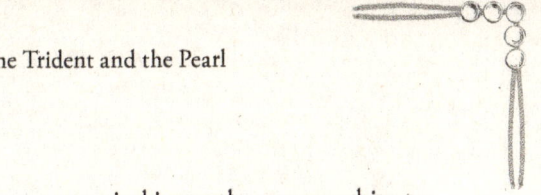

Without meaning to, my mind instantly compares him to Lieve, but it feels as impossible as comparing a fish to a bird. They are not the same. They cannot be. My beloved husband was a mortal man and this new husband of mine is as much above a mortal as a racehorse is above a goat.

"You mistake the point," I tell him firmly. "For you have not forgotten your purpose any more than I have, and no amount of harmony between us will matter in the end if you are god touched and must sail off after the wishes of your deity. Until you confess as much to me, the balance of our power swings entirely to you, and that I cannot allow."

He winces, but still he does not confess. I am insulted that he thinks to keep it from me.

And so, I am diligent. I mend nets. I gather fish. I cook what we need and put the rest with his catch in reed baskets to be taken wherever he takes it, but I am consumed by an ever-growing agitation to *act* that mixes with my salty grief and bitter resentment.

It comes to a head on the third week. I open a fish with the knife, skimming through its silver scales, watching blade and skin flash equally in the bright sun—and then, to my horror, the flesh splits open and in the mouth of the fish is a single copper coin.

I swallow hard and draw out the coin from the fish's mouth with reluctant fingers. It is identical to the omen before the storm, a Crocus Isles coin, stamped with the face of Okeanos. I stare at it a long time before I decide.

I can wait no longer.

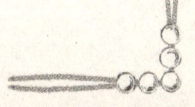

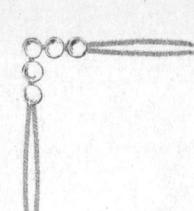

This time when I bite my fist and curl on my side of the bed at night—as I do every night—I do not cry myself to sleep. This time, I am waiting. I am going to test his magic for myself. He will not share his secrets with me, and so I must learn to use it myself. I must find a way to his god to take my revenge.

It is a very long time until Oke's breath evens out and I feel his body melt into the bed beside me. I am about to sneak from the embrace of the ragged blankets when he sits up with a start.

He's moving in the moonlight before I can react, flinging himself from the bed, half-dressed and barefoot. He limps out the door without a word, leaving it to bang in the wind behind him. I try to follow him. After all, he may be going to his god, but by the time I reach the door, he is out of sight.

I wait with my breath held, watching the water, but if he sails away on his boat, I do not see the gleam of white sail.

I wait what seems to be an hour and then one more just to be sure he is really gone. If I am to try something reckless and possibly fail at it, I do not want an audience. Eventually I slip from the warmth of the bed and out into the night. If he is not on the shore and not here, then this is my chance.

I do not know why I think I might work his magic. I have never been taught any such thing and I feel a bit of a fool as I make my way down to the dock through the bite of the night air, and yet...I saw his cousin do it, too.

It can be done.

And if they can move from place to place with the twist

of a hand, then can I not try it, too? I do not know what I will do with such power. But I know I cannot revenge myself on gods from this fair isle. And Oke will not take me home. He has said so. And—most relevant of all—now that I know disaster looms once more for my people, I cannot help but try to return to them by any means.

Something twists in my belly at the thought of the Crocus Isles in trouble. Something that links me still to that place. It's my blood and my bones and every happy memory I ever had, and while a queen has few friends, still there are those of whom I am truly fond. They may be guards and palace staff and minor nobles who hardly dare speak of what is dear to their hearts with someone of my station, but I have watched them live and grow and bear children as the years unfolded and the thought of any of them in distress etches pain across my heart.

Every choice I have ever made has been for them. What will happen if I do get my vengeance against the gods? Will they suffer for it? I must consider this before I act.

But not tonight. Tonight—while my husband is away—I will see if I can work magic, too.

I slip to the very end of the dock where the water-soaked wood is dark against a darker sea. Oke is not here. I am alone.

The moon is veiled by lacy threads of clouds and the surf pounds its familiar rhythm, but my heart races too quickly to fall in time. I put my toes on the edge of the dock just as Oke's cousin did, but then I think better of it and I swirl one

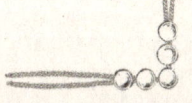

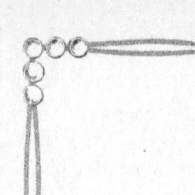

foot in the water instead. I bring to mind an image of the Crocus Isles, of my people, of my home. And—laughing at myself for being such a gullible fool—I lift my hand like I'm holding a bowl, and I twist my wrist.

I must have expected to fail, for success leaves me breathless.

The world spins so suddenly that I have to clap a hand over my mouth to keep from vomiting. I blink, lose my balance as my vision goes first black and then white. I glance off some hard surface, hit my head, see stars, and slump to my knees... in water.

Blinking hard, I wrench myself to my wobbling feet, splashing embarrassingly, and gasp, clutching at my head.

It has worked. Or at least, something has happened and I am no longer on Oke's island.

I am on the terrace of my old Winter Palace on the island of Calypsala, standing in one of the mosaic tide pools. My fingers find the marble banister and trace the carving I'd commissioned last year—ships setting out to sail.

I'm home. Really, home. It feels incredibly *right*.

I'm choked up for a moment. In my mind's eye I see my parents in this very place, speaking together in low voices as they often did so as not to disturb the peace as they breakfasted. I'm seeing it when I would drift out to the balcony to catch my breath during parties, tired from too many smiles and too many nuanced conversations. I'm seeing it as the terrace where Lieve would kiss my neck and draw me out into the sea to bathe.

I blink back tears and try not to indulge in too much

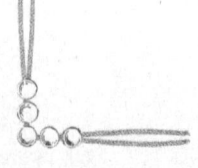

hope. I may be home, but I am not queen and this terrace is no longer mine. My place—if I have one here—will be helping somewhere else.

Even so, it is good to see it again.

I'm not in a hurry to leave. I linger a little, wanting to soak back into my world. A tiny pang of regret reminds me that Oke will return home and find me gone, but he was well enough before I came to his home and he will be well enough again without me. I will return to him once I have established that all is well here. If four weeks with that wound hasn't killed him, then I doubt he is going to die of it.

It's only when I reach my former bedroom that I frown.

Where are the guards? They ought to have been standing watch on that door. Why is this room in such disarray?

I'm frowning as I pick up my pace, leaving the room and entering the halls beyond, noticing how they echo, how they stand silent as the crypts filled with our ancestors. Why is that vase broken and the shards not gathered up? Why is that table overturned?

All the elation I felt on my arrival is leaking out of me. Something is terribly wrong here.

The smell of smoke hangs heavy in the air. I open doors as I race down the hall, looking in each one.

No one is in the library. No one in the studies set across from it. No one in the Green Room, where I used to receive scholarly guests. And every room is in chaos.

A book lies on its face in the hall. There's a blank spot on the wall where a tapestry of Queen Lyseries and the Great

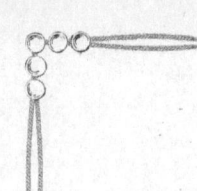

Fish used to hang—a gaping spot like a lost tooth from an otherwise tidy row. Someone has smashed one of the ornamental tables. Fragments are thrown about as if a great wind has blown through the hall, picking up bits of wood and parchment in equal measure and settling them like fallen leaves across the floor.

It is just as the coin in the fish's mouth predicted. Turmoil has struck my people and I was not here to prevent it. The floor seems to sway under my feet, but I know it is only my guilt making the world tilt and roll.

I clench my jaw, furious at myself for not trying to work the magic I saw sooner. Four weeks I lingered, mending nets, watching birds, and playing the good fisherman's wife...and what has happened here while I was flitting those weeks away?

I wonder for a moment if I am dreaming, but just as I start to fear I've somehow shifted my reality into some plane empty of human life, I stumble into the map room and there is someone here I know.

Turbote stands with a sack in his hands—a common grain sack—and he's stuffing priceless maps into it one after another.

"What are you doing?" I gasp, still not sure if I'm dreaming or if this is real. Somewhere in the distance is a rumbling that could be thunder or could be the feet of many people.

Turbote startles and turns. His hand flutters birdlike to his open mouth and he presses the back of it to his gasping lips as if he's afraid this is a dream.

"It cannot be," he whispers. "I have lost my mind."

"Turbote?" I ask in a wavering voice as he gathers me into his arms sobbing soundlessly.

"Coralys. My queen. Gods have mercy, it's you."

He's blinking back tears and I feel like someone has dropped heated lead through my chest. I push myself out of his clinging embrace.

I have never seen Turbote cry. I am not sure he cried at his own brother's funeral. I was there that day and he was stoic and firm. Now he ripples with spasms like a jellyfish swimming through the water.

"The gods have not abandoned us after all."

"You're a priest of Okeanos," I say, gripping his arm in a way that I hope imparts some kind of strength. "You will never be abandoned."

He laughs, a terrible hollow laugh.

"Okeanos? Whose fault do you think this is? We trusted him. We gave you up. And now disaster has struck."

"Disaster? What has happened?" I can't quite catch a full breath. Something in the distance rumbles again.

"You have to help us, Coralys," Turbote says, shaking hard. His eyes are watery and shadowed. Veins stand out blue on the backs of his hands. "They arrived in the night. Suddenly. There was no warning. They must have overwhelmed our fleet. They've been sacking the city. The guards are dead. Everything burns. The people are slaughtered in the streets."

That doesn't explain why there is no one here. Surely they would take refuge in the palace.

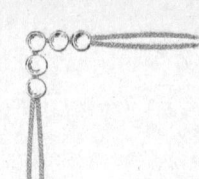

"Who has attacked us?" As far as I ever knew, we have no enemies. We are peaceful people with peaceful goals.

I steal to the window and look out.

Gods have mercy.

"It was too sudden. It was too fast." He's babbling. "There wasn't even time to pray. Not even time... not even time..."

What I didn't see from the tide pool I see from here. The city on fire, flames dancing in tentacle trails up what I know to be the major streets of the city. My heart begins to race and my body twitches as if urging me to run.

"Who?" I demand again.

"We don't know. They didn't say. They wear the tentacles of Okeanos and claim to be his scourge."

"That makes no sense. We are the people of Okeanos."

He must not be telling me something. Surely they could not be so utterly surprised.

"Are we?" he asks, his hands crumpling a precious map as he shudders. "Are we? He took our queen. He drowned our lands. And now, as we recover, he's taken the rest. No one else could render us so desolate. We have no other enemy with such power. We've failed him."

"Where is Delarte?" I ask, and it's only now that I notice Turbote is streaked in black soot. He's missing a sandal. He's wild-eyed and his hair sticks out in every direction. "Where is your king?"

He's not answering me. He's lost in his story.

"It started with a demand. From the sea god. A virgin sacrificed to the sea every night, or disaster would strike. We

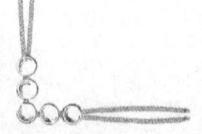

didn't listen. We thought it couldn't be true. That we would be asked for such a thing." He's shaking so hard it's like he's in a heavy wind. "And then they burned Tempest Reef." Tempest Reef is one of my five islands. "Gone in the night. Only five ships managed to flee to Calypsala. That night we threw a girl into the sea with a rock tied to her foot." I gasp, but he presses on. "We threw one in every night until the people revolted the day before yesterday under the urging of Gheric Rodehands. I did warn you of him. 'No more daughters,' they said, and look where we are. Look! Calypsala is lost. Delarte seized." I did not think it possible for his eyes to grow wilder, but they do now. "They cut out his tongue, Coralys. I watched them do it. They cut out the tongue of our king."

"This can't be real," I say, half to myself. My stomach sloshes queasily and my mouth is watering as if it is preparing to vomit. "I've only been gone a short time."

"A short time?" Turbote's laugh is hollow and nearly hysterical. "You've been gone for weeks. Terrible weeks. Do you know how long a week can stretch when you are in hell? Gods have mercy on us." He pauses and laughs again. "Or perhaps I ought to beg the gods abandon us. No longer touch our shores, O Great Okeanos! We cannot bear your presence."

I can't absorb this. It feels like madness. I grasp at practicality.

"You came for the maps," I remind him.

"Yes, the maps." He seems relieved that I noticed. "I came

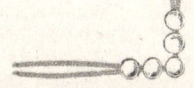

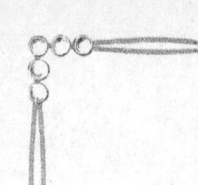

for the maps. They're priceless, you know." I do know, though I wouldn't risk my life for them. "Maybe they'll have some clue. Some place we can hide from his wrath. Some place safe."

"Do you have anyone waiting for you? Any way of escape?" I prompt.

I am looking at a man who threw innocent girls into the sea to drown. I am looking at him as he loses his mind.

"A fishing boat." He sounds like he isn't sure.

"You'd better get to it, then," I say, but he clings to my arm.

"Come with me. Please. We need you as queen, Coralys. It was your loss that started this madness." He's suddenly angry. His furious words gust hard into my face with his stinking breath. "Tradition be damned. Look what it got us. Look what madness has descended upon us."

I can see what he means. He is no longer sane himself.

"I'll take you to the boat," I say calmly. "Why don't I carry those maps?"

But he's not willing to give them up. Instead, he leads me crab-like across one hall and then across to another, never taking a straight line but darting from doorway to doorway until we reach the gardener's entrance. Then he grabs my arm and clings to me as we spill out onto the cobble courtyard.

I freeze.

Bodies litter the mosaic cobbles. Men and women lie where they fell in tangled garments and pools of fly-crusted blood. They look as though they were corralled here first.

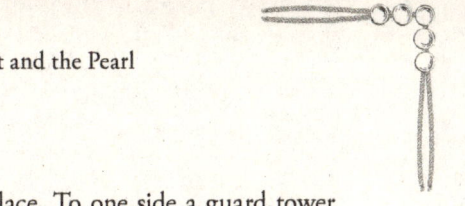

This explains the empty palace. To one side a guard tower is charred black and still smokes, and the smell of burning flesh hangs in the air. I gag and scramble to pull the tunic over my nose and mouth.

Gods have mercy. I see a face I recognize—a chambermaid—and look hastily away, blinking back tears. But they won't be pushed away. They streak my cheeks and I'm forced to scrub at them with my palm.

"Here," Turbote says. "This way. Hurry. They left the palace when there was resistance in the city, but they'll be back to finish looting it, you can be certain."

"Who is 'they'? We had no enemies threatening us. We had no reason to fear."

I can't grasp that all this has happened while I have been in my new husband's home. It makes no sense at all.

"What does it matter who they are?" Turbote's voice is almost a wail. "Don't be like Gherise."

I shoot him a quick glance. Gherise is...was...another of my advisors. Usually a rival to Turbote.

"He thought he could ask those questions. He thought he could demand answers of the raiders. Last I heard, they killed him on the docks."

He pulls me from the entry courtyard to the gardens. There are more bodies here and there is no avoiding them.

"Where is everyone?" I breathe. "Surely there are some others alive here?"

"Fled, or dead. They drove them to the city square," Turbote says.

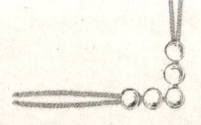

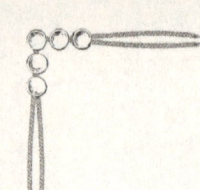

Now I am trembling just like him, my hands shaking badly, but it's not until we come to the center of the garden overlooking the turbulent sea that I find my legs won't carry me anymore.

We keep the anchor from the first ship of our people here in the center of the garden, where it is backdropped by the roar of the sea on the rocks. It held our people fast when first they came to this island and by tradition it will hold us fast until the end.

It is here still. Holding fast.

But lashed to its crusted frame is Delarte. He's wearing my pearl belt and crown, though they are badly askew. His dead eyes are sightless. Crusted blood traces down his chin and soaks the front of his tunic.

"They didn't even ask him any questions," Turbote says, hands fluttering again. "Just took the tongue and left him to die. I hid. I hid and I can't ever forgive myself for it."

I wasn't here.

And I can't ever forgive *myself* for that.

I wipe my sudden tears away harshly. I don't deserve the right to them.

There's a sound in the bushes and I look around for a weapon. The bodies have been stripped of anything like one.

I fumble for the belt pouch with the knife in it. A poor weapon, to be sure, but better than nothing. Both the knife and something else fall to the cobbles and I lunge after them, catching the black pearl in the tear-slick fingers of one hand and the knife in the other. My fingers on the pearl feel hot. I

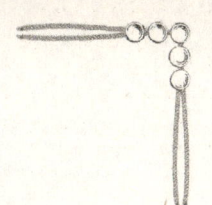

look down at it and see a wisp of smoke curling out from its glossy surface.

I'm just finding my feet when an unfamiliar voice slices through the air.

"Decorative, to be sure, but it won't last long in this heat. I prefer my monstrosities cast in bronze so that they last."

Fear runs cold and sudden down my spine, down the backs of my legs, dragging my courage with it as I find myself face-to-face with a... creature. A thing of nightmares. It stands with a finger to its chin as it regards Delarte.

Turbote tugs at my sleeve, clearly blind to the monster, but I can't seem to look away.

The thing is man to the waist and then his muscled torso ripples into the eight undulating tentacles of an octopus. Or rather, I should say the six tentacles, as two end in terrible mangled stumps as if something has chewed through them. His face is beautiful in a bold way and his skin terribly pale. It's pinkish in the face and neck, but slowly turns to a bluish white across the chest and belly until it becomes mottled over the skirt of his tentacles. He wears a silver torque and nothing else—and now surely this must be a dream, because I recognize him.

This is Vesuvius from the book—the one it claimed was God of the Sea.

I nearly swallow my own tongue at the sight of him. What does it mean that I can see a god?

"Is this your doing?" I ask him boldly, for I do not know how he has come to be here.

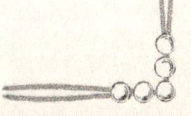

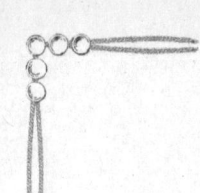

He stares at me blankly for a moment before curling a lip. "Surely not. I was always a more creative torturer than this."

He moves toward me and I raise two fingers in a warding sign. From the creature's body to the pearl in my hand runs a fine tracery of white mist. I have the most terrible suspicion that the monster is tied to this pearl. I have conjured him up, then. Somehow. Or conjured up his spirit, for the book named him dead.

"Stay back." I am proud that my voice barely shakes, but Turbote does not seem to notice the figure. He tugs again at my sleeve.

"Come, Coralys."

He's right. I have no weapon but my belt knife. I cannot fight this monster or any other. I take a wavering step backward.

"We could make a bargain, ragged woman," the monster suggests with a lifted eyebrow. "Whoever has killed your friend can be killed in turn. I was ever an excellent assassin."

"Did you come here from this pearl?" I ask him, opening my palm to reveal it. That ghostly tendril remains.

He smirks. "Where else?"

I want nothing to do with him, though—beyond his unnerving appearance, I cannot explain why. That he will kill me when I refuse him is almost certain, but still I prepare myself for a fight, clenching my belt knife in one hand and slipping the pearl back into my belt pouch to free my other hand.

The vision vanishes with that action, leaving only my

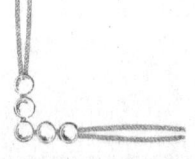

dead cousin hanging from the anchor—the symbol of the destruction of the people of the Crocus Isles lashed to the symbol of all our strength. I swallow, waiting for the nightmare to return.

I wait for one, two, three breaths and then—with a sense of overwhelming relief—I turn my back on my cousin and whatever is left of the god-monster's spirit, and I run.

Turbote clutches at my arm, steadying his old feet as we scramble through the gardens and down the wide stone steps toward where a small boat launch is carved into the shore. The Crocus Isles have always been a kingdom of peace. There was never any reason not to bring boats right to the edge of my palace. I wonder if they arrived this way first. If they spilled from ships now hidden elsewhere, pouring over the land like darkness during a storm.

A small fishing vessel waits for Turbote, hidden in the high rocks of the launch. People huddle on the deck as if to make themselves small. I can't see them clearly enough in my haste to recognize anyone. Unless that is Maevelys near the prow?

Beside me, Turbote stumbles. We're still on shore and we'll need to wade out past our waists in the water. I catch him and for a moment our eyes meet—sorrow and loss acknowledging pain and misery—and then someone calls from the boat, a sailor, I think. He's pointing behind us. I spin to look.

We have been discovered.

Our enemies—for that is who these men must be—race down from the gardens after us. They're armed and

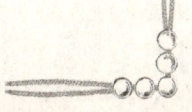

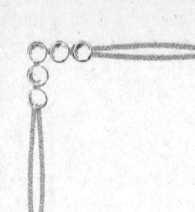

soot-streaked, and I've never seen that look in an eye before. It's a look that has long abandoned mercy. What I am in the eyes of those men, I do not know, but I am not a woman, a queen, a wife. I am a *thing* they have a will to alter.

I push Turbote ahead of me as fear claws up my throat and run as I have never run before. Our feet hit the surf just as the first of them clears the garden and reaches the steps.

"Hurry, hurry," Turbote chants as we crash through the waves to our waists. There's a better way to the boat if we stayed on land. But we don't have time for that way.

We're nearly there when one of the men draws level with me, his sword lifted as if to strike Turbote, who is a pace ahead of me. I don't think. There is not time for it.

I launch myself at the man, driving all my weight into his side, shoulder first. It hurts when I connect. He's wearing a hauberk under that surcoat. But I must have hit just right, because we go down together in the crashing waves.

I catch a glimpse of Turbote being caught by hands reaching from the boat, and then I'm in the surf, a tangle of limbs and steel and salt water. I can see nothing in the churned-up sand-filled waves. I catch a half a breath of water by mistake and everything burns—my nose, my mouth, my chest.

Gods have mercy. I will die here.

The sea catches me in its powerful embrace, dragging me under, demanding I surrender my life. I have never surrendered. I will not do it now. I will die fighting.

I try to twist my hand in a bowl shape, but it's caught in a tangle of fabric.

And then the figurative arms of the sea morph and become the very real arms of a man, and I am wrenched up from the waves and thrown behind his naked back. I stumble and shove handfuls of hair out of my face so that I might see. Water pours off my rescuer in rivulets as he soundlessly raises a hand.

The man I knocked over surges up from the waves with a roar, sword held expertly in a neat lunge. He is not alone. The others have caught up and they throw themselves forward in a wave of man and steel and sharpened blades. Their battle cries slice through the sound of their feet churning up the water and I'm frozen in helpless fear, watching violence come alive and set itself against me.

I'm already braced for the sound of flesh rent by steel, already swallowing down bile as I know I am next, when my defender flicks the first two fingers on his raised hand.

Inky tentacles shoot up from the waves in a gurgling froth of water as if the sea has grown roots into the air at the pace of several centuries of growth to the second. They jut and rise between the scrambling forms of our enemy, curling and lashing.

I feel the brush of slimy skin against my leg and barely hold back a startled cry, and just as I am looking up from the dark water, the nearest man—the one I knocked down—is snatched by a tentacle with lightning speed and dragged screaming beneath the waves.

I hear the sound I expected of steel hacking flesh, but it is not our flesh being attacked and all his furor does the man

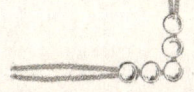

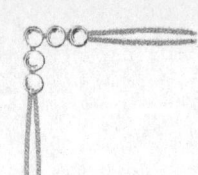

no good at all as the water churns red and white like a liquid banner of death.

Oke turns so calmly to me that I do not expect the molten rage in his pale eyes, but I should. For behind him his deep creatures have crawled up onto the tumbled shore and snatched a dozen men, one by screaming one, into their clutching grasp and dragged them beneath the swell. The men are drowned in inches of water, battered on the rocks like floundering ships, and left behind in floating, lifeless pieces. And the creatures, barnacle-crusted and slick with blood and water, pay no more mind to their screams than I pay to the call of the gull.

I gasp and then Oke sweeps me up in his arms like a man carrying his bride and plunges us both beneath the waves.

He drags me deeper and deeper.

I tug at his wrist, terrified of drowning, but it's no use, he's stronger than I am and bent on drawing us under the waves. The world spins and whirls—worse than could possibly be the case simply from the rip of the tides pulling on me—and I'm so disoriented that I can't tell up from down. Again the arms tighten, dragging me, pulling me, and then shoving my head by the back of the skull upward through the surface. My face breaks into air and I gulp in a hungry breath.

I'm relief and pain and panic all mixed into one.

Frantically, I spin in the water, trying to get my bearings, but there is no fishing boat. No dead enemies. No unnatural creatures where they ought not be. I'm on a lonely shoreline

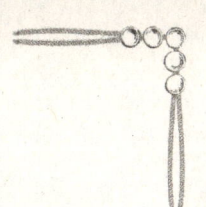

of rock and trees, the water deep and surrounding me rather than only waist-high.

"Coralys," pants a voice wetly beside me. I turn and gasp at the face of my husband, flushed with exertion. Something has left a ragged scratch down one of his cheeks.

I cough out water, heaving in a way that makes it hard to keep my head up, and then suddenly he's there, holding me up so I don't drown myself as I cough and cough.

"You rescued me?" I ask breathlessly when my lungs are clear.

He's speaking but I'm not listening. I keep seeing Turbote's fluttering hands. I keep seeing Delarte's corpse strung up across the anchor. I keep seeing the tentacles and my last glimpse of the sea where a huge many-toothed mouth had opened and sucked in a man's entire torso. I keep thinking the impossible.

"You were in the sea," Oke is saying as if that explains anything.

He pulls himself up onto slick rocks and reaches a hand back for mine. He grips it and drags me up on shore, and I'm trembling, shaking so hard that my teeth rattle. I can't seem to order my thoughts. They keep skittering away like drops of water on a hot surface. I'm dazed, dwelling on stupid details, jumping to wild conclusions.

But it cannot be... can it? Have I been so blind?

I watch him come out of the water. He's naked and his godwound in his leg looks worse than before. It has not scabbed over or mended and the skin around it is red and inflamed and hanging loose in ragged shreds.

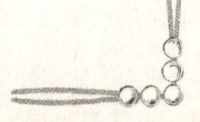

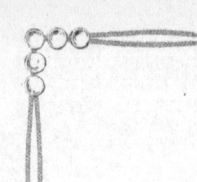

"It's easier to find things in the sea without anything in the way," Oke says as he lowers himself to a rock to catch his breath. "Clothing. Weapons. Anything."

"I don't care," I say, realizing it's true as I find my own rock and wrap my arms around my knees. I am shuddering apart like a ship on too strong a sea. I will never recover. And I can't hold it in anymore. I mean to say one thing, but an accusation springs to my lips instead.

"If you could find me and rescue me, then you knew somehow what was happening. Why didn't you warn them? If you could call up tentacles and snatch men from the surf, why did you not drag them *all* beneath the sea? What are you doing? No. Wait. What are you *failing* to do?"

My chest is heaving and it's not from trying to breathe again. It's all the emotions of the past four weeks coming together in this single point because I *know* now. This man is not the sea god's champion. No mere hero can call up monsters. No mortal man, however elevated, can command the seas.

He shakes his head. The scratch on his cheek is bleeding. A single red rivulet runs down his jaw and I shudder at the memory of Delarte, but it does not dissuade me.

"I found you because you called me and your call is loud. I have been doing what I can."

"And?" I press, tightening my arms around myself.

It's him. It's him who let my people die. Not just this time but every time. He spoke with me while my Lieve sank beneath the waves and offered me a bargain when it was too

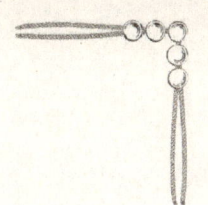

late. What was our misery to him? What was my loss? A lark? A joke?

And no wonder he would not confess to being god touched.

I am shaking with fury as I try to say the thing I've wanted to say all along. "What right do you have to choose who to spare and who to ignore? What right did you have to dismiss cries for help? What right did you have to withhold your protection? I don't want you picking me when you didn't pick *them*!"

Tears flow down my cheeks, but they are not tears of sorrow. They are distilled fury.

He tries to take my hand and I can't shake his grip away. I'm not sure if he realizes I'm trying to, because the expression on his face is tender and understanding as if he's comforting grief and guilt, as if he doesn't realize that all I feel right now is fury. I clasp his hand back tightly, twisting it so that our two hands are clenched like fists between us, unwilling to let him think I am weak. Unwilling to let him dominate me in this. My guts clench and then it comes pouring out.

"You're a god."

He pales.

"Stop lying to me," I practically shout, holding up our linked fists between us like a threat, a defiance. "Do you think I'm such a fool that I can't see? You're *the* god. Okeanos of the Sea."

He almost drops my hand, but I won't let him. He must not think he can turn me aside.

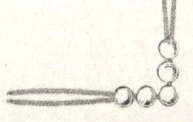

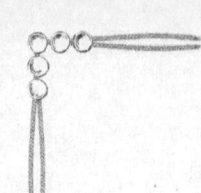

He shakes his head, but it's not denial of who he is. It's a defensive thing, like he's denying the underlying accusation—that this is his fault. That my dead are laid on his deck.

"Okeanos demanded human sacrifices." I fling the words at him. "And they gave them. And that was not enough. Still he sent his forces to mete out punishment."

He's a very good liar. His shock looks genuine.

"What?" He sounds breathless, as if he cannot bear to hear my answer when he asks, "Who told you this?"

"Turbote told me," I say. "I am certain it is true."

He's shaking his head. "It is not so. I can tell you now that it isn't."

He tries to take a step backward, but I step forward with him, keeping him close, not letting him distance himself from his guilt.

"I believe Turbote's words to me. Gods do as they please. They spare no pity. And the God of the Sea did this to my people." I'm choking on my own words, filled with a mixture of grief and fury that overwhelms me. "*You* did it. *You* had no pity on them, just as you had no pity on me. No pity on Lieve. You tried to make me trust you! You tried to make me fall in love with you."

He flinches back as if from a blow, but this time it is him who doesn't release my hand and I can't shake his grip free. He uses it to reel me toward him, until his face is inches from mine and I can read every twitch in it.

"All will be well, Coralys," he says intently. "I will make it well again."

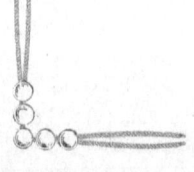

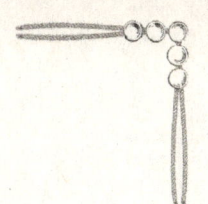

Another lie. He cannot fix what has been broken.

I sob silently, bowing into our tangled fists, biting my own knuckle to keep from making a sound. These are not tears of sadness. They're angry, furious, helpless tears steeped in hatred. I'm scared. I'm so scared of being helpless. I'm so scared that if I don't reef in my sails, I will give myself away. It takes me several breaths before I manage to gather control of myself again.

"All will not be well," I tell him grimly, wrenching myself from his embrace. "Because you have made it unwell, and you cannot stitch back together what has been broken."

"Cora." His hollow voice sounds like I've landed a blow to him, but I don't see how when I've spoken only the truth.

I point a shaking finger at him. "And you are who I hold responsible now. Not gods in some vague sense but *you*. Tell me you are not Okeanos. Tell me you are not the God of the Sea."

He flinches and that's just fine with me. He's shaking his head, his wet hair limned by moonlight. He is tight as a sail line.

"This is not the time," he says, and his eyes are desperate. "I must go. I don't have time for this."

"You don't have time? What will you do? Fish?" I scoff, shaking my head. "You said we wanted the same thing. You said we wanted to save our people. Are you not my people's god?"

He's trembling slightly now, too. Perhaps he is as angry with me as I am with him. Have I angered a god? He has not yet admitted it and I don't think he will.

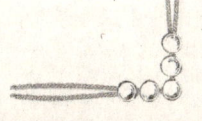

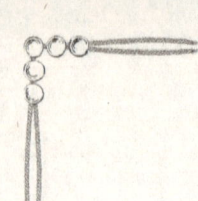

"That's why I must go, Coralys. And right now. I have not time to spare in dealing with you."

It feels like a slap, but he's right. My people are more important. We will deal with his guilt after he mitigates his failure.

"Are you going to rescue the survivors and bring them here?"

"No. I am not. And you must not, either. You barely survived your foray into that burning city today. Don't be a fool by going back. I will discover who these enemies of your people are. You stay here. Allow no one on our island. I will return."

He takes a step toward the sea, but I am vibrating with frustration.

"Discover?" I ask in a shuddering breath. "I am not asking for an investigation. I am asking that you go back and you save them like you saved me." My voice grows hard. "Or that you die trying."

Lieve died trying. And Okeanos did not spare him. I should not feel ashamed for holding him to the same standard.

His eyes harden like ice in a northern harbor. "Enough, woman. Is this about stopping what's happening on your islands? Or is this about vengeance for your lost power and dead husband?"

"Why can't it be both?" My voice is loud but it is small compared to the roar of the sea, and I'm furious at myself for not being strong enough.

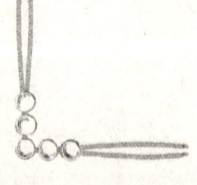

"How charming," he says, taking a step back from me to the edge of the dark rocks. "It must be a wonderful thing to judge justly without requiring evidence."

"I thought you had somewhere to go." I lace each syllable with poison.

His lip curls and he shakes his head at me in censure, and then, in a graceful dive, he leaps from the rocks and cuts a clean path into the sea. There is not even a splash to give evidence that he was ever here.

And I am left alone and shivering on the rocks with nothing to warm me but the sure knowledge that I have angered my husband and fought with him, but I have also narrowed my possible enemies from ten gods to one. And better still, I have a weapon I did not expect—a black pearl and a strange creature who offered to bargain with me.

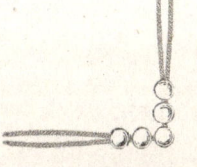

Chapter Twelve

I am lonely in a way that feels like a freezing wind blowing through my flesh and into my bones. It's both a physical loneliness and a loneliness of purpose, for I am the only one still alive who is trying to fulfill this goal—the preserving of my people through the sacrifice of my freedom.

I have never before been alone. As a girl, I had been cared for and tutored by a string of attendants from birth. As queen, there was a never-ending stream of people dressing me, feeding me, cleaning around me, or needing my ear, my word, or my signet ring to aid them. We all had the same goal. The same guiding purpose.

I'm haunted by the expression on Okeanos's face and the memory of his gentle touch as he drew me close when we fought—almost as if he was trying to comfort me while I was raging at him. And I am sick with the knowledge that

I was maneuvered into marriage by the very god who first drowned my husband and then drifted in to sweep me away like a bit of flotsam on the shore. It makes my head roar and my heart quicken.

I know how gods play with mortals. But this is a betrayal worse than when Epicus slew his father and fed his feet to the sharks. This is a betrayal worse than when Shimea slew her lover with the knife he gifted her to seal their bond. This is a betrayal worse than when Anticus stole his brother's kingdom when he was away, marrying his wife, adopting his son, and expunging his name from the histories. It is a worse betrayal because I have been betrayed by both my god and my husband.

I do not go back to the islands with a twist of my hand and magic. If there's even a shred of hope that Okeanos might fight for my people, then I do not want to distract him from that. I might feel with every breath the sting of his betrayal, but I am no fool. I nearly died in the waters with Turbote. I certainly will not live through that a second time.

And while I could go back later and be queen, that would negate my bargain and Okeanos might swallow my islands whole.

In my tangled fight with that enemy warrior, he left a nasty gouge in the flesh of my arm. I turn my attention to binding that wound. And as I do, I think of how a god can be killed. The warrior attacking me had tried and then those tentacles swept him aside. For such an act to succeed, it would have to be by surprise.

But even as I think this, I am reminded of Oke's hands

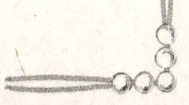

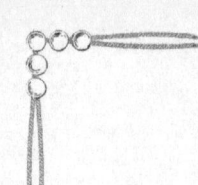

on mine—strong and sure—as I cast out heavy rope nets to fish. I remember how even that terrible godwound barely slowed him.

He could return home at any moment. And then what will I say to him? What will I *do* to him?

Emotion saws raw and hot through my chest, tugging me first one way and then another.

I could tell him that I must make him pay for what he did to Lieve and my people. I could still try to get my vengeance.

I saw the ruined faces of my people. Our entire island was ravaged, gone. I can only imagine how many other faces I would have recognized had I sifted through the dead.

Okeanos was their god. He knew exactly what he was doing when he stepped foot first on my dock. And he knew who I was when he bargained with me in that temple and then killed Lieve.

No matter how sweet or shy he has appeared over these past few weeks, it does not change any of that. He wears his face as he wears his pearls. Just another beautiful thing he clothes himself with—no more the truth of who he is than any garment might be.

I'll admit that I indulge in a few sobbing jags and some furious rock throwing as the only means of temporarily calming the storm inside my heart.

I do not like either of my options, but I must choose. Either I align myself with the god who ruined my people and my life, or I defy him and seek his destruction.

I know my own mettle. I know I do not give over easily. I

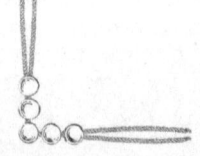

am almost certain to choose the second path, so why does it cause me guilt to think of it? Why does my mind shy away from the idea of taking Okeanos's life?

He deserves it entirely. He has failed terribly in his role as God of the Sea. Or he has intentionally used his position to benefit himself. Either way he has made himself my enemy. He has rent a hole in my heart so deep that no vengeance shall ever suffice, no penalty shall ever pay for what was lost to me. No matter how much I might like him as a man, he is also my traitor god.

Over the next days, I turn in my turmoil to the books. I am a fast reader, but not all of them are in a language I know. I am versed in Archaen—the language of my islands and most of the coast—High Archaen for holy works; Greillic; and some Farsadean. There are about thirty volumes written in none of those, and since they also have no woodcuts, I cannot tell what their subject is. I work my way through the others, one at a time, bringing them with me as I check my lines, wash my laundry, set my fire, and curl alone in my bed. It's cold when I'm the only one in it and the winds from the shore whip in through the open window and chill me to the bones until I bury myself beneath a heap of tattered pillows like a crab crawling under the sand.

I dredge out every bit of knowledge I can as I plot.

And through it all, I keep that black pearl close, and I think. I have not yet decided if what I saw was a hallucination brought on by trauma, for Turbote did not also see it, or a true creature.

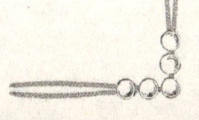

If he was real, then he is connected to this pearl. If he was real, then he offered to make a bargain with me to defeat my enemies. Do I dare to bargain with a monster or an ancient god or whatever this thing might be? I don't want to end up holding my own severed head, or manacled to six other women and thrown down a well, or any of the other things depicted in the books on Oke's shelves. I shudder at the thought.

Vesuvius is not in my childhood list of gods, though the song runs through my mind more than once as I consider him.

Take your breath for Aurelius,
Drink your drop for Okeanos,
Plant your seed for Glorian,
Give your kiss for El'Dorian,
Sing your song for Ordanus,
Strike your hammer for Alexandros,
Walk your trail for Pagetto,
Dig your grave for Treseano,
But for me it is Heskatan with her snorting horses,
And Markanos will guide me through battle's courses,
And your love will fade, my dear, as my death takes me
And in the Nightwaters, all ten gods I'll see.

Could that song have once said, "Drink your drop for Vesuvius"? And if it did, then how did Okeanos replace him? Is it truly as easy as just killing the god and taking his crown?

The Trident and the Pearl

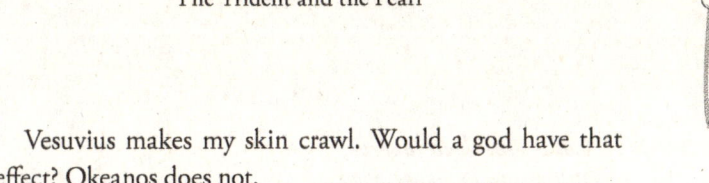

Vesuvius makes my skin crawl. Would a god have that effect? Okeanos does not.

What if Vesuvius attacks me? He could overpower me. He could kill me. Perhaps he could even trap me in that pearl with him—however that works.

But what if he says that he can help me kill a god? Surely we will both want revenge on the god who has destroyed us. Would working with him transform me into someone complicit in evil rather than a champion of the good?

A tiny voice in my mind reminds me that vengeance is rarely a "good," but it can go right back to where it came from. I do not require a conscience at the moment. And besides, my aim is higher than vengeance. My goal is justice, restoration, peace. Just not peace for Okeanos.

It is the sixth afternoon after Oke is gone and I am on the shore with a book on my knee, staring at the sea, that I take out the pearl and the thimble and look at them. The pearl is a normal black pearl. It has no mark to distinguish it, no way to expect it is anything but a precious bauble. I set it to the side on the sand and look at the thimble. This is even simpler and even stranger for its simplicity.

But I realize something as I stare at the thimble. In the time we have been married Oke has only asked me to do one thing. Fill this thimble with riches.

It's one of his tasks. I remember the first four very clearly.

Win a god's oath.
Wed the drowned queen.

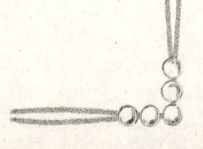

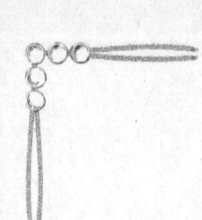

Collect the dead to serve.
Fill a thimble with riches.

Is it a test to determine if I can help him fulfill them? He has presented me with his fourth task in such a simple manner that it is hard to be certain.

Well. He and his test can both go and hang for all I care.

I am crying as I sit here, great, fat, angry tears as if my small saltwater contribution could match the salt of Okeanos's sea. The disparity reminds me of the gap between god and man, and that only makes me more furious. Bitterly, I catch my tears in the thimble, one by one until I fill it up.

I'm spiteful in catching them, in filling Oke's little thimble. I make sure to catch every one.

With care, I tuck the pearl back in my belt pouch and carry the little thimble back to the house and set it on the table. I'm perversely proud of myself. He asked for riches from me and instead I have given him evidence of what a pauper I am, for I have nothing left but my bitterness and rage. I've filled his thimble with both. He can choke on them when he gets back.

Oddly, the thought comforts me enough that I draw the pearl back out, and with a sigh, I confront my fears. Let's see what the soul of a dead god has to say for itself.

I leave the house and go out to the cliffs nearby in a spot where our home is hidden from view. I do not know why it feels important to protect it from this angry soul, but I do this almost reflexively. On this expanse of lichen-crusted

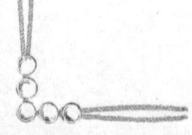

rock there's nothing to see but stone and sea and one large statue looming over us. A statue still sharp and unworn by the wind. She appears wise and strong with a bladelike nose and angry eyes, and she wears a shapeless robe as if femininity means nothing to her. I find the mood suits me well.

I repeat my actions from the last time, wiping my cheeks and then holding the pearl in my wet fist, and just like before, he emerges in a wisp of mist from a hot pearl.

He's large, towering over me. Had he a man's legs he'd be no taller than Oke, but his octopus lower half takes up a lot of space and it undulates and shifts, reminding me that I once saw an octopus squeeze through the circle formed of its keeper's forefinger and thumb. I shudder and he sneers.

"Here to bargain after all? What will you ask for, mortal woman? Will it be riches? Love? A crown?"

He's a study in contrasts, his upper half that of a beautiful but oddly light-skinned man, his face set with fine features and black hair. He has no beard or even the shadow of one. Were it not for the fact that he has six fluctuating legs, I would almost find him attractive. That, and the fact he is dead—a soul only. Or at least, I assume this to be the case.

One thing I know for certain. I must handle my dealings with this being with great care. If Okeanos would betray me, then this creature would betray me even more quickly given the chance. My goals are not safe with him.

"I had a crown once, for all the good it did me," I say carefully. "Who are you, exactly?"

"Who am I?" He darts like a striking snake, suddenly

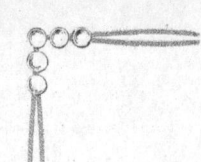

right in front of me, face an inch from mine. I control my features as if I see this kind of behavior every day. I wish—suddenly—that I'd brought a weapon with me. Or even a fishing net.

"You draw me forth beneath a statue that *I* made to honor the woman *I* killed so I might take her place and you have the gall to ask who I am? I am Vesuvius, God of the Sea, just as this was Chaolic, goddess before me."

I consider this. "All these statues are keepers of this island."

If the sound he makes is a laugh, I find it more chilling than welcoming. "Certainly. Keepers. That's what the gods are."

"The gods are not immortal, then?" I ask. A painful hope lights sharply in my chest.

"Gods are not easy to kill, mortal. Nor do they suffer age, wounds, illness, or other trials of mortal life, so we call ourselves immortal, for it is practically so."

He leans against the statue and studies a detail in how her hand is carved as if he hardly cares about our conversation.

"But you are dead."

"Mmm." It's a noncommittal answer, but I believe it is a yes.

"And you killed a god," I press.

He tips his head as if he allows a point to me.

"You killed this god," I say, gesturing toward the statue. Getting answers from him is like dislodging a barbed hook from a fish's mouth.

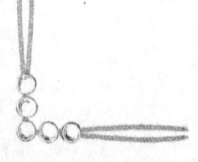

"I did."

"How?" I ask calmly.

"How, she asks," he says, and he laughs another of those grim laughs. "As if I will just tell you how to slay a god and take from him his power. If you want that, you'll bargain for it, little mortal."

I saunter a short ways away, collecting my thoughts. He practically thrums with annoyance as he waits for me.

"Are you trapped in that pearl?" I ask him. He does not answer, merely stares at me malevolently. I do not like the glitter in his eye. He sees an opportunity in me and I do not know what it is.

I tap my chin, thinking. I would prefer to know the rules of his imprisonment, but I do not think he will tell me unless it benefits him. I would prefer to know more about who offers me a bargain. I am terribly aware that this creature wishes to twist me to his own ends and that they may very well diverge from mine. But there is no one else who can tell me how to kill a god. And I know now that I must. Nothing else will satisfy the burning feeling that presses the air from my lungs moment by moment.

"What would you have in return for that knowledge?" I ask carefully.

He smiles, a terrible, cunning smile. I feel he is trapping me, but I can't see how.

"In return for the knowledge of how to kill a god?" he states carefully.

"And an understanding of where I might reach the gods

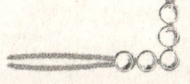

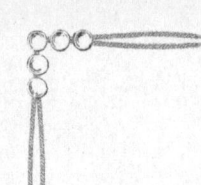

in order to do this deed," I add. After all, I have no idea where to find Okeanos since he left me here alone and I will need to find him if I am to kill him.

"Just any god or one in particular?"

This time I don't answer. This is not my first negotiation. He is fishing for useful information to use against me.

"The night after tomorrow will see the start of the Resurgence. All the gods will attend," he says with a second tip of his head. "There? See? I have given half of what you want for free. Bargain with me and I will tell you how to get there and how to kill a god and keep him dead."

I swallow. "I have heard of this Resurgence. I am told I must throw a finger into the sea to attend."

He barks a laugh. "Someone doesn't like you very much, mortal. Whose sandal are you sticking to, hmm?"

I shake my head. I am not so much a fool as to give him more information than he needs. He shrugs, acknowledging that, and peers at me for a long moment.

"You can certainly buy your way with blood and sacrifice. But there are other ways. Did you marry recently?" he asks with a feigned casualness that doesn't suit him at all.

"I did," I say warily. "I married a fisherman."

He nods, face blank. "Have you been much in the sea since then?"

I shrug, giving him no more than he is giving me.

He nods again, leaning against the rough statue with one elbow and looking out to sea.

"These are my terms, then," he says, and his voice takes

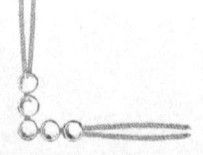

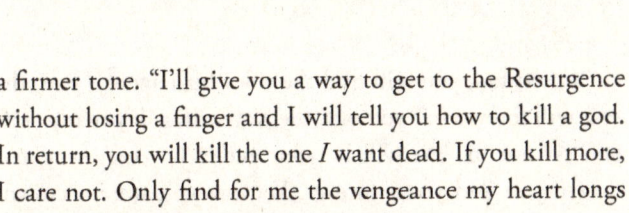

a firmer tone. "I'll give you a way to get to the Resurgence without losing a finger and I will tell you how to kill a god. In return, you will kill the one *I* want dead. If you kill more, I care not. Only find for me the vengeance my heart longs for and our bargain will be complete."

I clench my jaw. I don't like the little voice in the back of my head telling me that I ought not to work with this creature. And also that I probably shouldn't be agreeing to murder two gods. But shall I really say no to the only one who can give me what I'm asking for?

"If you are really the soul of a dead god, why don't you do this yourself?" I ask him, and he raises an eyebrow.

He shakes his hands and they ripple in the light. "I lost my corporeal form with my death, though my soul is trapped in that bauble you hold. I can't kill a god. You'll have to be my hands for me."

"What god would you have me kill?" I ask, finally driving to the heart of the matter.

"He who put me in this pearl. He who ruined everything," he says, stalking forward on his rippling tentacles. "Okeanos."

I shiver, but I keep my face straight. How is it that this is so convenient for me? There must be a sting in all this honey. But I cannot divine it.

"The sea god is powerful," I hedge, trying to keep my eyes and face blank. "It will be no easy task. What if I fail in doing it?"

He smiles like he was expecting this. He caresses each word of his reply with his tongue like he is savoring them.

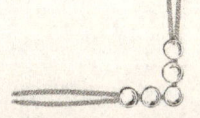

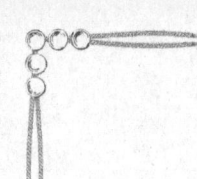

"If you fail, you will find the tides turn against you, the seas will forever spit you out, the waves drag down any craft you set out in. She will be your enemy in every way and drown you and yours forever. You say you wore a crown? Then that means your people, too, for their fate is bound up with yours."

"Then why bargain with you at all?" I ask coolly.

"To get what you want," he says as if I am a fool to even ask. "Or are there other dead gods offering you the means and opportunity to slay the divine?"

I take a long moment to think about this and he does not disturb my silence. I try to think logically. He is certainly hiding things from me, and given the chance he will absolutely work against me, will even kill me if he can. But he is right. There is no one else I can work with to get what I need. I try to weigh out the consequences against the necessity, but I'm looking at the green tossing sea and all I can see is Delarte streaked in blood. All I can see is Lieve sinking below the waves. All I can see is mad Turbote with his wild eyes and stories of killing innocent girls.

And it hardly takes any effort at all to say, "I will kill Okeanos, only tell me how it may be accomplished."

He snorts. "It's easy enough if you know the trick of it. You'll need to kill him with the weapon of a god."

I don't know if I'm more stunned or more furious at this. "Easy?"

"Once you're at the Resurgence and surrounded by gods, grab one of their weapons. They'll keep them close, but there

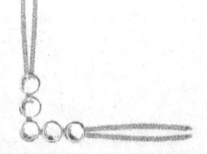

are ways that mortals might come close to the gods. Let one of them make you their pet if you must. And when you have it, you'll slay him like you might slay any mortal. The weapon of a god will part his flesh and make him as easy to kill as any man. Then—and do not forget this step—you will reach into the wound and draw out the pearl you find there and keep it. He will be entrapped as I am now. He will be at your service for all time. And your bargain with me will be fulfilled."

"You make it sound so simple," I say wryly.

He shrugs. "It is simple. In theory. It's the practice that's such a challenge."

"I should say so," I say, my lip twisting without meaning to, but my distaste only makes him mock me all the more.

"Look offended all you like, lady. You are the one who came to bargain with me. And I've already done as I agreed. Now you must do as you have promised. Kill Okeanos. Take his pearl. Do it swiftly and with a sure hand."

"You still haven't shown me how to get to this Resurgence," I remind him.

"Put your feet in the sea, fix the place you wish to go in your mind as fully as possible. Do this." Here, he twists his hand as if he is gripping a bowl but his fingers are shaped differently than I have seen before. I try to replicate the pattern. "You will be transported."

"Explain that more fully," I say firmly.

"This mortal plane is all you know. But the gods dwell on many planes layered over one another as a wet cloth hugs the

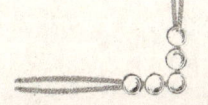

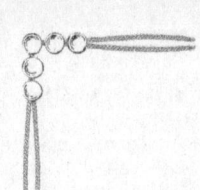

ground it's set upon. You can shift between these planes and to different locations. There's a trick to it—if you know it, you can go anywhere you like unless a god bars you from it."

I swallow against a dry throat. That I, a once-queen and definitely a mortal woman, would think I could mingle among gods and even kill one is out of the realm of reason. As if I am slipping my own moorings. But think, I remind myself, your life is already madness. Why fight against the current, when you can work with it to get what you want?

He slides across the rock over to the statue and leans against it again, sunning himself.

"Make a shape like this." He holds up his palm, fingers spread wide as if he cups a bowl, but the first two are crossed and I notice the others are subtly shaped. I imitate him. "You'll give it a one-quarter turn, at a speed of about one heartbeat. Flick your thumb at the end. And while you do it, tell the sea you belong to him and will not stand in his way and think of the Hall of the Gods. Surely you've heard of it in story and song."

"And if my imagination does not suffice?" I ask dryly.

"It won't matter. Thinking of it is what counts." He tilts his head to the side and closes his eyes for a moment as if he is counting, and when he opens his eyes, he is smiling that wicked smile again. "It's definitely in two nights. The Resurgence. You've made your bargain just in time."

I swallow down a lump in my throat. I've made a bargain. With what is inarguably a malevolent spirit. And now I must do as I have said I would and slay a god.

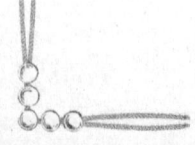

"I need a plan," I say. "To go in with no plan feels foolhardy."

"What do you want, lady?" He turns his sharp gaze on me, flicking out two tentacles in a way that makes me think he's mocking me. "Do you want the gods to send you a map of where they will sit? Do you want an engraved invitation? Shall they line up and let you choose from their weapons and then place their heads upon the table so you may sever them one by one? Do you think Incanus had a plan when he slew the dragon? How about Carthinus when he lopped off the five heads of the Leopard of Neb? Heroes don't have plans. They have intestinal fortitude, a willingness to think on their feet, and enough motivation to dive in and do what they must. You'll be going in blindfolded like any other hero. Use your brain if you have one. Adapt. Don't mewl to me about a plan. You cannot possibly know what you face until you arrive—and neither can I. But you've made your bargain with me for good or for ill and you owe me the death of one god whether you like it or not."

He glances at me curiously, as if weighing how his words have taken me, and then shrugs again and leaps. At first, I think he's attacking me and it's only when he somehow leaps back *into the pearl* that I realize he simply grew bored of me and left.

"Well, then," I say to an empty rock and a harsh-carved woman. "Steal a weapon. Kill a god. Take his pearl."

This list is as ridiculous as the one Oke has written.

His name makes something squeeze inside my chest. For

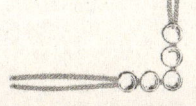

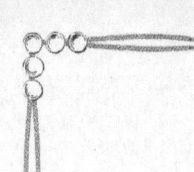

it is he whom I will be destroying if I really do this. When I do it.

I pause, nausea rolling over me in waves, my brow hot and suddenly slick.

"You can do this, Coralys," I tell myself. "You must do this."

Killing a god would constitute a great act of power. It makes sense that it terrifies me and feels impossible. Anything less would never work at all.

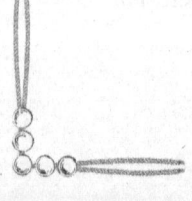

Chapter Thirteen

On the morning of the seventh day I go swimming. My chores are done, my nets out, and my plan laid. There are no weapons on this island, and so tomorrow I will dress in my husband's gifted chiton and I will stand in the water, twist my hand, and go to bluff the gods.

But for now, I will swim. And I will try to find in myself the inner reserves I will need to kill a man...a god...who I have lived with and liked. For that is the only way to take his authority and end this calamity that has befallen my people. And I do not lie to myself. I know that if I do this thing and succeed, then I will take his place.

But it's too much to grasp, and so I do not grasp it. I simply try to think of those I've lost and those who remain and try to plumb my own depths and discover if there might be a little more courage, a little more resolve that I might bring to

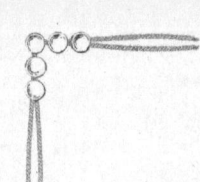

bear upon this task.

I think especially upon Lieve today. I see his sacrifice reflected in my own. I do not expect to survive tomorrow. I go only because I have seen a wreck and cannot abandon it to the waves, just as he did.

I do not go down to the sandy bay. I do not know why, but it does not feel right to be in that public entrance to our island. Instead, I find my way to a slender strip of beach beneath a rocky incline that looks like mismatched giant's steps, worn and washed by the sea.

Here, I step into the tossing surf and let it take me away as I have not since I was a young girl. Queens have little time to frolic and I have not swum for pleasure since I was crowned. I'm almost horrified by the delight I take in the feeling of my body slicing through the water, the grip of the waves against my hands, the slide of my fingers through their drag, and the way all of it cups and buoys my form. It is the closest feeling to the embrace of a lover that I know—and the closest to that I am ever likely to receive again now that my course is plotted and my goal set.

I fling myself into it with full abandon, and it is not until the tide is on its way out again that I follow the tumbled shells and stones back toward the dark swell of the land, my limbs languorous from happy exertion and my feet idly tracing the lace of the surf along the edge of the clear water. I wade for a while, glad that my mind idles without directed thought, akin almost to relief.

I'm waist-deep in the water when I sense something large

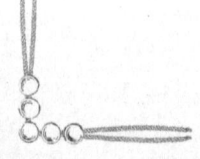

in the sea around me. My breath catches in my throat, fearing a shark or some other great fish, and then right in front of me, rising up out of the water, is Oke. Where he has come from, I cannot say, and unless he has aided my people, I hardly care.

He's bright and gleaming under the sun, his skin more weathered than I remember, the light stubble on his chin darker, the strands of his sun-bleached hair lighter. It's caught and tied in a knot at the back of his head and both it and his face run with rivulets of bright water.

Across the beam of his wide shoulders is slung a blue marlin—the finest example of the species I've ever seen, its black back and blue belly slashed through with a long splash of aqua across its broad side. The spear of its nose matches the spear slung across my husband's back, and for a moment, as he stands up to his waist in frothing water with that king fish across his shoulders, the sight of him is almost overwhelming. Perhaps someone ought to have made a statue of *him* on this island. How can someone so treacherous be so infinitely beautiful?

I flinch from his sudden glory. He looks more the God of the Sea than Vesuvius does, for all that the dead god has an octopus lower half. Okeanos fits the sea as well as the marlin does, as if the two of them and the water itself are all one tangled-up whole and that whole sears my vision, tricking my mind into thinking I'm seeing something too wonderful or worthy for me. How did I not know immediately that he was the God of the Sea?

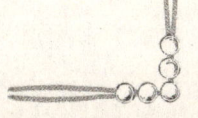

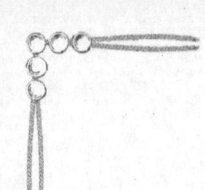

I draw in a strangled breath, and then the sensation is gone, leaving only a powerful man and a great fish, and the ever-changing, ever-powerful swell of the endless sea.

"Wife," Oke says, and he looks away suddenly as if he is reluctant to meet my eye. He flings the marlin to the shore and stalks through the water toward me, his gait twisted and slowed by his wound. "I would speak with you."

He is only wearing one pearl necklace—a fat one that sits over his naked shoulders like a collar—but it is made of three strands, and one strand is black pearls, which remind me a little too much of Vesuvius. I shift uncomfortably when I see them. My bargain with the soul of the dead god does not sit easily with me.

"What more is there to say?" I shift in the water as it licks around my waist. All my hard-won equanimity has dissolved with his words.

I wish things were simpler. I wish that in my plans for the future I was not ending the life of a husband, of a man, no matter how tenuous our actual bond might be. I think I could have liked this man well enough were I not burdened with a great fury, a greater shame, and an enduring loyalty to a people who once looked to me for help. And I think he could have made me a decent husband were he not a treacherous god.

I speak calmly. "Did you save our people? Did you cast down their enemies?"

He doesn't answer. And I feel the resolve in myself tighten.

"You filled my thimble." The words gust out of his mouth so quickly that it's hard for me to catch them.

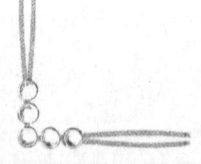

He must have been to the house, then. Why did he not leave the fish there? I feel my cheeks flush. My act of anger feels like a fit of tantrum now. I mean to kill him. And that is earnest business. To leave petty tokens first seems beneath me.

"I gave you all I have left," I say, and the words are more resigned than bitter.

He nods, looking sharply away, his eyes slightly glassy. "That is well, Queen Coralys."

Behind him the waves are growing larger, choppier, more ungovernable. I start toward the shore.

"I am no longer allowed that title," I say. I am thrown off by his emotion and gratitude when I expected resistance and reprisals. "And I don't forgive you. It changes nothing that I now know you are a god."

He sighs as if he has swum the whole breadth of the sea, only to find he must swim it again. His fingers tangle through his brown hair and he drags loose strands of it back from his face.

"You are more than vengeance and wrath, Coralys."

He's dismissed my whole purpose in one sentence, making it sound ridiculous instead of the high calling of my life now. And worse yet, the arguments he threw at me when last we spoke are ringing accusingly in my ears.

"You betrayed me," I whisper. I hate that I feel my cheeks heat at his words. They betray me, too.

"Do you know how you turn tragedy into hell, Coralys?"

His voice is sad and his broad shoulders slump a little.

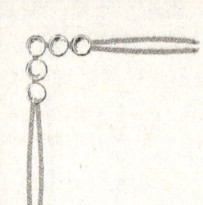

Somehow that slump and the way he looks so wistfully out across the sea make him appear younger and they pull at something in my belly. Something a little akin to sympathy. Something a little too close to understanding.

He has been standing waist-deep in the water. Now he strides forward, the water running from his form in rivulets until he stands on the beach with me. I swallow roughly, overwhelmed by a strange combination of hatred and fondness. Of distrust and longing. I am a wreck being pounded by the swell against the rocks in one direction and by furious rains in another, and I do not know which will sink me first.

His gaze is intent. It sends a little shiver down the backs of my thighs. "You turn tragedy into hell by turning to resentment to succor you. I want better for you than hell."

"How comforting." My words are dry and so is my mouth.

The wind around us picks up, rippling our hair and snapping our clothing like sailcloth. It brings with it dark clouds and turns the sea behind Oke the same green as his eyes.

I'm surprised when he snags my hand in his and kneels in front of me. He holds my hand as a courtier might, but then he turns it so the palm faces him and rests against his forehead. My stomach flips. I don't ask to be touched like this. Not by a man. Not by a god. And yet another part of me craves it. It wants to thread my fingers in that hair. It wants to give him what he's asking for.

"Forgive me," he says. His fingers are still tangled with mine as he presses my palm against his brow, and at first I think he's apologizing for the touch, but then I realize he

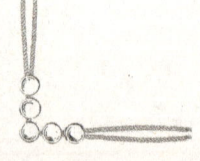

means this act to be some kind of almost religious blessing or absolving. "Forgive me, Queen Coralys, for being slow to answer the cries of your people and failing to drive their enemies away. Forgive me for their spilled blood." He seems to choke a moment on the words, and his other hand rises up and tightens on the strings of pearls he wears. "Forgive me for my failures."

I clear my throat and draw my palm away, untangling our fingers. Losing the touch fills me with an almost giddy relief and a terrible yawning loss all at once. I am suddenly unmoored. I expected a fight. I did not expect a plea. I am unprepared.

"Who are you to apologize for the deaths of my people? Who are you to ask my forgiveness when you've been spending lives like coin from a fool's purse?"

He looks away into the gathering storm, and when the flickering emotions on his face grow stronger, I begin to believe I might get some answers. He abandons kneeling to me and instead strides up the rock shore as the first raindrops fall, but as he moves he speaks in halting words.

"You have named me God of the Sea. You have named me Okeanos." He pauses, his eyes boring into mine. "But I am the son of a fisherman, Lady of the Sea. I lived with my family until I was a boy of eighteen, fishing and working hard under the hot gaze of the sun before the gods of heaven." His eyes plead for me to understand. "My father was a hardworking man with scarred hands and a quick smile. Stergios. He taught me everything about finding fish and luring

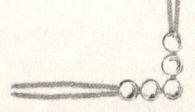

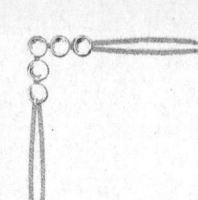

them into the nets, and he would joke that such was the way that he lured my mother into his home. My mother was Alai, daughter of a fish merchant. Together they raised four of us in a cottage no bigger than mine here, and I had planned to do the same. I had even chosen a girl I thought to make my wife. She was warm, kind, good to children. She lived in our small village."

The storm still brews above us but no rain has fallen yet, and when he flings himself onto a natural seat on the rock, he winces as if he has forgotten that he is wounded and ought to take care.

It does not stop the rush of his words. "A storm came one day—greater than any I've seen before or since. I was out in my boat, tending the nets, out of the sight of land. I could not make shore. I stayed low in my boat and fought the wind and rain for hours until I was near exhaustion."

This part clearly pains him and he looks away. I let my eyes linger.

"When I returned, there was nothing left. The storm had swept our island bare. The surge of the sea swallowed everything. A little wreckage was all that remained and not a soul survived." He swallows. "I waited for survivors seven days. And then, desperate, I prayed."

My heart squeezes. This is my story, too.

"It is possible it was hubris that gave me the boldness to ask the God of the Sea for the souls of my family back. But I think it was only love." His hand squeezes into a fist and then, spasming, releases again. The lines on his face are

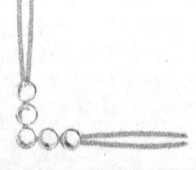

deeper, the expression stark with remembered pain. "That is not how he took it, though. Vesuvius descended upon me and just as hope was lighting my eyes, he struck me hard, shoved my face into the sand, and told me to clean his name from my mouth. I will not deny that I tried to fight back—struggled with all my might—but it was for nothing. In the end, he stripped me bare with his own hands. Is that an honor, do you think? For a god to pay such special attention to your humiliation?"

This is my exact story. He has stripped me bare. Can he not see it? I'm trembling a little, whether from rage for what was done to me or rage at what was done to him, I don't know.

His voice is desolate. "He took from me all I had left. My boat. My nets. My spear. And he left me in the sand naked and with nothing."

And I am thinking of Vesuvius. I am thinking of his tentacles and the look in his eye when he told me he wanted only one god dead. He wants to strip this man twice. I shudder.

Okeanos is silent for a long time and I'm silent with him, both our breaths trembling together under the gathering storm. He's beautiful in his tragedy. I am overwhelmed by mine. And when the first drops of rain fall, it is as if the heavens mourn with us.

Oke gusts a wry laugh. "*He* found me then. Offered me what the God of the Sea would not. Gave me a home and a place and the soul of Vesuvius."

A cold creeping sensation runs through me. I have been

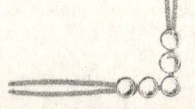

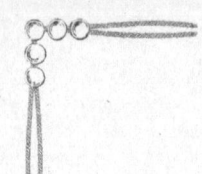

consorting with his enemy and now I sit here and hear his confession. What would he do to me if he knew?

"I can never turn on him." Oke looks out to the horizon again now, his gaze steady and fixed as if he is saying a vow. I don't know who he means, some friend, perhaps, but it hardly signifies. For it is not a matter of who he will betray but who will betray him, and I feel my face grow hot, for it is I. "Not after all he's done for me. No matter who is standing against us."

"No matter who?" I ask softly.

"Yes." He clenches his jaw even tighter. The muscle in it pulses and highlights all the other unforgiving lines of his face. The rain is coming down on us gently. It's warm as it plasters our hair to our faces.

"But you cannot give that loyalty to my people?" I ask, for while I feel absolute sympathy for his tale, I am still implacable. He is both betrayed and betrayer. He has not helped my people. He has not stood in the way of calamity. He is either cruel or incompetent. Either way he must be dragged down so that someone else—someone who will truly shelter them—can take his place.

"I have given my loyalty to your people—and more besides," he says, and he is not looking at me, he is looking far into the distance. "I am working to build them a safe place. A place where they can be free of all this."

The words spring from my lips before my thoughts are fully formed. "They had a safe place, on their islands, where I ruled."

He's shaking his head. "Not safe enough."

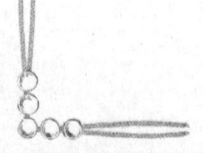

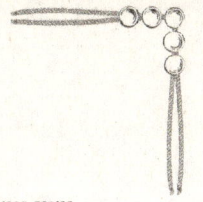

"Not when you do not defend it," I spit at him. Any sympathy I had is washed away with the rain.

"There is not enough space on the Crocus Isles." He glances at me then. "All the people of the sea are mine, not merely the few you consider your own."

"The few—" It's like he's snatched the breath from my lungs. "You should be out there fighting for them. Defending them. Guarding them. Not... building some fortress somewhere. Besides, I have watched you. You fish. You waste your time with me. You are not building anything. You are not doing *anything*."

He shakes his head in denial, but he does not look at me. "We aren't so different, you and I. We both cannot walk away when those we love are hurt."

"We are entirely different," I say, shaking. I came so close to being moved by him and his story. I am aghast at myself.

"Work with me," he pleads.

Does he think I can forget so soon all he has destroyed? I cannot allow him to be our god.

And when he reaches out a tentative finger and strokes the outside edge of my smallest finger nearest to him, this ghost of a movement stabs me like a knife, for I see the lonely boy—his family and hopes lost forever—but I also see the incompetent god who I must tear down so that he might be replaced with another.

"Help me build this fortress for your people and mine," he implores gently. "You have guessed who I am. Now divine the purpose in what I have done."

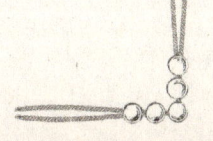

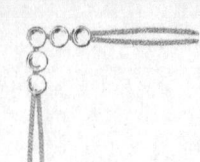

But I dare not let him see my heart. I must keep him trusting me. I must keep him at his ease. For no mortal weapon will kill a god, and I must have the tools I require before I act.

So I look at him and smile, and it must seem like a yes, for his features soften.

"Will you come fishing with me?" His request is so unexpected that I feel my brows raise and his half smile wavers as if he cannot tell what my answer will be.

I do not want to fish. I want to scream at him and demand he do better. I want to scream at the sky and sob until my eyes and nose are raw.

"If it is important to you, I will."

"Then we will go now."

And he looks so boyish when he bites his lip that my heart aches to comfort him, but I do not. Because I must not. Not only because his every betrayal shreds my heart into more tiny pieces but because I must kill him with my own hands and imprison his soul. There is no other way. I must betray him as he has betrayed me.

"Whatever course you take, Coralys." He pauses, swallows, and then looks me directly in the eye. And I feel a tingling sensation down my spine, for it is as if he can see to my heart. "Whatever course. Please know I absolve you of guilt."

And then he turns and leads me along the shore, scooping up the marlin as he passes, and I have the oddest sensation that he can do exactly that.

We fish and it hurts that we almost fit together. It rubs at

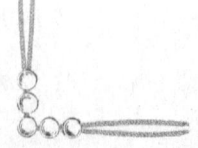

me like a too-small shoe, because we two could have made an excellent pairing, a strong partnership in any circumstance but this one.

But we are on opposite sides in an impossible war.

We do not eat supper. We are neither of us hungry. The fish go into a tide pool where they'll wait for Oke to either kill and smoke them or set them free.

We slip, instead, into dry clothing and drape ourselves like seaweed over the large bed, and I'm not sure if he sleeps, but once again, I do not.

I do, however, dream. I dream of a sea where instead of fish, you pull possibilities free. I pull out Lieve's soul and we live in this cottage happily together swimming and fishing. But Lieve of the dream is hollow and lifeless as if my memory cannot do him justice. And the life I see in my imagination feels just as empty. When I finally hear Oke's breath even out, I bite my lip hard and hope that I do not lose my courage when I do what comes next.

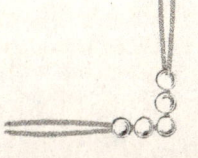

Chapter Fourteen

I slip from Oke's warm bed into the chill of the hour before dawn. The cold nips at my flesh and a last stealthy glance at him bites at my conscience, but whatever I owe him for these past weeks pales beside what I owe my people and the memory of Lieve.

I mean to leave Oke then, but he rouses, his eyes narrowing when he sees me creeping from the bed. He's quick to join me despite his wound. I try very hard not to look at it. It will be my one advantage against him if he becomes aware of what I mean to do.

"I must leave to deal with a matter today," he says mildly as we check my nets for fish, hauling them up dripping and heavy in the rose-pink light of morning. My fingers are growing calluses like his from handling the rough ropes. He guides my work, teaching me as we go with small gestures and nods. "Would you come with me? Or would you remain here and when I return we can discuss together my plans to build a refuge for our people?"

It's an offer of a truce. And I wish I could take it. But when I think of his refuge, all I think is Refuge from what? For is he not the source of so many of my people's woes? Is he not the one who has brought storm and calamity upon us?

He will be dead and that will be the end of it.

"And where do you go, husband?" I ask, begging my face not to show the path my mind has taken. I gather the fish from the net and put them in a reed basket. They flop and dance in the crisp morning air, flinging arcs of water droplets out like golden strings of pearls in the morning sun. I must brace my feet on rounded stones as I catch them and slide them back in place.

And I realize in this moment that it is not only that I am angry and hurt beyond expressing. I am also afraid. I see in him the end of my people, my culture, my very islands. All at the hand of their god. For who is there on whom to call, when your god cannot help? Where do your prayers go, when your god is not listening?

And I cannot leave my beloved people to the fear that has me so tightly in its grip. I must go. I must set this in motion. And I must not let him know what I am about.

"I must treat with my enemies," he says gently, an echo of my mental list, but he does not look at me. Gold burnishes his face and glints in his green eyes, and he is so sober he could be one of the guarding statues. "I must carve out a little more time for us to act."

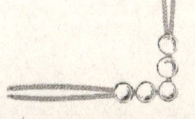

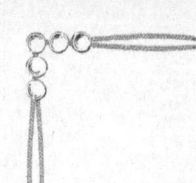

"I wish you well," I say, not meeting his eyes, tasting the lie on my tongue.

He bobs his head in acknowledgment but says nothing more.

And yet he still hovers at my side all day—there as I clean fish and cook them, as I wash clothing and hang it to dry, as I sweep the house. When I turn, I brush against him; when I lean over something to study it, I feel his breath on my neck. He helps me at each task with gentle efficiency until I feel like I might scream. I need him to *go*. I do not dare twist my hand and shift realms with him here. He would follow. I know it. And then what? Would he guess my purpose? Would he find a way to stop me? I think this is exactly why he remains so close and so sharp-eyed.

It is midafternoon and the day has grown bright and furious when I finally run out of things to do and he moves in front of me so that I have to look into his jade eyes.

"I beg you forget your revenge," he says, and his jaw clenches as if this is taking an effort to ask. He hunches forward as he speaks, the muscles of his shoulders seeming larger with the movement and its accompanying intensity.

He knows, then. Or he suspects. A surge of cold fear lances through me, flooding me from forehead to feet.

"You wish for it still, do you not? To have your revenge on me. To destroy my plans and bring me down. Because of the calamity your people face, the death of your husband, the loss of your crown."

I say nothing.

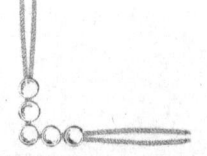

"You know I am your god and your husband, and yet you plot against me. You will not take my word that I am bent on your good and the good of those you love."

To my utter surprise he leans close and draws me to him with a hand at the small of my back. He is warm and firm with muscle. I'm so taken aback that I gape at him like a fresh-caught fish. I see in his eyes the unexpected. Longing. Desire.

"Hostility is the last thing I wish to see grow between your heart and mine. Leave it, wife."

"And what will I be, then?" I ask, a little breathlessly. "Faithless? Fickle? I am neither of those things."

I shiver against his touch, regretting that I must reject it and him in the most violent way possible.

"You'll be my wife."

"What would you have me do? What?" I press, frustration acid on my tongue. "Forget my dead husband and my suffering people, and live a happy life with you here in the sun and by the sea?"

His hand at the small of my back tightens in what I think might be matching turmoil, and the movement hitches me a little closer as he shakes his head. His brow so close to mine that I can feel his hair brush my cheek. He is very alive. Almost inhumanly alive, and I feel myself pulse in time with the rhythm of his heart. His words are forced, tight, frustrated.

"I would have you stand by my side and be my wife in more than name."

I'm surprised that he would bare himself so knowing I

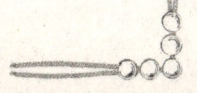

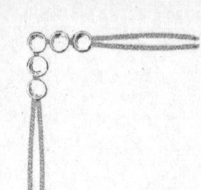

must shatter any hope of such a thing. That he would draw so near to she who waits like a snake in the grass. Surely he realizes. Surely this is why he has hovered so near and waited so long. Did he truly believe he could seduce me into trusting him? Now? When my heart is set?

I slip from his arms, putting distance between us, and the look I give him is firm and set.

"Had I not so great a cause, I might very well have given you that. But it is too late."

He nods. "I must attend to my duties, then. As you must attend to yours."

And I feel every place that he no longer touches like the shock of cold spray on the skin. His pleas have changed nothing except for how much it will hurt us both when I take his life and all his dreams from him.

He gathers his things quickly and I watch from the cottage as he leaves on his boat. The wind is rough today, and it shakes the little craft in sprays of silver as it drags it off to the deeper sea.

And then—at long last—he is gone and I'm free.

I make my way back down to the water—not the beach and not the rocky steps where I bathed in the sea. Both those places are too full of Oke, and to betray him there feels doubly wrong. Instead, I slip out in a different direction past the statue where I called up Vesuvius, down the toothlike jagged rocks that make me feel as if I am crawling into some great creature's mouth, and down to where an unhappy sea foams against the shore.

The Trident and the Pearl

All along this half bay, the waters have washed up spew from lands beyond: battered timbers, tumbled bits of glass, a handmade buoy with the sign of Okeanos carved painstakingly into the surface and then worn away by the waves. Little tokens of lands far away that I'll never see now that I've chosen this course.

I step into the surf and let it tickle my shins. Now that the moment is here, I find I'm not quite ready. But I do not have the time nor the patience to wait for my heart to be ready. I screw up my mouth, fix my courage, and take the black pearl from my pouch and stare at it a moment. I'm not sure I want that horrible dead god with me for this after all. I leave it clenched in one fist, close if I need it, but unopened.

My hand is shaking as I raise it in the cupped shape Vesuvius showed me. I know I am afraid. But is anything truly worth doing not a little terrifying?

Before I can think my way out of it, I twist my hand the way I was shown. The world around me shimmers and reels, and I blink hard to recover myself, expecting to be in the home of the gods.

I am not.

Instead, before I can gasp in a breath or see my surroundings, water rises in a forceful swell, sweeping my feet out from under me, curling upward and then crashing down again like the mouth of a monster bent on destroying me. I am swept up and rolled under the powerful wave. Panic clutches me, but I fight it back and scramble for footing. There was ground beneath my feet a moment ago.

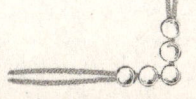

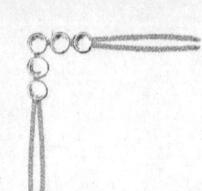

I find it suddenly as the water recedes and pull myself upright between sharp rocks that rise through the water like the spine of some great dead creature.

I gasp for air and claw against one of the rocks, choking and heaving on the salt water I swallowed. I must be in the wrong place. I must have done it wrong. As my anxiety rises, the water rises, too, and then I'm smashed again under an angry wave.

I lose my grip on the rock and tumble, knocked hard on the head so that I nearly lose my grip on the pearl. For the second time in a fortnight I think I may very well drown. By luck alone, my grasping fingers find the rock again and I claw myself free of the drag of the dark waters and suck in a breath, forcing myself to remain calm until the wave recedes and my heartbeat becomes manageable.

I must find higher ground.

I drag myself up the spinelike rock, only to have the waters chase me upward yet again, until I've climbed twice my height and I'm still ankle-deep in water.

I wobble there on the top of one of the rocky ridges and look outward at a string of white islands connected to this spiny ridge as if they are the ribs of a massive dead creature. I think I see structures carved from the white stone on some of them, and in the distance there is a rock that rises high above the rest, but I am drenched and bedraggled and to reach it I must swim from rock to rock along this jutting spine.

I have a long path to take. The sun is sinking. My dress is ruined, and I fear the power of the waves will sweep me away.

I need guidance. I must not be too proud for it. This is nothing like anything I would have expected from the home of a god. It is lonely and howling.

With an effort, I unfurl my fist and reveal the pearl. It does not take much work to cry. I'm on the edge already, certain I've done something wrong and trapped myself in some lonely shell of a world. Didn't Vesuvius say they were layered one over the other like wet cloth? Perhaps I have gone through too many layers. There is only one who can advise me, but when my tear drops onto the pearl and Vesuvius springs out along a thread of smoke, I wonder if I've made a mistake.

Vesuvius takes one look at me and laughs. The stumps of his two missing tentacles look worse than before. They're crusted over, swollen, and discolored.

"This is your paradise? How diverting."

"Paradise? You said nothing of paradise." My voice sounds harsh, even to me. But in seeing him I'm suddenly very aware of what a disaster this is. My fine white chiton clings to me uncomfortably, twisting around my calves and tripping me up, and my hair is tangled around my arms like strands of seaweed. Even if I make it to the meeting of the gods, I will hardly be inconspicuous.

Vesuvius's gaze is sharp. Always sharp. I fight the urge to step back from what it might reveal. I must be very wary with him near.

"You have done as you said you would. I see no problem. The Resurgence awaits."

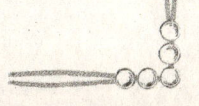

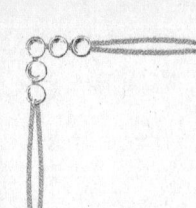

"No." My voice is bitter with embarrassment. "I have done it wrong and there's no one here."

He sneers, but his attention is only half on me. He's looking around him greedily as if he could eat the view.

"The Resurgence takes place in a plane between the other planes—a half-world of shadow and imagination. Each one to enter sees it differently. You've envisioned it as some dead creature upon which you will crawl. Fitting for a woman who looks like she's been vomited up by the sea." He gestures as if to indicate my garments. "As you do."

I skip over his criticism. "So this is the fruit of my own imagination?"

He pauses, his beautiful face twisting with a humor I do not share. "It's the fruit of someone's imagination. If not yours, then perhaps the God of the Sea's. This does seem to reflect his spartan heart. I'll have you know that when I was God of the Sea, every inch of my heavens were packed with lovely servants and sumptuous repast. The sea is not a lonely wild place, but one full of bounty and power. In my heaven, there were no barriers to traverse to its very heart. Here, I think you'll need to battle your way forward with every step, or it may very well smash you to wreckage on its rocks."

I suck in a fortifying breath. Can nothing be simple? "A fine guide you are. You have left out key elements."

"I am not your nursemaid. Fight or don't fight. What difference does it make to me?"

"The waters rise each time I move forward," I say tightly. "Have you an explanation for how to deal with that?"

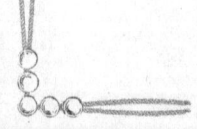

He smirks and I feel my heart grow thick with hate for him.

"With every word you show me more of my enemy. Perhaps fear is what he is troubled by most. Perhaps your very emotions stir up his seas. A child's defense, to be sure, but Okeanos was never very sophisticated. I suggest attempting to be calm. If that is even something you can achieve."

"And where will I find the gods?" I snap. "Should I imagine them up, too?"

He lifts a brow at me like he might not answer me after I've taken that tone with him.

"Try to stop thinking like a petulant mortal and more like a god-slayer. They'll be within the heart of this place." He nods ahead of us to where the rock rises and some structure looms high above the sea. "I hear tell that Okeanos is always late, so that will give you time to go in there and bluff your way into the midst of the rest of them."

"Are you certain they will be here?"

"This is the Resurgence. If anyone fails to attend, he'll lose not only his standing but his power, and a god without power isn't a god for long." His mouth twists sourly. "Trust me on this. They will be here. And you will find them. Just stop dallying in the waters like a fish. I will come with you."

"Won't your presence alert them?"

"None can see me but she who holds my prison." He looks at where the sun hangs low in the sky. "Unless you mean to waste both our chances, best hurry."

But I do not trust him and do not want him with me for

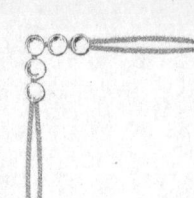

this journey. And even if I did, I would need both hands for the effort. I slide his pearl back into my pouch and set to work clambering along the sharp rocks.

I will not relate how many times I fall, nor how often I cut open my knees, my elbows, and even my palms. The rocks are sharp and uninviting, and every time worry threatens me, the waves only grow higher. I am forced to set aside all concern for what I will face when I arrive and focus solely on the minute-to-minute work of traversing this spinelike ridge of pale rock. The cold spray of the ocean is unforgiving, chilling my fingers until I cannot feel the rock I grip and making everything slick as if instead of rock I am fighting with living eels.

By the time I reach the towering structure ahead every muscle in my body is shaking and my heartbeat is loud in my mind.

I drag myself from the dark waters, my flesh all goosebumped and frigid and my soft chiton shredded by rocks and pink with blood.

It is no matter. I have arrived and that is all for which I could have asked.

What appeared only a rocky rise from afar is an awe-inspiring place from a closer view. A nearly circular isle of white stone is ringed by colossal statues at least five times my own height. I immediately recognize them as images of the gods—ten statues, one for each of them. And from the open mouth of each statue pours a fountain of water that runs down the stone, leaving a residue of iron and lichen before trickling to the ground where it washes into the sea.

The Trident and the Pearl

It is not exactly a room or a hall. These statues would provide no cover at all from the elements, but they serve like a perimeter around a great room and in the center of this room is laid a table.

The table is large enough for an army to feast and laid upon it is a banquet fit for a magnificent harvest year. A whole tuna lies carved on one end, its carmine flesh sliced delicately and a half lemon placed over one eye, and at the other end of the table sits an entire roast pig on a silver platter, though its eyes are replaced with cherries rather than lemons.

I'd be salivating except for what lies in the center.

It's not a fish.

It's not a roast beast.

It's a dead woman.

Gods, but I hope she's dead. My heart speeds as I catch sight of her, and I swallow hard, looking in every direction before creeping forward to examine her.

She's sprawled out across the table, her long silver-pale curls tangling between bunches of grapes and sweating pitchers of melon juice. Someone has laid a shell over each of her eyes, but no one bothered to lay anything over the jagged slash across her throat. From its gory center a dozen golden flowers—not yellow, but actual burnished gold—spring up, multiplying even as I watch them. They smell of honey and frankincense and they are the only thing that moves. Her chest is still, the breath plucked away already.

In one hand, wrapped around her fingers, are chains of

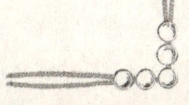

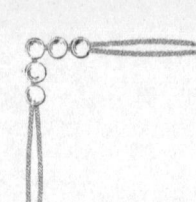

cabochon rubies, fat as hen eggs and cranberry red, just like the blood that drips from her throat and trickles down the side of the table.

She is terribly beautiful. So beautiful that I feel almost as if she can't be real, but her pale skin—bluish in the extremities—tells a different story, and her beautifully stitched chiton is torn nearly to her hip and stained pink with watered blood.

Fighting sharp stings of fear, I hurry back to the nearest statue and duck behind it, crouching low to hide myself behind his great stone foot. This table must be laid for the gods, and this poor lady laid out with it. I dare not let them see me when they come. All thought of bluffing my way into their company evaporates with the very real dead woman on their table. That could be me…will be me…unless I can find another way, and the only way to do that will be to watch and wait for the right moment.

I shrink farther against the back side of the statue's foot. How ironic that I should hide behind the image of he who I aim to destroy, but here I am, taking refuge in the shadow of Okeanos as I wait for the gods to arrive.

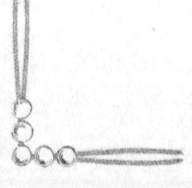

Chapter Fifteen

Though I watch all around me, the arrival of the first god still takes me by surprise. There's a faint sound similar to someone opening a wine bottle and at the base of the statue of Aurelius, God of the Air, a man appears.

My fingers wrap tensely around the base of Okeanos's statue, but I am very still, barely even breathing.

The statue of Aurelius is easy to recognize. He's always depicted as a young man in a very short chiton, a crown of olive leaves on his head and three arrows in one hand. It's only when the man appears that I realize I've seen the real Aurelius in the flesh before.

This man carries no arrows and the crown he wears is gold and glittering; his chiton is the color of wine and his chlamys worked with silver and gold thread in an olive leaf pattern, but it is the same man I met on the docks of Oke's island. The very same one who suggested I cut off my own finger and throw it in the sea. I can see now why Oke was so nervous about him.

My eyes keep passing over his face as if they are too afraid to latch on to his terrible beauty and hold there. I must force them to stay on him and force my shoulders straight. This is not my god. Nor is he the one I want dead. All I need from the God of the Air is to escape his notice.

Aurelius strides into the room from the base of the statue where he has materialized. He moves like a wounded lion, stalking with a slight hitch in his step, his lithe muscles flowing as he looks around him quickly and then hurries to the table. One hand rises and lingers just over the body of the dead woman and then he draws it back, swallowing visibly.

His eyes narrow as he looks around the room a second time, and my heart picks up speed. Will he see me hiding here?

To my relief, there's a second pop and beneath the rough-hewn statue of Markanos, God of War, emerges a man dressed in continental armor—a muscle cuirass and flowing cape, crested galea and embossed greaves. A large ruby dangles from one ear. He's older than we are, maybe twice the age of Aurelius—though if they are both gods, then they are ageless—with the barrel-chested look of a fit older man who has maintained his looks. His face is hewn from rock, his features almost ugly, yet they possess the grandeur of rough-cut mountain peaks. It's a beauty hard to define, and impossible to reproduce.

The Trident and the Pearl

He's flanked by a pair of mortal men bearing swords. They're both blindfolded, though they move at his back in perfect synchronization. Rethgar and Rothgar—the blind guardians of War. I am witnessing legends come to life.

A stab of fear shoots through me. If they find me spying, what pain may be visited on me by an angry war god? Surely they will not spare me.

My knees wobble as Markanos's eyes flicker over my hiding place, but just like Aurelius he strides to the table, his eyes narrowing as they take in the dead woman.

"El'Dorian?" His words come out in a growl, but his face is troubled rather than furious.

One of my hands flies up to cover my mouth before I can stop it.

The dead woman is the Goddess of Love and Virginity. I steal a quick glance at her statue—the only one without water pouring from its open mouth. Its joyful expression looks nothing like the dead woman, and its hands are full of blooming flowers, where she has flowers growing in her death wound.

Three gods. Only seven more, a hysterical voice in my head says, and the child's song begins to sing in my mind as Markanos's hand drifts to the hilt of his sword.

Take your breath for Aurelius,
Drink your drop for Okeanos,
Plant your seed for Glorian,
Give your kiss for El'Dorian,

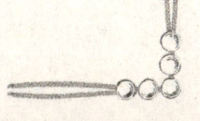

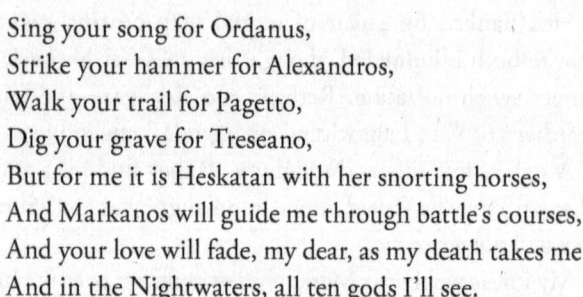

Sing your song for Ordanus,
Strike your hammer for Alexandros,
Walk your trail for Pagetto,
Dig your grave for Treseano,
But for me it is Heskatan with her snorting horses,
And Markanos will guide me through battle's courses,
And your love will fade, my dear, as my death takes me
And in the Nightwaters, all ten gods I'll see.

I want to laugh and I know it's simply the strain of seeing actual gods that makes me feel that way. No one will be giving El'Dorian kisses now.

"You shouldn't have killed her, Aurelius," the God of War says grimly, but before he draws his sword the God of the Air lifts a palm in peace.

"Hold your wrath, War. This is no work of mine. What grudge have I ever had against the beauty of El'Dorian?"

The God of War frowns at the corpse on the table. His hand trembles on the hilt of his sword. He is unsettled by this and so is Aurelius, though they speak so calmly.

"If it is not you, then it must be one of the others," Markanos says in a low voice, but he does not take a seat; rather, he withdraws back to lean against the feet of his own statue, Rethgar and Rothgar following him. He rubs at a pair of parallel lines in his forehead, but they do not fade away. "We will wait and see what they have to say for themselves."

I can't tear my eyes away from Markanos. He looks exactly as I would have expected him to look. It's said he

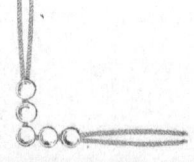

was dropped into a battlefield by a great stork and that in his wrath he leveled both armies and claimed all the lands from the Elephant Spire to the Frigid Plains as his personal territory; for the gods own pieces of us mortals. We are broken up by them into flocks and herds—or, in Okeanos's case, schools of fish—and each attends to his own like a shepherd. Or like a butcher.

Another pop startles me and three gods arrive at once. The first one I see is Glorian, arguably one of the most powerful gods. She is just as lovely as Aurelius, but where he is dark-haired, pale, and ephemeral, she is golden and lush.

Glorian is crowned with uncut emeralds, her golden-red hair wraps around her limbs in thick curls, and flanking her—odd for the Goddess of Plenty and Growing Things—is a whole squadron of burnished soldiers, their spears in hand, their shields gleaming. But their peaked helms don't disguise the faraway looks in their eyes. It is as if they are not exactly here in mind in the same way that they are in body. My subjects were never *things* to me, and it makes me feel tight and worried to see these people treated so.

"An army, Glorian?" Markanos says from where he lingers, leaning against his statue. "That's not like you. Do you know something we do not? Something about the death of our sister, perhaps?"

"She's no sister to me. Not one of you is my family."

"Harsh," Aurelius murmurs with a raised brow, but she carries on.

"Only Aurelius was even a god when I joined your ranks,"

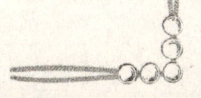

Glorian says, but I see she pales as she says it, and the goddess who emerged beside her has a distinctly green look around the edges of her brown face. "Forgive me if I do not trust you, God of War, even in this neutral place. I have seen how your worshippers posture at my borders. There are whispers that King Torfang assembles a secret army and eyes the olive groves of Pescatore with greed. Shall I trust you when you assemble against me, Markanos?"

I miss the details of Markanos's denial. I'm too busy looking at the others who arrived with the goddess Glorian.

Her companions are Heskatan of the Hill Countries, Goddess of Horses, and Pagetto, Goddess of Travelers. I identify them both easily—though it is still shocking to see gods living and breathing before me when I was not certain they even existed only weeks ago.

Heskatan is a very dark woman, whose long hair hides most of her face. She is silent and grave and her eyes never leave the corpse of El'Dorian. She is the only one who has not arrived on foot. She is mounted on a wide-chested black horse, and when she dismounts, she feeds him treats from her hand.

With her is Pagetto, a goddess with sharp eyes and a voluptuous figure. Her hair is shaved entirely and a cap woven of gold and dripping gems is worn in its place.

"Leave us our small defenses, Markanos," Pagetto says in a purring voice. "You cannot be the only one to bring your guards. Look at the table. If El'Dorian brought mortals along, perhaps she would not be laid out like dinner."

Despite her words about guards, she has brought only one companion—a woman so veiled that I can see nothing but her eyes, bearing a large snake. The snake wraps around both the woman and Pagetto at once, its pale yellow skin roiling and writhing as if it has recently eaten and its prey is still within. For a moment, a shape very like a human face passes across the snake's pale midsection.

I count silently to myself. Six gods are here. Each of them as nebulous in their morality as a fish or a bird—I see no heroes or even villains, only strange and elevated beings. But if I have met six, then four more remain. And one is Okeanos. My palms sweat at the thought that he could be here at any moment. And then what? Shall I dart out and snatch a weapon from one of the gods before he notices? While every statue of the gods carries some weapon as decoration, so far only Aurelius, Heskatan, and Markanos are visibly armed. Could I steal a sword while they are distracted with the death of one of their own?

"If El'Dorian is dead, then where is her heir?" Glorian asks incisively. She looks around, peering at the bases of the statues, and I shrink back a little more. "Did either of you think to look, or were you just going to sit there?"

Despite her accusation, Aurelius lifts a pitcher, carefully disentangles one of the dead goddess's curls, and pours himself a drink.

Pagetto shudders delicately.

"It's been ages since someone killed one of us," she says in her bell-like voice. "Who was the last?"

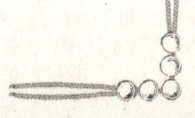

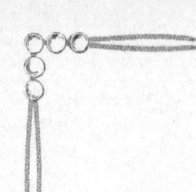

"Okeanos, killing Vesuvius." It's the first time Heskatan has spoken. Her voice is soft, barely above a whisper.

"And what a shame that was," a new voice says as one more god arrives. "I always liked Vesuvius. He had this trick he did with severed heads at parties that was truly unexpected."

This voice is exactly what you would expect from a god appearing under the statue of Treseano, God of Death. Just like the towering statue above him, he carries a mace and a sack. I hope I never know what is in the sack. It squirms in a way that makes me very uncomfortable.

Treseano is middle-aged and short and he walks like he doesn't want to commit to just one direction. I get the distinct impression that the other gods shrink away from him. He leads twenty retainers, all dressed in black cowled cassocks. All with their mouths sewn shut. His priests. I hear they do that to themselves, placing each stitch as part of a rite of passage. Even knowing they chose it, it makes me shudder.

"You too, Treseano?" Markanos asks accusingly. "Since when did we bring armies to this place?"

"Not since the last god war," Treseano replies. "It looks to me as if this one is kicking off sooner than expected."

He gestures flippantly at El'Dorian and takes a seat beside Aurelius at the table, scooping up a handful of grapes and eating them one by one as he speaks. His priests remain at the foot of his statue, but he doesn't set down the wriggling sack he carries.

"No one is at war," Pagetto says urgently, taking the seat

opposite him with a very straight spine. I can see even from here that she doesn't like to sit at the table with a reminder splayed out across it that even gods die, but she does. She must hold a weak position among them if she must pretend at equanimity when she clearly does not feel it.

Glorian and Markanos don't have to pretend. They stand by their statues as if they each have one foot out the door.

Three more are left. Ordanus, God of Music and Art; Alexandros of the Hammer, God of Smiths; and Okeanos, God of the Sea.

My palms are sweating. Just a little while longer and he will be here.

"Are you really going to eat?" Glorian asks them, her mouth twisting. "With poor El'Dorian laid out like that and both Markanos and Alexandros posturing as if they mean to make war, do you really plan to sit and feast together?"

"I'm not posturing," a bold male voice says, and a tall, golden-haired man steps out from the foot of the statue of Alexandros. His chlamys is black and clasped at the shoulder with a complicated silver fibula pin. A hammer is slung across his back. "War is coming. My smiths feel it in the pounding of their hammers, and you all know well that we cannot take part in the wars of man directly. To fail to prepare our worshippers to face what is coming is to be blind and deaf to the pleas of their hearts."

"Well said," says Aurelius, toasting him.

"Where's Ordanus?" Alexandros asks—he's as muscled as you'd expect from a god of blacksmiths and

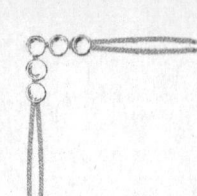

silverworkers—pulling out a chair and offering a goblet to Pagetto, who receives it very reluctantly. He takes a place beside her, leaving only three standing.

"I think we've lost the important thread in all these greetings," Markanos growls. "What matters is not whose followers threaten who or what wars might arise—all that will come in time."

"If you have anything to do with it," Alexandros mutters, and Aurelius lifts his glass to toast him again.

"What matters," Markanos says, speaking over them, "is who killed El'Dorian."

"Most likely it's some mortal who wanted her place," Glorian says eventually, and she seems to steel herself before finally taking a place at the foot of the table. It's as far from the corpse as it is possible to be, but even so she grimaces.

"Heavens forfend." The second-to-last god has arrived and he stares in horror at El'Dorian as he strides from the base of his statue. Ordanus, God of Music and Art, doesn't carry the harp he's depicted with, but the two harpists following him make up for it. One is male and one is female and they are both young and lovely, dressed in blue-trimmed robes, playing as they follow him.

Ordanus is worshipped along the coast wherever Okeanos is not. I've been in dozens of his temples and heard his priests and priestesses play at coronations and ceremonies all my life. To see him in the flesh fills me with awe.

Ordanus's harpists sway to the music, their gazes fixed into the distance. I am starting to see that the servants of the

gods are kept intentionally at a distance. They are mute in this assembly, no more noted than furniture.

I remember visiting a temple of Ordanus on the Ivory Shore that had a choir of a hundred souls, and their song was so divine that I would not leave until they'd sung their entire selection. Every song was in praise of this deity, and it feels like a rope burn to think this is how little he cares.

It's only when I hear someone say, "But it rather showed your hand to attack the Crocus Isles outright, don't you think?" that my attention is suddenly riveted in place.

What have I missed? Who attacked our islands? I try to peek around the statue again, but I have moved too quickly. Across the room, Markanos freezes and then grunts, and with a decisive leap, he bursts forward, crosses to the table in two strides, vaults over it, and is in front of me before I have unfrozen enough to flee.

He reaches down, seizes me by the hair, and drags me to my feet.

"Little murderess," he says with a curling lip. "Good evening. I am Markanos, soon to be your executioner as I take revenge for El'Dorian."

"I didn't kill anyone," I say in a rush, but he's already slid his sword from its scabbard and he has the edge pressed to my throat.

"How long have you been hiding, listening to us?" His voice is low and threatening.

I say nothing. No answer to that question will please him.

"We could hold a court," Glorian says from her seat at the

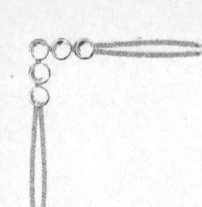

table. She is watching us tensely. "After you check to be sure there aren't more mortals crawling around here. If one slipped in, who knows how many others might have entered our plane?"

"Why complicate things?" Markanos says easily, turning his sword in a casual but showy trick that spins it around his palm and back into his grip. I can imagine him doing that with my blood still dripping from it. "She is here where none but the blood of a god can enter unless they are brought in our entourages. She is the one who killed El'Dorian, however she managed such a task. Where are you hiding your god weapon, mortal woman?"

He drags me forward, out in front of the statue of Okeanos. It looms over me, a great, shirtless figure holding a fishing spear in one hand and a string of pearls in the other. I nearly laugh at the irony of it; I may very well be slain for a crime I didn't commit...yet. For while I have not killed a god, I certainly came here to do just that.

The dark humor of it twists my lips into a smile, and when Markanos's eyes meet mine, it seems my smile is the wrong expression to be wearing. He grits his teeth and draws his sword back. I'm just inhaling my last breath when a sudden hand yanks me backward by the chiton and another catches Markanos's arm, as the blow he's been threatening finally comes down.

I gasp as I stumble backward and crash into a solid body built like a wall. I am pulled all at once against the chest of a god. I can tell that's what he is. His power weakens my knees. And I know this touch, this scent.

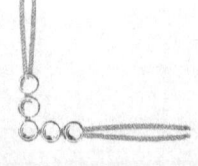

"Okeanos," Markanos says, sounding surprised and a bit disappointed. "You're late. And you're interfering. I was about to dispatch this mortal."

My mouth is dry—and not just because I was almost murdered a moment ago. My husband is here at last. He knows I want revenge. Will he understand that I came here to find the opportunity for it?

The rhythm of my heart is erratic.

"In that case, I *am* late," Okeanos says, and my breath gusts out in sorrow. "I nearly missed saving you from a dreadful mistake, my friend."

The word "mistake" sounds louder than all the others, and with it I finally steel myself and force myself to turn.

His iron grip slackens enough to let me look at him, and as I turn, our gazes meet.

"You came," he mouths to me. He knows. And the way he looks into my eyes is vulnerable and intimate and it makes my lips part and my stomach flip over.

He swallows, and when he makes his announcement, his voice is strained. "This is my wife."

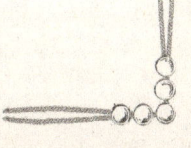

Chapter Sixteen

I choke and I am not the only one. Around the room curses and exclamations ring out. At first, I think the gods are that horrified by our marriage, but then I see the color has drained from their faces for another reason.

Every eye is glued to the godwound in Oke's thigh—every eye but his.

He shoves back Markanos's sword and whispers, "El'Dorian?"

"Dead," Markanos says, staring at his wound.

He has intentionally torn his breeches in such a way that the wound—ragged-edged and bloody—shows plainly to all. Strange that he would keep it a secret from my advisors only to show it so dramatically here.

His eyes wrench from mine and flick from face to face. His trap has been sprung. He's looking for their reactions as

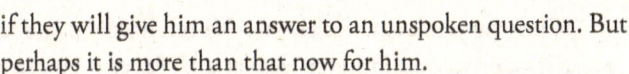

if they will give him an answer to an unspoken question. But perhaps it is more than that now for him.

"Who killed her?" His voice is upset enough that I feel a twist of jealousy—though why I would be jealous that the god I want to murder might care about a dead woman, I do not know.

"We thought it was this mortal you claim as wife," Markanos says gruffly.

"If it were, then she would be Goddess of Love and Virginity, and it would hardly be your place to kill her," Oke says as Markanos lowers his sword.

The God of War shrugs awkwardly. "I liked El'Dorian. And besides, whoever murdered her ruined our meal."

"It's not ruined," Aurelius says from his place at the table. He has thrown one leg indolently over the arm of his chair. "The wine is excellent."

Whatever else they say is lost on me. Could the one who wounded Okeanos and the one who killed El'Dorian be the same?

And if he had succeeded, would he have become god to our people? It is unsettling to think our fate can be decided by the bickering of deities and that we would have no chance to influence our future at all.

"Why do you all sit at table when El'Dorian flowers upon your meal?" Okeanos says in a tight voice. A muscle in his jaw jumps when he clenches it. He leans against one of the chairs, seeming casual, but I note how he takes a little weight off his wounded leg.

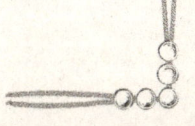

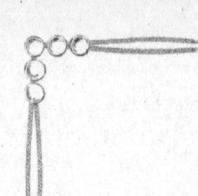

"While we yet live, we celebrate. We can hardly pause for every loss, or we would never feast at all," Pagetto says neutrally, but I can tell she's shaken, because her wine has dribbled from her goblet onto El'Dorian's shoulder. "And look, even you, marked as you are by a cruel wound, are not killed by it."

"Do you wish me so?" My husband's tone is light, but his body is tense.

"Fate forfend," she says, a little breathlessly. "But how do you stand before us so wounded?"

"One of you," Okeanos says grimly, "has underestimated me."

It's such a preposterously mild statement for what's happened that a surprised laugh slips from my mouth.

They all turn to me at once and frown.

"I think, husband, that *all* have underestimated you," I say coolly.

"And you, Coralys?" he asks me as if it is just we two and not an entire audience. "Have you underestimated me?"

"You did say you absolved me of all guilt," I remind him.

Outside the ring of looming god statues, the sky is darkening and the wind kicks up, swirling the sea into waves that crash against the white rock. I am not distracted by them. I look steadily into my husband's eyes and I cannot read the expression he wears. He's gripped by a powerful emotion—I can only imagine it must be fury—but when he answers, he does not sound angry, merely determined.

"It is so, Coralys." He clears his throat and turns away

from me to the others. "As courageous as it no doubt is to scream into the abyss and mock death by feasting at a table laid with our dead friend, I have no care to join you in it."

"It's tradition," Glorian counters, but I notice she has yet to eat, and her retainers hug close to her back as if they fear for her safety.

"Tradition to eat over the dead?" Okeanos presses.

"Tradition to break bread with one another," Glorian says, her voice still tight. "Even in the face of incursions and brewing wars. Even in the face of insults and mortal losses. All of which are stirring now." She looks down at his wound speculatively. "Even in the face of grievous wounds inflicted by brothers."

"Brothers or *sisters*?" Okeanos murmurs, and she does not meet his eye.

Markanos coughs. "We could break tradition. This one time." He looks upward. "Heaven forfend we incur the wrath of the King of Heaven."

King of Heaven? Is this a real being or a superstition? I am mystified by the pronouncement. I have never heard of that name, not in our religious ceremonies, not in my libraries or reading. Not even in the books of Okeanos's library, but it seems to suit the others, for they stand almost as one.

"The tuna was off anyway," Pagetto says with a false note of bravado in her voice. I do not think she tasted the tuna.

Oke ignores her. "We will perform the Resurgence. We will do our duty, and then we will leave."

When Aurelius clears his throat, his voice is light as if he

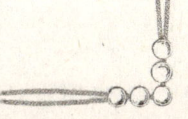

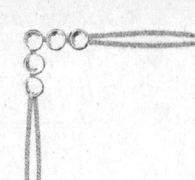

is trying very hard not to weight it with anything. "You'll leave tonight, Okeanos?"

Everyone stills, looking toward him.

Okeanos grimaces with half his mouth. "I will leave the next morning. As will my wife. As will any of you who possess the sense with which you ascended to godhood." He flicks his gaze to me. "No god will remain a god for long without the blessing of the King of Heaven."

So, he believes, too.

"Speaking of wives," Alexandros says, crossing the floor to Okeanos. His golden head is held high. "You have married, Okeanos. And you have brought your short-lived bride here." He lifts an eyebrow. "How fortuitous. Tell us, what tempted you to take a mortal to wife when none of the rest of us have made ourselves so vulnerable?"

Oke shifts so that his body is between me and Alexandros. I feel a twinge of guilt shiver through me.

"My wife is not what is at issue here."

"Though she *was* hiding behind the statuary," Aurelius says, sotto voce.

"Far more important is the question—who killed a goddess and left her here in our meeting place? And what will we do about it?"

"We are all of us god-killers. And what's one more dead?" Treseano asks around a mouthful of some flaky pastry.

"One more might be you," Okeanos says mildly.

"It won't be."

Though I feel chilled at the idea of a violent god murdering

other gods, it is no more chilling than when a god watched my islands ravaged by storms and did nothing, when the waves choked my Lieve and no one came to help, when the fires swept across Calypsala and not a single divinity extinguished them, so they will forgive me if I am somewhat preoccupied by greater, heavier murders than the one done to El'Dorian. She was never my god, anyway.

Okeanos makes the ancient holy sign suddenly—the same he'd made on his little boat before he confessed to me that he had enemies bent on his harm. He had not exaggerated his situation. But I find I do not much care. After all, I am one of his enemies.

"Then I demand my right as one of the divine council to force the Resurgence at once. May each be washed of the past, relieved of the present, propelled to the future, and may it be done immediately, and done well, and done for a time and half a time," he intones, as if speaking holy words.

They must have the authority of law, for the others put down their food, grimacing.

"We will still discuss this wife of yours and why she hid here spying on us instead of arriving with you," Alexandros says, and his words seem threatening when he looms so close to Oke. "Even if it must wait until after proceedings occur."

My husband is silent, silent enough that it sounds like a retort.

There's a moment and then Treseano spreads his hands, mollifying. "I'm not one to humor anyone, but he's spoiling my appetite with that miserable wound. I propose we

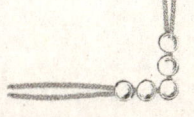

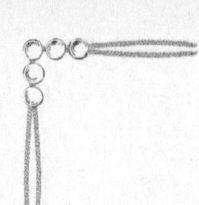

expedite the ceremonies and then we may make proper work of some repast while the sea goes off to sulk. Who would have thought he'd be more isolated and miserable married than he was unmarried?" He waves an indolent hand. "But then who has ever predicted what the tides might bring?"

There is no grumbling as there would be with humans. No dithering or discussing. There is a small grunt of annoyance from Markanos and a lifted eyebrow from Alexandros, but together they walk toward a spur of ground that splits off from this gathering place and toward another raised island carved from another heap of rock. The rock curves up from the sea like the arch of a rib and forms a delicate bridge. Around it, the waves surge and spray, the storm only growing as mauve twilight fills the sky.

Glorian is last to leave but us, her huge procession trailing after her. She spares me one hard glance that sends a spike of fear down my spine.

I swallow hard, my knees trembling as I take the first steps onto the stone bridge. I don't remember seeing it here when I arrived, but I wasn't looking for other islands. I was only looking to my goal—the death of a god.

Okeanos, as if oblivious to where we march, grips my hand like a sailor grips a line in a storm, as if somehow I will keep him from being blown to his death, though surely he knows—he must know—that nothing at all has changed. And though I must be sensible and wait for a moment when we are alone, when he trusts me, and when I have a god weapon, I am still just as determined to spill out his life as

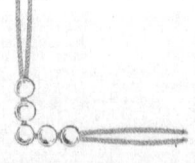

whoever spilled out El'Dorian's. I dare not do otherwise, not even now that I have met the gods themselves in all their terrible glory and strange familiarity.

"What are you doing?" I murmur as we walk, him with a pronounced limp.

"What are *you* doing?" he repeats back, and he is right. I cannot question him when I will not allow him to question me. We must both march to our fates on our own. We are married in name only, never in heart.

Chapter Seventeen

How could any other island be more impressive than the one with the towering statues of the gods? And yet the one we reach next is glorious, formed by ten arches that together make a kind of cupola with a round circle open to the moon above in the very center. It shines down directly onto an altar formed of the round dish of the earth herself perched on the backs of ten miniature forms of the gods. I wonder if those figures change with the change of the gods and if next time it will only have nine figures and El'Dorian's will simply disappear.

We all gather around the strange earth altar in a loose circle and proceedings begin—a string of sacrifices and pronouncements that would mesmerize even the most jaded of mortals.

I ask Okeanos to tell me who this King of Heaven is, but

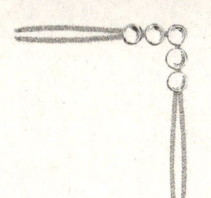

he shakes his head minutely and keeps his lips pressed close together. There is no idle chatter in this sacred place.

Markanos makes his obeisances first, moving up to the altar. I have to look away. Each time I see one of the gods, it is a renewed struggle not to bend beneath the glory of the divine. I hate it. And I hate how unrelenting it is, like the line of a song repeating again and again in my head until I am sick to death of it.

He declares, "This I lay on your altar, King of Heaven, my icy lands are yours. My mountains bow. I am your servant."

He does as he says, laying an offering on the altar—a sword made of crystal, I think. It's gorgeously wrought, though I doubt it would stand up to any true abuse. It's hard not to wonder at the strangeness of the gods worshipping someone higher still. Is he real, or have they invented him? Must even a god have someone to worship?

The view between the open-walled pillars of this temple shifts from the view of the sea to an eagle's-eye view of the territories of Markanos as he lays his treasure down. His lands are vast and gorgeous. His armies are assembled in ranks, his cities mighty, his crenellated towers a powerful defense of his people, his fields of wheat growing, swelling, harvested, fallow again, his herds rushing across the land as the seasons ebb and flow behind them. I have the strangest sense that he lays all that—the year, the harvests, the people and their lives—along with the crystal sword upon the altar. They are all one—his very identity and all his treasure represented in that one gift. And when the sword goes up

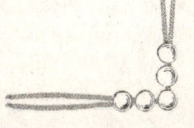

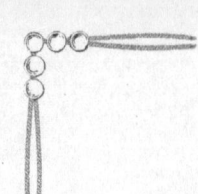

in a bright white pillar of fire and is no more, I can feel the power surge back into him, feel how it enlivens his otherworldly glory to such a degree that I must look away. For a bare moment, I glimpse a golden corona around his head.

I cannot stand to even look at his face for a full breath as he states very calmly, as if this is something that has happened so frequently it barely needs noting, "I have no declarations of lands won or lost, of new allegiances or progeny."

I'm breathless. Made so by his decadent majesty and by my consciousness of my own unworthy position here.

And yet.

And yet, I am undaunted in my goal.

These ten who I have known all my life as gods are not what I imagine a god to be. They offer their sacrifices to this King of Heaven and his power is granted back to them to use as they manage his world—like lords stewarding fiefdoms. That much Okeanos whispers to me and I am reminded of the story he told me earlier of how he'd railed against Vesuvius and been given his revenge by some great benefactor. Did he mean this shadowy deity?

Okeanos's attention is intent upon the proceedings, as devout as any priest I've ever seen—far more so than Turbote, who I have seen secretly wipe a dripping nose on his vestments.

This Resurgence is not meant for mortal eyes. It leaves me gasping and small, my mind dizzy and struggling before these magnificent gods for all that they pretend to abase themselves with their sacrifices. I'm ashamed to say I am

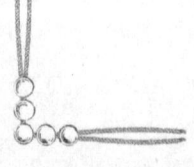

too... temporally limited... to fully grasp all that is taking place. I'm grateful when Okeanos grips my upper arm as if to steady me, no matter how foolish it may seem. It is the only thing grounding me.

The gods parade one after another, offering spectacular gifts on this altar of theirs to this lord they claim. Each time we see the swooping view of their worshippers and wealth, and I get the sense that I am seeing only the tiniest breath of what they are showing. There are conversations and nuances and exchanges going on around me all the while and my mortal eyes are too dim, my mortal ears too dull, my mortal reflexes far too slow to see them all.

Of them all, I adore Heskatan's offering the most. She gave the horse she brought with her, and to my delight, her horse fledged, displaying great wings of golden feathers the moment before he was placed, trembling, upon that altar. For a bare instant I felt as though anything might be possible—and then he was gone and she was glorified, and I could taste the loss of him in the air I inhaled like the smell of the earth after a strong rain.

I am catching only the barest edge of what is so elaborately woven before me. And each time, when they are through, the sudden glory descends on them that I cannot bear to see and the same golden corona rings their blessed heads.

I am mortal. My flesh is temporary. I feel hatred deep in my bones for the disparity. I am small before it. The only thing worthy in me is this desire to hold my people together.

But entranced as I may be, I have not lost my head. I

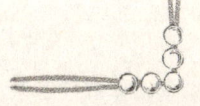

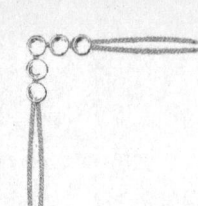

have counted the weapons I might use—Markanos's heavy sword, Alexandros's hammer, Aurelius's blade, and Heskatan's double-headed axe. I see no possibility of stealing any of them.

With a sinking feeling deep in my core, I note that my husband is still carrying his fishing spear strapped to his back, though he has no cause to fish here. The meaning slaps me in the face. It is his god weapon and it has been there the whole time, leaning against the wall of our little cottage when he was asleep in bed. At any time I could have taken it up and slain Okeanos. What a fool I am. I need not have come here at all. Did Vesuvius realize this when he asked me if I'd been recently married? And if he did, what motive had he for sending me here?

There's nothing I can do about the dead god's potential betrayal. I must be sensible. I am here now and the fishing spear may yet be the easiest weapon to take, for perhaps I can convince my husband to trust me. After all, I have slept at his side so innocently all these many nights. Mayhap I can put him at his ease and lead him to believe this night is no different from the rest.

I school my expression to mild interest, desperately keeping all my emotions deep inside where they will be unreadable to these great beings who care no more for me than a buzzing gnat.

Okeanos shifts and I know he is next. To my surprise he draws me with him. I want to protest, but my tongue cleaves to the roof of my mouth.

"All that is mine I give to honor the King of Heaven," he says a little awkwardly.

I am beginning to realize that while powerful among the gods, Okeanos is shy. This attention makes him reticent. What he lays on the altar is a single pearl, pure white. It seems lowly and terribly mortal compared to the offerings of the others. I frown, concerned.

But Okeanos's offering is accepted, and with it, I gasp, for I see my kingdom and *all* the kingdoms of the sea through the view between the pillars of the white temple of Okeanos. They make me feel an almost physical thirst as I gaze down on their glories. But just as I am beginning to smile with the joy of teeming seas, prosperous cities, and hearty ships, the view we are offered sweeps across the green waves to watch the great storm swell over my island and my people fall beneath the waves, drown, and die.

My hand moves to my throat in horror. I can't quite breathe. My ears roar with loss to where I can hear nothing of the murmurs of the other gods. I am lashed to the sight of this. This is the betrayal that has gutted me reenacted, and if I had any qualm that I may have misjudged, may have over-reacted, it is extinguished.

We are betrayed at the hands of our god.

Invaders sweep over not just the one island I witnessed, but three more, and with them fire consumes whole cities. My whole body tightens as my people are herded onto ships and stolen away. And it's only a glimpse, only a glimpse, but we sweep out to the Andalappo Isles, and they, too, are torn

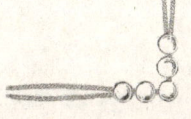

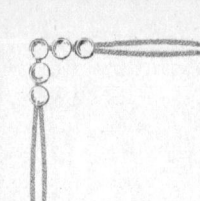

apart by raiders and fire and sword. We sweep still farther to where the sea has risen up and swelled in one great wave over the Pentalumus Peninsula. Men and women wash away like particles of sand along the shore, just as insignificant, just as tumbled under the waves to rise no more.

Betrayed. Utterly.

I am gasping as I hear Okeanos declare, "I declare a loss of eight cities, three islands, and the nation of Ghant Eliore."

Lost or ruined by his own hand? I turn my face to his that he might see in my baleful eyes the judgment he deserves, but he does not look at me. His expression is stony and unmoving. And it only fuels what roars in my heart.

I've watched him clean fish while cities burned. I've watched him sleep while lives were lost. We spent an evening watching jellyfish. I feel not a shred of pity for him. My resolve hardens like his face and my blood burns with every pulse of my racing heart.

I will manage this godhood much better than he does. He has been wasting time speaking sweetly to his new wife and all the while his kingdom has been ravaged and swept from his grasp.

He looks to me a little uncertainly as he says, "And I declare I have gained a bride, a wife, a full equal."

The blood in my ears roars. I smile reassuringly and absolutely falsely. I cannot stop my shaking, but I can force my mouth into an upward bow. Within, my heart howls.

"Yes," I agree.

And I hate him for the flicker of hope I see in his eyes. For

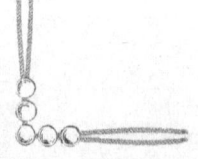

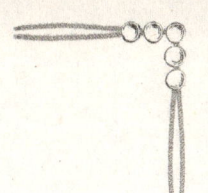

how he almost smiles, for how he looks away, intent on the scenes of his ruined kingdom as if he has any right to even look at them after all he's done.

And I hate their King of Heaven, too, whoever he is, because the glory comes down and Okeanos fills with it, and his golden corona is so bright that I can't even look, can't even think, as he pulls me away so that Aurelius might take his turn.

"Well done, wife of mine," he murmurs, but he can stuff his "well dones" down his own throat and gag on them. Or I can do that for him if he finds it too difficult.

I'm too upset to watch Aurelius place his gift on the altar. I can't even say what it is.

I'm so deep in thought that I do not notice the rest of the ceremony. It is pageantry and ritualistic observance and drama and I care for none of it. The ceremony ends, the glory fades, and I am just beginning to wonder what comes next when I hear someone gasp, and I look up in time to see Treseano leap onto the altar.

His face is still glowing and bright from the power that has descended upon him, and as he spins to face us all, adopting a wide, half-crouched stance, he still carries the squirming burlap sack over one shoulder.

"What nonsense is this, Treseano?" Alexandros begins, but the God of Death is looking around the circle.

"Someone is killing gods," he says grimly, his gaze flicking to the side, and I can't tell if it is Aurelius or Pagetto he has glanced at, but it seems to grow his courage. "And

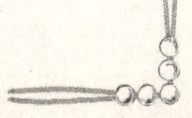

it is not me, though death is my purview." He pauses long enough that Alexandros opens his mouth to speak again and once more he is interrupted. His jaw shuts with an audible snap as Treseano raises his voice. "Now that we have received our blessings, it is time to speak freely."

"Though perhaps not standing on the king's altar," Glorian murmurs, and is ignored.

"The King of Heaven," Treseano says, glaring down at us, "has not prevented this murder, nor has he seen fit to establish an heir for El'Dorian's worshippers. I am no malevolent force. No revolutionary. But I put to you this: Why do we worship a king at all when *we* are gods?"

"Why, indeed," Aurelius murmurs, flicking a hand out and flourishing a dagger as if he is bored by the proceedings.

"For the sake of vows made and powers granted," Markanos says dismissively, but Aurelius tosses the dagger at him. Markanos catches it with a glare.

"I'd hear the rest of Treseano's speech," the God of the Air says. "He seems to have thought well on the matter."

"I'd hear from him, too," Heskatan murmurs, and there are nods from Alexandros and Pagetto. That's half of them.

But why am I surprised? Betrayal is the spice of the day, it would seem. Okeanos betrays his people. I betray him. Why should these other gods not betray this mysterious King of Heaven?

Beside me, Okeanos stiffens, and his voice is very low. "I'll have no part in treachery."

"Who is speaking of treachery?" Treseano rumbles,

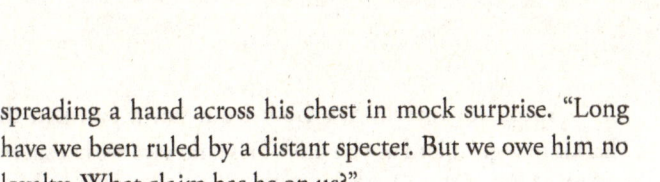

spreading a hand across his chest in mock surprise. "Long have we been ruled by a distant specter. But we owe him no loyalty. What claim has he on us?"

"The claim of his blessing granted just now," Okeanos returns.

Glorian makes a sound of assent, and I see a nod from Ordanus.

"Make up your mind tonight," Treseano says brazenly from his perch on the altar. "Those who do not stand with me, stand against me."

"This is madness," Glorian says. "Why disrupt things when all goes so well? We've had bounty and plenty for a handful of centuries in a row and I've found I like the taste of it."

"'Well,' you say?" Treseano scoffs. "For you, perhaps. Tell El'Dorian it has gone well."

"But surely her murderer is among us," Glorian says. "Or a mortal has slain her and taken her place and will soon make an appearance."

"Reveal her murderer, then. I'm waiting," Treseano taunts her, and then strikes a dramatic waiting pose. "No? Then let us seek justice of our own. Let us tear down the King of Heaven and take his place. Who is he to rule over us and do it so poorly?"

I swallow. His thoughts echo my own. I can hardly disdain Treseano for wanting what I want: Justice. Protection. Basic competence.

"This has all the seeming of a ruse," Okeanos says. "Who speaks through you, Treseano?"

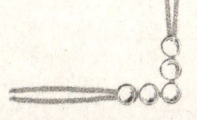

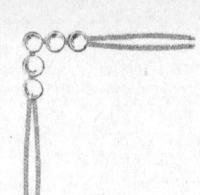

"I speak for myself, Sea God. I am not a pawn in the hands of a great lord as you are," Treseano says with a sneer.

"And I stand with Death," Aurelius says mildly, drawing out a second tiny dagger and trimming his nails with it. "The time has come, I think. Change breathes in the wind and wafts into the air."

I watch Okeanos out of the corner of my eye and wish I'd been taken as a bride by someone else. Someone who truly did understand what matters in this world as the god beside me never will. Someone with the ambition to do something about it instead of entrenching themselves in useless loyalty.

"Enough," Okeanos says in a low tone, startling me. He is lovely and terrible with the glory of the heavens still shining in a corona around his head. "This will not happen."

"It is not for you to say." Treseano adjusts his grip on his mace.

Like lightning, Alexandros draws his hammer, and Aurelius pockets his tiny dagger and slips his spatha from its sheath. I'm counting in my head, trying to keep track of them all.

"It's for all of us to say," Treseano says, staring down my husband for a long moment until Alexandros shifts his weight to his left foot and spins slightly to his right. Now his back is to Aurelius, his weapon up, and both of them stand with their backs to Treseano as if they have become his honor guard.

"Is this war, then?" Markanos says, and he sounds far too excited.

"What else would it be?" Treseano calls back in what is clearly a taunt.

The Trident and the Pearl

I take a stumbling step backward, sensing violence in the air. I'm only just in time.

Markanos bulls past me, sword in hand, and as he dashes forward, Treseano leaps from the altar, flinging his bag out. From it tumbles a writhing black creature. It looks almost like an oversize leech, black and glossy, large as a ship's cat. It wriggles toward Markanos at the same moment that Treseano roars a battle cry.

Okeanos has dropped his grip on me and my vision is seared by the glory of the gods. Too many of them are moving too quickly. It sends bursts of pain through my skull, shattering my perception into short little snatches.

I don't dare let that glory pin me in place, I shuffle backward blindly, feeling for one of the uprights to dodge behind. I am unarmed and very, very mortal.

There's a roar just in front of me as Markanos's two blind companions—Rethgar and Rothgar—tear into Treseano's host.

"For glory!" they shout as they burst into the ranks of the sewn-mouthed priests.

"No!" Markanos exclaims, but he is too late.

These are mortals.

They scream and die like mortals, butchered on both sides by a sudden fury of sharp blades and gasping intensity. They fight for their gods. And neither side dares cower when their devotion is so high.

It has always been so that priests or monks or even heroes will give their lives for the glory of the gods, flinging

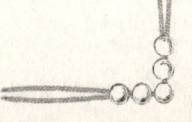

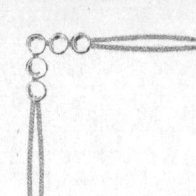

themselves into certain death for the promise of an unrivaled afterlife, but I have never seen it done with such flagrant abandon before. It is as if they came here to die and must race one another to do it.

On the mortal plane the gods are forbidden from directly murdering mortals or ruling them as a king would and so they have always fought and acted through our monarchs and armies. But this is not the mortal plane, and I did not expect that the gods would spend their mortal followers so cheaply.

Something hot hits my legs and I look down. A spray of blood streaks across my skirt. I try to shake it off, as if that is what is important right now, but my brain is not working properly. It is not offering me the right kind of options.

I force my eyes to look up and my legs to stumble backward.

A single one of Markanos's guards drops beneath a heap of Glorian's followers right in front of me. They've fallen on him like gulls upon a rotting fish. His screams grow fainter and then cut off.

I should run. I cannot make my legs so much as twitch.

With a sudden howl, the head of one of Ordanus's harpists goes spiraling through the air in an arc over the mass of gathered bodies. It seems heavier than I would have guessed.

Ordanus shouts angrily, and a wave of sound bursts across the mortals, bursts across me, and I'm clutching at my ringing ears, all sound ripped away.

The world around me is a grunting, ripping tangle of

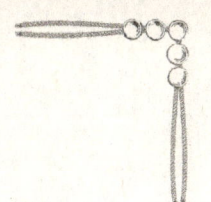

fighting limbs and terrible carnage. Feet squeak on marble as they slip in blood.

I don't know when I stopped breathing, but the world is spinning and my vision is narrowing. I'm afraid that if I turn, my back will be exposed, but if I don't run... My heels strike the wall behind me and I'm trapped. There's no way to flee with a wall at my back.

A hand reaches toward me from the crowd and one of Treseano's sewn-mouthed ghouls bursts from the tumult toward me. I just have time to suck in a breath for a scream when someone curses fierce and furious beside me.

One of the gods strides through the masses, scattering mortals like fish scatter before a dolphin. His shadow falls over me, and I flinch back before I realize it is Okeanos stepping between me and the fight. He flicks a hand and a wave rises from the sea, swells over the edge of the pale island, and sweeps the sewn-mouthed villain over the other side.

Okeanos strides into the mess, hindered by his limp, but not stopped. He grabs Ordanus by the hair and drags him up from the ground as he plants his spear into one mortal warrior—one of Treseano's, I think. His waves rush again over the masses, flattening some to their knees and sending some over the side like they swept aside the sewn-mouthed priest. Before Okeanos, the last mortals fall, or still, twitching in fear and death.

"Enough." The sea god's words are calm, quiet. Treseano strides forward, but Okeanos points his spear at him in warning, roaring, "I told you. Enough. Have you not been

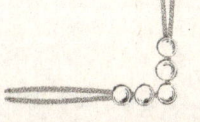

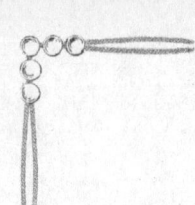

sated on sufficient blood this night? Restrain yourself, or watch me cut your throat with your own sword."

Treseano stops.

So do the rest, frozen in place, wary as they watch these two gods stare at each other. My eyes flick to Aurelius and I frown. He is untouched, leaning against one upright as if he is merely a spectator like me.

"The declaration has been made," Okeanos says grimly. His wound is worse. Blood pours down his leg. "We've all heard it. You will have your god war and you will have your revolt against heaven. But we are all of us here until morning. Or have you forgotten that our godhood and the powers just renewed are dependent on keeping vigil here this night? Will you spend every hour fighting to the death, or shall we call a truce until we return to our holdings below?"

"I have not forgotten," Glorian says airily. I hadn't even noticed her there, but she's close to Okeanos. She has not a speck of blood on her. Shocking, considering her entire entourage lies in shreds before her slippered feet.

"Then you know," Okeanos says, and his voice is the thunder of the breakers upon the rocks. His voice is the angry sea. "If you leave before the proper time, you will lose your godhood."

She looks away but she does not speak again.

None of them do. They simply look one to another as if to divine each one's intent.

Okeanos turns now to Treseano, barely leashed fury in his voice. "This is impulsively done. You will think better of it come the dawn."

"You call the planning of centuries impulse?" Treseano asks, flicking the tip of his sword free of blood. But his words smack of the same posturing that led him to eat food laid out beside a corpse.

"Centuries?" Okeanos looks around him, flint-faced. "This looks like the planning of a single moment."

Treseano smirks, glancing over his shoulder as if to include everyone in his taunt. "And yet your islands are burned. And you have done nothing. Or did you lie when you tallied them up for the King of Heaven?"

Okeanos's cheeks flush dark.

"Oh yes," Treseano continues. "Your people are ripped from you—and you stand there impotent. What is the sea but a holding tank for water no one wants or needs? We cannot grow our crops with it. We cannot succor our people. It is refuse, and your home is the place where refuse is stored." Treseano flicks a finger, screwing up his mouth in an expression of disgust. "Have your night of peace. Have your calm before the storm. I'll not break it and neither will those with me. We have no need. When dawn breaks, we will leave and everything you love will come to an end."

He turns his back as if he has nothing to fear from any of them, and I see Okeanos's hand tremble as if he wishes he could thrust his spear right into it. But Treseano walks down the temple steps and out of sight and Aurelius and Alexandros follow, a single step behind him. I do not see what the other gods do. I admit I am shaking too hard to keep track.

I blink away the black dots swirling across my vision and

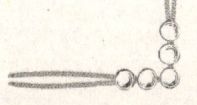

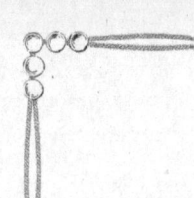

it takes me a moment to compose myself. I have just watched men and women butchered like fish on the docks. It could have been me. I hold the contents of my stomach down by sheer force of will, tasting acid.

When at last I have charge of myself, I catch a glimpse of Markanos and Okeanos sharing a weighted look before the God of War marches away. The only one left is Ordanus, holding the severed head of his musician in both palms and looking lost. He sits heavily on the altar, still clasping the head, his eyes staring into the blank eyes of the mortal. They are very large.

"Fair Andrane's voice lit the sky and flushed the flowers of the field," he says in a way that is almost a song.

"You should have taken better care not to bring him to such a place as this, then," Okeanos says gruffly, and then he turns and grips my arm, and I let him.

I didn't realize I was crying, but of course I am. Silently, thank the gods.

Or don't thank them. This is, after all, entirely their fault.

Chapter Eighteen

This plane of the gods makes no logical sense, though I'm too shaken to dwell on its strangeness. We backtrack—me with shaking limbs and a set expression, and Okeanos with a grim jaw and easy grace—to the island with the tall statues. In silence, we follow another small archipelago of pale spinelike rocks. I scrape my palms twice as I scramble to keep up with Okeanos. He hardly seems to notice how difficult it is to traverse this non-path.

Eventually we emerge at the end of the spine to where a group of small islands hang in the air wreathed in mist, connected only by ridges of crenellated rocks that can be climbed like stairs if you are a god or a mountain goat.

I stare at the nearest hanging island as we circumnavigate it. Watching a chunk of rock hang over the water supported only by a slender branch of stone the width of my wrist

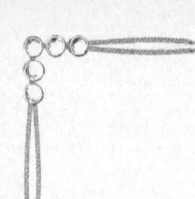

makes my stomach flip. The mist is too thick to see what lies upon each island and it even muffles sound so that when Pagetto and Glorian disappear up an arch of rock ahead of us, they are lost to us entirely.

I'm sweaty almost immediately, my muscles trembling as I leap from rock to rock, trying not to tumble into the dark waters. To my shame, Okeanos catches me when I slip on a spur of rock, one hand supporting my lower back while the other catches my elbow. Every muscle tenses at his touch. He is a god. He still glows with power. I just watched the gods cut down mortals like overgrown grass. And he is touching me. My stomach swims with the knowledge of that.

Elaborate lanterns hang from the bottom of each island, lit with an otherworldly flame. They cast stark shadows on Okeanos's face so I cannot divine his thoughts as he leads us to the highest hanging island and helps me to scramble up the last nearly vertical climb.

I crawl over the edge of the rock and sit a moment, gasping as I collect myself. The island is double the size of Oke's cottage and boasts a large bed, the headboard of which is made of silver-inlaid coral; two inlaid chests, again with a spreading coral motif; a little table laid out with crystal bottles of drink; and a cunningly crafted wardrobe carved like dancing waves. The wardrobe is set with mother-of-pearl, and between the swirling panels, little carved fish poke out in unexpected places. On either side of the wardrobe someone has set carved statues of a pair of swordfish leaping.

I am disheveled, tattered, abraded, and streaked in other

people's blood. I do not look very queenlike and certainly do not look like the wife of a god—even a god like Okeanos who is as responsible for the deaths of thousands as if he had murdered them himself.

I wipe my face with a hand and swallow down a spike of fear before reaching a trembling hand into my belt pouch. I hope I have not lost Vesuvius's pearl. I may need him yet. I draw the pearl out as Okeanos is hauling himself over the lip of the island, his shoulders tense with the effort. He leaves a trail of blood—this time not only from his wound but from the carnage he helped to create. His fishing spear remains in one hand. It's stained with killing.

I must have been crying without realizing it, for the moment I draw Vesuvius's pearl out of the pouch, he slips from it in a searing stream of mist. He takes one look at Okeanos and the expression on his face is crowing delight mixed with animosity. One finger presses over his lips as he looks at me, and swallowing, I tuck the pearl deeper into my fist.

He's no ally of mine, but if I have to run, if I have a chance to kill, he might be the tool I need in that moment.

"We must tarry here until morning," Okeanos says distractedly. "The blessing of the King of Heaven is not complete unless a night is spent under his roof. Markanos told me once of a god who left before it was completed. Bareus, God of Fire."

"There is no God of Fire," I say between chattering teeth. What is wrong with me?

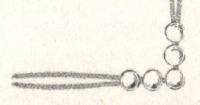

"Certainly not anymore. Not all gods are replaced when they pass. Sometimes, they just cease to exist at all," Okeanos murmurs. "Can you calm yourself, Coralys?"

In Okeanos's terribly glowing face, I can almost make out those familiar green eyes. I can almost remember the kind fisherman I married, but trying to put the two of them together in my mind makes me shudder even more.

I just watched thirty people smashed to unrecognizable pieces. I just watched a god idly pick up the head of a man as a child might pick up the piece of a vase he broke—a little regretfully, but with no intention of preventing it from happening a second time. Still shaking uncontrollably from witnessing such a horror, I have followed Okeanos onto this impossible island and felt his hands touch me as if he were a mortal man and not a god. But I must not let myself forget the truth—that evil can have a lovely face, that horror can be an artist.

"What is this place?" I whisper.

"It looks different to each one," he says. Behind him, Vesuvius has drifted over to the table and peers at the food laid out upon it. "But I think you see it as I do—as an island of refuge."

He reaches for me as if to wipe a tear from my cheek, but I flinch back and he winces. I am in no mood to be touched. And if I am to do what comes next, I must not forget what he is.

Hesitantly, he returns to pacing.

"Surely now you see why my goal is to build a refuge for

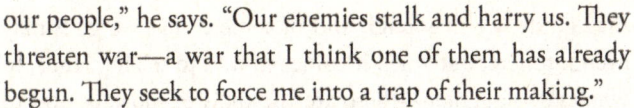

our people," he says. "Our enemies stalk and harry us. They threaten war—a war that I think one of them has already begun. They seek to force me into a trap of their making."

"*Our* enemies?"

Vesuvius snorts and I am grateful he can only be perceived by me. He's propped against one of the swordfish, his tentacles swelling out and rippling back with each motion of the sea.

"Our enemies," Okeanos repeats, stilling for a moment and looking at me. His green eyes are lit by his halo and his nose and jaw are both sharper in the bright light. "Let us speak plainly, for you know my heart and all my secrets. I told you, Coralys, that I had a people I would save. I bid you help me. They are the folk of the sea, and their enemies are my enemies...and yours." He bites his lip, looking pained. "You have seen my failure to hold back their attackers."

I have seen it, yes. I am bleeding out with the pain of it and scalded by the fear it will continue while he seems to take it in stride. It is no surprise that he does not mourn. What are mortals to the gods except playthings to be discarded when they are not presently wanted? But I cannot allow my people to be playing pieces to him as I have been. No matter how clever his ideas or noble his goals, he's lost sight of them as individual people. They are not a school of fish to be judged as a whole, a few individuals lost for the good of the rest. They are each one precious. Like Lieve was to me.

He goes on, "I have made every effort, but as you have seen tonight, we are constrained by the laws of heaven. We

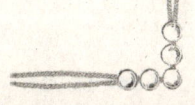

may guide, we may tend, and in some things we gods may even interfere, but when it comes to war, to seizing lands, to wholesale slaughter—these are the tools of mortals, and to use them, or even counter them, requires the work of mortal hands. I confess the loss of you as queen of the Crocus Isles has cost me an ally in this, but perhaps you see that as my wife you can work with me. That is why you came here tonight, is it not, though you were late to the decision?"

My breath freezes in my lungs. He does not suspect. He thinks I came here to work with him as he asked me to before he left. I am very, very still.

"Together we can build this refuge. Together we can find the source of our people's misery and excise it." He's back to looking into the distance, thinking. "Which god is calling us out? Who is it that endangers our plan?"

"Okeanos lies," Vesuvius says, examining one tentacle as one might examine their fingernails. I look at him and he lifts a brow at me as if he is patiently waiting for a child to catch up with his explanation. "This is his chance to firmly pin you in place and secure your oath to help him. Don't do it. You have seen with your own eyes what he has done to the ones you love. Do you really think it is these nebulous enemies who have swept away the lives of your people? Was it Aurelius's banner that flew over the raiders on your island? Was it Treseano who claimed you as his reluctant bride?"

He is right. I will not be so dazzled by beauty and majesty that I forget what I know to be true. But I do not trust Vesuvius.

I draw myself up and speak. "If all that you say is true, then tell me how you care about a people you watched wrecked by a storm while you did nothing to save or succor them."

"You refer to when your husband was killed." His tone is sharp, decisive.

I flinch but he goes on.

"I was delayed. You have seen my godwound." His voice is burred. "I couldn't come sooner, though I tried."

But I am not having this. "You intentionally delayed until I struck a bargain with you. You forced a marriage to further your own ends and in the process many were lost. It was manipulation, plain and simple."

He lifts his hands. "You blame me falsely. I made no bargain with you until we spoke our wedding vows. You were tricked by another." He stops, considering. "Possibly someone with a hold on your kingdom so that he could maneuver a mortal into power in order to steal it from me."

"That's not possible," I say, shaking with anger. Now he's just inventing conspiracies. Who else will he pretend has power over the sea except the God of the Sea?

He grimaces. "When I wed you, I did it properly in the old way. If I meant to trap you, I would never have granted you such power. How else do you think you are here now on the plane of the gods if not because I opened it to you?"

"Am I to credit you for that?" My voice is trembling. "Should I believe it was coincidence that I made this bargain and then you swept in just in time to save me from myself?"

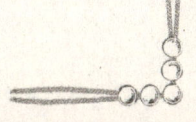

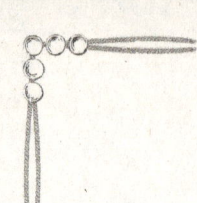

He runs a hand through his hair. "Yes. Exactly. You are to believe that you made the bargain with another, and that upon seeing it had been made, I chose to marry you myself to prevent a worse fate. I am not responsible for the storm or the lives lost."

My retort is like a whipcrack. "Then what are you responsible for? For doing nothing? For inaction?"

He's circling the floating island, agitated. I have to keep turning so that he is in view, and every time he passes Vesuvius, the former sea god taps his lips as if to remind me to keep him a secret.

"Lies," Vesuvius mouths when I catch his eye. "All lies."

"Imagine you were wed to one bent on the destruction of your islands," Okeanos says, his shoulders thrown back proudly as he presses his point. "What paths might a marriage to their queen suddenly open? What gates might fling wide? The moment I saw that vulnerability, I shored it up. I was late to stop the storm, late to save those innocents washed away, but I prevented a second trap from springing." He softens, stills, faces me. He's almost pleading. "We want the same thing, Queen Coralys. We want our people safe. Can you not see it?"

"He's very good at this," Vesuvius murmurs from the corner. "I almost believe him. But do not forget, from the start his neglect doomed your people. He killed his rival and he claimed you for his own. Likely, he has been watching you. Perhaps even for years. Gods do this." I shiver at that thought. I treasure my privacy and to think someone powerful has

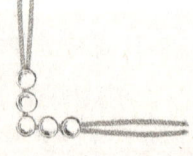

breached it leaves me ill. "And then they maneuver that weak mortal into a place where they cannot say no and they take them for their own pleasure. He'll be surprised, I think, to find you are not easily shunted into place."

I swallow. Almost, I could believe Okeanos. He is so very sincere. But Vesuvius's conclusions are also my own.

And if Okeanos really cares only for his people, then why did he list out towns and cities lost when the other gods claimed no gains? Glorian had been worried about armies gathering on her borders. But Okeanos had sounded more worried about dead El'Dorian. Was that because he thought the lives of his peers more important than a few thousand mortals in his care?

I am not a fool to be turned by a pretty face and honeyed words.

"If all you want is my people's safety, then why did you allow their islands to burn?" I challenge Okeanos. "Why not prevent the murder of Delarte?"

Okeanos is shaking his head before I've finished. "I was not able." He's speaking slowly, catching my gaze with his and holding it, and the look in his eyes is so open and trusting that it twists me. I keep seeing flashes of the man I was starting to know and it feels like finding a snake in your clothing. "You know this to be true. You were there. And you have lived these many days with me while I've laid bare my heart to you."

"Weak." Vesuvius's mouth forms a grim line. He flows out of his corner and takes a place behind Okeanos, studying him as he speaks.

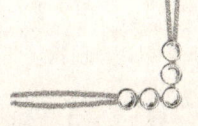

"You could have told me who you were right away. Or confessed it when I first threw the truth in your face," I say. "You could have brought me with you to help if that was what you meant to do. We could have stayed on the Crocus Isles and ruled them together."

He slices the air with his hand as if slicing through my argument. "That was never an option. We have bigger things to achieve than ruling just one island nation. I plan to show you all that godhood entails. I plan to induct you into every part of it. I want only to give you time to mourn first and time to move past your understandable thirst for vengeance. You did not hide that desire from me. Tell me, Coralys"—his voice stutters over my name—"do you want that vengeance still?"

I keep my face very smooth, but he seems to read the lie in it, for he is immediately distressed. He looks at me aghast.

"What will vengeance help? You will end up dead by my hand as I defend myself. And I will be shattered by the misery of it. And your people will have lost two champions for their cause in one fell blow."

He pauses, breath heaving, and leans both hands on the bed, looking across it at me. I do not believe him. He is too beautiful and altogether too earnest. I am being manipulated with every flick of his green gaze into mine. My heart bending to his, wanting to trust, wanting to open myself in turn. It is that very softening and wanting that galvanizes me. I must act and act soon before I cannot tell truth from lies anymore.

His breath calms a little and he tries again, his tone almost wheedling.

"I'd hoped to persuade you. Over time. As I have said. When you had finished mourning your husband and I could appeal to your reason." He grimaces. "I had not yet realized you would not use it for me."

He has said the wrong thing. He has brought Lieve into this. My vision is dark with fury.

"I possess no reason? Is that what you credit to me?" I scoff.

"You misunderstand," he says, but I will not listen.

"*Your* reasoning is full of holes. If you are beset by enemies, then where are they now? We're vulnerable on this island in the fog and no one has come for us. Why have they not claimed your territory in that Resurgence ceremony when they might have? Why have they not finished the job they started?"

He growls but does not answer. He has returned to pacing, as if that helps him think.

His clothing sticks to his very impressive figure and I study it with intent. He looks too strong for me to kill, despite the wound in his thigh that dribbles onto the stone like ink. But he has given me no other option. His explanation is not believable, and far from promising to stop in his headlong plunge into ruin, he seeks only to justify himself in it. I have never killed before and I worry that when the moment comes, I will not have the fortitude.

"I do not know which of them is set against me. The

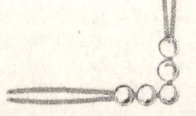

evidence is conflicting. Am I being driven by prejudice? By emotion?" He's back to his puzzle as if he's solved me and can move on. "Perhaps more than one conspires against me. Two could harry me from the darkness more effectively. If I tear down the obvious contender, that may very well snap the trap and then whoever else wages war against me from the cover of the shadows might overwhelm my people while I am distracted. I must be patient. I must let them lead me to the others before I strike. I require a plan."

His head snaps up and he looks me in the eye. I don't know who he means by "the obvious," for none of this is obvious to me. I stare at him stone-faced.

He clears his throat and takes a half step toward me, hesitating at the last moment. "We both know that you are a strong and capable queen. And I have given you a share of my power and all the explanations you could possibly desire. You must be my partner in this. You have the power to help me, even now, to turn the tides that swell over your islands and folk. As my wife and equal, you may even now join with me to repel our enemies and stand firm on our shores. You are indeed a woman of reason. Admirable, strong, honorable in every way. Say you understand and can set aside my failures and work with me to get what you've wanted all along."

And again, I want to believe him. I can imagine myself at his side, fighting for my people. Standing against the gods who strike at them. We could work hand in hand as we did when we fished together. It's a breath-snatching offer.

"Your people have only one enemy," Vesuvius reminds

me quietly. I had almost forgotten he was there. "And it's not plotting, or malice, or the schemes of the gods. It's this incompetent guardian, too obsessed with his own place and interests to protect them. Even now, listen to his words. He speaks of himself and his enemies. He speaks nothing of prosperity for the Crocus Isles."

I do not trust the dead sea god any more than the live one. I jam his pearl back into my belt pouch before Vesuvius sees anything else and Okeanos frowns, watching me, though he couldn't possibly see what item I'm slipping into the pocket. I've held that pearl in my palm this whole time.

The monster vanishes.

"Coralys," Okeanos says, his voice half growl and half plea. He crosses the space between us in two long strides and takes my face between his gentle hands, and I wish the gap was so easy to bridge. I wish it could be so simple. "Drowned Queen. Harbor in this mad storm. I lay my whole self before you. Will you not be my wife in more than name? Will you not work with me? Choose me?"

He leans in close, his breath mingling with mine, and I can't think. I can't see clearly. For a moment, I see only him.

"Come," he pleads, his lips nearly brushing mine as he speaks.

He takes me in his arms and holds me so reverently. His gaze is deep with emotion and it seeks to penetrate past my every defense. But I am terrified. And the more vulnerable he is, the more my breath hitches and my heart pounds. The more I lose the control I so desperately need.

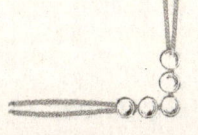

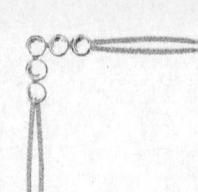

"Do not continue doubting me," he whispers. "Believe that I am who I say I am. That I want what you want. That I want you."

And then the whisper turns to a kiss. Delicate, gentle. As if his pleading has turned from words to action and continues in this tender embrace. And I don't stop him. I should, but I don't. I let him taste me and persuade me and savor me. And to my shame, I savor it, too, for when again will I ever kiss a god? When again will I ever know that they taste of wine and honey and rays of sunshine on the sea?

And when he draws back and our eyelashes flutter open, I bite my tongue and tell him the only thing I can think to say.

"Be patient with me, and I will give you an answer."

His smile is quick as a darting fish. He believes he has triumphed.

But I have not answered the way he thinks. Because whether Okeanos has enemies or not. Whether they try to kill him or not. Whether he needs my help or not. He is a liability. He is an anchor dragging on the ship and he must be cut loose. Nothing has changed except the depth of my understanding of this situation and how much it will hurt to destroy this man I am coming to soften toward. While he lives, my folk will never be free.

I must not be his partner.

I must be his murderer.

I have grown so calm that Okeanos has begun to smile again. His smile makes my heart want to open like a flower to the sun. What a traitorous organ. I pay it no mind.

"You'll ally with me," he says as his smile grows. He's overly eager, overly trusting, and it masks for him my true intent. And he looks so sincere that it makes me ill. "You—of all people—will want this, too, will move the heavens and the earth to achieve it, will stand with me against any storm. We will not fail, you and I."

Well. I won't fail. I can guarantee that.

I might vomit right here. With the taste of wine and honey still on my lips and the brush of his kiss still tingling through my core.

But I smile with him and I contribute to his planning as he thinks through how to escape the trap of his enemies and spring it on them instead, catching all of them at once. His shoulders seem less stooped and his eyes are lighter with every suggestion I make to his plan. He believes I am *for* him. I am a better liar than I knew.

We plot together well into the night and it feels like a fairy tale I am telling a child, for it will never come to pass. I do it with an eye ever on his fishing spear—his god weapon. He keeps it in hand, allowing me no opportunity to snatch it up. But eventually even the God of the Sea grows weary, and when he proposes we sleep the rest of the night, I agree. I curl up on my side of the bed and he curls up on the other.

No one has tried to attack us here on the island. No one needs to.

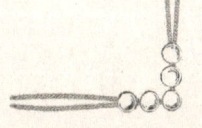

Chapter Nineteen

I wait in the darkness, clutching to my chest all my little certainties. I must be right to do this. There is no other way.

I keep coming back to the same thought. Who do I really care about? The people who depend on me even now to return and save them, or one faulty man with a boyish smile? I know my duty. I know what is right. Fortunately, they align, even if my weak flesh balks at the idea of staining my hands in his rich god-blood.

We all of us worship gods. Some we make. Some we inherit. Some by necessity. Some by design. But there comes a time when we must set them aside, or if they will not be set aside, then they must be slain.

Okeanos is warm beside me, and the way his breath moves in and out carries the comfort of sleeping next to another person. My body is drawn to the safety implied in that.

Without meaning to, I move closer and closer. Close enough that my cheek touches his hair. And then his breath evens out, and as I tense to spring up, he moves, suddenly, and flings a leg and arm over me in a sleepy, possessive cuddle.

He's warm and soft with life, heavy with muscle. His even breath is against my cheek. I feel the scratch of his barely there beard tickle my ear. His forehead nuzzles against my temple like a small child might nestle into comfort. He smells of salt and faraway spices and *man*. Not like a god at all. His limbs, long and lax in sleep, are heavy on me. Vulnerable, like a puppy cuddled on my lap, but this puppy is a dangerous one. Dangerous, not only for all he has done and will do, but dangerous because he is making my heart hurt.

He's bleeding on me. He's warming me. He tugs me in tight against him without waking as if it gives him succor to draw so near.

My belly flips and rolls as if I've swallowed a mackerel whole and living and it seeks its way out. I want to be sick. I will be sick and sick and sick forever.

But my mind brings back the image of Delarte strung across the anchor, his tongue cut out, the scent of blood thick in the air. Of Lieve disappearing beneath the waves and his body cold and lifeless in my arms thereafter. Of Turbote driven mad by horror, his hand clutching at me. And with those images fresh behind my eyelids, I slip out from under Oke's tender embrace, away from where his warm chest softly shifts with his breath, and out into the cold of the night.

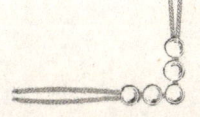

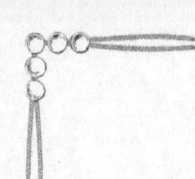

The moon watches me—the only one who does—her eye wide open with scandalized anticipation. Waves beat upon the shore outside our bedroom, as if they might hammer on a door to wake my husband in time. But they are too slow.

Everything is too slow except me.

Already, I have slipped from the bed, my feet cold on the mosaic floor. Already, my hand wraps delicately around the shaft of the fishing spear.

I creep back up onto the bed, the silk of the bedcovering sliding under my limbs, but this time I do not lie down. I stand, shifting to secure a strong footing. I will have only one chance. I must do this well.

I pick my spot.

Okeanos wears no shirt to sleep, only the pearl cuirass. I see every rib. I choose a place between them.

The spear feels weighted with a thousand intentions when I lift it high. I do not yet know if I can kill like this.

My throat is suddenly clogged. It's hard to breathe.

I choke for a moment until I remember it was hard for Lieve to breathe, too, when the waves clawed down his throat.

The thought is enough to decide me.

I plunge the spear down as hard as I can. I hit my mark, lean my weight into the spear, and feel it pierce through the resistance of vulnerable flesh, glancing off bones, through viscera into the clogging thickness of the feather mattress below. And I hold the haft firm and unmoving just as I have been taught to do with a great fish on the end of a harpoon, leaning all my weight into the intention.

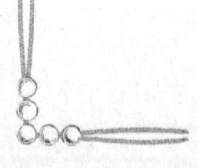

Okeanos spasms against the spear. His blood spurts hot down his side, spilling across skin made pale by moonlight and soaking into the sheets. And just as my breath crystallizes in my throat, his eyes spring open like twin traps and he drags in a choking inhale before coughing—hard—body curling possessively around the spear shaft, hands fumbling for it until his fingers catch and stick. Blood droplets decorate his pretty lips and spatter my pillow.

"Cora," he gasps. "Coralys."

I cannot breathe.

His expression is panicked and his head jerks in a rough circle, his arms flailing out and knocking over a waist-high vase positioned beside the bed. It smashes on the floor, making me flinch at the clatter, and then his eyes find me and he sags.

I realize, a little sickly, that he thought me harmed, that he was panicked for my sake, not the sake of the spear I've thrust through him. A wave of nausea washes over me, my stomach heaves, and my eyes smart sharply, but I came here for this. It's been my only hope since I lost Lieve. I'd be both craven and gutless to come to the task and refuse it now. Wouldn't I?

"Oh god," I say in a gasp. "Oh god, I'm so sorry."

What irony—to pray to your god as you murder him.

I lean my weight hard on the spear, not giving an inch as our eyes lock, and to my horror he grips the spear in both hands and uses it to slide his body up the wooden haft so he can face me nearly nose to nose. The iron scent of blood

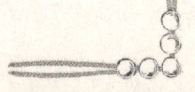

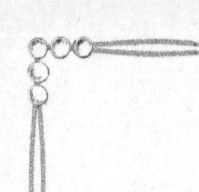

hangs thick between us and the droplets on his lips are black as inkblots in the moonlight.

He feels his side, lifts a hand, and looks at how it's dark with blood. Pain fills his face before he turns again to me. I know what he sees: me with lips parted in horror, eyes wide, and yet unmerciful.

"I hoped for better from you." His words are punctuated with rough breaths as if they are vital to say before the end and he must force them out.

My own voice trembles like grass in a gale. "This is the best I have to give."

He nods sharply, as if he accepts that, and then with one hand he wrenches the pearl cuirass from his throat and thrusts it at me.

"Yours," he gasps, pain etching lines on his face that were not there before. "You must take them."

A few pearls spill free of the string, but I reach out and take the rest from him. Slick as they are with his blood, they are hard to hold. I string them through my belt.

To my horror, he has climbed the spear farther. He is unthinkably strong. And now he grips my jaw in one bloody hand. His breath is ragged just like mine. My bones feel terribly delicate in his powerful grip and my breath flutters like a bird. I think he could break me even now with a snap of his wrist. But he only looks at me for a long moment before shuddering.

"The clock," he says, as if whatever he saw in my eyes compels him. He's struggling to speak. "It's in the clock and

the book. Look in the library. Finish the work. Save our people. Whatever you think you've gained here is only loss, but perhaps it is not too late. Four tasks are already complete. Remember that."

He lets go of my face as suddenly as he forced the embrace.

I am shuddering with the horror of what I've done.

"Now flee," he gasps, the strength of his face stark in the moonlight. "As fast as you can." He bites back a moan. "Your safety lies in the sea."

It's only when he slumps that I realize how much effort it took for him to stay upright. He lets go his grip on the spear and falls into the bed, his arms sprawled limply akimbo, and there's no more tension on the spear anymore. There's no more light in his glassy open eyes.

The sound that escapes my lips is more of a faint cry than a sigh.

But someone is scrambling up the rocks that lead to our island. They must have heard the breaking vase.

"Okeanos?" a male voice calls.

I'm choking on my own breath, it's coming so quickly. I let go of the spear and feel for Okeanos's pulse and there's nothing there. Nothing.

Panic claws up my throat and the waters are rising.

I can't be discovered like this.

They'll be certain I killed El'Dorian, too—that I'm this god-killer they so fear—and I don't know what that will mean beyond certain execution.

I scramble from the bed, tripping on the sheets, and

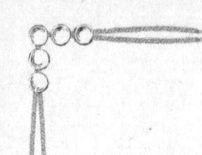

stagger across the stone floor, running and skidding to the edge of the island as fast as my feet can carry me.

Behind me, I hear another call. The voices are getting closer. Someone gasps a curse.

But I am quicker.

I reach the edge and I fling myself into the water below as one might fling a line of rope, only to remember that I don't know how to get back. I hit the water with a slapping belly flop and then rise, fumbling with my belt pouch as I hear a second person scrambling up the rocks.

"What's happened, Markanos? Is he there?" The words are harsh and male, but I don't know whose they are.

I pull Vesuvius's pearl from my pouch and it takes no effort to wake him. Not when my tears are flowing so freely. I almost drop the pearl twice I am shaking so hard as I bob in the waves.

"What is—?"

I silence him with a quick gesture. He looks past me and his eyes widen with sudden delight.

"Tell me how to get out of here," I demand in a harsh whisper even as the voices behind me rise.

Above me someone curses even more loudly and he's joined by the second voice. They've found Okeanos.

Vesuvius laughs soundlessly and the contortions of his face and body repel me even as I gesture again for silence. With a shrug and a triumphant grin he shows me a new hand movement, and the moment I see it, I copy it, praying I'll escape to anywhere but here.

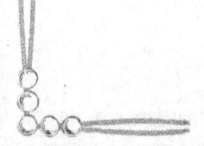

The Trident and the Pearl

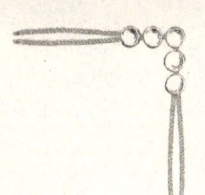

Footsteps slap on the rock above me as the world spins in its almost-familiar way and shifts me between planes.

I rock with nausea as I grip the deadly black pearl in one hand and what's left of my sanity in the other, and I hope, hope, hope they cannot catch me.

I've left a husband dead. Sprawled on his own bed. Murdered by my hand.

And there is nothing before me but bleak emptiness and the heavy guilt I'll carry forever.

His death was supposed to heal the world of ill. It was supposed to fix all the mistakes that came before—maybe it still will—but right now it feels like it's not just me or my islands drowning, but all the world, and I am queen of the flood, queen of the drowned, queen of damnation itself.

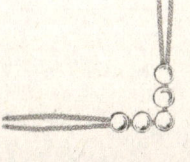

Chapter Twenty

The sea opens to me the moment I shift in it, and I am momentarily too stunned to move another inch.

As I merge back to Okeanos's home plane awareness sweeps over me, dragging me down and drowning me under the pull of it. I am the sea and the sea is me. It is in my bones and heart.

I feel every line of the shore where the waters lap against the rock, every fish slicing through the waves, every ripping, tearing attack of one creature upon another, every youngling spawned, every slide of fish against fish, every tumble of rock and murmur of the great movements beneath the floor of the sea. I feel it as one feels one's own flesh.

I am freezing cold and laced with sharp ice. I am warm and balmy and tranquil. I am the hard grey of the north and the sultry azure of the south.

It is utterly overwhelming.

I am the sea.

I am sliced by the hulls of ships, the calls of fishermen echo over my surface, and with it comes their joys and worries as they catch or fail to catch. I am told the names of children as they are born into the waves, feel their startled first breaths and cries. I know the creak of the rigging and hear the worried curses of captains carving paths through froth and bubbles. And I feel the despair of the drowning, the misery of the hungry holding empty nets, the pounding of wave after wave over the exhausted who can barely stay afloat.

I am the sea.

The sea is me.

And this is not a thing for mortals, I tell myself as I shudder under the pale grey dawn of a rainy day.

This is not a thing for *me*, I tell myself in a panic.

I am gasping when I blink back to consciousness, overwhelmed by sensation and emotion. I am on all fours in the water, the tide lapping up to my chin. Drenched and clammy, my fingers pale and wrinkled, I feel as if I have spent an entire day within the brine.

My hair is crisp with salt. My breath comes fast and painful as if this is the first breath I've drawn all night. It is a little terrifying to realize you have inadvertently become a body of water.

I shudder and look at my hands. They are not covered in blood. They are pale and dimpled from the sand and yet they look worse than if they showed the evidence of murder.

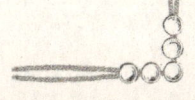

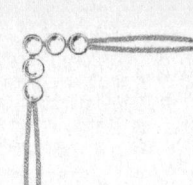

Distractedly, I drag strands of seaweed from my hair and shoulders.

I have killed a god and now I am one. I can't say that I like it much. But this was never about what I liked.

I drag myself up onto the shore of Oke's island breathless and gasping. This shift feels worse than the others, as if something is being ripped from me. I do not care that the jagged rocks bite my palms and cut my flesh.

I have abandoned the Resurgence before dawn. I don't know what that means. Maybe nothing. Maybe everything. I know only that I am cold to the bone and not just because I shiver as I pull myself up the shore in the midst of a pounding rain, a triumphant laughing Vesuvius dragging himself with me. Has he been with me all along? It felt like I was hours in the sea, but perhaps it was mere moments. I blink at him in stunned silence.

"You did it, you ragged mortal wretch," he calls over a crack of thunder. He's kicking his tentacles out in celebration. "You killed a god. Are you proud of yourself? Does your heart dance now?"

My heart does not dance. My heart feels as if it is dead by drowning, bloated and pale, adrift and abandoned, a thing washed up with the tide to dry in a crust of salt upon the sand.

I killed him.

Oh gods, I killed Okeanos.

I heave out the contents of my stomach onto the rocks, feeling again the shudder of Okeanos's body around the

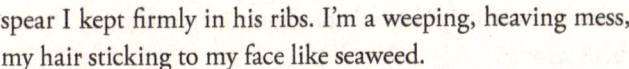

spear I kept firmly in his ribs. I'm a weeping, heaving mess, my hair sticking to my face like seaweed.

The rain washes away my filth as quickly as it comes up. It's as ashamed of me as I am.

"You are a god now," Vesuvius crows. He's not looking at me. He's looking around him and his eyes are hungry with greed. "You have no limits."

I laugh, harsh and bitter. I have no limits? Does he jest? Surely my conscience has had no limits. And what is there to brag about in that? I sit heavily on the rock and turn my face up to the black sky and torrents of rain.

"Where's the pearl you took from him?" Vesuvius asks.

"There was no pearl."

He looks at me, aghast, but I do not care about pearls right now.

I am a god. What a terrible joke. A drowned god, just as I was a drowned queen. Puddles fill around me and little rivulets trail around my feet. I lie in them limp as a sodden cloth.

I had not really considered what it would be to take Okeanos's place. It was obvious, if I'd stopped to think, but my mind was on justice and revenge, not on seeking power. I had thought only of protecting my people, of grasping the opportunity to be a better ruler for them.

I wish I had thought of what came next because there is no happily-ever-after at the end of my story. No magic to pour down like rain and wash away all the tangled mess of revenge and bitter resentment. If this is a fairy tale and I have

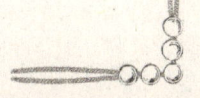

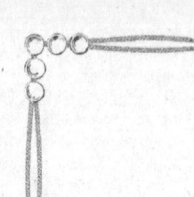

slain the villain and freed the slumbering kingdom, then it is all wrong.

In the end, I do not have the strength to find my way back to Oke's cottage. I do not even have the strength to determine where I am on the island. Instead, I use the last of my energy to drag my body farther up the shore, through the streams and puddles, and to collapse at the feet of one of the looming statue guardians. This is one of a mighty warrior whose beard whips around him in a dreamed wind and whose eyes watch for far-off threats. I make out his features in the flashes of lightning, set a cheek against his cold foot, and wish the rain could wash me clean or wash me away entirely.

Vesuvius follows me, sliding across the rock with sinuous grace. "What will we do first, Queen of the Sea? Shall we raise a palace for you and fill it with mortal slaves? Shall we draw up riches and glories, command armies, and engage in a great campaign? I consult your wishes."

I shove Vesuvius's pearl back into my pouch roughly.

I'll have none of that. I did not do this for power and glory.

I murdered a man who trusted me. He put himself in my power because we said vows together and bound our souls and futures into one. I broke those vows tonight. He gave me the ultimate gift between man and woman—complete vulnerability in every aspect of life—and I returned it with violence. I can never wash the guilt of that away.

I lean on the feet of the statue, a dull malaise settling over

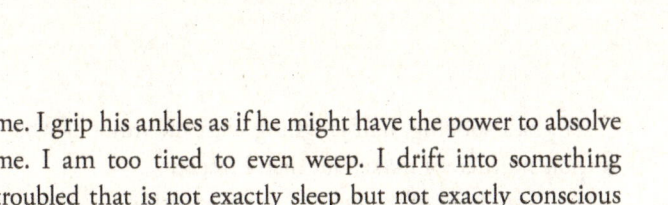

me. I grip his ankles as if he might have the power to absolve me. I am too tired to even weep. I drift into something troubled that is not exactly sleep but not exactly conscious thought, either.

I keep seeing Okeanos again and again as I drift in and out of darkness, and the look in his eyes when he said he thought better of me stings like salt in a deep wound.

Eventually I weep. It's quick and harsh and then it is gone, a storm across the waters of the sea.

But there's no changing what has happened. You can't put a soul back into ruined flesh, and shouldn't even if you could. And if killing Okeanos was meant to save my people, then the job is only half done.

I take hold of myself and force myself out of melancholy. I have work to do.

The storm is easing, the torrents have calmed to a drip, and I shiver uncontrollably as the rain slithers down my back. Becoming a god has not shielded me from discomfort or pain. And I am almost certainly a god.

But there is work to do whether I am a god or not.

I wipe my eyes roughly, drag myself to my feet, and snatch up the pearl necklace from the ground where it has worked its way free of my belt in the night. In my haste, the string breaks and I'm on my knees in a moment, scooping up pearls in my hands, fishing them out of puddles, frantically searching for every last one as if saving his pearls can atone for taking his life.

I hate myself.

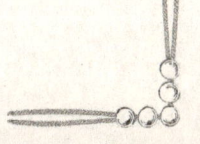

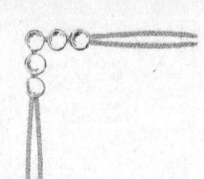

I'm half sobbing, half laughing with the irony of what a terrible murderer I make, but then I freeze.

Souls spill out of the pearls I touch, drifting up, growing, and then popping to life like bubbles in the surf.

I shuffle back, gasping as they emerge, one after another. Some are very human-looking, dressed like the statues I've seen around the island. Others are strangely monstrous like Vesuvius, waving tentacles or thrashing on the shore in ways that suggest they were meant to remain underwater.

I'd thought idly of whether all Oke's pearls might be prisons and I'd never really believed... but they must be and I'm holding a string of hundreds of them. And he gave them to me when he lay dying.

"Hark. Okeanos is dead," one of the souls says, sounding worried. He peers down at me as if studying a strange creature pulled from the depths. He's a man—I think—though his beard seems more like the body of a jellyfish than a thing made of hair. Long, slender tendrils flow from his beard weightlessly as if he is underwater. "His heir parades herself before us. Is she hale enough of mind, think ye?"

I'm frozen in fear as I look from face to face. There are too many to keep track of at once.

Another is speaking, a beautiful woman like the shadows between the waves. "There will be a hard age ahead for the people of the sea. We're only ever as strong as our god, and this one is not stout."

"What about the work?" a third asks anxiously, crowding in. They're all peering at me, studying me. "The great work?"

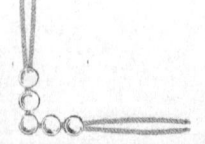

The Trident and the Pearl

I step backward another step, but they follow as quickly as I move. I'm breathing a little too quickly, feeling a little too pressed. Are they all dead gods?

One looks like a man drowned. He wears a crown that's very like the one in my great-grandfather's portrait. I lock eyes with him and he squints as if I am a puzzle he is working out.

"She looks so innocent for a murderer," he says, frowning. "You're certain she's the heir?"

"She opened the pearls, didn't she? Is that his blood smeared on her face, do you think?"

I rub my cheek with one hand. They're all speaking over one another and they aren't as clear and defined as Vesuvius was. Some of these souls are wispy and barely there, their voices so faint they could be the wind, while others seem close and living.

Hurriedly, watching in every direction at once so that they don't touch me, I start to shove the cuirass into my belt pouch. It's not going to fit. Not all of it. I twist and jam, trying to push it in, spirits winking out one by one.

They are murmuring together, but I don't want to hear these things. I work faster, jamming them into my belt pouch by the handful until I have only a few left and I cannot possibly fit those into the overfull leather bag.

They've grown quiet, those who are left, watching me owlishly.

I spread these pearls left out on the rock, out of breath, frantic. I grab a sharp-edged stone the size of my fist, and try

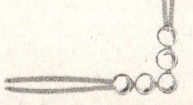

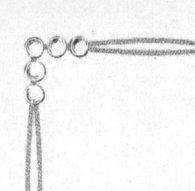

to smash them with it. I'm hammering and hammering until I can hardly see through my tears and fury. They're not what I thought they were. I'm not who I thought I was.

And they are not breaking.

They are not even chipping.

"That's what I did, too, when I found out," a female voice says when I pause. "I tried to smash them all."

"Found out what?" I ask, without thinking, my hands shaking so hard that the rock clatters.

"That I was a god and a miserable one at that."

I look up. She's crouched across from me—the only one left. I think I recognize her. Her statue down at the dock is submerged up to the chin at high tide, but low tide reveals all but her barnacle-encrusted feet. Her statue wears a regal wrapped-cloth dress, but her soul's version is nearly translucent and stitched with herons picked out with silver thread. I can well believe she was a goddess. Her dark brown skin gleams flawlessly as if she has been polished.

"It doesn't work," she tells me aridly. "They aren't real pearls."

"Nothing about this is real," I say, wiping my eyes on my damp tunic to avoid my hands.

She laughs. "You only wish that were true. A word of advice: You don't have to put them in your bag to dismiss us. You can just wipe the tears off the pearl and stop touching it. I learned that the hard way. Took me a month. But then, I was always more stubborn than sensible. Most of us are."

I feel my face go hot. I'm sensible enough, thank you.

"So, you were also a god," I say, my eyes narrowing. "Do you know what comes next?"

"Next?" Her smile is mocking and she spreads her hands. "Now you rule. Over the sea. Over the people. Over the islands. And you try not to fail, for there's no one to call for help if you do."

"How do I rule?" I ask, insistent. "How do other gods rule?"

She shakes her head as if my question is stupid. "Fish. Answer prayers. Keep the worst away."

My confusion must show on my face, because she sighs and shifts, settling down to sit beside me with her arms hugging her legs as she looks out to sea.

"You're the sea now, girl. Not symbolically—though of course that, too—but you are literally the sea, as Okeanos was before you. What is done to the sea is done to you. What is done to you is done to the sea.

"If you fish and catch, then your people will find bounty. If you fish and catch nothing, they'll have lean years. If you rage and scream, they will endure storms and heavy seas. If you are sunny, so will their lives be.

"If you are set upon and wounded but not slain, then they will be wounded, too, by fleets or raiders, disease or despair, it matters not—they'll be as ruined as you are to the same degree unless you can turn the tides again."

I feel a lump in my throat. Oke bore that terrible wound. And my people were beset by both a storm and an invasion. I had never considered that the two might be related.

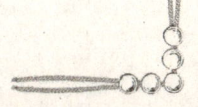

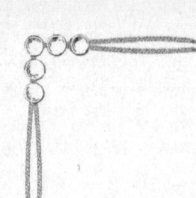

"It is a terrible thing to be a god," she says, not noticing how still I am. "No mortal can ever be ready for the task. But that is who you are now, so go—be the sea. Be the God of the Sea. And try not to ruin it before someone else wrests the role from your snatching hands."

She starts to fade. I grab at her, but I am too late and she winks out like a dying candle.

With a sigh, I give her up and gather the rest of the pearls in my palms.

Oke's island is like a shell when the hermit crab has crawled away to find a new home. The waves wash in and out. The sand drifts where it wills. There is nothing here but the lonely echo of the wind.

But if I am to be a god now, I will determine to be the best god there ever was.

I cross the threshold of the cottage into what was once Okeanos's home and life. I remember him standing beside me at the table scaling fish. His hands had worked with sure efficiency despite his pain.

"I did not expect to survive the encounter," I whisper to myself as I dry the remaining pearls on a stray cloth, watching their spirits wink out one by one, and then fling the pearls on the table, emptying my belt pouch of all but the black one. "I did not expect to really take his place. And yet here I am."

I remember Oke sitting on that chest talking to me. I remember sharing that bed. I feel sick all over again.

Something shining catches my eye and I frown, snatching

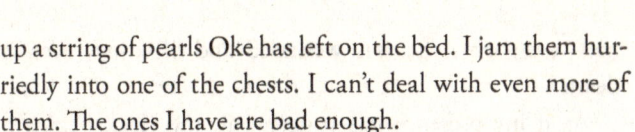

up a string of pearls Oke has left on the bed. I jam them hurriedly into one of the chests. I can't deal with even more of them. The ones I have are bad enough.

I wash hastily and dress in a fresh tunic, throwing the ragged, bloodstained chiton in the corner to deal with later.

I do not want to fulfill Okeanos's last wish. I don't even know why. I don't hate him in the same way that I did before. It's hard to hate a man you've killed. His blood that spilled hot across the blankets and painted my skin has left me hollow, spent, like the heart of a tree where a fire has burned but not reached the outer rings. I am charred and crumbling while without I am perfectly whole.

But I square my shoulders, pull out the book, draw down the lever, and hurry down into the darkness on my own.

The room has not changed. There are treasures in small alcoves and on plinths. Little scraps of crowns and scepters, swords and goblets. I am ignorant of their history or purpose beyond the obvious, and whoever placed them here seemed to attach such historic significance or perhaps honor to them that they have not cleaned them or polished them. Some are broken and were not repaired. Oke said that it was all here when he arrived. I could ask the pearls, perhaps, but I never want to see another god again, living or dead.

Perhaps Okeanos wandered these same rooms after he killed Vesuvius and raised himself up as a god. I wonder what he thought of the water clock the first time he saw it.

I wonder if he felt as small as I do right now. But I can't imagine him feeling small. He always seemed steady to

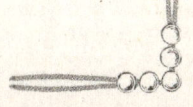

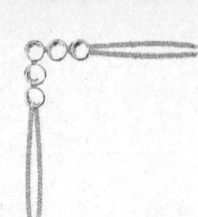

me—even when he was wounded and bleeding, even in death.

As if my presence has triggered it, the clock begins to move and the water pours into the mouth of the sea god's serpent, spinning him so that he falls headfirst into the water and turns back up again, but though the clock cycles as if to turn the hour, the little rays on the top of the clock stay exactly the same. Four blacked out. Six white.

I frown. There were only three rays blacked out last time I was here and clearly they are not keeping track of the hours that pass. Oke mentioned something about four when he was telling me to find something hidden in this clock. He told me four were complete.

Interestingly, the face of the clock's statue is still missing—gouged out in lurid chunks—but its body has warped to a more androgynous form. Or perhaps that is only my perception shifting it. Down here, away from everything else, it is so hard to tell.

I examine the clock, running my hands around the base of it. There are no hidden catches that I can find. No secret riddles. No lever or button or anything else that I can see. But I know there's something here somewhere, or Oke would not have asked me to look for it.

I could ask Vesuvius, perhaps. But his laughing triumph still echoes in my mind and twists my stomach. Vesuvius must only be let out as a last resort. I do not want to become like him and I fear it may already be too late.

I'll simply have to figure this out for myself. Oke would

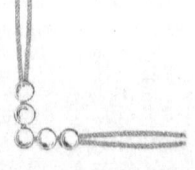

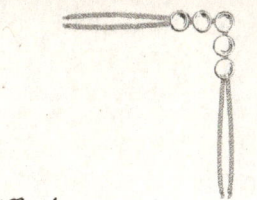

not have sent me here if he thought it was too difficult a puzzle to solve on my own.

I study the base of the clock where a series of small images are carved in the clock's base. Birds, fish, the sun, the moon, stars, boats, the images are endless, but when I find the little wave carved into it I remember Okeanos's words, "Your safety lies in the sea," and when I press the wave symbol, there's a click and a drawer slides out a finger's width.

I pry the drawer open the rest of the way and within I find three rolls of parchment. I unroll the first right there on the floor and immediately wish I had not.

It is so delicate that the edges flake, leaving little fibers along the mosaic floor. Drawn on the parchment in intricate detail is a lighthouse.

It is depicted from the side and then the top, and then a separate sketch is drawn of every floor of the ten it is meant to have. I have never seen the like. It looks almost like a living thing, gripping the rock with its tentacles, flaring fins soaring above the eyelike light. And yet it is terribly beautiful, delicately worked, gorgeously rendered. Flowering tracery windows of epic proportion fill the walls. When occupied, the whole house would be lit like a crystal spire gleaming out into the night. It snatches my breath clean away.

And it hits me like a fist to the chest. This is the place of safety he's been trying to build for his people. This is the refuge he was trying to convince me to construct with him. I should have known this would be his last request. I frown at it, annoyed, for it cost him his life and his godhood, and in

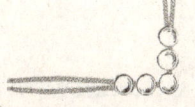

that moment I had thought was so intimate, as he lay there dying, it was this for which he yearned.

I cannot make out the labeling. It is in a language and script I've never read. But I recognize it from one of the books I'd seen in the library above. And there are notes below in a sharp, masculine hand that bear the words *Curse of the Great Lighthouse* and a repeat of the list I found before. The list of ten terrible tasks.

Win a god's oath.
Wed the drowned queen.
Collect the dead to serve.
Fill a thimble with riches.
Heal the crown of the sea.
Turn the betrayer's heart.
Mend time with golden stitches.
Drink the ocean dry.
Spin moonlight into silver.
Split the seven seas in twain.

Oke has completed four of those, just as he said. Which means the rest are mine to tackle if I mean to honor his mad request.

I shake my head and return to the upper level of the cottage, carrying with me the only weapon I found below—a strange bronze trident—verdant green all over from corrosion. It's not much of a weapon, but it's the best I can do. I lean it against the wall beside my bed and go to the bookshelf, and

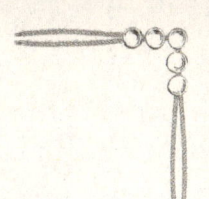

in a matter of minutes I find the book, *Curse of the Great Lighthouse*, which I had believed to be a fictional tale.

It details that a great lighthouse was lost beneath the sea when the gods together cursed a race of sailors and their greatest achievement—a lighthouse of such grandeur it blocked the paths of magic and bargain, offering a sanctuary to all who would avoid the strength of both blessing and cursing. It speaks of the jealousy of the gods and their determination to be turned away from no door—not even the door of a single human sanctuary. They sank the lighthouse and buried it beneath the waves forever, exacting terrible punishments upon the sailors who had built it.

There is a section toward the end that strikes a chord. I read it twice over.

> "It is said that the Great Lighthouse will never return to us again except by an act of wondrous and terrible magic that might draw it up from the depths of the sea. But who could achieve such a wonder? For to do such a thing would require the power of a god. And no god would bless a place where they are not welcome."

I applaud Oke's reasoning, but there is no way to give him what he wants. These tasks are labeled impossible for a reason. And I have a people to rule over and help to prosper and save. I do not have time—nor his ambition—for something so whimsical as raising a lighthouse. If he had hoped I would take up his mantle, he must think again.

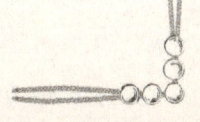

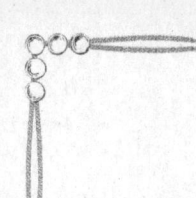

I need something useful to occupy me, something to take my mind off death and great works of magic and dead souls, so I fix the pearl cuirass, threading the beads one by one back onto their string. But it does nothing to solve the roiling storm in my heart or the doubt creeping in. When I reach Vesuvius's pearl, I pause, hold it up, and sigh. It does not go on the strings with the others. It remains in my belt pouch. I cannot explain why, only that it must be so.

It's long past noon when I curl up in the bed again. I just need a moment to rest, just a moment to escape being myself.

I curl around the pearl cuirass the way that Oke curled around the weapon that killed him and I choke on a silent sob of shame before I shake myself out of it.

Tomorrow, I will go and see my people. I will catalog their troubles and needs, and I will set about righting them. That, alone, will make up for murder. For what could be a greater end than the salvation of my people? I must not lose sight of all I have gained.

But though I try to comfort myself with that, I do not sleep. The crushing weight of guilt presses on me as if someone has carved my god statue already and has laid it over me.

I am stained and ruined, my heart in tatters, my conscience shredded. When *I* die, there will be no pearl. How could there be when I've ruined any soul I might have had?

But I am not ready to bend. Not to sorrow and not to shame.

Tomorrow, I must rise and find a way to be a better god

than Okeanos ever was, and if I do not know how, then I will simply learn. After all, I did not know how to *kill* a god and I achieved that. Certainly I can learn how to *be* one.

I tell myself this over and over and over until eventually I fall into a fitful sleep.

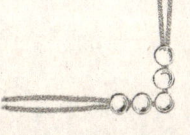

Chapter Twenty-One

I wake to a throat clearing.

I sit up so quickly that the pearl cuirass rattles and I must push long tendrils of hair from my face so I can see.

I laid no defenses last night, not knowing I would need them. Even the trident is not close to hand. It slipped to the floor in the night. And now here is an enemy in my very room, lounging on one of the chests as if this is how he spends every morning.

"Awake?" Markanos asks. He does not smile. He only runs a finger down the flat of the sword he has laid upon the table. It whines like the rim of a water glass. "Did you dream red dreams of murder and the shedding of blood?"

"So many," I agree, a little breathlessly. If he's come to intimidate me, he's welcome to leave straight off. I offer him a cold smile. "And you? Did you dream of slaughter?"

"I *am* the God of War," he says, resting his palm over the flat of his sword. He makes a sudden twisting move and the sword dances across his forearm like I've seen men dance daggers over their knuckles. It's an almost charming thing to do. Almost playful.

But not quite.

"Charmed as I am by your presence," I say tightly, "I am not receiving visitors."

"Murderesses rarely do," he agrees with a companionable smile as if we share a secret.

I say nothing. I will not deny I killed Okeanos. Any fool will know that. I went to bed with him on an island and only I left. I sit here now in Okeanos's bed and Okeanos does not. This mystery is hardly a party riddle with a surprise solution.

"And you a murderess twice over," he says, watching me as a cat watches koi in a pond.

"I did not kill El'Dorian, if that is what you suggest. Was she your sister that you love her so?"

"No." He's watching me as if waiting for me to say more.

"A lover?" I quirk a brow.

"It is not for her that I have come today."

Ah.

"If you've come to avenge the death of Okeanos," I say as coolly as I can, though I choke a little on my late husband's name, "then have done with it. You're the one here with the sword and the armor and the muscles. I think we both know how this ends."

It seems I won't need to learn to be a god after all.

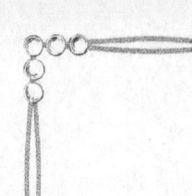

My heart is beating so hard that it is all I can hear.

He spins the sword again.

I hold my breath. Is there a place in the Nightwaters for people like me? And if there is, is it as terrible as they say? One priest told me that when a murderer dies and finds the afterlife, the terrors of the Nightwaters kill him in the way he killed his victims, only over and over and over again forever. How will I feel when I'm skewered to a bed for the thousandth time?

Markanos slams his hand on the flat of his blade, it stops twirling abruptly, and he smiles at my involuntary flinch.

"If Okeanos is gone from the land of the living," he says very slowly, "then that is a revelation to me."

I wait. I know there is more, though I cannot fathom what mad game this god is playing at. Surely he knows my husband is dead. I most certainly do.

He leans back with his legs spread out the way fighting men like to sit. Some say it's very masculine. I have long believed it is because their backs pain them. Every action wears a path on the body and the way of the sword is no less harsh than the way of the washerwoman or the way of the midwife.

His voice is a quiet rumble. "I saw him in the flesh not an hour ago."

I do not gasp. I do not flinch. I do nothing to give away my surprise except for hold my tongue.

If Okeanos lives, then perhaps I am not a god at all. I am only playing at one. Perhaps it is only my imagination

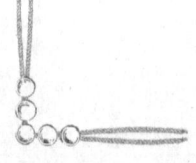

that paints blood on my hands and guilt on my heart. But I doubt it is so.

More likely, this is Markanos's cruel joke. More likely, they are all laughing even now from that terrible plane where I left them, casting lots to see which of them will swoop down and devour me. Perhaps Markanos won the toss.

"And here you are in Okeanos's house. In his bed." He flicks a finger and his eyes narrow. "Wearing his pearls. His wife in all but devotion, it would seem."

"If you're not here to kill me," I say with a raised eyebrow, "then I wonder at your presence here at all."

He pauses, tapping a finger on the table, and then seems to make up his mind and speaks all in a rush. "Take it away. Set him free."

Now I am truly worried, for there is a kind of pleading in his voice. I don't understand the request.

"Okeanos is as free as he'll ever be," I say quietly.

The dead, of course, are the freest of all.

He stands so quickly that I scramble backward across the bed, the blankets tangling in my legs, the bed swinging wildly on its hanging chains. I have no defense and I'm vulnerable here sprawled before him like an offering.

"Have it your way." He is flushed in the cheeks like I've made him angry and he snatches up his sword and slices it through the air at the same time that he cups his hand like a bowl, twists it, and is gone.

Well.

I have been visited by a violent god and survived. I will

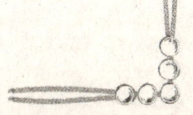

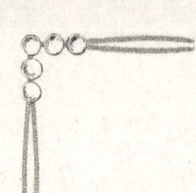

have to remember that my home—my very bed—is not the sanctuary it had been while Okeanos was alive.

I am not sure what to make of Markanos's mad statements. He spoke to my husband? Not an hour ago? He wants me to free him?

From what, exactly? Is it possible that Markanos ran into the room after I'd slain my husband, scooped up the pearl—that I did not see when I skewered Okeanos with my spear—and then spoke to his soul?

That is the only explanation that makes any sense. And if there is a way to release these souls from their pearls, then I do not know it yet.

I will not let it worry me. Today is about returning to my people. Today is about making things right. I dare not let anything else distract me.

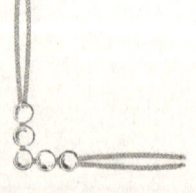

Chapter Twenty-Two

I prepare as much as I can. I dress my hair, wear the pearl cuirass, and find the cleanest of Okeanos's clothing.

After changing my mind three times, I even bring out Vesuvius.

He is of little help.

"Unless you've called me forth to parade before me the body of my enemy and to let me watch while you hang him up for the nations to ridicule, I have no interest in your company," he says, looking me up and down with a grimace. "You look terrible."

I ignore his insults. "I am about to meet my people as their god. Any advice you have to give would be helpful. How do I access the power of a god? How do I channel it to their needs?"

"Everything is bought with a price," he says, circling me as if he is judging a new purchase.

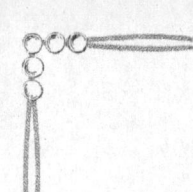

"And what is your price for this information?" I ask, setting my jaw with distaste.

"Tell me something interesting," he suggests. "Tell me something I won't already know."

I weigh my options. I think Vesuvius is trapped in this pearl and that he cannot harm my plans or tell them to another, but I am not entirely certain of it. I choose something I think cannot harm me.

"Markanos visited me here this morning."

He lifts an eyebrow. "Interesting. Will you wed again, Drowned Queen? Are you entertaining suitors?"

I remain silent and he gives me a close-mouthed smile. "Very well, then let me say it again and we shall see if your weak mind can catch my meaning. Everything is bought with a price. If you need something for your folk, then you will pay for it. A small price for a small thing, a great sacrifice for a great thing."

"As if you would sacrifice for anything," I scoff.

He leans in close so that if he had a corporeal form I would be smelling his breath in my face. I do not flinch back, though every bit of me wants to.

"You'll never know the sacrifices I've made, little queen. You have not the mind to appreciate them, but let me spell out one my predecessor chose and see if it enlightens you. She was a weak god, but perhaps you can strive to her mediocre level. Her people were set upon by raiders one night and scattered. She built them a great light in a tower that would guide their ships home but burn up any enemy ship it

touched. The price was steep. To make the light stay lit only for her people, and to make it deadly to all others, she had to feel the fire in her bones the entire time it burned. They say she screamed in agony, roped to the altar of her temple for a full three days as her priests poured water over her again and again as it hissed up in clouds of steam. I wish I'd seen it. Not that it would have stayed my hand."

I am thinking of Okeanos's Lighthouse despite myself. Would his ten tasks have ever been enough? Or would he have had to suffer perpetually for it, too?

"And you—of course—would never choose such a sacrifice," I say. I can't quite help myself. He brings out the worst in me.

His lip twists with scorn. "You constantly underestimate me. I was a sight to behold in my prime that would have left you weak and trembling with desire."

And that's why you don't taunt the vile. They always find a way to twist it back upon you.

"She'd do it again, of course," I say, trying to be generous. "And so would any god. To save their people."

He snorts, flicking his gaze to mine as if we are sharing a joke.

"You have your dead husband's pearls. Open any one of them and make that same lackwit comment, and watch them tell you the same thing. Their folk are dead thousands upon thousands of years now. Would they save them again, having lived so long and seen so much? Never. They were just people. No more worthy than the ones I burned up. No

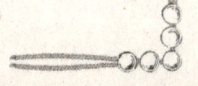

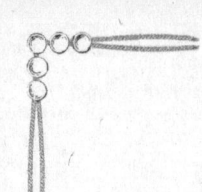

more worthy than the thousands of others that creep across the great shoulders of the earth like bugs across a carcass. They are nothing but a tide to turn and direct as suits you, to nurture and grow or devastate as the turn of your temper dictates. You are a god now, Drowned Queen. Consider thinking like one."

I frown. I am determined I will never be so coldhearted as he.

"As for the technique. You cannot know what you must give until you know what you need." He waves a hand dismissively. "Then the cost will equal the act. Unless you judge it wrong. If you choose too small a thing to exchange, then the working will collapse. Too great a thing, and you'll have... strange results. That, I look forward to."

This time his smile is false as fool's gold and it is all teeth.

"Do they still speak of the rain of fish in Quetorum in your time?"

I shake my head and his smile grows. "That came from a god choosing too great a sacrifice when his people's nets came in empty. They say godhood is not for the overly dramatic, though I've always thought it was wasted on anyone else."

He vanishes then as if he's grown tired of me, and I am left alone to go and find what manner of sacrifice will be required to restore my people.

I know this will be hard, but I am a woman who does hard things. I always have been, and knowing it will be a challenge doesn't daunt me. This is what I've worked so hard for and now it will finally fruit.

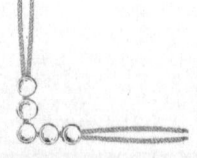

I make my way down to the docks, feeling the loneliness of my position. I half wonder if Okeanos was pleased to take a wife if only to fill the air with a sound other than that of screaming gulls. If he was, I suppose he changed his mind about that around the time his wife plunged a spear through him. But I see him everywhere here. On the path. On the dock. On the little boat he's left for me, tied up to the pier.

He told me he went back to save my people after we fought. We will see about that. Maybe he paid a price too small and that was why their attackers succeeded. Or maybe he didn't try to pay at all. Maybe he lied to me. Maybe he was saving it all for his obsession with an ancient Lighthouse sunk beneath the waves.

I step into the water, determined to make the shift to my people's islands—and I gasp.

The sea opens to me the moment my foot steps into it and I am stunned all over again. It embraces me, singing to me, speaking to me, and in it I hear whispers like snatches of voices... like prayers? I cannot pick one from another in the flood of them, only an insistent battering like a great wind beating on the door of my house. Somewhere far off, I feel a sense of ill or infection but that, too, I cannot quite pinpoint. It is like emerging from a cave into a sunlit courtyard packed with people. There are too many emotions and sensations to absorb them all at once.

I twist my hand urgently, panic flaring at my heightened senses, and the stomach-twisting feeling of shifting from one place to another is almost a relief.

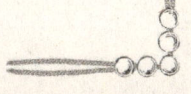

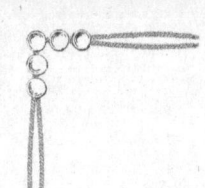

I stand quickly when I've reached my destination and hurry out of the water and up a moss-clad rock upon the shore. Dead trees lay tangled around it, their white digits reaching bone-like to the sky. This is not where I intended. I have shifted somehow while I was insensible.

The coastline here has a ragged hunger to its uneven edges. The sea in this place chops viciously at the land, eating it by bites season after season. I snort. Perhaps I came here because I was hungry and this is the result. But my attempt at a joke does nothing to make me feel at ease.

Until I realize that I don't need anyone to tell me where I am. I dip a toe back into the water and I feel the sea again. It tells me everything.

I am on the shores of Talasa. Up there is the temple dedicated to Okeanos.

I am home.

I can't help myself; I turn to where Lieve was lost in the sea like metal turns to a lodestone. But this time the sea is me, and I shudder as I feel the memory of his last thrashing as he fought the high waves. I buckle and bend to cup his form as he sinks deeper, his lungs full of me, his fingers clawing runnels through me.

I swallow and force my mind onward. But I cannot help but wonder if, during our first meeting, Oke was experiencing this haunted, filthy feeling having just lived through the deaths of so many in his sea.

It takes all my willpower to turn from the pounding surf and mount the steps to the temple. I do not know why I take

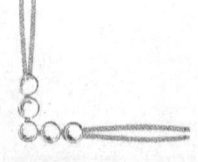

this path, only that it seems the obvious one. After all, who should the God of the Sea inquire of her people from if not her priests?

But the island is deserted. No one is on the docks. The devastated homes have not been repaired. Gulls pick at the refuse still surrounding them.

When I reach the top of the steps and find the temple and look up at the glorious statue of Okeanos—a true likeness and yet not; resplendent, and yet far too perfect for the god I knew—I notice something I've never seen before. There is a little lighthouse pattern carved around the bottom of the dais on which the statue stands. Was that always there?

So intent am I upon it that I almost startle out of my skin when a wide-eyed child taps me on the shoulder. She's holding the hand of a man and they're dressed in the clothing of the temple. The girl holds out a white bundle to me.

"You look lost," the man says. Deep lines mar his face, but he isn't old. He's barely older than me and I think he is the child's father. She carries his likeness.

"Are you a priest of Okeanos? Of the sea?" I correct myself.

"I was," he says, looking away sadly. "On the isle of Calypsala. But I heard the others had abandoned this temple." He shrugs. "It seemed wrong to not have a caretaker here."

"A waste," I agree, and I can't keep the tears out of my voice. "Where is everyone?"

He shakes his head sadly. "With the loss of Queen Coralys,

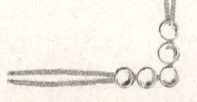

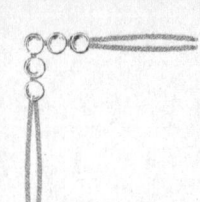

no one wanted to serve in this temple. It is said to be a bad omen, a place where our queen was led astray and duped, for why else would her bargain have failed? When the raiders attacked Calypsala and slaughtered our king, that was further proof. The temple was abandoned and the people have fled to the capital for succor. Perhaps it is for the best. There are rumors that there may be war soon on the mainland."

"War?" I say warily, but I know he is right. Was that not Glorian's complaint? That her rivals were raising up secret armies?

"While I, a priest of Okeanos, should embrace a return to religious dedication, I fear that it is only an excuse. They say nations are aligning according to their patron gods. They say—" He glances at the girl as if he doesn't want to say more with her there. In a calmer, quieter tone he says, "I'm sure we're safe here. Why don't you give the lady the dress and go play with the goats?"

The girl offers me the bundle again.

"Thank you," I tell her, and she's gone in a flash.

"Not all who wear pearls can afford to give them up, and the body needs clothing," the priest says, glancing at the pearl cuirass I wear.

I finger it nervously. Does he know these are not real pearls? He looks away as if he doesn't dare look at them.

They have offered me a peplos—one in good repair, fit for a minor noble or well-off merchant. I cannot pay him for it and I feel ashamed.

"Thank you," I say, for thanks is all I have to give.

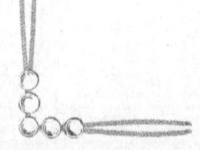

"If you'll take my advice, lady, you'll stay," he says a little shyly. "There are many homes on the island that could be fixed. We keep goats and bees and there is enough food for one more. Don't go to the mainland. Don't get caught up in this strange war." He drops his voice and he checks over his shoulder to be sure the girl is really gone. "The gods are best left alone for the most part. You'd be safer here."

"In a temple?" I ask in disbelief.

"In Okeanos's Temple," the man—a priest, I suppose—says with the kind of reverence I've never before heard in a voice. "I met him once."

I lift an eyebrow in doubt, but he raises a finger.

"I truly did, lady. I prayed to him when the raiders killed my wife not a month back." There's a tightness to his mouth as he says it and something cold fills me. I saw what those raiders did. I know of what he speaks. And just like him, I lost a partner only a short time ago. The pain in his eyes is echoed in mine. "He made me a promise. He told me he would make us a place where we could be safe. All of us. If we would just hold on."

I point to the lighthouses at the base of the dais. "Have those always been there?"

And his eyes widen as he realizes I know exactly what he's talking about, and he has to clear his throat to answer.

"For as long as I have been here. But I cannot say if they were here before that." He pauses and it is a pregnant pause indeed. "Have you ever met Okeanos, then, great God of the Sea, mighty and benevolent?"

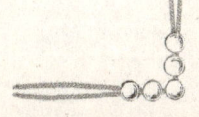

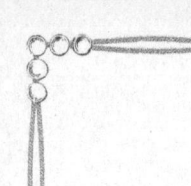

I snort and turn away. "I should hope so. I am his wife."

I do not stay long after that. Seeing the hope mingled with disbelief in his eyes is too much for me. There is a war out there somewhere, god against god. I know it is real. And I know there will never be a place of safety for this man and his child because I killed the one who was building the Lighthouse meant to be that place of safety.

I flee Talasa and I do not look back.

I feel as though I am sinking, sinking, sinking.

War is brewing. And my people may become caught in it. I must find out more. I must find someone I know.

I no longer need anyone to instruct me on how to turn my hand now that I am the sea. I can find any place as long as the waves lap the land there. I go immediately to my other islands. I start with Tempest Reef, skipping from place to place along her shore. Her cities are silent and dark. Her docks empty. I move faster and faster, gripped with panic. Next is Bon Verdas. There will be life here. There must be.

I am right. There are fishing sloops and a tiny wash of light spilling across the bay. This was never a large city nor a wealthy one. But our dye makers and merchants are based there and foundries make bells and other ship equipment. There may be someone I know close by.

I flow out of the sea, dressed now in the gift of the priest. It is good. I am less noticeable wearing a dress than I had been in an overlarge tunic.

My heart is in my throat, my lungs burn and ache with every panicked breath, but I know what has drawn me here.

I felt him in the water. I hurry to a bay just south of the city and step from the water there just as Turbote steps from a small tide pool, supported by his son, Frexole, and Garnet, who was chief steward of the Royal House.

"Turbote," I say.

"Goddess, have mercy," my old advisor breathes, startled. He drops to a knee, his old bones clicking in a way that makes me flinch. The men with him hurry to join him.

He does not know me. I touch my cheek on instinct, wondering if I have changed in appearance. My breath stills in my lungs as I realize that somehow I have taken on that same nature of the gods that once bid me to bow. Surely I am a god to these people, and if a god, then responsible for them.

No one cares that I try to stop them, that I gesture for them to rise, nor do they give me even a moment to speak. Their chests heave with sudden anxiety and their faces are etched with the same. Never did they act so when I was queen.

"We abase ourselves. Please. Ask no more of us. We cannot bear it," Turbote manages to gasp.

"Turbote, it is I," I say, uncertain.

"She speaks your name," Garnet whispers in horror.

"It is I, Coralys," I try again.

"Great Goddess, spare us your wrath," Turbote murmurs. He looks up into my face and there is not a shred of recognition there. How can he not see me? I have given him my name. He appears almost guilty. "Do not ask more from us."

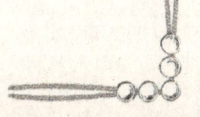

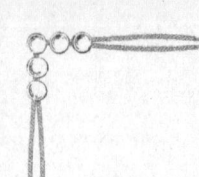

My words are as uncertain as my thoughts. "Has what has been asked of you been too hard?"

I am confused by their reaction to me. The priest and the girl only saw a lost lady. These three act as though they have met the guardian of the afterlife carrying a blazing sword. They keep their eyes averted and Garnet is covering his face.

"Never, never, Goddess." Turbote makes a holy sign across his chest. "Did we not offer up the daughter of Prexot only yesterday to the God of the Sea?"

I rock backward in horror. But that would have been me. And I did not ask for that.

I hold up a hand. My mouth is so dry I must wet my lips to speak.

"You must stop such things immediately. You must make no human sacrifices."

"We would never hold back what belongs to the gods, Great Lady," he says, lifting both hands reverently.

I feel ill. I want to shake Turbote. I want to scream that he lies.

And with a pang I remember how he told me that Okeanos demanded the same thing of him.

And I believed him.

My tongue tastes acid, and bile rises, burning in my chest. Perhaps Okeanos was not the liar I thought he was.

"If we stop," Turbote's son says in a reverent hush, "then things will only grow worse. Already our babies are stillborn, our nets are empty, our houses catch fire, and there is no

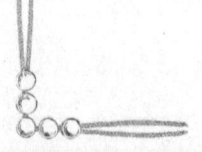

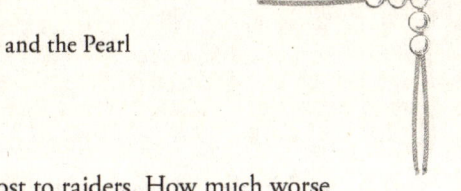

rain. Already our lands are lost to raiders. How much worse if we fail to worship Okeanos, God of the Sea?"

"But Okeanos is dead," I whisper in despair before I realize I have said it. "And even if he were not, he would not ask this of you."

Turbote looks at me square in the face for the first time since I arrived and I see sheer terror in his eyes. "Was he not here only this morning? Did he not demand our sacrifice?"

"Did he?" I echo.

Markanos did say that my husband was not dead. But I felt for his pulse and it was not there. I felt his death gasp as if it were a knife in my own chest. This makes no sense to me. Besides which, now that I know who Okeanos is, I know he would not ask for virgin sacrifices. Or any human sacrifice. I may place blame at his feet for many things, but never that.

Someone must be impersonating my husband. And for them to do it so swiftly, it must be a god who knows he is dead.

"Honored Goddess, only tell us what more you want," Turbote begs, cringing, and I blink away the black stars that dance across my vision.

I feel sick. I think... it's possible... that I might have been wrong about Okeanos. About this one thing, at least.

Turbote's still spewing his words up and I wish I'd never come here. "Do not fear we will buck your will. Did we not exile Gheric Rodehands for trying to take what was the

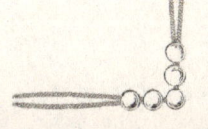

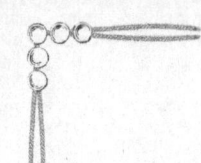

gods'? He and the thousand who stood with him? We will deny you nothing."

Gheric Rodehands. Again. I shoot Turbote a suspicious look. His mistrust of this political rival is long-standing. Even as queen I had to prevent him from laying a punishment on Gheric Rodehands for his talk against a monarchy. I see Turbote has wasted no time in quickly dispatching his rivals.

"How did he take from the gods?" I ask warily.

"He stole back the sacrifices, O Shining One," Garnet murmurs. "He took from your hand what we held in keeping to offer to the depths."

They exiled him for *saving* the girls they were throwing into the sea? This grows worse and worse.

"You will invite him back," I say sternly. "You will need every possible ally here when the storm comes."

If there truly is a god war, it will come to these islands as well. No place on earth will be spared.

"We will deny you nothing," Turbote repeats. "Only please...please, if you will, plead with Okeanos for us that we might have full nets again."

"I make you no promises," I say abruptly, for I am choking on what I have heard. This is worse than madness. They exiled people. Because they refused to submit to insanity. They killed others. For nothing. "But you must promise me not to sacrifice any more people to the sea."

"That," Turbote says earnestly, "we will never agree to do. We must obey the gods."

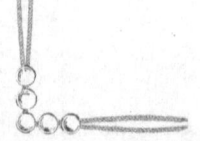

The Trident and the Pearl

But I am a god and he is not obeying me.

I turn back to the sea, sick and reeling. I must find whoever is impersonating my dead husband and issuing such grim orders in his place, and I must determine if I still have a people left to save or if they have all become as corrupt as my old advisor.

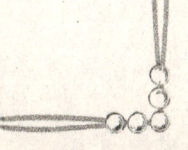

Chapter Twenty-Three

I return to my home—for that is what Okeanos's island has become for me. I no longer feel at home in the Crocus Isles. My people have filled it with their virgin sacrifices and god wars, and I do not yet know how to turn them away from those things.

I'm exhausted, alone, and out of sorts. I almost wish I could drag Vesuvius out of his pearl just so I could have someone to talk to about what I've seen, but I'm not quite that desperate yet.

I collapse into my bed dirty and despairing. My people cower and do evil in my name. Others are dead because of things they said I ordered them to do. The damage done is irrevocable. My only bright light this night was a lonely priest and a little girl carrying a ball of fabric and even they are threatened by the actions of others who mean to start a war.

Is this what Oke dealt with when he was God of the Sea? No wonder he paid no mind to my accusations. It seems that mortals lay any number of things at our feet.

But I am Coralys, the Drowned Queen, and I do not give up. So, the next morning, I rise early and I fish. I fish all day. I do not know if I must keep my catch to fill my people's nets, but I do not want to risk it, so at the end of the day the dock is heaped with the silvery bodies of dead fish.

I cook one for my dinner, collapse into bed, and do it again the next day and the next and the next. It is a full seven days that I fish from the moment dawn breaks until the moment the sun falls into darkness. I fish until my hands are red and blistered and aching from seawater and rough ropes. I fish until the catch stacked on the docks reeks and rots and fills my harbor with gulls. I fish until I know Oke's boat like I know my own bones. I fish until I fear I have caught every fish that ever existed.

I fish and I think about gods and men and how people seem to worship whatever is the most convenient for them. And I think about how I killed a god and nothing changed. It only made things worse. I wish I hadn't been so hasty. I wish I'd gone with him that morning of the Resurgence instead of going off on my own. I wish I'd shown even a little humility, but then I wouldn't be here, would I? Because humble people don't decide that they're going to kill gods and take their places. Or if they do, then they're not called humble anymore.

Only then, after I've done all I can, worn, weary, and filthy, do I set out to find my people again.

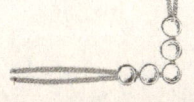

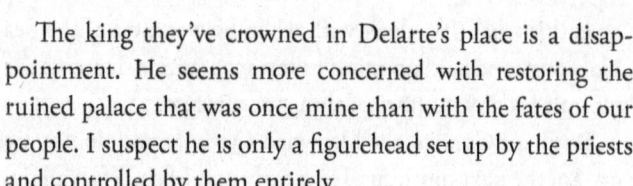

The king they've crowned in Delarte's place is a disappointment. He seems more concerned with restoring the ruined palace that was once mine than with the fates of our people. I suspect he is only a figurehead set up by the priests and controlled by them entirely.

I find him in his palace, where he cowers and abases himself. I never enjoyed being bowed to, and it is growing so thin now that my temper feels as frayed as Oke's bedding.

"We honor you, Goddess. Spare us your wrath."

There's more. I don't listen to it all because it's the same as it was with Turbote. He refuses to stop killing helpless victims. He refuses to listen when I counsel him against war.

"But our enemies are amassing on the coast, Great Goddess," he says. I have told him I am Coralys, but he will not call me by name. "It is said there are so many ships in the harbor of Bel Amos that an entire forest was leveled to make their masts." This is patently untrue as rumors of war have only been a few months in the making. No one levels a forest in a month. "If we do not choose a side, we will be forgotten. Our time of glory is now. Let the Crocus Isles go down in history as the great land of Okeanos, God of the Sea. Is it not right and good to fight for the honor of the gods?"

"It is not either of those things," I snap. "And Okeanos is not your god anymore. I am."

"Of course, Wife of Okeanos. Your great bounty has blessed us."

I still don't know how that name slipped out, but someone said it the last time I was on the islands and now the

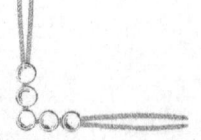

name is everywhere. I glance over my shoulder at the sea. Already, I wish I were back within it rather than here. Oke's hermit ways are becoming more and more appealing to me.

"Our nets have been full to bursting. All are fed and our wealth grows."

Good. There will be no more hungry children. No more refugees with nothing to eat. I'm just beginning to smile when he wipes the expression from my face.

"With this bounty we grow rich enough to foot a navy. A navy of almost every able-bodied man and boy. They will sail for the mainland, where we will slay anyone who stands against Okeanos. Our allies in the Andalappo Isles have sent an ambassador begging for our support and we will give it wholeheartedly."

"What?" I roar, and I don't mean to do it. I don't. But he wants to kill in the name of his god. He'll kill and say it was me—or my dead husband, which amounts to the same thing. My fraying temper dissolves like mist in the sun. "You will send no ships."

"I cannot rescind my orders. I have made promises. I have written irrevocable commands." He's white-faced and shaking and he doesn't meet my eyes—thank the gods. If he did, I might throttle him for what he's doing.

"Then at least bring back Gheric Rodehands as I ordered Turbote to do the last time I was here. He and his thousand followers might help fill the gap left by the men you'll send away."

With the actual leaders of my people in such shambles,

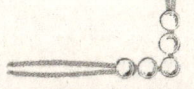

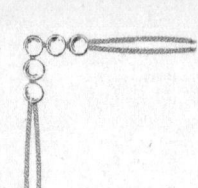

the man might be their only hope for a government not intent on murdering its own people.

His hands shake, but still he defies me. "We will never tolerate the heretics on our shores. Trust that we honor you in that. We reject them for all time."

I leave without another word, leaping into the sea like a diving bird does. I am furious. But what am I to do? Punish them? Force their obedience?

If I do that, then it is not the king who will suffer, it is the very peasants whose cries and prayers have motivated me to feed them.

I am starting to be able to pick out their individual prayers when I am in the sea and they cry to me day and night for help. Just the few weeks since I was their queen are awash with trouble and there is no end to those who reach in faith for help with it. I could go to each one and bless them individually, but the moment I turned to the next in line, the very bounty I gave them would be seized by these corrupt rulers for the war they hope is coming. I cannot solve their individual problems without solving them at the source. This is all a tangled knot I cannot untie.

Frustrated, I slice though the sea, feeling for the prows of the ships, and when I find them being built in the harbors, their waiting weapons stacked high on the shores, I set about stymieing them. Wave after wave I send against the ships. A ship swamps and then another, pounded in their builder's cradles until they are nothing but splinters. But the next day when I return, the debris is being cleared away and

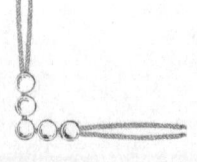

new timbers brought to replace what was ruined. They will not stop until every mast is broken and every scrap of wood destroyed. And then what? Will I see my islands stripped bare and impoverished to keep them out of this looming war?

I crawl home, spent and bitter, to lie on my bed miserable and alone. An escape from magic, from gods, from those who would speak for gods is beginning to have an appeal after all.

Mortals. What terrible creatures they are. Almost as bad as the gods themselves. Do none of them care that they will break themselves upon the cliffs of war and that—just like the ships—there will be nothing left of them? How many nations have broken that way? How many cultures lost forever due to the arrogance and overreach of their leaders?

And so I listen. Every day I sit on a rock by the water before I go out fishing, and I listen. I do what I can. I find lost fishermen and guide them safely home. I find a missing child swept away by a strange tide. But I am powerless to help with so many things. How can I return a drowned friend? How will I bless a barren womb, repair a spoiled fortune, bring home a shipment of silks safe?

I also read the books Oke left behind. Especially the book about the Lighthouse. He was not wrong to set me to them, for by them I learn how to find the shipment of silks upon the sea, how to nudge a ship just so to avoid a storm—how to push smaller squalls away and bend the current where it must go. Small things, but each one eats at me.

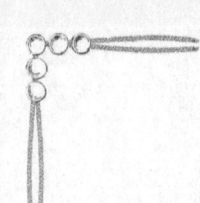

Sarah K. L. Wilson

To bend the squall, I give my voice for a day and find myself breathless at every task until I must take to my bed and draw in slow thready gasps thinking I will die of lack of air. To guide the ship, I must lose my own balance for an hour. My twisted ankle is enough sign that I do not operate well without balance.

I wish I knew how to change the hearts of kings and counselors and seduce them into peace over war, but I still have not learned it. I hate the idea that Okeanos might have been able to do just that—that if he were not dead, he might have stopped this from happening in a way I cannot. Bigger works require more from me. When, finally, I can tackle them, I am left trembling and vomiting for six whole days because I shove the red plague from the coastal cities along the Rust Coast.

I lie miserable in the water, so hot I think I will melt away when I listen to the prayer of a priest from Saint Flagra's Nation and relieve them of their terrible drought. I am so certain that day that I am dying that I whisper my thoughts to the sky and hope they carry to the Nightwaters, where Lieve dwells. But by evening I am recovered and I sleep in my bed as if nothing ever happened.

I would gladly pay the same price to turn the hearts of those rulers. If only I knew how.

I hear murmurs of war coming in every port and on every ship. It feels like my chance to keep us out of it is slipping away while I am caught up in all these other tasks. Their worried voices dance across the surface of my waters and I

feel them in my very bones, but I know they are fully committed to preparations now. To extract them would mean their ruin and maybe even their deaths.

Worst of all is the sea serpent.

It is possibly a month into my tenure as God of the Sea when I'm arrested by a prayer. I am fishing—with the men all gone and having sold their surplus of fish to pay for this useless war, there's nothing left for the women and children unless I fish for them. I feel sometimes like I am always fishing. I dream of fish at night. I see them when I try to look at the books. I've put away my pearls and the dress and everything else and all I do is fish in that old raggedy tunic and think of how Oke told me he was a fisherman. The Fisher King. It's becoming glaringly obvious why he claimed that title.

Today, I am fishing tuna. After that first seven-day, I learned I *can* toss them back and only save one small one for my own supper. I'm pulling up a glorious yellowfin tuna when I hear the prayer.

"God of the Sea, save us!"

I have learned the trick of moving quickly from one place to another, and it's a simple thing to put one hand in the water and the other into the shape of a bowl and twist it to find the supplicant. I expect someone drowning or in trouble.

Things are not quite so simple when I arrive.

There's a ship on her side, wallowing in the waves, her sailors scattered all out behind her in a trail. It is they who plead for my help. Squeezing the ship's middle is the largest

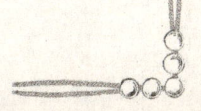

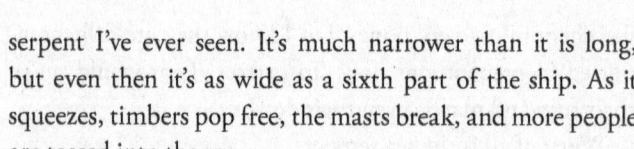

serpent I've ever seen. It's much narrower than it is long, but even then it's as wide as a sixth part of the ship. As it squeezes, timbers pop free, the masts break, and more people are tossed into the sea.

This is certainly a job for a god. If only I knew how to manage it. I stand up in my fishing boat and try to get a better look. The head is deep below the heaving water. We're only seeing rings of body right now.

I have the strange bronze trident with me. I hope it will be enough to kill a serpent. If it was Vesuvius's weapon, then it is a god weapon, but I don't know if that still means it is special if the god in question is dead. I brace it in one hand and start to steer the boat toward the disaster with the other. I will have to leap from the boat onto the creature's coils and stab it, I suppose, and if that doesn't work, I'll have to swim down and find its head and stab it somewhere more vulnerable. I can't see any other way to deal with this monster.

I'm about to lunge forward and begin when she speaks into my mind.

Will you harm me, God of the Sea? She sounds uncertain.

Not if you leave my people alone, I tell it back.

Your people? Glorian of Growing Things has taken great bites out of your entire eastern coast. I hear half of it belongs now to her and not to you at all. And Alexandros the Toolmaker arrives to take his own piece of the northern one. You are squeezed and soon will be broken, ready to pop with a little more pressure. The creature laughs. *You will have no people, Drowned Queen. Even I have heard that.*

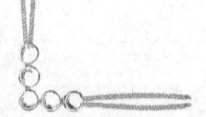

The Trident and the Pearl

I am so stunned that I hardly know what to say, but I'm not as stunned as the sea serpent believes I am. She is so pleased she has surprised me that she does not notice how close my boat has drawn to her shining scales, or how I am bracing my trident to strike. She lifts her head from the water and brackish fluid pours through the tendrils of her beard and foams around her curving jaw. She opens her mouth to scoop me up, but I kick the tiller hard, and as my little boat surges to the side, I plunge Vesuvius's trident through her skin and into her throat. And just like I killed a god, I kill a sea serpent, though not nearly as neatly.

She drags me through the water as I twist the trident, plunging me under, wrapping her tail around my side and squeezing, squeezing, squeezing until I think I might burst. The fight is a blur of desperation and intent, but to my credit, I remember I am the sea. When she squeezes me, I squeeze back, my waters gripping and throttling her as she throttles me until I manage to twist my trident into place and drive it through her eye.

When her grip on me falls lax, it's all I can do to rip my trident free and drag myself back into the little fishing boat. I cannot breathe properly. My ribs slowly find their places and pop back into them and around me are the cries of the living as they rush to rescue the dead and the horrible smell of bursting bubbles filled with a rotting seaweed scent that are the only reminder that these waters churned with a living, breathing monster just moments ago.

This is madness. All of it.

I drag myself back to my island somehow and pull my broken body up onto shore and lie upon the rocks until finally I can breathe and my limbs—to my surprise—function properly again. I could have sworn I had a broken shoulder and clavicle, and at least a half dozen ribs, but they are all functional by midnight and painless by morning.

I hope the people made it to safety once the sea serpent was dragged from their hull. A good god would have stayed and been sure. A good god wouldn't have been too damaged to help. A good god would have never let it happen in the first place.

But me? I make a terrible god. Worse, I am realizing, than Okeanos. Worse than Glorian. Worse than Aurelius. Possibly even worse than Vesuvius, and that is a very great claim indeed.

I am the very worst of gods.

My only comfort is that the sea seems to love me.

When all has gone wrong, I lay drifting in the water. I won't lie and pretend this part is not excellent. It is the balm to my aching soul, the sweet in all the bitterness. I close my eyes and feel the movement of the humpback whales in their pods, feel the dart and dash of the dolphins, and the great joy of the anemones on the reefs. And for a moment, I am blissful. I dance with the bubbles that roil up where the seals dive and moan. I laugh with the hoot of the sea lion. I fall into sonorous rhythm with the penguin in his march. I snap at nothing with the shark. I am the sea.

I feel the great inky quaking of the monsters of the depths

and I bid them go back to sleep. I feel them only when they murmur, but I sense them always—great creatures who sleep deep in the beneath, underpinning all the ocean with their power. I am their sea, too.

Sometimes I feel something more out there far off in the ocean—that same murky sense of dread and pain I felt the first time and from which I shy away. I do not want to know what gives off such terrible misery. I am afraid that if I find out, it will become my responsibility to fix it, and that whatever the solution is will most certainly mean my taking on that vast well of pain. I have had enough pain. I am ready to live without it for quite some time. I can try it again later, when things are less fraught with trouble.

And once—only once—I think I might sense the Lighthouse just under the skim of sand in the deep Pleitas Trench. It, too, is far away and it feels like a wind chime sounds, haunting me all day and well into the night—enough that I draw out Oke's notes again and read of his Lighthouse project and wonder if he was a dreamer, or a madman, or merely a visionary slain before his work was done. It has become clear to me that he was, in fact, trying to build a paradise-like refuge for his people. And that he was not lying to me about any of the claims he made. And maybe, just maybe, I might give him his wish after all and find a way to draw this Lighthouse back up from beneath the waves.

For just a moment, I think of Oke's distant gaze and I think we could have shared this—that I would not have had to bear the burden of it alone—had I not been so certain that

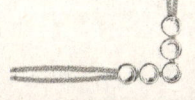

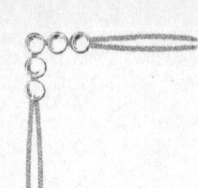

he was lying to me and that his death was vital to changing the course of things. The thought guts me and I must thrust it away as I do every time the conclusion creeps closer—the knowledge I'll not be able to avoid forever, the understanding that I already see even if I'm struggling to accept.

I was wrong.

I killed for no good reason.

For the god I hoped to supplant was only replaced with a worse god... and that one is me.

It is two moons into my reign as goddess that I go looking for the rebel Gheric Rodehands. I have given up on Turbote. Given up on the prince of the Andalappos, who is now king of the Crocus Isles. I have learned both of them serve only themselves. They make up what the God of the Sea has "told them" out of whole cloth and then demand obedience from the people despite my orders to the contrary. I have asked for none of what they claim I have required. I have asked them for nothing at all. Everything they tell the people is a lie, and I fear that if I see Turbote again, I may kill him. I have found no evidence of someone else giving him orders—no "Okeanos" pulling his strings. I do not know if he has gone mad from the terrible horrors he lived through or if he is the villain he seems, intent on the deaths of others to shore up his own power.

I cannot quite seem to calm my fury where he is concerned, and I am beginning to fear that one day I will sharpen this trident and go looking for him. He has not stopped his terrifying demand of drowning virgins. And the

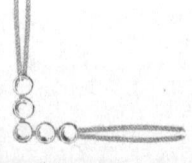

The Trident and the Pearl

last five I've drawn from the depths at the very last minute cursed the God of the Sea—and Okeanos specifically—with the first breath they drew back into their salt-soaked lungs. It was not easy to find them safe places to hide, and to my despair, I could not convince them that the tragedy they had lived through was not ordered by the dead god they blame.

Because of all this, Gheric Rodehands is my people's last hope of a mortal who might be made into a king. He certainly can do no worse than those who have already claimed the title. I have been watching him from afar, and now, it would seem, is the time to speak.

He's young. Twenty-five, perhaps. Not good-looking, not particularly powerful of body, but his people hang on his every word. I wait until he is in the sea cleaning fish—he's not too good to work with his hands—and I meet him there.

He freezes when he sees me, but after a breath he returns to what he's doing. I'm frequently curious to see how mortals will react to me. I have looked into my shell of rainwater and my face is no different than it was when I was queen, but sometimes in the right light I do think that perhaps it glows a little. It does not seem enough of a change to explain the reactions of mortals. Some—like Turbote, who still does not recognize me—act as though I am as distant from them as the heavens are from the earth. Others, like the innocent child of the priest of Okeanos or this leader of the people, simply shrug and carry on with their work. I have not yet figured out if it is something I am doing, or some attitude they have, or merely a quirk of vision from one to the next.

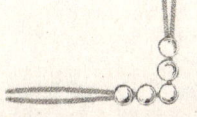

"The Lighthouse," Gheric says confidently when I explain who I am, and this time it's my turn to freeze. "Casavar the priest told me about it." His eyes blaze as he speaks on about the man—the one I met in Okeanos's Temple who gave me my peplos. "If such a thing were possible, I would lead our people to it. All who remain. And we would be free of these looming god wars that threaten to ravage the land. We'd be free, too, of the moods and whims of those who were meant to protect us but seem only set on ruining us." His smile is grim and sad. "But of course, it's only a tale."

He tells me of other things as well, and tries to sway me to his cause. Were I mortal still, I might join it. Were I queen, I'd make him a captain or advisor despite his clear disdain for the monarchy. He's very persuasive. But I am neither mortal nor queen and even the memory of me has left the lips of the people. They do not speak of Coralys except in cursing the gods for taking me and leaving them to their current fates. There is a small group of people who believe I was the first of Turbote's virgin sacrifices—foolish, since I was not a virgin and since Turbote had nothing to do with my choice to abdicate. To everyone who meets me now, I am only Okeanos's wife. They will not call me Coralys no matter how often I remind them.

I go home from my meeting with Gheric deep in thought.

"Can I bring up the Lighthouse from the depths?" I ask the helpful woman from the pearl that night, drawing her out from her prison, but she only laughs at me.

I ask them one by one—each resident of each pearl—and

each one laughs or shakes his head or tells me I'm a fool. Even those who look at me with wistful eyes as if they wish it could be so say the same thing.

"It's too late," they say. "There was a chance, but that is gone now."

At last, I even ask Vesuvius.

"The Great Lighthouse?" He sneers at me, but there is a light in his eye that tells me I've piqued his interest. "Better to ask for the soul of your dead husband back."

And I do not know if it is his words that trigger it, but that night I dream of Oke drowning with no one to save him. I leap into the inky water, but when I reach for him, there is nothing to be found but a dull, festering ache.

When I wake, the dream is still with me and I realize the ache I felt is familiar. It is that infection I've been sensing in the sea that I do not wish to explore.

I go about my work that day pretending I don't know what I'm going to do, but when evening comes, I can no longer deny it. I must know. I must know if Markanos told the truth and Oke yet lives in some form or another. I must know if his life is connected to that dreadful pain and sorrow I feel at the center of the sea. And if it is, then I must beg him to explain to me how to drag his Lighthouse up from the depths. I must know if there is any other way than that ridiculous list of impossible tasks. And I must do it now before I make a greater mess of things than I have already.

Chapter Twenty-Four

I heard a story once of a woman who wed a man who visited her only at night. She was forbidden to see his face, which was no matter since he only attended her in the dark. The man was the most winsome of lovers and one day the woman awoke to realize she had fallen in love with him. How could she be in love with a man whose face she did not know? Fearing he may be a monster, she brought to bed with her a tiny mirror, and when her husband slept, she angled the mirror to catch the light of the moon and shine it on his face. He was beautiful indeed—so beautiful that it broke her heart. And it broke his, too, for he opened his eyes, saw her betrayal, and immediately turned into a gull and flew away squawking, leaving her only a feather to remember him by. And there the story ended with broken hearts and some god-man off scavenging fish guts along the shore.

That story is different than mine, for I am not in love with Okeanos and no one has ripped him from my arms but myself. And yet, it echoes in the same way, for I looked to see the monster and found beauty instead. Or perhaps I did find a monster when I looked for him...only that monster was me.

I wear the belted tunic and the pearls. I never feel completely safe taking the pearls off anymore, and the tunic will give me free movement if this turns out to be like the encounter with the sea monster. I do not think that Oke would have the witlessness to turn into a gull, but I could very well see him as a sea monster intent on cracking every rib in my possession. I bring with me the trident with which I killed the last sea monster. It is the only weapon I have, but more than that, it is a symbol to myself that I can do some things, still.

The walk down to the shore feels long and heavy as if I already know what I will find when I travel to the painful miasma I feel in the center of my sea.

I don't take the boat. I can't explain why. I simply have a wrenching feeling that whatever I find might require quick flight, and besides, I feel safer with the arms of the sea wrapped around me. I feel more whole when I can move with its every current. More real in its briny depths.

I step into the waves. They're shockingly peaceful today, painted in lacy white foam on the edge of dappled green water. Like his eyes, I think, when I was murdering him. But I won't dwell on that now.

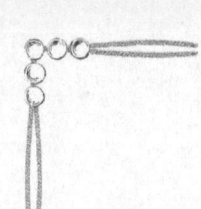

I slip into the water and I hardly need turn my hand anymore to move where I wish. I am the sea and the sea is me. I think of the misery and darkness and churning pain I've been feeling somewhere out there in the sea like an itch on my back, and then suddenly we are there and I am bucking against a sensation like a knife down my throat.

Whatever I perceived from afar is magnified here. While at first it had felt like a patch of darkness, and then later like a canker with something rotten within it, now I have become certain that a terrible evil is being spun out in that place. It taints my waters and clouds my power with something akin to pain. I have a feeling I know what it is and the thought makes my stomach clench and twist. But if I am to address it, then I must go to the source.

I have arrived underwater. The dark roots of a small island are before me and here the sea is churned black with activity. Fish of a hundred colors and shapes dart in and out of the bubble-cloaked shadows. I make out the undulating body of a ray, the stinger of a jellyfish, the smooth fin of a shark—they're such a tangle that I can hardly pick out one creature from another. But there are hundreds here and they are feeding on something dangling from the surface.

I would have to muscle through a wall of fish to see what they are feasting upon. I will take a more oblique approach and see if I can observe without being observed in turn.

I clamber up the backside of the island. It is a small island—hardly bigger than a large fishing sloop. To one side of it, a massive anchor juts out from the rock at a very odd angle. One

of its arms is swallowed entirely by the black rock as if it was lowered into hot lava, sealed in its embrace, and then jetted up on a stream of hot rock to form this island. The anchor bears a crossbar that is thick with a patina of rust, shellfish, and barnacles. Washed around it are massive clumps of kelp rotting in the sun while birds stand in a solemn line along the anchor's crossbar like witnesses before an execution.

But it is not the anchor that draws me, trembling, toward it, but the man lashed to it, hands above his head, rings around his wrists with rivets placed right through the flesh of them so he might not move his hands at all from where they are pinned to the anchor. His legs dangle waist-deep in the thrashing water and I see now what has driven the fish to such frenzy. They feast upon him as they ought only feast upon the dead.

But of course he *is* dead.

I should know, since I am the one who killed him.

In the wound on his thigh, fat barnacles have taken up residence, peeking through the gaping flesh. I look on him aghast, trembling all over. My trident falls to the rock, clattering and then slipping into the waves, but I find that I cannot care.

He looks up at the sound, and our eyes meet with a clash. In his is a spark so very alive, so very powerful, that though he is the one bound and captive, I am the one with the sudden spark of fear in her inmost heart.

"You live," I gasp, barely able to draw a new breath.

His face is a thunderhead. "I mislike this, wife."

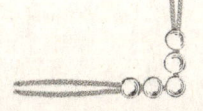

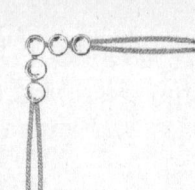

Understatement. How very...godlike of him. My fingers start to tremble.

"How are you alive? I felt you quiver and die by my own hand."

He's frowning at me, his eyes running all over my exposed body. In his worn tunic, there's quite a lot of it to see.

"You are bruised and wounded," he says, fixated on my skin.

I look down. I hadn't even noticed the bruises. And he's right. There's a gash I left unbandaged on my leg. His gaze darts up to mine, questioning.

"You must be in relentless pain," I say, shuddering at the cloud of red in the water. It is his flesh the sea creatures feast on, but he is stoic and hard on the surface, his face a mask he wears in front of whatever he feels.

"The bruises," he presses. "Where did they come from? Has someone assaulted you?"

I choke on a surprised laugh. "I am simply very bad at being a god."

The frown on his face disappears and he nods to himself. I feel a sense of shame as if I've disappointed him.

"How are you alive?" I ask again. My arms snake around me as if I can protect myself from the evidence of what I've done.

This time he smiles—a rueful, cynical smile. It's only there for an instant and then the mask is back.

"I wed you in the old way. While you live, I cannot die—not entirely. Your life binds my soul to this place."

"This place exactly?" I press, squatting down now so that

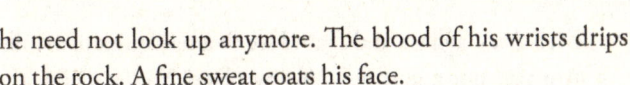

he need not look up anymore. The blood of his wrists drips on the rock. A fine sweat coats his face.

"No, wife. That is the work of an old friend. Can you guess which one? He has anchored my soul to this rock. In the sea, but not the sea. Feasted on by sea creatures all day, only to be restored by god-power at night. An endless cycle of pain and torment fit only for a dethroned god."

I reel back in horror and his face ripples with some emotion he tries to hide from me.

"This... I did not intend this," I say in a small voice.

"You wanted me dead. You did not stop to think what that might mean. For both of us."

"I did not," I admit a little shakily.

His lips are pressed firmly together, his face hard. Surely he is furious with me. Surely he would take his vengeance if he could. I brace myself for whatever words he'll fling at me, but he remains silent.

"Why would someone do this to you?" I ask, standing to look at how firmly he is secured. If he was placed here by a god, may he not be freed by one?

I examine his bonds without touching him. His hands are purple and grey as if they are nothing but one great bruise. I want to rip them from their restraints, but even hovering close I can feel a great power emanating from the rivets that repels my touch.

He pauses as if weighing his words and one eyebrow quirks. "I have not agreed to support Treseano's rebellion or to twist my wife's intentions to gain support for it."

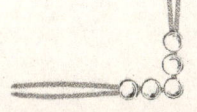

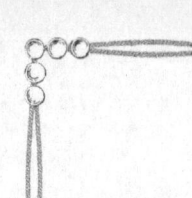

"Me?" I say, aghast, and again I see that tiny quirk of a smile.

"Are you not a god now, in my place? You are new and inexperienced, but the sea is powerful and you will be also, given time. Those ranked against us hope to stymie the sea before that comes about."

"But they haven't approached me."

"They will."

I search his eyes, looking for condemnation, for bitterness, for fury. Were I him, I would want revenge. I see none of those things. There's tight pain there. But I do not feel the sharp flickers of fury I expect.

"Coralys. Your tears honor me. But do not cry."

"Do not cry?" I exclaim as my arms snake around me again and I hold myself together with them. I had not meant to weep, but I also do not mean to shake and I am shaking uncontrollably. "Look what I have done to you."

He watches me silently, his breath catching a little, his only concession to the agony of being slowly eaten alive.

"I killed you. Or I thought I did."

"Oh, I am certainly dead," he agrees, and now there is a flicker of something dangerous in his eyes. "But dead gods don't just go away. They linger. And their souls are trapped, or contained, or set to endure torture forever. I would not recommend godhood. It is not for the craven or the weak."

I choke on a sob. And still he's watching me, weighing me, skin tightening around his eyes.

"I don't understand why you aren't furious with me." My voice feels like it comes from someone else.

"When you take a wounded thing to your breast, there's always the risk that they'll bite. I had thought...hoped...I could convince you to help me. Together, I think we could have turned the tides of history." He looks away now, musing. It's like he's speaking to himself. "It felt like such an excellent opportunity. A queen of the sea. Who better to help me to succeed at the great task? She'd want it, too, I thought. A Lighthouse to guard her people. She kept saying she wanted them safe. What could make them safer? And it was part of the list of great acts to marry you. Wed the drowned queen. It was such a tidy solution. Would you really have preferred to marry whoever else might have turned up on the docks?" He looks at me now with soulful eyes. "It might have been Aurelius. Or Treseano and whatever he keeps in that horrible sack. It might have been *you* chained like this when he was done with you. I thought I could do better for you than that. Was I so wrong?"

"No," I say miserably. "If you'd just *told me*."

He looks away and I can't read what is behind his careful mask.

"Mistakes were made by both of us. I didn't bet on you being a recent widow. I didn't bet on you mourning a dead husband. It seemed...wise...to wait. To allow you time to grieve. Not to force things. Maybe it was selfish."

"Selfish?" I move a little closer and flinch when he turns sharply to catch my eye again.

"I waited to be wed to you more fully. Out of respect. Out of what I thought was kindness." He bites his lower lip in

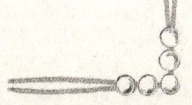

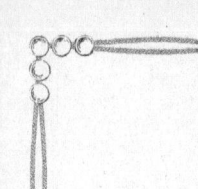

a way that reminds me that he kissed me before I betrayed him.

"Out of the hindrance of a wound in an inconvenient spot," I counter, because as touching as his words are, I'm not about to be lured by half-truths.

He shakes his head. I see his arm twitch like he wants to make that chopping gesture he does when he's in disagreement.

"Do me the honor of more credit than that. Marriage to a god is eternal. I had time to win your favor. I just didn't bet on you killing me first."

He's sweating worse now, and when I glance at the water, the blood is staining it more deeply red. Does he really do this every single day? I feel lightheaded for a moment and must fight to keep my wits about me.

"I thought the dead would feel nothing, even had they not crossed yet to the Nightwaters, and yet you are tortured here," I say, twisting my hands one in another.

"Don't fuss over my pain, Coralys. It's nothing. Here, come here."

He sounds worried and I realize I'm crying again. I dash my tears away. Unhelpful things.

"Tell me what troubles you," he says gravely. His face is full of understanding. His muscles flex against his bonds, standing out sharply, as if he would like to embrace me even now. "Is it the work of leading the people?"

I shake my head, appalled; *he* is what troubles me.

"In part," I say, and then I tell him about how I have done

so far. Of my failures. Of how our enemies encroach. Of how the people creatively interpret my every move and don't see me as a god at all—or at least pay no mind to my warnings or pleas.

"You found the book and my list?" he asks me gently. "Of tasks?"

I nod wearily.

He nods, too, but his seems more like he's trying to convince himself of something. "Just five of those tasks are enough to do a great wonder, Lady of the Sea. They could perform a miracle, change the course of time. They might raise the dead." I feel my breath hitch at that. "How much more might ten achieve? I think they could draw that Lighthouse back up and shield our people forever. And you can still do that. Somehow—I never expected it for a moment—but somehow the task you accomplished was added to mine. You do not have to start afresh. It will be harder without me, but not impossible."

Now, his eyes glow. He wants this more than he wants to be free of torture. More than anything.

"I saw the list," I say. "And if I'm not much mistaken you've done—or we've done—three of the tasks. You married the drowned queen and collected the dead to serve you, and I filled a thimble with riches."

I'm a little smitten by his smile. I dare anyone not to be.

"Four tasks," he murmurs. "For you won a god's oath—mine, when I swore to you that I would be your husband."

"That seems unfair to complete two tasks at once."

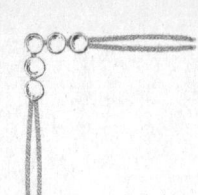

"Ah, but I did not need to bind my soul to you, nor did you need to wed, so both count."

"And you would like me to complete all ten and raise your Lighthouse as a sanctuary for our people."

His face is full of longing. "More than anything."

"But if you know who has you tied here, I can make him free you," I say, leaning toward him. I want to end his pain. "And then we can work on raising this Lighthouse together."

He's already shaking his head. "To do that you'd need to kill another god." I start to interrupt, but he speaks over me. "Which would be harder if you don't have their trust as you had mine. Nearly impossible, as the gods are dividing into sides to fight and they will be suspicious of everyone—but especially someone who has just murdered her husband."

I flush at that. "It's not the only way. You said five tasks would restore a life."

He nods, but he doesn't look happy. "And they would. But I beg you not to spend them on me, for how else will we raise the Lighthouse? We would have to complete all five a second time in a different way—did you read that in the story of Princess Kilinippa?—and while perhaps we could find a new way to collect our dead to serve than by trapping their souls in pearls, we'll have quite a hard time finding a second drowned queen to wed. Unless, like Plector, you're willing to drown an innocent mortal woman."

I swallow. I still think it would be easier to redo five tasks with his help than to do six without him.

To distract myself and delay answering, I stand and

examine his restraints. They burn my fingers and cannot be moved by any power I possess. I close my eyes and try to feel for what bargain I might offer to set them free. Can I be ill and draw in the pain myself? Can I pay by taking his place for a time or by stabbing through my own wrists with spikes? But there is no offer I can make to free him. Each one I think of dissolves away in the certain knowledge it is not enough.

"No mortal tool will cut those and nor will your power take them away," Okeanos says earnestly. "I am not the first god to face such a fate, nor will I be the last. If I was whole, perhaps... but I am not whole." He pauses. "Forget me. Forget this place. Finish the tasks and raise the Lighthouse. Give our people a place of safety that cannot be snatched from them."

I say nothing, stubbornly staring at his prison.

"Coralys," he says, and still I ignore him. "Cora."

The tender way he says my name finally draws my gaze.

"Oke," I say belligerently, and the tiniest flicker of a smile shows in the corner of his mouth. Maybe it's all he can manage in so much torment.

"You cannot change the past. You cannot take back what you've done. You cannot absolve yourself with your actions now. Not even by freeing me."

I shiver.

"But tell me this. Do you still believe me guilty of the crimes you thought were mine?"

"No." My voice is small.

"Do you think I mean to harm your people?"

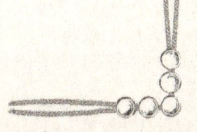

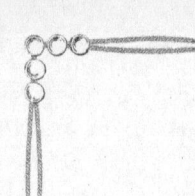

"No." None has planned more to save them. I steal a look at his green eyes and feel as though I have been stabbed right through.

"Do you think I mean to harm you?" he says gently, and his eyes are so deep, so careful in how he holds my gaze that I choke a little.

"No."

"That is enough for me," he says quietly, and when I look at his face again his eyes are very serious. "I need nothing more from you. Though I would like it if you finished the work, I don't require it. Do you understand? Do you...do you know what I'm trying to say?"

"I think I do," I say, but I'm shaking again, and rivers of sweat run from his temple and drip down his jaw and I know it is all he can do to keep from screaming.

"Good."

He has forgiven me, I think. Absolved me. Never has he felt so godlike as he does now, as he forgives a sinner with a simple word.

He clears his throat. "Do not pursue more revenge. Please. It will bring neither of us satisfaction. Promise me this."

I am silent. It is not in my nature to make such a promise. But when his eyes catch mine again, I must swallow, because he ought to be able to ask me anything and receive a yes after what I've done. He has the right to ask this of me.

"Yes," I say faintly. I look away, no longer able to meet the intensity of his gaze. "I will look to your Lighthouse."

"You are doing a better job than you think," he says, and

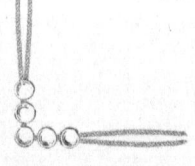

it's the gentleness that breaks me—that he's offering me kindness when it ought to be offered to him.

I squeeze my eyes shut and I think of what I can do for him. I can't get revenge. I can't free him from the anchor. I can't stop the creatures from coming to eat him...but maybe I can offer him guardians to drive them away?

I look into his stormy eyes one last time and I say, "I'll fix this."

And then I make my bargain and the world seems very far away; my legs grow very long, and my skin so hard I can feel nothing at all, my clothing and the pearl cuirass slip down my body and I must scramble to escape their cloying grasp. I think I hear him call my name, but words mean nothing to me anymore. I slip into the water like a stone but not before I see two massive crabs tearing into Oke's torturers and ripping them to pieces.

Chapter Twenty-Five

I emerge from the water dripping and in a foul temper. It is no delight to be a crab. I still feel as though I ought to have more legs than I do and the balance of my body is all wrong.

I creep sideways from the sea, my human feet soft and slippery on the smooth rock, and stop dead.

Someone has lit a driftwood fire of blue-and-purple flames. That someone sits on the far side of it from Okeanos and both of them are lit by the dancing light. It's a strangely companionable situation. My trident lays beside my husband on the rocks, as close as if he set it there.

My eyes snap to Okeanos's bare muscled chest. The wound I gave him is yet set into the flesh, ragged and unhealed. He is still strung up by his hands and they twist painfully in their tethers. Even with the sea creatures driven away by my sacrifice, he must be in agony. He sits though, not at ease, but not in as much visible pain as he was before, and his eyes watch me with a hunger that makes me uncomfortable.

"You must not do that again," he tells me gently over the soft patter of water running from my slick body and dripping on the rock. It mingles with the mellow crackle of the fire. He is always so very gentle, this new husband of mine. "You will waste your days paying for my comfort and your days must be better spent. *You* must be better spent."

"How desperately romantic you are, Okeanos, telling a woman she must be spent like a coin in your purse." Okeanos's visitor is Markanos. He lounges on the rocks like he plans to stay here a long time. "Is this why you've never taken a lover? Do you repel them thus with such vinegar words? I could teach you better. My reputation in romance is only exceeded by my reputation in battle—as you would know if you sought any company but my own."

I am frozen, staring at him. If he tries to kill me again, I suppose I could dive beneath the waves, a crustacean indistinguishable from the others. I don't think I'm fast enough to retrieve the trident before he might stab me. My breath comes quickly. Awareness of my limitations is a clamp around my throat and yet...

"What are you doing to my husband?" I ask quietly, but I put a threat in my voice.

Markanos laughs. "Feeding him wine, naked queen. And some kind of pastry with salmon in it."

He holds up both for me to see before turning to dribble a little wine in Okeanos's mouth.

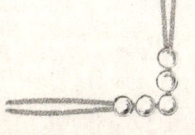

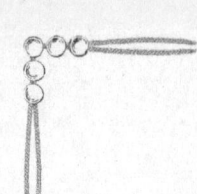

The sea god offers me a wry look, swallowing the wine with calm acceptance.

"Someone must see to his needs," Markanos taunts. "Not all of us choose to be crabs."

A wave rises up over the shore and slaps hard when it comes down, splashing on Markanos and sizzling across part of the fire with a puff of steam that clouds the air.

I take that cue to scoop up my tunic, belt, and cuirass from where they fell when I transformed and I quickly dress. To their credit, neither man watches me.

"Are you insulting my wife?" Okeanos asks in a restrained voice. Does he still have some control over the waves? I try to sense it within myself, for if I am the sea, then I should feel any hold he has on me, but I cannot. Either that was coincidence—unlikely—or his grip remains on the reins of the ocean and I cannot sense it, for we are too intermingled.

The thought gives me pause, but I must drag my gaze back to Oke's almost instantly, for his words are thick with some emotion I can't read when he says, "Wife, I must confess, not once in the centuries that I have been a god has another offered her safety for mine or her comfort to ease my pain. Or seen me as a man in need of succor or kindness. The last to do such for me was my mortal mother. I am... humbled by your gift."

His words are sweet, as is the look in his eyes when he offers them. I stop dead at what I was doing—fumbling with the buckle of my belt. I'm taken aback. If generous gifts are new to him, sweetness is not new to me. My Lieve was a

good friend—strong, kind, tender. I cannot compare him with another. It is not fair to do so, and yet what I see in Okeanos's eyes is the same as what I knew from Lieve. He shows me a facet of vulnerability so endearing it hurts, aches, cuts something deep inside me. I wince because I can feel how it affects me. It makes me want to open myself up in kind, to accept what is being offered and return it.

Our gazes meet and mingle for a long moment, and I feel as though I am breathing in time with him, as though I am thinking in time with him. Unbidden, the memory of his kiss returns and my lips are suddenly dry.

I love my husband, I remind myself. I love Lieve.

My breathing is heavy and uneven.

"Leave off," Markanos mutters, shaking his soaked arm with a grimace. The water sloshes from his sleeve as from a jug. "Tortured you may be. Dead in all but spirit, certainly. But I'll not have the legendary Okeanos debase himself to a mere mortal queen." He turns to me and I force my attention to him. Anything to recover my self-control. "Do you not know him whom you have married? I think you do not, for all you try to buy him with petty gifts." He stuffs one of his salmon pastries into Okeanos's mouth to silence the start of a protest. As if that's not petty. He's one to talk. "Let me enlighten you, Drowned Queen. Okeanos, God of the Sea, is the greatest god of the pantheon. I have watched him single-handedly turn back a fleet of eighty ships launched to invade his islands. He settled them with one careless flick of a wrist and the storm that arose swamped them, sank them, and swallowed up the survivors."

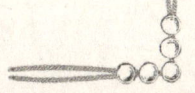

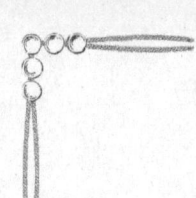

I inhale sharply through my nose and out of the corner of my eye I see Oke stiffen. He knows how I feel about careless violence.

"Is this so?" I ask. I feel as if I balance on a taut rope.

Markanos is undeterred. "Did not Aurelius try to take his holdings not fifty years ago? And did Okeanos not hammer those temples of the air to dust beneath the pounding of his breakers? He led the vanguard himself, a dozen mad sea priests charged from behind his banner, all of them mounted on giant squid. They rippled up the shore, unstoppable, terrifying, trailing a wake of salt water and blood as they ripped Aurelius's temple apart."

"I would have heard of that," I say dryly.

My tone may be the only dry thing on the island. Waves whip up around us, pounding the shore, and it is not *my* emotions that whip them up. I slide a side look toward Okeanos, and his glowering brows knit tight together.

"You *have* heard of that," Markanos says with a rumbling laugh. "They blamed it on a storm. A very precise storm that destroyed the temple entirely."

Fine. I did hear of it, but he is wrong. It was not so precise. It leveled half the city.

"And the innocents swept up in the chaos?" I ask, but he's not listening to me.

"I'll not bother listing the Battle of the Shoal Reef, or the matter of the dispute between Heskatan and the Scarlet Ram. I'll not list for you the kings he set up and tore down, the counselors tricked or judged, their bodies washed

overboard to bloat upon the waters when they ignored his words. I will not list the nations saved and ruined, the shores pounded to nothing, the islands swallowed up, or fellow gods bowed under the power he brings to bear. I may be God of War, but my friend is God of the Sea and well does he hold his spear and trim his sail, for he reigns with strength and justice, and in the end nothing in all the world compares to the power of the deeps."

In the silence after this declaration, Oke's quiet voice sounds loud.

"The innocents haunt me still, Coralys."

Oke has eyes only for me and I shift uncomfortably at the emotion in them. I believe he is sorrowful over the loss of these people. But what good is that beside their suffering?

Markanos scoffs. "The pair of you have your sails trimmed the same, I see. Forget the past. Let us speak instead of more dire things. Treseano and his rebellion, for instance. It's clear now that he is the one who murdered El'Dorian, knowing as well as any of us that she would side with you, Okeanos. I always thought her sweet on you, Goddess of Virginity or not. Wine, Drowned Queen?"

How does everyone know that name for me?

He holds up a goblet with a single raised eyebrow, but I shake my head. One of my feet is still in the sea, poised to flee. I still do not trust that he will not catch my hand and tie me up beside my husband. I do not trust this god at all.

He shrugs and drains the goblet himself. He certainly loves to hear his own voice.

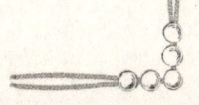

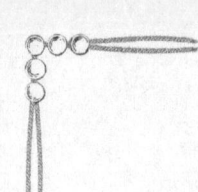

"Treseano has tied you up fairly, Okeanos, that is a certainty. I thought at first it was your woman who wove these magic knots, despite your protests to the contrary." He flicks one of Okeanos's chains and I flinch. "But if she's paying a price to keep the creatures from eating you heels-to-heart every day, then it must not be her who has affixed you so, and if not her, then it must be him."

"Did I not tell you so?" the sea god asks.

Markanos keeps talking as if he wasn't interrupted. "He'll bring you to heel to serve his rebellion one way or another. Has he sent his dog back begging yet?"

The waves calm slightly as if Oke's emotions have calmed with them.

"If you mean Aurelius," Oke says carefully, "I will not name him dog to any man, but he was here this morning demanding again my submission."

Was he, now?

"Was it not Aurelius who found my corpse with you?" Oke continues. "I think he hoped to find my pearl within it."

I will never take it in stride that he is dead but not dead, that I killed him and yet he discusses it as if it is merely misfortune as he eats and drinks from the hand of Markanos with a gouge from my spear still set into his flesh. He's shockingly alive-looking for someone who is dead, though I do see that his skin is very pale, almost grey, and his eyes are glassy in a way they were not in life.

"Then we shall both be glad there was nothing to find." Markanos grits his teeth and drags more driftwood over, throwing

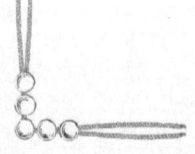

it on the fire, creating a swirling plume of sparks. They dance and extinguish just like all my plans and assumptions.

"You are friends, then?" I ask, looking from Okeanos to Markanos and back. It's an odd kind of friendship if that's what it is.

Oke nods. "Yes."

"I would not trouble myself so much as this for an enemy and there'd be a knife in the gullet at the end of the night," Markanos agrees.

"Yes, I believe that's what you threatened *me* with," I say acerbically. "Twice."

"You did murder the greatest of my friends, girl." He sits again, sprawling on a driftwood log he must have brought here himself, for it was not on the island when I arrived in the daylight.

"The only of your friends." Oke quirks a smile. How does he smile right now—even tightly, painfully? He's still chained. He's still dead.

"Greatest," Markanos corrects. "I did have Rothgar and Rethgar." For a moment his expression is haunted and then he blinks it away and is back to good humor. "Did I not just list a portion of your exploits? You forget, girl, or you never knew and you ought to know, what a powerful god you married and murdered. He's so humble he'll not tell you himself. You met him at his worst."

I look Okeanos up and down and raise a brow. Oke makes a face that suggests he wishes he could hide from my gaze but is trapped in place.

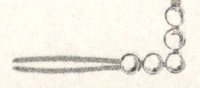

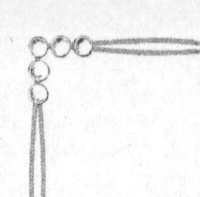

"You met him besieged by shadow enemies, outmaneuvered, unmanned..."

"I think that description suffices," Oke tries to interject.

"Outclassed and outplayed," Markanos charges onward, seemingly unaware of the tightness around Oke's mouth. "Wounded in a way bound to bring any man shame. This is not him at his best. He was...he is yet, even now that he is dead...the greatest of us, and you did a dread deed when you drove your spear through his heart."

I am still looking Oke steadily in the eye. He looks away sharply. Embarrassed. Shy. And it's that shyness that makes me believe Markanos.

"There's more to power than violent deeds, God of War," Oke says grimly.

"Well, if that is a prompting to tell your bloodstained bride of how you saved her own reign in its early days, I'm happy to oblige," Markanos says, and there is something challenging in his eyes when he looks at me. "Did you not find it odd, unworthy queen, that your nation found fish in plenty in the Blasted Year? That half the world strained under the heat of the sun that year, and they fainted and died of heat and starvation, and yet there your isles sat, in blowsy plenty, barely acknowledging the miracle of what your god did for you."

"That was you?" I ask Oke, a little breathlessly, for I remember that year well. I know how I smiled and smiled in public and fretted behind closed doors, certain the famine would take us, too, if our nets began to fail even once.

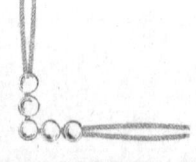

He does not look at me and that is all the answer I need.

I take a single step toward him then, and he exhales. How long was he holding his breath?

"If you are his friend, then why is he still a prisoner here?" I ask Markanos. "Are you not a god? Can you not set your will into the world and free him?"

The God of War laughs and draws a whale-bone pipe from a little leather satchel he has with him. He makes a show of packing it, tamping it, lighting it, and offering a puff to Oke before answering me.

"I could ask you the same. I *did* ask you, if you'll recall."

"When? When did you ask this?" Oke's voice is sharp, but his friend speaks right over him.

"This is not an enchantment easily untangled, paltry queen, because the power of it lies in his death. If he was not dead, he could not be held this way."

"I am yet unaware of a way to raise the dead," I say grimly, and he wiggles the fingers of his hand dismissively.

"You're new yet. New enough that your eyes are still closed and you stumble with each step. You're like as not to break your own neck as survive to grow. He won't tell me why he wed you. We don't marry as a rule. Last I heard a god had wed was well before my time. Before even Aurelius or Glorian or Heskatan, and they are the oldest of us. No one would open themselves up to the chance of such treachery. None but our hubris-bloated friend here. But it is for that reason that I'm here. I would try my hand at freeing him and I would have your help."

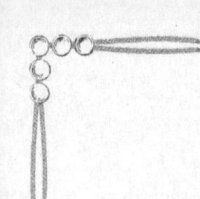

"She's already committed to helping me with my task," Okeanos says sharply. There's fear showing in how he holds his limbs so rigidly. "Nothing must take precedence over that."

"While he is bound here," Markanos says, ignoring Oke, "the rebellion grows. Those of us who do not like it are isolated and harried on every side. We need Okeanos back. When his power is full, there is none who dare defy him. I would have your help to free him from his bonds so he might stand shoulder to shoulder with us."

"The rebellion will fail," Okeanos says. "You have no need of me. But my people need their sanctuary."

Markanos growls in his throat as if they have covered this ground before and now he has lost patience. "You are too single-minded, Okeanos. Take pity on us all and have a moment's self-interest."

"Can I speak a moment with my husband?" I ask Markanos. I'm still wary of him, but I won't reject an offer of alliance.

He shrugs. "Do as you must."

But he goes nowhere, simply leans back in his seat and savors the smoke of his pipe. I must creep very close to Okeanos and squat down to speak to him privately.

"Oke," I begin, trying to compose my thoughts. He's very cold so close to me. The fire paints him with a wash of violet light, a pretense at life and health, but the Okeanos I remember warmed the bed and the air around him. This one is but a cold shell. I shiver.

"Coralys." For a moment his eyes are unguarded.

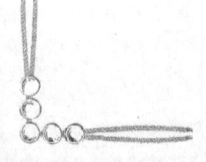

There are so many words we aren't saying. Mine are full of regret. Full of guilt. His are full of something else—something I'm terrified to name.

"Keep your promise to me," he begs.

I look away, swallowing. "One of the tasks on the list is to heal the Crown of the Sea. Who is that but you? I can keep my promise to you *and* help Markanos."

"That's a girl," Markanos says from his place on the log. I shoot him a poisoned look. He is not helping. "We don't have much time. If we're going to free this seaweed-encrusted god, then we must leave now. While our enemies are distracted. Before their plans are in place."

"If you can heal me while you attend my tasks, that is well and good, but, Coralys, I beg you," Oke says, lurching violently toward me. His restraints hold him back, but I feel his cold breath on my cheek and look directly into his green eyes. "Don't waste your time on me alone. Not as a crab. Not as a woman. Go home. Fulfill the tasks. Save our people as you said you would. Don't follow the lead of my old friend. His heart carries him down the wrong path."

I won't promise him that. How can I?

But now his eyes are frantic and my heart squeezes. How can I deny him this request when I've taken everything else from him?

I feel terribly torn. I would like to fulfill his requirements while giving him back his freedom—maybe even his life. And that could absolve me of my guilt and still save my people in the end. For surely he would do a better job of being

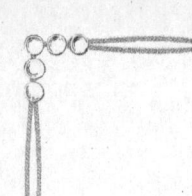

their god and lifting their Lighthouse than I would. I want both things at once.

I stand abruptly.

"We must make ready to leave, Markanos of War."

"So we must." The God of War stands, dusting off his trousers and knocking the ash from his pipe.

Okeanos spasms against his bonds, his face a rictus of pain. He barks a short, hard curse. But my back is already turned to him.

I hear a sharp inward draw of breath as he gets himself under control, speaking then in a tight tone to my back. "No matter what you feel for me—no matter what pity or regret—it cannot outweigh the needs of our people."

He's right, of course. He must be right.

I speak quickly so that I won't have to think too hard about what I am saying. "I give you my word that my primary aim will be to raise your Lighthouse, Okeanos. But I will do it my way."

"And I will help, of course," Markanos surprises me by saying.

I'm distracted for a moment by a small wave that moves up a little farther on the land than it ought to be able to go. It laps gently across my foot and then it is gone. I stare at it. I feel as if I've relived a moment of my life. My mouth is falling open and my breath draws in long and slow. Oh. Oh no.

I hear sand being kicked over the fire and then a hand is in mine before I can shake it off, and Markanos says bluntly, "We'll go to your island and make a plan before we act."

And then a sword is slashing through the air and we're both taken far from the tiny island in the middle of the sea. The last thing I hear is Okeanos's rasping breath going in and out of his ruined chest, and I wish I'd made no promise to him at all.

Chapter Twenty-Six

That wave. That single lapping wave. My mind is stuck on it.

When I had lived seventeen summers, I went out on the water in a small craft all alone but for a guard. I should not have gone out and I'd been warned many times to keep to shore unless I was well attended, but though I was princess and honored and loved, one thing I had very little of was adventure. I went out that day seeking it, and I would not even have taken Cyrus but that he found me as I was casting off and leapt aboard.

"You must not sail on your own, Princess," he'd said, and then refused to answer any other question or obey any order. He was one of my guards, well my senior, and stubborn with duty, so in the end I took him with me. It was that or not go at all, and I was desperate for a taste of freedom.

Our excursion was a beautiful hour or two of my hand alone guiding where I went, my eye alone seeking out beauty, my joy alone choosing the winds to embrace. Almost, I could forget the glowering guard in the prow of the boat, lost in the beauty of a sea and sky as blue as lapis stones and great puffing clouds of stark white. We were off Talasa, the smallest of our islands, and there were few other craft at sea. I left them all in my wake and made for open water.

And it was only when I was far enough out that no other sails were in sight and the island had grown small off to starboard, that a squall whipped up out of nowhere. It swamped our boat and flipped her over so quickly that the world became a blur of dark bubbled brine and gasping, aching lungs.

To this day I do not know how I found Cyrus under the waves or how I managed to haul his unconscious bulk up onto the hull of the boat. I must have been gifted some strength beyond that allotted to mortals. Eventually I dragged myself up, too, and lay there slung over the keel alongside him, gasping, bruised, and exhausted. He lived. He breathed. But I was the only one aware and thus the only one to know that our boat was drifting farther and farther from land.

I could have tried to swim back. I might have even made it to shore. I was young and strong and a good swimmer. I could have tried to flip the boat over and get back in. Unlikely. It was heavy and I was already worn out. Besides, either way, it meant abandoning Cyrus to death and I found that I could not abandon him to save myself.

I knew full well that I had risked too much for the sake of adventure and it was my fault alone that he lay there insensible beside me, vulnerable to the elements, and the trick of fate that brought us there. It felt like hours that I lay there, my heart pounding, breath rasping, guilt and fear tearing me apart inside.

Only that time I'd stayed with the man who was suffering because of me. I had not walked away and abandoned him to his fate.

I'd sat up on the keel of the boat, looking desperately around me, and I'd tried to paddle us to shore with my hands. I'd begged and pleaded that we would survive. I'd beat the water out of Cyrus's lungs and I'd crouched there on the hull heaving with sobs, afraid and certain we would die. But I couldn't leave him. Not when he was helpless and alone. I wouldn't. I wouldn't.

And then there'd been a little wave. A wave I'd forgotten until I'd seen it again just now. It rippled up over my foot as if asking a question, and at my muffled sob it receded, and as it left, the wind changed.

It took hours—hours of me clutching Cyrus to keep him aboard and subtly shifting my weight to keep the boat from turning and dumping us into the water—but by the time the wind and waves stopped pushing hard to shore we had reached the land, and with shaking limbs and trembling breath, we'd come ashore, for Cyrus had revived by then and, moaning, realized our near miss from the jaws of death.

They'd had a ceremony to honor him. I'd said nothing

about that and neither had he, though he met my eyes once. Behind them, he barely concealed a hint of terror that I might deny what was being said of him. That I might tell everyone the truth of what had happened. But how could I? He would not have been out there at all but for me. If he was honored as a hero now—the man who saved the reckless princess's life and brought her home again—and if I was scolded like a foolish child who nearly killed herself and another man, well, that was better than the alternative. Because I was responsible for what had happened. And if it were ever discovered that Cyrus was not the hero of the story, that he had not saved me from the waters but had needed to be saved, he would certainly be dismissed from service and I knew he had nowhere else to go.

And so I stood silent and took the judging looks and firm chastisement while they hailed Cyrus's courage. I stood in the water with the rest of them as he received his honors and his laurel and I kept my mouth sealed shut. And I could have sworn there was a little wave then, too, that washed up, curious, questing, lapping at my knees.

I'd forgotten about that wave. But it comes back now with the memories and I have to swallow hard on what it stirs up in me. I'm not making the right choice this time, am I? This time, I've left the drowning man in the water. I've left him to suffer. And he made me promise to save myself. It's all wrong.

I grit my teeth and try very hard not to think more on Cyrus and the boat and Okeanos and the island as we spin back to my home island and Markanos releases my hand.

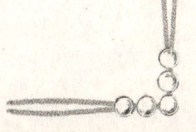

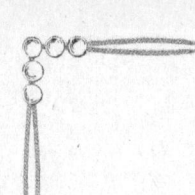

We both come out of the spin gasping in the dark of night. There is very little moon. We have returned to Oke's island. To my island.

"That's the statue of Ochum," Markanos says as we arrive. "Did Okeanos tell you the story?"

"No," I say shortly.

I want him to get to the point and take his leave. My ship has gone wildly off the course I set for it and I am anxious to find some equilibrium. My husband is not dead and he says things that make my heart race for him even while it still mourns for Lieve. I'm tangled up and confused and I've gone and made a promise to help him in his all-consuming quest. I need time to sit with that.

Markanos ignores my tone, telling his story instead. Isn't that just like gods. They always think their priorities are the only ones.

"Ithman was a king at the time, I think. Or close to. He attacks Ochum, the God of the Sea. Ambush. Fabulous fight. They wrestle in the water, thrashing, fighting. You wouldn't think you could drown a sea god, and you shouldn't be able to, but somehow he drowns him, right?"

"I thought only god weapons could kill the gods," I say.

This time his laugh sounds nasty. "Who told you that? It's an easy way to do it but not the only way. Anyway, Ithman drags his body up on shore and leaves it there while he rejoices. He's done it. He's a god. He feels the sea rushing into him from all around and he can't help himself. Raises his hands and summons all water to him. That's his downfall

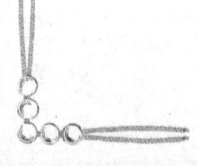

of course. It's always in that moment of victory that you can be bitten hard by fate." He pauses to laugh a moment and I frown at him. I'm not quite as amused as he is by stories of murder. "So he's rejoicing, arms high, calling all the water to him, and he calls the water right out of Ochum's lungs. The dead sea god revives. You've been around the sea enough to know that's possible, right? A man can be dead. Fully dead...and then you can bring them back. Happens sometimes with drowning. So Ochum's not dead anymore. Takes back his godhood. Great, right? I always thought so. Ithman hardly has time to blink and he's mortal again. You'd think Ochum would kill him, but he figures it's the best kind of joke. Puts Ithman in a tower prison. Can never touch the sea again. That's cruelty right there. That's revenge. Sometimes on a cold night I tell that story. Always warms the heart."

I shiver.

"Is he still there?"

"Who?"

"Ithman. Or was it just a legend?"

He laughs. "I don't actually know. Fitting, though, that we come out here and see this statue, don't you think?" He looks at me, and his features are bolder than ever in the light of the moon. "After all, you've killed Okeanos and he's not quite dead and here's a reminder that he could come back and snatch your godhood back."

"We're married," I say thickly, not certain if he's threatening me or if he considers this a joke, too.

"So you are." His eye is sharp as he looks at me. "So you

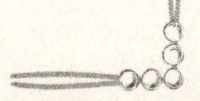

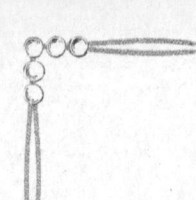

are indeed. You should guard this island better. You are ripe for an assassination attempt."

I raise an eyebrow at him. Of all the gods, he has been the most threatening to me. Who would I guard against but him?

"If they have tried to persuade Okeanos, they may try to persuade you," Markanos says coolly. "And they may do so violently. All the protections he put on this place died with him. Best be on your guard."

"I think our enemies more subtle than that," I tell him, though I am a little worried at his assessment. I have had guards to protect me all my life, but now there is only me and the sea. "Come to the cottage and we will talk. I have limited time."

To my relief, he follows me. "Limited time? Surely you jest."

"When dawn breaks, I'll be a crab again for the daylight hours. If I fail to make that bargain, then our friend will be eaten alive for yet another day."

"Forget being a crab," Markanos says as he walks. "It's a waste of time."

But I don't answer him. I simply lead him to the cottage as calmly and regally as possible. I must make this plan with him. I need a powerful ally. Markanos is my only option to fill that role.

I open the cottage, offer him a seat, and begin to brew tea.

"Let us be clear," he tells me as he sprawls on the same seat he sat on to threaten me so many mornings ago. "I do not want to play games or raise lighthouses or any other

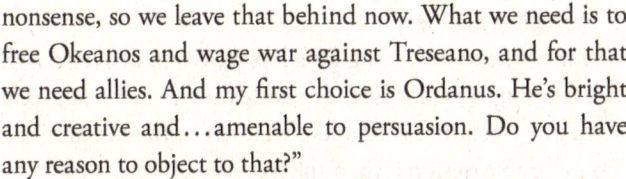

nonsense, so we leave that behind now. What we need is to free Okeanos and wage war against Treseano, and for that we need allies. And my first choice is Ordanus. He's bright and creative and…amenable to persuasion. Do you have any reason to object to that?"

"None."

I arrange a pair of cups on the table, weighing my words with care. How much should I share with him?

"We could free Okeanos *and* complete one of his tasks," I say carefully.

"I don't want to hear about his fool ambitions," Markanos says.

But they fill my mind, and for two reasons. Firstly, because I have agreed to help Okeanos raise this Lighthouse and I have never been one to go back on my word. But secondly, because I can still feel his eyes on me, still feel his longing that this be accomplished, and I can no more fail him in this than I can fail him in seeing him freed from his torture. His face fills my memory, his words my heart, and it's like I'm soaked in him and can't get dry. It's like he's seeping right into my bones. I could not be free of him now if I never saw him again. I could not be free of him if I slipped into the Nightwaters myself.

And so, as I brew our tea, and listen to Markanos try to explain why Ordanus might be a valuable ally, I am thinking of how if I were to heal Okeanos, it would also mean healing the Crown of the Sea. I'm thinking of how I can accomplish his task while making him whole.

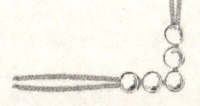

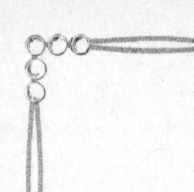

Which is madness.

I'm a wife in mourning for a lost husband. I have no right to be letting myself soften for another. And yet I am. I feel it with every breath. I soften like fruit left in the sun and I am no more able to stop it than the fruit can.

I'm still struggling over that when I surface to find Markanos is still trying to persuade me.

"Ordanus, for all his foolish-seeming ways, has ever been an untangler of what is tangled. A solver of puzzles and clever tricks. You can't love art without understanding the basis of what makes a thing beautiful and that's usually its own kind of puzzle. So we'll visit Ordanus and see if he can shed a little light on the matter of how to free Okeanos."

"Why would he?" I ask grimly, trying to return to the task at hand. "It seems to me that all the gods but Okeanos have lined up in a row against this King of Heaven. Oke has made himself their enemy by virtue of his faithfulness and none of them can stand it."

He offers me a mocking half smile. "Oke, is it? Stay your pet names. Ordanus sits on the marker post, neither jumping one way nor the other. And you're a fool to think all of them are against your husband. There are ways to oppose a thing quietly. Not everyone dramatically kills a perfectly good husband just to make a point.

"Ordanus will hear our request. Chances are, he will even help, if only to restore the balance again and stay firmly in the middle. Trust me. I have tried to take Ordanus's territory before. He is a formidable enemy. Slippery and difficult to

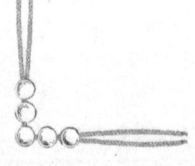

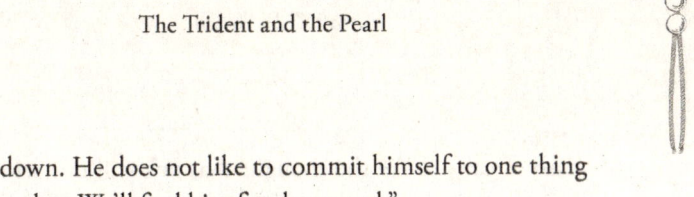

pin down. He does not like to commit himself to one thing or another. We'll find him firmly neutral."

I nod. I would never have guessed this of the God of Art. I would have expected...I don't know...dreaminess, perhaps?

"Is that your god weapon?" Markanos points to my trident as he takes a sip and I hand it to him. "Hmm. This is Vesuvius's trident. Terrible thing. I'd hate to have it score *my* flesh. I suspect there's more to it than the usual. Vesuvius was a tricksome monster when he ruled the blue, and I tremble to think what he might now be plotting in the Nightwaters. How did you come by it?"

"Okeanos has a host of strange items laid up in a storeroom."

Markanos gives me a sharp look. "And he did not warn you to stay away from them?"

"He might have," I say. What business is it of his? Besides, this trident gave me victory over the sea serpent. I will not give it up. Especially not now when I might need it.

"Well, if you took it up as your first weapon as a god, then it's yours now," Markanos says. "Let's see what we can do with it."

He has the trident cleaned and sharpened and the shaft free of burrs very quickly. I sip my tea quietly and watch. I am growing tired and my thoughts are far away.

Now that I know it was Okeanos who saw and saved me in my youth, who was there when no other was, who later knew what I had done when all else believed a different

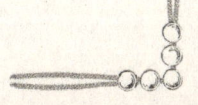

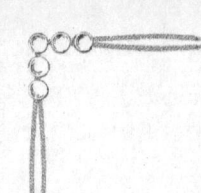

story, I can't shake the thought that he's still one with the sea, watching my actions and knowing everything that happens while he is tortured far away. Is there a way that I might watch him—watch *over* him in return?

"Have a care with this trident," Markanos says, frowning as he finishes his work. "It sings to me of a dark power. I think it could pin a thing so well in place that it could stitch a soul back into the world of the living."

"Truly?" I ask, not certain if I believe him. "How would you know?"

"I am God of War, Drowned Queen. I can feel the heart of a weapon in a way you never could. Tell me, have you used it?"

"I killed a sea serpent with it," I say uneasily as he hands it back to me. "What do you expect me to do with it now?"

"Stick it in your enemies."

A laugh gusts from me without any conscious thought. "So simple?"

"It usually is. It's only people who insist on complicating things. Death is as simple as breathing. Now. We have a plan. You have a weapon. I will return tomorrow at dusk and we will see what Ordanus might reveal to us."

"Why not now?" I ask. I'm exhausted but unwilling to let such an opportunity pass.

"Because I am tired and so are you," Markanos says with a wry twist to his lips. "Besides, war has begun on the mainland. I have prayers to attend. I'll not leave my people without my aid. Get some rest. Don't play crab all day."

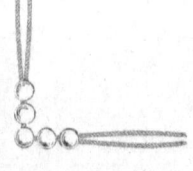

The Trident and the Pearl

And with that, he rises, slices the air with his sword, and is gone.

I follow his lead, spending the rest of the night trying to do my best to answer what small prayers I can. My people are stirred up. We've lost trading ships close to where Alexandros and Glorian fight along disputed shores, merchants far from home when hostilities broke out, and traders who thought to profit on the chaos, and there's little I can do to ease their pain except help the passage of those in flight.

When dawn rises, I am a crab again. I cannot be otherwise because far away there is an ache in the sea that I am failing to mend, and I fear that if I do not find some way to heal it, then I will lose it entirely.

Chapter Twenty-Seven

Markanos comes to collect me at dusk. I am ready for him: neat, tidy, dressed in fresh clothing, and carrying my trident as he asked.

"Let us find Ordanus," he says when he sees me standing on the shore.

The evening is cold and I have found a piece of cloth and a simple pin to wear as a chlamys over the belted tunic. My hair and the chlamys both billow in the shore wind, and it carries to me the scent of the fire he lit last night. It was still smoldering when I walked past it, turning my stomach with the twin realities that I have an enemy who wants me dead and that keeping him at bay will require violence.

"We will ask him what he knows and see if he can help us. Expect opulence and extravagance. Our brother Ordanus is not one for stark simplicity."

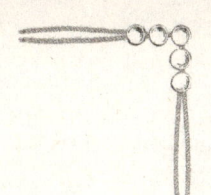

I nod. This should be easy and yet I am nervous to visit a god. I have not been to the home of one except for Okeanos.

"Follow my lead and be as silent as you can be," Markanos says, watching me with narrowed eyes as if he thinks I am about to burst forth into speech. I meet his eye steadily and he snorts before grabbing my hand and cupping it with his. He twists it as he slashes his sword.

I find it interesting that his way of shifting between planes seems to be linked to his sword slash just as mine is connected to the sea.

I have grown so used to Oke's cottage that I have almost begun to think that all the gods might live in such simple domestic circumstances. How foolish of me.

Ordanus is God of Art and Music, and when we arrive at his home, I can see he has embraced his role with his whole heart.

Ordanus's home is set along a lakeshore, and it follows the flow of the shore, hugging its curves, straightening with its sharper lines. It is sculpted from honeywood and round river stones. Flowering vines creep up the sides and hang along the edges of the roof. There are stained glass windows everywhere—whole walls of them depicting fanciful creatures of land and sea and sky locked in battle or embrace or rising in glory. Music ripples from wind chimes like none I've ever heard, filling the air as we pass. It seems to me that the very house sings to me.

Markanos is looking in every direction at once, on guard despite the pastoral setting.

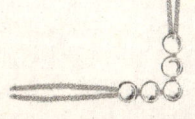

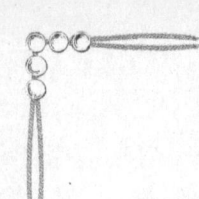

"It's oddly quiet," he says calmly.

We curve around a waterfall past a low pool of koi fish and a wall made entirely of shaped metal figures. One blows a trumpet from his place standing on the back of a lion. Another is playing drums that are giant turtles. A pair of girls play harps as they are carried on a sheet borne by a flock of birds. It's whimsical and beautiful and I could stare at it for hours.

"Where are his dancers and musicians?" Markanos murmurs. He has pitched his voice very low and he holds one palm out, pressing down in the air as if trying to keep me quiet.

I am soundless as I follow him through the door and into a vaulted cedarwood room full of gleaming instruments on stands. The smell of the place fills me with a quiet longing to hear the music play. My eyes linger on one instrument after another, each more spectacular and rare than the last.

Our footsteps are masked by carefully patterned rugs, and it's only when we've reached the other side to a room just as large but covered from floor to ceiling and then across the ceiling with paintings, that I realize it is very quiet here. For such a very large place, there are no servants. No musicians. No artists. No one at all.

I find myself copying Markanos's careful, quiet tread. We slip through the rooms like ghosts. In the distance, I hear a tinkling sound that I cannot place. It sends little shivers up my spine.

We pass through another door to a well-lit gallery with

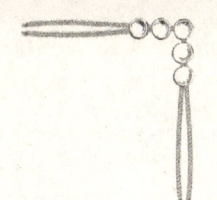

floor-to-ceiling stained glass windows in a geometric pattern. It's a pottery room. There are shelves and plinths for the pieces. Shelves that are empty.

I gasp.

Earthenware shards cover the floor and run up the sides of the room, and the items on display are not the only thing smashed. People—mortals—are dead throughout, pinned to the walls with shards of broken crockery. I don't know what killed them or who, but I know that the woman hanging on the wall nearly at the height of the ceiling was not just hovering in the air there when this happened. She is skewered to the plaster like she is a painting, too.

There is one single item untouched, the shards seeming by chance to have missed it—a clay platter on a plinth upon which is the severed head of a mortal. I recognize this horror as the slain musician Ordanus had mourned at the Resurgence. He's kept the head here like a memento.

I shudder, but what is one horror in a room of horrors? For this is not all.

In the center of the room, in a perfect circle bare of anything else—pottery, people, blood, anything—lies Ordanus.

He does not lie in a natural way. His limbs are bent wrong and so is his back. He's pinned to the ground, speared through by half of a waist-high vase, his eyes wide and terrified. His fingers scrabble across the bare rug like a pair of blanched crabs.

"Markanos," Ordanus gasps.

Oh gods, he's alive.

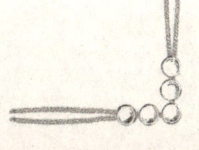

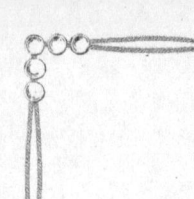

A string of bloody drool falls from the edge of his mouth and hits the perfect circle of the bare floor.

I can smell blood and offal all through the room. It's enough that I stumble and clamp my free hand over my mouth. My foot crunches on broken earthenware and I fight back sudden tears of pain as a single shard goes through my bare foot.

This has happened recently. Moments ago, if I am to judge. Some of those trickles of blood from the humans hung high on the walls have not yet dripped all the way to the floor.

But we heard no sound on our arrival and the other rooms are intact. There is some mad power at work here—something wrought by a god.

I'm shaking, terror snatching control of my limbs from me.

"Ordanus," Markanos says grimly, but there's nothing sentimental about his tone, nothing even verging on compassion. He makes a single circle around the room, peering into shadows, sword ready, as I pick the shard of pottery out of my foot and limp into the bare circle. When he's done, he seems to be entirely at his ease as he saunters over to Ordanus and squats down beside the dying god. "Who killed you, brother?"

A roar splits the air from behind us. I straighten, both hands tightening on the haft of the trident. I spin to look behind me, but there's nothing there. I turn again, searching and seeing nothing, but Markanos is faster. He must see something I do not.

He's on his feet in a moment, throwing me to the ground behind him so that I sprawl beside Ordanus, nearly brushing his cooling flesh as I pick myself up. His overlarge eyes—beautiful in life and dripping with charm—watch me from inches away and I want to vomit as I force myself to my feet again.

"Wife of Okeanos." Ordanus laughs threadily, leaking more blood. My stomach rolls over as he whispers to me, his plump lips forming each word lovingly. "Two. He has two now."

Two? What is that supposed to mean?

The sound of pottery breaking behind me fuels my rise as only terror can.

I spin around and see Markanos struck in the chest by a creature—the strange leechlike thing I saw at the Resurgence. It is formed like a tangle of black gleaming ropes that slide over one another but shaped more like an eel with a long shadow tail and a mouth that opens to show row upon row of gleaming inky teeth. The creature's flesh swells outward and then draws tight and lands another blow directly to Markanos's chest. My ally bucks hard from the hit, air knocked out of his lungs, grappling to try to keep his feet. The weight of his opponent nearly bowls him over.

It's Treseano's monster. Which means the God of Death must be here somewhere, and Ordanus said there were two. Where is the other one?

I adjust my grip on the trident, looking left and right, and then there it is, emerging from a shadow where it was

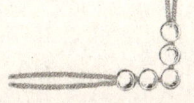

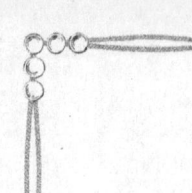

hidden. It's a second rope creature, and this one is shooting right toward me.

I'm seeing things in little bursts between heartbeats, they're happening so quickly.

Heartbeat. A shadowy figure twitches behind the roiling creature. I identify him as Treseano. He's holding an empty sack and moving quickly, sprinting in a circle around the room from shadow to shadow.

Heartbeat. This tangled rope thing is trailing from the sack as if it originated there. Its tail is nothing but black braided smoke.

Heartbeat. I anchor the trident, suck in a breath, and try to aim the tip toward the creature, but it weaves frenetically and I can't adjust the angle quick enough. I can only hope that a god weapon will be enough to turn the balance in my untrained favor.

Heartbeat. The creature twists away from the trident at the last second as if it is playing with me. Its tapering ragged tail flicks out as it flies past, sweeping my legs and sending me off-balance. I wouldn't have thought smoke could strike so hard or hurt so much. Pain sears through my vision, but I hold my trident tightly as I fall directly upon the dying god. I press up from his flesh, desperate to find my feet, horrified that I've touched him at all. I want to scream, but I don't dare waste my breath.

He meets my eye for a moment as I awkwardly stand and he laughs a bloody, gurgling laugh.

"Treseano's bag has two monsters," he whispers as if this is a joke that only this pretty god-man finds funny.

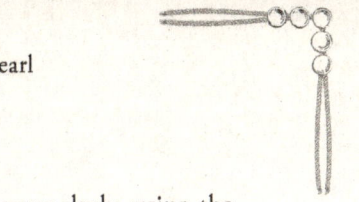

"Yes, that seems obvious now," I agree dryly, using the trident to drag me up.

I can't believe I'm talking to a dying god about this instead of... well, of his death, his hopes, his fears. It feels like eating dinner on a table with dead El'Dorian there like a macabre centerpiece. Like her, tiny golden flowers are forming and budding in the blood that drips from his lips to the floor. His laughter sprays it farther, like dandelion seeds.

He has something else jammed in his chest—some kind of dagger with a strange guard. It's in there so deeply that there's barely a fingerbreadth of hilt showing. It must be a god weapon, or how would he be dying now?

Ordanus is still talking, his words thick and slow. I don't dare linger when the creature is certainly coming back, but I can't look away from his dying words.

"What do you think he bought with the price of agreeing to carry... two of them?"

Something otherworldly screams. I wrench my gaze from Ordanus's, scanning the room for the enemy. Markanos has one creature by the throat and he's shaking it brutally. There's a bite on his arm that's flicking blood out with every shake.

I've lost track of Treseano. The other creature has turned around and launches itself at me again. I bring up the trident and try to thrust it at the inky strands. I feel it catch, but the force is more than I expected and it bowls me over, tumbling me to the ground.

My elbow crashes against the floor and my hand is

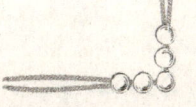

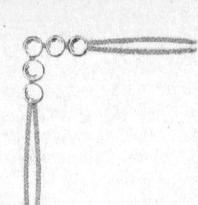

suddenly numb. The tail of the creature wraps around my torso, throttling me hard. I gasp jaggedly, my ribs creaking, my breath snatched away, panic clawing up my throat. And then I'm twisting the trident, sliding my hands down the haft so they're closer to the spear points and I can angle it to thrust into the tangle of smoky strands. I manage one strike, two, and then the creature drops me suddenly and my head smacks hard on the ground.

I rise, blinking back stars, clawing across the ground to catch up the trident again.

I am just in time to see the black...thing...cover Ordanus's face. I drag myself back to my feet, swaying hard, vision flickering with black stars, and then I draw the trident back and jam it into the shadow as hard as I can. It bunches and gleams like a leech as thick as my torso but I twist the skewer, twisting, twisting, until it shrieks, yanking itself quickly from the grip of my weapon and leaping away.

It's gone so suddenly that my trident pushes through the air where it was and clangs against the marble floor.

Ordanus's eyes are glazed with death. His mouth gapes even farther open. Repulsed, I stumble backward, my panicked breath loud in my ears.

There's a sharp curse and then Markanos is beside me, examining the dead god.

"But why kill Ordanus?" he mutters as I spin, expecting another attack, but there's no one there. Not in the room. Not on the ceiling. I'm shivering so hard that my teeth rattle, but I don't feel cold. "And why El'Dorian? Neither one

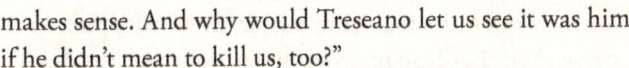

makes sense. And why would Treseano let us see it was him if he didn't mean to kill us, too?"

"Maybe he did," I say grimly. "He certainly made an effort."

"Then why not finish the job?" Markanos grumbles, shaking blood from his blade. "If he wanted us dead, *you*, at least, could be dead. Why stop now? Why gather up those two creatures instead of using them for their purpose?"

I swallow. "Ordanus didn't think he wanted to be using them. He seemed to think that carrying them was a price he was paying to create a working."

Markanos pauses, looking from the wound to me and then back again. "Well, then maybe that is why. He was killed to keep him silent on the matter. Not to hide his killer. Treseano has a secret, it would seem."

"But we know what working he has paid for," I say, suddenly uncertain. "He's paying to keep Okeanos tied to the anchor."

Markanos frowns, his eyes still glued to the dead god. "They might not know that we know that. Or—perhaps things are not what we think. Either way, another of us is dead. And in the middle of a rebellion, that's a deeply concerning thing. Ordanus might have been an ally given enough time."

"Maybe that's why they killed him, then," I suggest.

He grunts.

"Who will be God of Music now?" I ask, feeling a sudden sadness wash over me. Ordanus was never my god. But

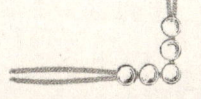

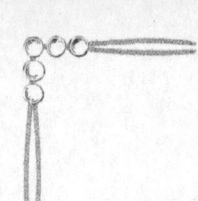

somewhere on the mainland people are worshipping in his name. And they'll go on worshipping, long past the death of the god they claimed it is for.

Markanos gives me a long look. "You can claim his lands and people if you want them. And if you love music enough. Or art."

I'm already shaking my head. My words are thick with emotions I don't want to have.

"I don't want any of this. I didn't come for any of this."

Markanos shrugs. He hardly seems to care that Ordanus is dead. It's a far cry from how torn up he was over El Dorian.

"Then the King of Heaven will call someone else to fill his place. Or it will be left abandoned. We need not trouble ourselves with it for now. We have learned what we must tonight—that Treseano is certainly the one binding Okeanos in place and that he will kill to prevent others from either revealing that or joining against his rebellion. I think our next move is clear."

"Finding a different ally," I say at the same moment that he says the opposite.

"Hunting down Treseano directly. This second creature in his sack may very well be payment to bind Okeanos—as you have suggested. It makes the most sense of what we've seen. And perhaps that first creature in the sack at the Resurgence was from the original wound to the sea god. We will confront Treseano and destroy them both."

"We?" I ask, thinking about my terrible performance in the fight we just had, but he isn't listening to me. He is lost in

thought, looking like he might just stand here in the middle of this carnage and think all night.

"We need to do something about the dead," I say. I can't stop my teeth from chattering.

"What? Oh. Yes. Them." He pauses for a moment before making a brushing-away motion with his hand. "Light the place on fire."

I stare at him, mouth open.

"We're too far away to flood it, Sea God," he says impatiently. "Just light a nice fire. There are all kinds of canvases in the next room."

"You mean the priceless paintings?" I can't help that my voice is shrill. "There's surely a better way than simply torching things all the time. Even for a God of War."

He shrugs. He's still lost in thought. I open my mouth to argue, but the smell of smoke is already in the air. It seems that Markanos is not the only one who believes that flames cover over a multitude of violences.

Nervously, I grip my trident tighter.

"Could those things kill Treseano? Those things in the bag."

I can't stop thinking of how they ripped at me. Their twisting torsos looked like braided roots mixed with shadows, but they tightened around me like snakes. I shiver at the memory.

He's distracted when he answers. "Oh no, they are there to torment him. Otherwise, how could he use them to torment others?"

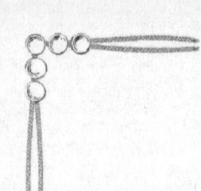

"That makes no sense." I'm out of patience. I hurry to the door, but it's closed and jammed shut. My heart begins to pound. Are we trapped? "Aren't they just two animals he somehow needs to keep alive?"

Markanos snorts. He's digging the dagger out of Ordanus's chest, an activity I don't wish to watch. I stand back, nervously watching the doors. If they so much as twitch, I'll attack.

"I wager he wishes that were so every morning, but these creatures are not his friends. He can bind them in the sack, it would seem, but they will fight him every step of the way, looking for their opportunity to tighten around him and choke his life out or fasten those maws full of teeth on his flesh and tear out a chunk. They're soul saps. They'll drain a little of his life and sense of well-being every single day until he's nothing but a twitching husk, and he must be ever vigilant that they don't do more than that. Perhaps he withdrew from this skirmish so precipitously for that very reason. I was just beginning to enjoy myself."

I shudder. "Even as part of an exchange for magic, that feels like a steep price."

I glance back to see Markanos cleaning the dagger and examining it.

"Treseano's," he says to my raised eyebrow.

"I thought he bore a mace," I reply, trying to keep my gorge down.

"A man can own more than one weapon, Drowned Queen. And of course the price is steep. If Treseano paid for something that will hurt a person day after day—as we

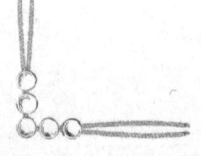

think he did—then he must pay the price of feeding these monsters a bit of his soul every day. And he must tend them faithfully or risk seeing his work undone."

"Can they be killed?"

"Anything can be killed." He winks at me. "You of all people know that. How we will kill them is another question. I've never heard tell of a soul sap dying while its victim remained alive."

"This is madness," I mutter. There's no way out of the room except through the door or out the stained glass windows. Smoke rolls in from under the door and I'm done with waiting for Markanos.

I raise my trident, breaking one of the windows, but far from letting fresh air in, the room suddenly seems smokier than ever.

Markanos seems to notice for the first time what's happening. He looks up, grabs my hand in his to form a bowl, and distractedly twists them together, and we're whirling away again without a single explanation or argument. I suppose I should be used to men just taking me wherever they please, but instead it irritates me. My lips press firmly together in censure.

When we arrive on the shore of Oke's island again, I grasp at the dock's upright and suck in huge gasps of fresh air. My lungs are hot and clogged from smoke and the smell of blood, and without another word to my so-called friend, I leap into the water, desperate to be cleaned of everything I've seen these last hours.

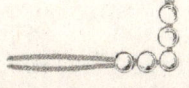

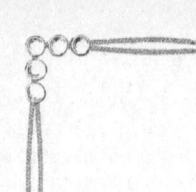

I wash myself in the sea. I wash out all the blood and dirt and soot and tears. But this time, as I plunge beneath the surf, I can feel Okeanos in the water wondering why I am smoky and smelling of blood. I can feel his confusion and then, over top of that, a deep peace as if the God of the Sea himself is trying to calm me.

I do not want to be calm. I do not want to be told how to feel.

I clamber out of the water.

Markanos stands there looking grim. "You'll need sleep if you're planning to be a crab all day. Get that done now and be ready for me at dusk tomorrow. Together, we'll hunt Treseano and his creatures. You're not much in a fight, but you're still God of the Sea. Let us accomplish this task, free Okeanos, and then I can fight the bigger war we're in with my friend instead of his useless wife."

I'm so stunned that I have nothing to say. He wants me to work with him after insulting me and ordering me about. Typical. He starts to swipe his sword and then stops.

"I'm angry about Ordanus. He wasn't a friend, but he's been a god nearly as long as me. I don't like changes." He glares at me—a change—as if he'd like to wipe me out, too.

"Fear not," I say grimly. "I'll just be here doing useless things until you return to kill more gods."

What else does he want me to say? It must be exactly that, because he snorts, slices the air with his sword, and is gone.

I don't even go up to the cottage to sleep. I just collapse on the beach, and the tide must rise farther than I expect,

The Trident and the Pearl

because I dream of Oke in the sea trying to comfort me as I cry. But when I wake up, it is not his arms trying to wrap around me but rather the swirl of the waves reaching, reaching forever for the shore.

The first ray of dawn spills golden across the water's surface and I just have time to gasp before I have six more legs and the sand is suddenly very close and the sea very deep.

Chapter Twenty-Eight

My body needs very little now that I am a god—not food, though it enjoys eating; not as much rest, though I am feeling worn and wrung out. When I shudder back into a human body, the light is fading from the sky. Any moment now, Markanos will be here wanting to hunt Treseano with me. Any moment now, the madness will begin again.

Time spent as a crab is a strangely thoughtless time focused solely on eating and moving, on avoiding danger and dancing from shadow to shadow. I do not think when I am in this state as I do when I am a woman...or a god. But the moment my mind is my own again I am flooded with all the thoughts I might have had when I was not myself.

Primary among them is this: In the Crocus Isles, everything we do of importance is done in the sea. And Okeanos

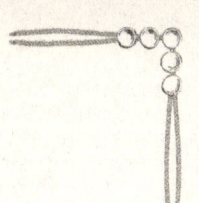

is the sea. How much of my life did he know before he ever met me?

But more than that, I am growing worried, for if I am the sea and he is the sea, together, the sea is half-dead. I do not want that half—whatever it is—to be lost to us entirely. The death of Ordanus shook me more than I expected. I am still trembling with it, still reliving the moments he whispered to me as around him all the mortals he loved died. If such a thing was done to him at his full power and in the safety of his refuge, then what might be happening to Okeanos while I am away?

I look at the fading sun and grimace. I do not have the time to go and check on his welfare, and yet I do not have the heart not to do it. Markanos can wait a few minutes. Just a few.

I dress quickly and then race up to the cottage to gather a lantern, knife, and flint. At the last moment, I fill a flask with fresh water, too. When I'm satisfied that I have all I need, I fly back down the steps, barely paying attention to what is happening around me, hit the water with a splash, and twist my hand as I'm moving.

It's as natural as breathing to me to move in this way, now. I almost don't feel nauseated when I land on his shore and find Okeanos there, limned in the light of the rising moon.

I can just pick him out as I bend to light the lantern.

"Coralys." His voice is rough, parched. I'm glad I brought the water.

The moment the lantern is lit I lift it and I gasp. My

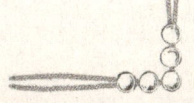

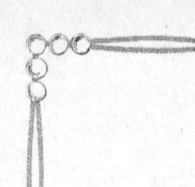

husband is not alone. There are two corpses, one on either side of him, and their blood is smeared across the rocks surrounding him, seaweed tangled around one man's leg and another strand of it clutched in the other man's hands. There's a sword flung to one side, but it is the only weapon I see.

"You've been busy," I say calmly, lifting the lantern higher and checking around the anchor with my heart in my throat. "How did you kill these men? You are chained here."

"My legs are free."

I don't know whether to laugh or cry.

"There are no more," he assures me, and I hurry to his side, setting the lantern down and bringing him water. He drinks deeply from the skin I hold to his lips, and when he is done, he sighs. "Are you well?"

"Am *I* well?" I ask in a slightly caustic tone. "I am not the one surrounded by corpses." I pause, thinking of yesterday, and amend my statement. "At the moment, at least. Who are these who attacked you?"

He makes a movement that might have been a shrug if his hands were not pinned above him. He's beautiful in the moonlight. The stark contrast makes the line of his neck and jaw strong and masculine. It highlights every swell and dip of his flesh.

I swallow. I have always considered myself an unflappable woman, calm and cool in a crisis, but all this is growing to be too much.

"They attacked you...here...while you were helpless?"

"It's the best time to attack," Oke says calmly. "When your enemy is helpless."

"And these are your enemies?" I am stalling for time. I do not know how to respond to this. Hysterics seem like a bad idea even though they keep suggesting themselves to me.

"Generally those who try to kill you are considered enemies, yes. These ones, I think, were merely sent to see that I was still chained and report back to their master. Unfortunately, ambition is never far from any man's heart and they hoped to do better than merely observe me." He sounds very tired. "What are you doing here, Coralys?"

"I was worried someone might try to harm you," I say in a small voice. My eyes are back on the dead. They wear dark clothing. Nothing distinguishable. Neither has a belt pouch. There is no boat here. One is fairer-skinned than the other. Beyond that, they are both so average in looks I would struggle to find them in a crowd. "It seems I had every right to be concerned."

"You are worried for me?" He says it like it is a joke and my eyes snap up to his. They are so very green in the dancing light of the lantern. The warmth of the light adds a flush to his skin, shades the hollow of his throat, dances over the spill of his hair across one cheek.

"They could have killed you."

He shakes his head minutely like this isn't important. How powerful was he in life that he thinks killing two men while dead and trapped is hardly worth acknowledging?

"They're mortals. It was cruel to send them against me. I

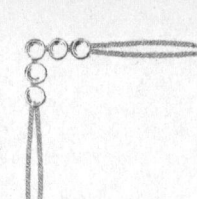

was God of the Sea a long time, Coralys. Why do you think my captor pinned me here and fled? Why is he not here gloating when you come to see me? He fears me still."

"What would these two have done to you if you had not killed them?" I ask, concern making me frown. "Can mortals truly hurt a dead god?"

"They could do all the vicious things beasts do to a man when he is vulnerable to their knives. My enemy does not like to be thwarted and this was simply a message." He is very calm. "Which reminds me, you took my torture yesterday. I asked you not to do that."

I have always hidden emotion in action. I do not like facing the idea that I might not want this man dead—that I might need him to be alive—and so I busy myself with dragging the corpses away and throwing them into the sea. I cannot leave them to rot beside him.

I speak as I work, not looking at him. "You were there. The day I was seventeen and my boat was swamped and I had to pull my guard from the sea. You were there, weren't you?"

He sighs. "By now, you must know what it is to be the sea."

"You were there," I say firmly. "You pushed my boat back to shore."

But though my words dwell on this one incident, my mind is spooling out and showing me others. The time my negotiations with the Andalappo Isles were going poorly and the waves kicked up at just the right moment that I could

remind their king that we were the heart of the sea and that they needed us for trade and so we forged that alliance—the most important one of my reign, and it couldn't have happened without that.

The time the Spice Coast sent pirates running through our waters. They kept disappearing before they could destroy our ships. I had thought I was so clever when I identified them as ships of the Spice Coast navy and not pirates at all. A wave had rocked one suddenly as I was watching, revealing a bit of the paint beneath the waterline of their ships. I'd known immediately what I was seeing. And I'd thought it was my bravery and cleverness that landed me on the deck of their "captain" Hoffness's ship. I negotiated his surrender with the promise of an alliance and a reminder that we were protected by the God of the Sea.

Now, I know Okeanos orchestrated that.

All the successes of my reign are playing out in my mind in little bursts, little flashes of memory, but I'm seeing them through a new lens and they sting. He was there for every one. He's been there watching and pushing. I would not have been the queen I was without such influence.

I'm breathless by the time the second corpse falls into the water, and I want to pretend it is from dragging the bodies, but of course it's not.

It's only when they've both slipped beneath the sea that I realize he hasn't answered my question.

"It was you," I say firmly, refusing to let him avoid this question. "You who pushed my boat back to shore."

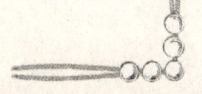

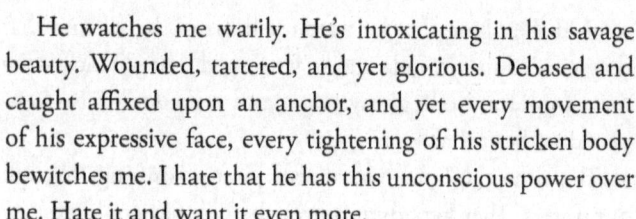

He watches me warily. He's intoxicating in his savage beauty. Wounded, tattered, and yet glorious. Debased and caught affixed upon an anchor, and yet every movement of his expressive face, every tightening of his stricken body bewitches me. I hate that he has this unconscious power over me. Hate it and want it even more.

"Whatever you think of me, surely you must agree that I am not the kind of monster who would glory in the death of a young woman fighting to keep another alive."

I am not wrong. He was there. Which means he was there for all the other times, too.

I feel the blood drain from my face and I straighten, staring into his eyes as if there might be an answer there.

"Why did you let him get the credit for your act of courage?" he asks me.

"He would have been dismissed. Or worse. The people loved me. If they thought he'd endangered their princess..."

I let my words trail off.

"You were always one to let others take the credit, but your actions were forever for them," he says. "When you tricked that pirate ship into a negotiation, for instance. That was all your guidance, but you let your advisor take the credit. He was honored in a ceremony in my sea. I remember this."

I can't stop staring at him. He's admitting aloud what I just realized is true. That he has known me all my life and I had no idea. That he has meddled in my life for reasons of his own. Even if they are benign, I feel suddenly vulnerable and afraid.

"You've known me all this time." It is hard to keep my voice from trembling. I don't take the step backward deliberately, but I take it. "You've been watching me all this time. Should I not be wary of this?"

His thick brows knit together, and his words come out harsh, almost derisive. "You can see a drifting woman about to be dragged off to die in the sea and you can help her without some sordid ulterior motive, Coralys. What are you suggesting? That I, who could have any mortal woman I wished for, was pining for a woman married to another?"

"I wasn't married then," I say, and my words half break in the speaking, but he speaks right over me.

"That I couldn't see a piece of myself in the heart of someone else without being overcome with the need to put a piece of myself in them more literally?"

I flush. I had, indeed, feared it was something like that.

"You do me an injustice," he says, and his eyes cut away and it is like a cut to my flesh. "And you accredit a very large worth to yourself."

I gasp, stung, but I have to know. I have to. I can't leave it like this.

And so, in a trembling voice, I force the words out.

"Were you there for all of it? Did you help me with every triumph I had as queen? Were none of them entirely my own?"

He does not reply, but his broad shoulders hunch forward a little, pulling against his bonds, and his muscles tighten, flexing everything from his rigid, powerful neck down across

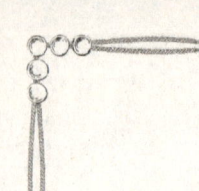

his ruined chest and along the trail of his midline to where the sight of him is lost beneath the surf. It is as if my words have been like the shock of an eel and the mere flesh and muscle of his body—perfect though it is—cannot bear up against them.

"Could I have done any of it without your aid?"

He still will not look at me, but he whispers, "You were an excellent queen, Coralys of the Crocus Isles. Your people could not have asked for better."

I feel my cheeks grow hot, for even as an excellent queen I required help. I am choking on these revelations. They do not go down easily.

I try to put my own self aside and think clearly, but it is so very hard to do. I am still aching from the harshness of this knowledge.

I must not lose Okeanos. Now more than ever, I am certain that all will be lost if he sinks beneath the waves of death. For who will save our people then? If I needed his help when I was queen, how much more so now that I am a god?

I bite my tongue and he, too, says nothing more. But I am not content to leave it so.

There is too much between this god-man and I. And I know, as I know my own soul, that we two are too much like a matched set of lodestones. We cannot dwell in peace side by side with nothing between us but friendship or common task. We cannot even live as a peaceful pair like Lieve and I did with our shared understanding and mutual support

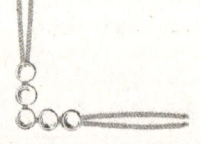

bearing us through many years. We two are not meant for such gentle dealings.

He must either be my greatest adversary or the dearly desired of my soul, and I have already tried the path of murder.

I will not take that path again.

But neither can I walk away. Neither can I abandon him here to his suffering knowing nothing of the turbulence raging in my soul, for I know what I am about to do is a betrayal of everything—of who I was and what I stood for, of my husband who never was anything but good to me, of my own actions just months ago. And yet I must seal this commitment as surely as the sun must rise in the morning.

I study him, biting my lip, letting my eyes linger for just a moment on the firm lines and tempting softness of his flesh. It's torn and abused and yet somehow that very ugliness makes all the rest of him that much more decadent. I swallow, my throat thick with desire, badly wanting to taste the sea along the lines the moon has suggested to me with her flagrant silver outlines.

I do not know if I am furious with him, or if I want to sink my whole self into his embrace. And I am unsettled by my own indecision. I am naked and vulnerable at this revelation, that I want to hide from eyes that see too much, that I want to exact justice for his meddling.

And yet.

I have never been a passive woman. I am not one now. The moment his throat bobs teasingly and his brow peaks

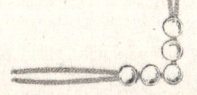

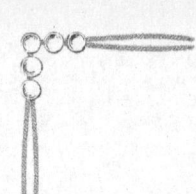

upward in a question, or perhaps a provocation, it is too much for me.

I stride toward him, sink to my knees at his side, take his glorious cold face forcefully between my hands, and with all my boldness brought to bear I set my lips to his. It starts like defiance, like a statement that he does not get to make all the decisions. But it is not defiant for long, for he meets me with unwarranted tenderness, and under his ardor I melt. My lips slide open, a tiny surrender, and I curve one possessive leg over his waist, straddling him.

For a moment my cheeks are hot with my boldness, my audacity shifts into uncertainty. I am almost resolved to draw back again, but just before I pull away, I feel him meet me, opening his mouth to me and making a subtle sound in the back of his throat. His kiss is forceful as if he is meeting my audacity with his own, wanting as I want, taking as I take, reverencing me just as I worship him.

He still tastes like a god, though I have stolen that from him forever. Though he is cold with death he is alive to my touch. My thumbs caress his cheekbones, his chin, his jaw. One of my hands slides down his neck and twists into his hair, and his shiver feels like my own joy.

And it is too much. It is too much for any mortal. It's too much for me as a god. I'm shaking with conflicting emotions like a ship torn between wind and surf. I draw back with a gasp and his low moan bites into me like an accusation. What have I done? I have no right.

I untangle myself from him, stumble backward, and land

clumsily on the rock. I have yet to draw a breath. The air feels stuck in my chest.

"Coralys." My name is a whisper on his lips, and I see by the look in his eye that he wishes he could reach for me, chase after me, sweep me back into his embrace, and I'm undone.

I bite back a sob of guilt and desire all tangled into a poison draft and force myself to take another step backward and into the sea.

"Cora." This time it is a plea. And I do not know if he is pleading with me to stay or to go, to take him or to leave him alone.

I do not know. And I cannot ask. Not now.

I turn quickly so I do not need to be burned by his molten gaze, and I leave him alone on the rocks, slip into the sea, and I flee. And it's only when I am miles and miles and miles away from the booming silence of all he hasn't said that I can breathe again.

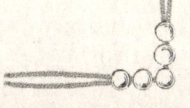

Chapter Twenty-Nine

I overshoot the dock and end up on a part of the island I've never visited. It's a lonely spot, not in the sea exactly, but hidden in a crevice between two rocks where ocean water laps in through a crack. I'm heaving with emotion, so tangled up in my mind that I can't tell up from down, and for a moment, I fear I'm not on our island at all, but when I hold my lantern up, I nearly scream at the visage before me.

It's Vesuvius. In statue form.

As a statue, he has all eight legs. Two of them pin a man in place while two more tear a woman in half. On all this island, none of the other statues are so grotesque. It is most certainly his face on the figure, but his usual cunning mockery is highlighted in such a way as to make it twist into both genius and cruelty and his handsome face is stark and bleak. The sculptor of this piece is an artist who ought to be revered. Every nuance of terror and horror show in Vesuvius's victims' faces and the white marble fingers curl precisely as the hands of a man would, dimpling the woman's thigh in a way so realistic that I can almost hear her screams.

I lift the lantern higher, anything to block out how my body still tingles from head to foot from that bold embrace, how my heart is racing, how I wish I had the courage to turn around and go back and do it again.

The golden glow bathes the statue and picks out details I had not seen before—the waves frothing up around the figures, foaming, formed with such care that they almost seem to move in the flickering of the lantern light.

My tongue cleaves to the roof of my mouth as I study it intently. I reach out and run my fingers over the ragged edges of the waves. I know as certainly as if he had admitted it to me himself that this is the creation of Okeanos. No one alive could hate Vesuvius as the artist of this statue did. I recall Okeanos's words to me: "Is that an honor, do you think? For a god to pay such special attention to your humiliation?"

And in my heart what I feel for the former sea god crystallizes into something like its own kind of hate. The gut-level revulsion of knowing that someone has been cruel to one you would be tender toward.

I can hear his every whispered word as I look at the shadows dancing across his face. Would I have believed Okeanos's explanation at the Resurgence if it had only been him and me in our bedroom together and not Vesuvius, too, whispering to me that my husband was speaking lies?

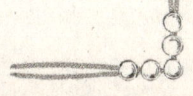

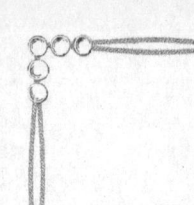

I do not know, but I find I am shaking off the last vestiges of my stolen kiss. Instead, I am trembling as I look upon Vesuvius. Perhaps I am furious with myself. Perhaps I am guilty and frustrated, I do not know, but I pick up a rock and fling it at the statue with a roar.

It falls to the ground without so much as chipping the marble and splits into two chunks when a voice behind me says, "You would have had to make one for Okeanos if he were properly dead. I wonder what you would have made for him. Would you have shown his honor and strength? Or would you have been blinded by hatred?"

Of course it is Markanos, god of self-righteousness. The swirling winds take the edges of his hair and cloak and ripple them as if the air itself would toy with him. I manage to calm my breathing enough to answer, but my cheeks are hot, my emotions more tangled than rope all thrown together in one barrel.

"Do you think Okeanos is blinded by hatred of his predecessor? I do not. The mood of this statue seems clear to me. And accurate."

Markanos shrugs.

"How did you become friends with the God of the Sea?" I ask him. I've wondered all along.

"With Okeanos?" He lifts a brow before coming over to the statue. "A wrestling match. He beat me. It was a fine display and one of the fiercest of my life. I keep telling you that you're not seeing him at his best. Brought low by a woman. It happens."

I do not give any credence to his words. But despite his arrogance, I am still determined to work with him. Tonight, we hunt Treseano and hopefully destroy the monsters he carries, free Okeanos, and at the same time heal the Crown of the Sea—fulfilling one of Okeanos's ten impossible tasks.

I pull myself together and employ my most imperious tone. "How did you find me here?"

Markanos barks a laugh. Everything he does is writ large. He's speaking to me, but he's handling the statue, tracing the perfect lines with his blunt fingers as if he can appreciate it better by touch than by sight. I get the feeling he's that kind of a person—hands-on, unable to simply watch a thing without diving in himself. Perhaps that is why he is friends with Okeanos. Perhaps he was not content to watch the man storm through time and history without involving himself in the story.

"You did something violent. Threw a rock, perhaps, or smashed something. Violence draws me like a moth to flame. I could feel you out here, though I'm surprised you weren't on the dock to meet me. I was waiting there as we agreed." His tone changes as his palm skims over the end of one of Vesuvius's tentacles. "I must say, I had no idea Okeanos was such an artist. Perhaps it is Ordanus who should have befriended him and not I."

"Rather too late for that, I think," I say tightly. I can't blink away the deluge of memories at the name of the God of Art. I dare not dwell on them, or I will be sick again and lose my nerve for what comes next.

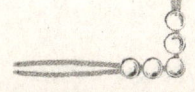

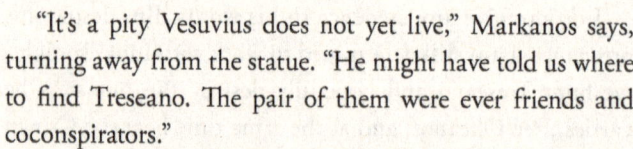

"It's a pity Vesuvius does not yet live," Markanos says, turning away from the statue. "He might have told us where to find Treseano. The pair of them were ever friends and coconspirators."

"Are we still going to look for him, then?" I ask, not meeting his gaze. I want to find Treseano, don't I? I want to free Okeanos and heal his wound and get us that much closer to raising his refuge. And yet I'm afraid of it, too. What might a free Oke do to me if one in bondage drives me to such madness?

Markanos shrugs. "Of course. I don't know how we'll find him, but it hardly matters. We'll search. And eventually we'll discover him."

I give him a look of disgust. No planning. No foresight. Typical. But then, I've planned nothing, either. Instead, I spent the time I should have been doing that chasing down a man who had no right to be watching me all these years and then succumbing to passion for him. I can hardly blame Markanos when I am such a mess.

I set down the lantern, lean my trident against the statue, and reach into the pouch at my side to draw out the black pearl. If Vesuvius knows where Treseano might wait, then Vesuvius will tell us. And that will be an end of his value to me.

It doesn't take much to work up tears to spill on the pearl. Just thinking of what Lieve would think if he'd seen what I'd done—especially if he knew all the torrid thoughts that accompanied my kiss, the heightened thirst that fills me even now—is enough to make them flow freely. I am deeply ashamed.

Markanos watches me, seeming to be amused. He won't

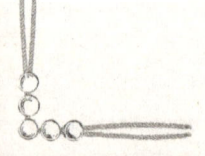

see the dead god, of course, so I look like a madwoman. But maybe he knows what I am doing, because he allows it, lounging against the statue of the screaming woman. I feel my cheeks grow hot, but there's no time for quibbling.

"Vesuvius," I say as the dead god appears to me.

Out of the corner of my eye, I see the war god raise an eyebrow.

Vesuvius's spirit face matches his statue. In the flickering light of the lantern, both carry the exact same mockery, but when his gaze finds the marble image of himself, his expression is transformed to one of singular delight.

"I've never seen it before," he says, and sounds a little breathless. "Who would have thought Okeanos had it in him to honor me thus?"

He sounds very pleased for someone who has clearly been set in memory for all time as a vicious torturer, and hidden in a crevice besides, so that only the most persistent—or someone like me who came here by accident—will ever see it.

Casually, Markanos picks up my trident and spins it in his hands. He can't see Vesuvius—but he can hear me talking to the former sea god and he is not looking at me as if I am mad. He seems more interested in swishing the weapon through the air as if testing its balance.

"You cannot keep calling me up from the grave as if I were your cupbearer," Vesuvius says in a silky manner that tells me this is merely the beginning of a negotiation.

"You were friends with Treseano, God of Treachery and Death. Or so Markanos keeps telling me."

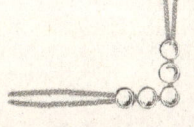

"Fitting, don't you think?" Vesuvius asks, skittering over the rock to get closer to his own statue. He runs a hand over the man carved forever in a pose of agony within the grasp of his stone tentacles and he smiles.

"We would like to know where he might go if he were hiding something."

Vesuvius looks back and forth between Markanos and me.

"We, is it? You move very quickly, Drowned Queen. Two dead husbands and already another one on the way. I commend you. Can I assume you have already looked at Treseano's home? Knocked on the door? Invited yourselves in? No?" He looks at me wide-eyed. "Maybe try those things first."

"We already found him at Ordanus's house. Where that god lay dying."

Vesuvius goes very still.

"So we can only assume he will not make himself so easy a target."

Vesuvius waves a tentacle idly, first as a gesture, but then he seems fascinated by it, and he twists it back and forth to admire.

"And yet you are here. At your home. Admiring my form set into the rock. Gods are arrogant people. They like to be where they can be found."

I turn to Markanos. "He says to look at Treseano's home."

Markanos flicks one of the points of the trident. "What do you think I was doing all day while you were playing crustacean?"

Vesuvius turns at that and regards me through narrowed

eyes. "Crustacean? Such a hard creature for such a well-rotted heart to dwell in. Tell me, Coralys, God of the Sea. What would tempt you to such a course?"

I clench my jaw. I will tell him nothing more than I must.

"Tell him to tell us where Treseano hides," Markanos breaks in. He is still unconcerned that I am having a conversation with a dead god he cannot see. "He will know. The pair of them were hand in glove a few centuries ago."

Vesuvius leans in close so that his lips nearly touch Markanos's cheek, and he whispers, "I could touch him and he'd never know. I adore that kind of power."

I roll my eyes. We both know he cannot. His threat is empty.

Markanos's jaw clenches as if he suspects exactly what is happening right now. His hands grip the trident a little tighter.

"Just tell us, Vesuvius," I say.

"I don't think I will. There's nothing I want that you can trade for that information."

He's just starting to smile when Markanos moves so quickly that I'm still sucking in a surprised breath when he's finished. He pivots sharply to his left, arms arcing perfectly, my trident an extension of them, and in a very neat spin and strike he's pinned Vesuvius to his own statue with the trident.

Vesuvius's cry is more surprise than pain, but even so he's stuck in place, thrashing on the end of the trident's barbs.

My breath hitches with surprise.

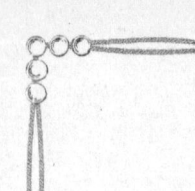

Markanos is breathing a little quickly, but I don't think it's from exertion.

"Got you, squid," he says with the manner of a man trying to exert strict control over himself.

"I did not think spirits could be affected physically." I'm struggling not to sound breathless.

Vesuvius has frozen in place, his eyes narrowed as they flick from Markanos to me and then back.

"By a normal weapon, no, but this trident belonged to Vesuvius himself and it had a storied reputation. I told you before: It was said he could pin the souls of the dead to the mortal plane."

"How charming," I say stiffly.

"It really was. I was the toast of the night at dinner parties," Vesuvius says, but his voice is tight. I do not know if it is tight with pain—for can a spirit experience pain?—or simply with fear of what Markanos might do next, for the God of War is no longer blind to him. I see it in the sparkle of Markanos's eye.

Vesuvius cannot escape his weapon. He thrashes hard against it and the trident shudders, making a small snapping sound. It doesn't matter. The dead god is still pinned in place.

"I think you'd better tell Markanos what he needs to know." My tone is grim. I feel that is justified.

Vesuvius waits a beat, looking through slitted eyes at both me and Markanos, but I know he'll find no softening here, and eventually he seems to realize that, too.

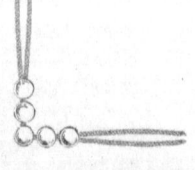

"Do you remember the plane where the Resurgence took place?" He directs his comment to me with an innocent look in his widening eyes. "The one where you chose to become a murderer?" My belly flips guiltily at those words. "I am very proud of you for that, by the way."

"Get on with it," I murmur, and Markanos, taking that as a cue, twists the trident.

Vesuvius flinches and his voice sounds strained. "That's where he'll be. He likes how malleable it is there. And how impossible it is for mortals to survive long without direct sponsorship from a god. The combination appeals to him when he is in distress."

"You brought *me* there when I was still mortal," I say without inflection. "And no god was watching over me until Okeanos arrived."

"Yes." He smiles and I could almost swear there's blood in his mouth, staining his teeth. "Wasn't that fun?"

"The Resurgence?" Markanos asks. "I suppose that makes an odd kind of sense."

"What if he's lying to us?" I ask Markanos.

The God of War shrugs. "What if he is? We'll try somewhere else tomorrow. We're gods. To us the centuries are as days."

He pulls the trident out of Vesuvius with a tug. Hurriedly, I wipe my tears from the pearl. The last thing I want is an angry Vesuvius near me. I hope those wounds don't last in him forever, but given the wound in Oke's chest, I feel like such a hope might be only a salve to my own conscience.

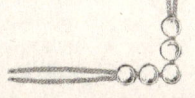

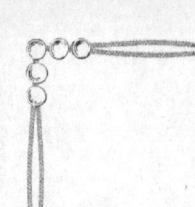

Vesuvius meets my eyes, panting and tense. I wipe the pearl on my clothing again, hoping to dismiss his spirit now that the trident is out of him. Perhaps I am too damp, or I'm missing a droplet of water, because he is still here, staring at me.

His eyebrows lift. "Is that a portent in the sky, God of War?"

Markanos turns to look, and I shove the pearl into my belt pouch instead—best to be thorough—and when I look up Vesuvius is gone as he should be.

How very odd.

"Just a Hunter's Moon," Markanos says as he turns back. He jams the trident into my empty hands. One of the prongs is broken off, a finger's width of metal missing. It looks like the jagged edge of a broken tooth.

Markanos clears his throat.

"I'll shift us to Treseano," he says firmly, and before I have time to protest that I'm not ready, he's taking my hand again, forming a bowl, and slashing his sword through the air.

Chapter Thirty

I am not overly fond of Okeanos's friend and his overbearing demeanor, but I will say this for him as an ally—he does not treat me as disposable. Before I'm even blinking back to awareness on this new plane, he's already sprung in front of me, sword drawn in a defensive posture.

"First we'll try where Treseano stays when he is here," Markanos says, already moving.

We've arrived under his statue in the common area of the stark white island. There is no table and no dead goddess displayed this time, and yet I'm just as tense.

Water still trickles from the mouths of the towering statues. This time, I look and confirm that Ordanus's mouth is as dry as El'Dorian's. Who will they be replaced by and how soon? I can't help but look over at the statue of Okeanos. I had stood under its shadow last time and I had not had the chance to properly appreciate it, but here it is in all its glory, and I'm struck again by his beauty and power and otherworldliness and the horror that I tried to shatter all that. There is no image of me beside him and his fountain still dribbles out a finger-thick runnel. I do not know what to make of that.

"So the gods have assigned places here, then?" I ask, trying to steady myself by focusing on the task at hand.

"Of course. We must sleep one night here every epoch. We've each staked out a place of our own. Did you not sleep here in Okeanos's bed?" He makes a solid point. "And people—even gods—like familiarity. Especially here, where we're disconnected from the world beyond. Fortunately, there are few places to hide here."

He gives me a weighted look at that and I return it.

I follow him out across the stone bridge that curves like a rib. Last time I was here, the sun was setting, painting this white bridge in soft color, but now it is fully dark and only the illumination of the faraway lanterns lights our path. I grit my teeth and place my feet with care. Though there is water nearby, I can't seem to properly feel the sea. It's as if it is a very long way away even though it ought to be right here. I can feel the echo of it, but it is like a memory of a friend long passed to the Nightwaters.

Okeanos used the power of the sea to fight when he was here, but I am not certain that it will be available to me. It seems too far away.

I take in a long breath to steady myself. There is no room

for anything less than courage. I have already lost everything. I have already gambled my life and soul. What is one more venture to forward my goal? I reach for the tide, feel it reach back, and I allow myself a very slight smile. Well and good. I hold my trident in both hands as Markanos keeps talking, not even noticing my battle and triumph over the tide.

"That's why he'll be on his island here. People seek the comfort of familiarity. They can't help it. It's instinctual. A smart man might think he'd choose to hide on my island or yours, but he'll hide on his own. It's his. Familiar. Right."

"I don't understand why he's here at all," I grumble. "Isn't he leading a rebellion? If he was not at home, then it makes more sense that he would be with an ally."

"The gods are not so friendly as that, Wife of Okeanos." Markanos laughs. "Offering succor to another god would be like taking a serpent to the breast. It will not end well. And even if that were not the case, he would still be here. Why go to all the trouble of luring us out just to hide when we fall into his hands?"

He helps me over a part of the rib that is tricky to navigate both because of its slick surface and strange curvature. I offer him a wry smile of gratitude.

"I don't see how you think he lured us here. We are hunting *him*," I say.

He raises an eyebrow. "Of course he's luring us. That's what the attack was—in part, at least. I don't think he would have cried if it succeeded, but he had to have guessed it might fail. My prowess in battle is well known, as is my thirst for

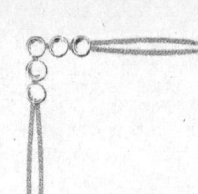

action. He is certainly luring me out to ground he is more familiar with so that he might strike when he is most likely to win."

"And is he most likely to win here?" I can't keep the dryness from my tone.

"No one is likely to win if they oppose me." He seems very sanguine for someone who believes he is walking into a trap.

"I would think he would have lured you to his home, then," I say.

Markanos grunts. I shoot him a sideways glance. He has no answer for that, and for some reason it makes the hairs on the back of my neck stand up. Something is not quite right here.

"And what do you expect me to do when we find him?" I ask, feigning diffidence. I haven't told him that I don't know how to fight. I would have assumed he could already tell by looking at me and seeing my performance so far.

"What I expect from you," Markanos says, still leading the way, "is for you to provoke just one of those creatures. You don't have to kill it. Keep it distracted long enough for me to sort out the other one and engage Treseano in battle."

"And how will I keep its eye on me?" I ask tightly.

"Don't die too quickly."

That seems to be all he has to share and I'm almost grateful. It's hard enough to hold on to my nerve without too many instructions distracting me.

We have crossed the rib and are on the other side where

the islands hang cloaked in mist and lit by their elaborate hanging lanterns. I watch the cloaked heaviness with wary eyes, feeling that at any moment one of those terrible black creatures might shoot out of the mist and wrap me in its sinuous body. I can still feel the bruises where it squeezed me yesterday and I taste acid in my mouth at the memory of it.

"Tuck in behind me," Markanos growls to me. "My job is to look ahead for a sign of the enemy. Your job is to scan the islands as we pass and to keep an eye behind us. We'll aim straight for Treseano's island, but it is grouped among those farthest from here."

"My job sounds a lot harder to manage," I say, trying to look everywhere at once.

"Do you think so? If you'd been with me when we took Grentale Castle, you wouldn't be saying that. The first vanguard caught an arrow in the eye. The second was done in by boiling oil through a murder hole. Didn't hit him head-on, just splashed. Terrible way to die. I can hear his screams still if I try to recall it and it was nigh on a thousand years before now. Third man took a blade to the gullet. That was Brennicus, my best friend, a wrestler."

"A wrestler?"

"Mmm." He sounds lost in thought. "It was he who found me a place in the army. I carry his dagger yet." He pats his hip. "I was fourth in the vanguard. I stepped over him as he bled out and took the day. That was before I was a god, of course, but I did love war even then."

"You loved it?" I whisper, aghast. My eyes are trying

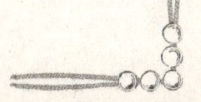

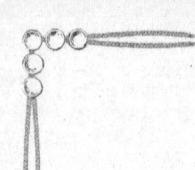

to discern if that is something moving or if it is simply a shadow.

"I was good at it. We tend to love doing things we're good at." He shrugs uncomfortably. "I won't say I didn't mourn my friends who died. Mourned them for centuries—and that's longer than most mortals are remembered, but I wouldn't be God of War if I didn't love the work. It's the strategy of it, the quick responses, the gut instincts that surge up, the way you're gambling with the biggest stakes possible—lives and nations. It's addictive. And more than that. Hate injustice? War is the quick end to that. Want a tyrant overthrown? War."

"You're oversimplifying."

"I am speaking what I know. I am the God of War because I respect it and know its worth. Do not you love the sea?"

"Of course. But all of us from the Crocus Isles love the sea. It's our lifeblood."

"Mm-hmm. And even if you slew Okeanos, if you didn't love the sea with all your heart, you could never be god of it."

"Then why did you suggest I could take over from Ordanus? Did you think I could love music and art that way?"

He shrugs. "You'd learn the love of it fast, or you'd die along the way. Same with war for me. I don't fuss much about it. We love what we love, and we make it our god."

"No, we make ourselves gods," I say absently. I could have sworn that shadow moved a moment ago along that hanging island closest to us. It takes all my courage to keep moving forward as the shadows pulse around us.

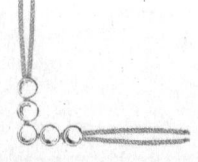

"Yes. We do," Markanos argues, oblivious to my concern. "Because we love ourselves. It was my idea to become a god. I went out and looked for Lichenchus, who was God of War before me, and it took me forty grim years to find him and slay him."

He's silent then for a while as we make our way forward. Twice he creeps up a set of stairs to check an island platform—both are empty of living things, though they are elaborately furnished and bear enough of the taste of their owners that one can guess whose they are. I am certain that the first is Glorian's. It's decked with pillows and woven cloths depicting large flowers and birds and there is a raised garden filled with pale decorative grasses and night-blooming flowers. The second is dark and stark as the mood of Heskatan. It boasts four separate wardrobes laid out much like walls, a raised box bed one must climb a ladder to enter, and a beautifully stitched saddle displayed on its own stand.

Markanos grunts at each empty island, but I do not think he expected them to be occupied. We both know we will find Treseano in his own place.

Even so, I feel eyes on my back. But though the feeling grows with each step, every time I twist to look, nothing is there.

I swallow as Markanos takes up his talk again. I think it comforts him to speak. It only makes me more edgy. Water laps against the rocks we traverse and the sound cloaks any we make—and any an attacker might make.

"I'm just stating the obvious," he says as if I have argued

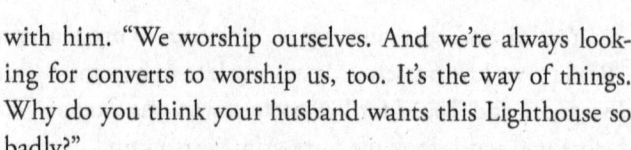

with him. "We worship ourselves. And we're always looking for converts to worship us, too. It's the way of things. Why do you think your husband wants this Lighthouse so badly?"

"To keep his people safe," I say. Did I hear a faint splash?

"To make a lasting name for himself," Markanos says. "To be revered. The original makers of the thing couldn't keep it. If he can prove he can—well, that would be an accomplishment."

He falls silent as we clamber over more jutting rocks and arrive at a new island, and I don't need Markanos to tell me whose this is. He watches it intently and I try to keep watch behind us and to the sides. My eyes keep flicking forward toward the island, though. It is set low and close to the mist-wreathed sea so that the lantern of the next island over hangs high enough above this island that it casts it in stark light.

I wish I could see through the mists. Worry claws up my throat as Markanos presses a single finger to his lips and then begins to mount the rocks that form a rough set of steps up to the island.

We are still climbing when I feel something brush my leg. With my heart in my throat, I twist to look over my shoulder, trident at the ready, but there's nothing in the mist.

"Markanos," I whisper, and then the creature is upon me.

It leaps from the mist at the same moment that Markanos leaps over the lip of the island and vanishes from sight, and I'm pinned clutching the nearly vertical rocks that rise up like teeth and form ragged steps from the riblike bridge to

this island. I must hold on with one hand; I dare not let go, or I will lose my balance and any hope I have of defending myself. My other hand grips the trident in a tight, white-knuckled fist.

The creature swirls out from the mist, cloaked at first so that it looks pewter grey but then growing darker until it is upon me—a black mass of writhing strands, eel-like and yet made of shadow. It opens its many-toothed mouth and roars, and its breath gusts over me in a cloud of soporific spice. I did not expect this, but I still manage to lurch to the side and land a glancing blow with the trident as it plunges past. I do not think it expected me to be able to maneuver at all. It will not be fooled twice.

It swims through the air, defying all logic and gravity, and turns around for another strike. I throw my efforts into scaling farther up the toothlike white rock. Chalky powder breaks free and coats my palms, and I do gain ground but not quickly enough.

Above me, up on the island, Markanos grunts, but there is no time to wonder how he is faring. The creature plunges out of the mist again, unharmed by my strike. It bunches up and then elongates, thrusting forward, its mouth open and roaring. Again, I feel the rush of its spiced breath against my face, but this time I try to get my trident angled right as I brace myself against the rock. I get the weapon up just in time and it sticks into the creature's flesh, but I've hit it too far back to prevent it from snapping at me, catching my left thigh with its vicious teeth.

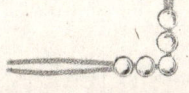

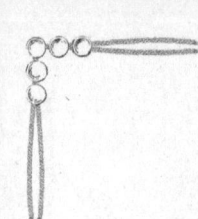

I scream as they dig in and tear, ripping and shredding the flesh. I twist the trident, almost on instinct, and the attack abruptly stops, but the pain hasn't ended and I'm fighting to keep my mind focused as it floods over me.

My breath rasps harshly in my ears and my muscles scream as I hold on to both the weapon and the rock, fighting against the creature as it rears back, nearly taking my trident with it. It's all I can do to hold on, and as the creature rips itself off my weapon black spots dance across my vision.

I can't fight it successfully here on the rocks. I'm too stationary. I'm too vulnerable. But if I couldn't climb while fighting before, I certainly can't now. I fight a wave of panic. No, I won't give in to that. I can think this through.

I look down at the pewter water below, judge how far I'll fall if I let go, and hear the faint echo of the sea. It's not my ocean, but it knows me.

I fling my mind toward it, calling to that echo and begging it to rise and bear me upward. If I could just reach the island above, I would have a chance, even wounded and inexperienced.

The creature has gathered itself up again, keening in a way that sounds like rocks scraping together mixed with a howl. I grit my teeth and pull at that echo, pulling and pulling as the creature bunches again and rushes forward.

It's not going to work. I don't have enough connection with this water. I try to swing my trident back up, but I've left it too long and all I see is teeth.

I gasp, pulling at the echo with all my mental strength—and

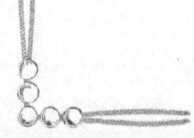

then like a dam bursting the water calls back and the sea rises in a sudden upward swell, catching both me and the creature up with a force so powerful that it snatches my breath, soaks me entirely, floods over us both, and lifts us. To my relief, we're flung apart.

In the sudden tumult of bubbles and brackish water flooding my nose and mouth, I kick, propelling myself toward where the island must be. We're above it, I think, but before I can orient myself we're already descending, the wave receding as quickly as it rose.

I smack into the rock, biting my tongue and tasting blood. But I'm scrambling up on the wet rock before I even finish catching my first breath. I'm still coughing up water as I adjust my grip on the trident.

The creature has landed right beside me. It's sliding across the wet rock and standing up like some snakes do.

I don't hesitate. I leap forward and thrust the trident into it while it is stunned and vulnerable.

My trident is a god weapon. It pins the creature in place, and panting, I step neatly to the side so it cannot shred my leg any more than it already has. I twist the trident as I saw Markanos do. The creature shudders. Screwing up all my courage, I rip the trident out, and as fast as I can I stab again, and again, and again until the shadow creature lies still and shriveled on the rocky floor.

I've killed it. I've killed it. Thank the heavens.

I'm panting, dripping blood, my dress ripped and my hair wild. Pain flares hot and insistent through my leg and up

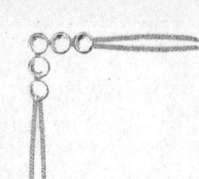

into my torso. It's only then that I flick my gaze desperately around the rest of the island.

"So that's how you killed him," Markanos says, his eyes locked on the dead creature. He's soaked, too. "Suits you."

The other creature hangs limply from his hand like a fur bought at market and there's a light of admiration in his eyes as if for once I've pleased him.

"Well done, Coralys."

But that is not what draws the gasping cry from me.

Behind Markanos, the room is laid out—a bed, a wardrobe, a chest, and a large fountain. And over the arm of the decorative statue is what is left of Treseano.

That horrible black sack he used to carry has been jammed over his head, as if he were crammed into it face-first. I know he is dead, for golden flowers spill out of the bag and drift to swirl in the dark pool beneath the fountain.

I am suddenly ill. He's been here all along as his creatures fought us, a grisly spectator. I swallow bile as too much warmth sweeps over me.

"Not much of a battle when your opponent is already dead," Markanos says, but I note how his hand shakes and his face has paled in the faint light. He strides across to the corpse, his rounded shoulders heavy as if he is very tired. I try to follow, but my leg is in agony, and when I look down at it, I'm momentarily frozen by the sight.

The flesh across my thigh is shredded, hanging in loose scraps of meat. I can see the bone—so much of it, stark and white against red flesh and tattered brown skin.

My hands start to tremble. I can't quite focus.

"Come and look at this," Markanos demands hoarsely.

"My leg," I gasp.

"Don't be such a mortal," he sneers, but I do not think his heart is in it. He is trembling visibly.

With great effort I abandon my wound and hobble over to him, fear a cold clamp around my heart.

"What makes this death different than the others?" I ask him.

"What makes the death of the leader of the rebellion significant?" Markanos asks as he rips the sack off Treseano's head. "Only that he was who we thought was behind all of this and now he is a corpse before us."

The dead god's eyes are open and staring. His dark skin has gone a terrible grey and something has left round marks on his neck and face—what's left of it. Half his face is as shredded as my leg and probably from the same source. Was some jewelry pressed against his cheek when he died, perhaps? I see nothing that would make such a distinctive mark.

"That makes no sense. Why would someone kill him and release Okeanos? Surely half the gods stand with him, and if others have chosen my husband's side, then they haven't made themselves known."

Markanos doesn't answer. He looks away and I see him swallow violently twice as if he is trying to hold down his bile.

"What makes this different than El'Dorian?" I press him. "You did not look so ill when you found her."

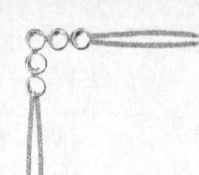

"Because she was just one god," he spits out, still not looking at me. "Now four are dead. Who is next? Me?"

"I didn't think gods could die," I say stupidly.

Markanos barks a despairing laugh. "Because they rarely do. Once in a dozen centuries, perhaps. Never four at once."

He wipes his forehead anxiously and then realizes he is still carrying the shadow creature.

"I need to look to my people," he says suddenly, taking a step backward. It's the most uncertain I've ever seen him. "I need to discover if there is some threat I've overlooked. I need to be sure..."

"But, Markanos," I say, fighting to stay conscious as my physical situation becomes unbearable. "We need to think this through. Who has killed Treseano and what does it mean that he's dead?"

"It means your husband is free. Is that not enough for you?" he roars, spinning to face me.

"Someone is killing gods. On both sides of this rebellion," I say in a small voice. The pain of my ruined leg washes over me in burning waves, nausea shudders through me, and my vision narrows to blackness. "We don't dare just run from here. We have to consider. We have to protect ourselves from betrayal."

"That's rich, coming from the woman who slew my friend while he slept," Markanos spits out, his face bleak, and before I can respond, he slashes his sword through the air and he's gone. I'm left on this lonely island with nothing but a dead god hanging from a statue, a dead monster shriveling on the

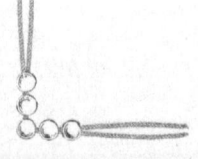

ground nearby, and the ghosts of my past clinging to everything I see.

I try to search Treseano for any kind of clue as to who has killed him, but there is nothing to find but what we've already seen, and if it would be obvious to someone else, it is not to me.

It takes all my willpower to force my leg to carry me to the edge of the island and to fall from there into the sea. All my efforts are spent in moving, in not panicking, in not fainting, and in reaching the salt.

The second I fall into the water, gasping with relief at the smell of the ocean and the way it hugs my flesh, I twist my hand and rush through the water back to home, washing up like flotsam on the shore of my island. I don't know where on the shore I arrive. I don't care. I crawl up the stone and collapse, clutching my ruined leg with both hands as if I can press the flesh back to the bone.

I'm sobbing, my breath in my chest panicked and rushing in and out far too fast. I black out.

I'm in and out of consciousness several times before I stumble up to the cottage.

I must not die like this. Not like this. Not when I've achieved nothing and my people and nation are as shredded as my leg. I must hold on for them, for Oke.

My thoughts are scattered and hard to grasp, sliced from me by pain and fear.

I collapse on the swinging bed and try to tend my leg. The flesh hangs in uneven scraps from the bone and I don't

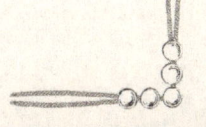

know how to put them back together again. I flinch back from the idea of cutting my skin and muscle away to trim what's left, even if they are mostly hanging free already. The very thought overwhelms me, and my head spins, my stomach revolts, and I lay back on the pillows, gasping in harsh breaths, and let sweet blackness claim me.

Chapter Thirty-One

I wake muzzy and disoriented, blinking in the white light. It's day. That means something. Something about the deeps of the sea and too many legs, but I can't remember what it is. I pull myself up onto my elbows, dragging my hair—curling with sweat damp—out of my face. I look down the bed at my legs. There are two. They both look perfectly well.

It's only as I stare at them that I remember how they looked last night and must sprint out the door of the cottage to empty my stomach into the weeds. The sharp morning breeze kicks up against my suddenly flushed face, and I take long, aching breaths, my eyes growing wider and wider as I look at my naked legs.

They are whole.

How is that possible?

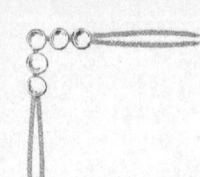

But that's the secret to how they torment Oke, is it not? Eaten all day, healed in the night. It's the one thing that, apparently, I can get right as a god. I heal. Shockingly fast. And it makes all the god corpses I've seen that much more grisly, knowing that if that final blow had not been dealt, that they could have dragged themselves out of bed the next morning in the same way—whole and well as if nothing had ever happened.

It takes me some time to gather myself together enough to wash and dress. My hands still shake as I work. We had thought—or perhaps hoped—that Treseano's creatures were the key to Oke's healing and freedom. Which means, if we are right, then he could be freed by the death of one, healed by the death of the other, and if fortune has graced me with her spice-laden smile, then that might have even completed one of Oke's tasks and brought him that much closer to the desire of his heart—the ancient Lighthouse.

I should be able to go straight to his island in the sea and bring him home. It is strange that he is not here already, in fact.

I frown.

Unless, perhaps, he is healed of the godwound, and freed of the anchor, but the effects linger? Perhaps he is unconscious, healing, but dead to the world as I was only a short time ago?

I should go and check.

I gather up what I'll need, preparing fish and flasks of water, blankets and extra clothing. I bring a lantern and fuel,

and the trident. I'm anxious, my thoughts skittering one way and then the next, and at the same time I'm excited. I want to see him. And not just as I've always seen him, but whole and healthy—free finally of torture and imprisonment—and smiling at me. The thought of it makes my breath catch a little, and I have to shake my head at myself.

Just do the work, Coralys. Be glad if he welcomes you at all. He'll still be half-dead and bound to you. You can't fix that no matter what you do.

But I am still looking forward to seeing the expression in his eyes when I announce to him that we're one step closer to his goal.

I check and double-check my tunic. It's terribly water-stained and wrinkled, but it's still the most presentable thing I have to wear. I am a god now. I ought to at least have a wardrobe. I'll fix that as soon as I can.

But not today.

I'm still shivering with nerves and the aftershock of last night as I make my way down to the dock for the last time. I want to leave from there in case Okeanos still comes back on his own. I watch for him anxiously, and I'm about to make a bowl shape with my hand when the air on the dock seems to ripple and then Markanos is there, chest heaving, arms shaking. There is blood on his sword.

He takes in the boat and supplies and me in one single glance.

"You're going to Okeanos," he says shortly.

"Of course. We've freed him."

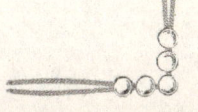

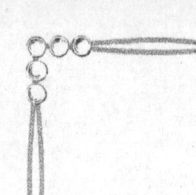

We're both assuming so. Assuming that was the purpose of Treseano's second monster. I hope we were right.

He nods curtly, not looking at me. I give him a moment, but this is no time for standing around.

"If you wish to wait here for our return, you're welcome to stay," I say, trying to hint that I will go one way or the other.

"Wait," he says, taking a half stride forward and finally looking up at me. "I've been thinking all night. He's doing five impossible tasks. Like Plector. Like Kilinippa."

"Yes," I agree, but I'm struggling to keep the impatience out of my voice. Why is he here? Why will he not let me get on with it?

"You could raise the dead with five tasks."

"So everyone keeps saying," I agree dryly, and then wait again. Eventually I sigh and I am the one who speaks. "If you are here to remind me that I owe our success to you, then consider it noted. We owe you a debt and I will make certain it is repaid in full."

"No, of course not," Markanos says, and he sounds sincere. "But you're going to him to tell him you've completed one of his tasks?"

"If we're right, and it freed him, he should be back here by now," I say. The back of my neck itches. I feel like there's something I just am not seeing. "And his wound should be healed on top of that. I'm... I worry for his safety."

"You worry for the safety of the man you murdered?" He smirks at me.

"If something has happened to him, well then, his

impossible tasks won't be credited to our collective score and I'll be back down to two," I say defensively, but his gaze is hard as it bores into me. I hope he cannot see the truth. I hope he cannot see that I am starting to feel attached to the other God of the Sea.

"If you care about him at all, Wife of Okeanos, then you'll take a different path." Markanos is stern, as if he thinks I need a lecture and he's the one to give it. "You may have freed him and healed him, but he's still dead."

My cheeks are on fire. I will never live down my poor judgment in killing the man. "Your point?"

"I heard you give your word to him that you'd help him with his Lighthouse," he says. "I want you to break that promise. As long as he's no longer God of the Sea, just a dead man hanging on by a thread of life to you, he's vulnerable and so are you. We need strong allies in this god war, and the pair of you are a liability. So. Raise the dead. Bring Okeanos back to life. Let him rule and reign over the sea beside you and let him worry about his Lighthouse when this war is over. He'd never ask it of you. But I will."

My head is whirling with the idea. He's right. His friend is not just free and healed, but he could live again if I agree to this.

"I'm sure there's something you want. You did not marry him for love or the desire to possess." His face screws up like he's bitten a lemon, and when he speaks, it is with effort. "If you free my friend from his death, I will do everything in my power to ensure you get whatever it is you really want. I can

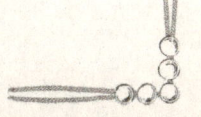

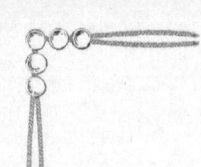

see by the light in your eyes there is *something*. I assure you that never have I met a task too great for me or an enemy too powerful. Simply name your price and I will meet it."

"I'll not be bought. My decision is my own." I shake my head.

"Fair enough," he says lightly. "Then do it without provocation. Do it because you are brave and honorable, the wife of the great Okeanos."

And it's not that I don't feel the pull. Of course I do, but I also know what Okeanos would say—that he can't replicate the tasks and if I use them on bringing him back, then I will destroy his life's work. Is it not his right to choose between himself and the work he cared about?

"How could I even do that? I don't know how to assign them. I was counting on Oke to direct me." It's an easy out, an excuse, and I know it.

"Do what they do in the legends. Both Kilinippa and Plector prayed to the heavens, 'Accept these five gifts, a work for each finger of my hand, and give to me this boon I ask of thee.' I know because Okeanos made me read that fool book."

I bite at my lip, suddenly fearful of the upcoming meeting.

"You don't really believe there is some great deity above even the gods," I say.

"Don't I?" Markanos's smile is twisting and ironic. "Did you not see the glory descend and our power renewed? If that wasn't a god greater than gods, then what was it?"

"Magic," I suggest. "The nature of that place."

"Come and find me when you're done," Markanos says, ignoring my argument entirely, and it feels anticlimactic somehow.

"You're not going to come with me and find out yourself?" I allow a sting in my tone. After all, he breezed in here, wounded me, and now he will leave as if it is no matter to him at all?

His face goes red and blotchy. "Alexandros made an inroad into my territory while I was distracted by Ordanus. Everything is chaos now. The god war has begun. The nations that have been building armies are ready to fight. If you listen to the prayers of your people, I am willing to bet that they, too, may be sailing forth to battle."

I feel my breath hitch at his words and a tingle run down my spine. Like him, I've been distracted, and last night when I was in the water, I was in too much pain to hear any kind of prayers. My gaze slips to where frothy green licks the docks and I can't seem to let the breath out.

"Besides, this is on you, Drowned Queen. Only you can employ the tasks to wrench your husband back into godhood."

"But the god-killer," I protest. "Whoever it is may be laying traps for us even now."

"Seven hells, woman. One thing at a time. If we don't take hold of the reins of the mortal lands, it won't matter which of us he targets next. You aren't a god without your followers!"

And he doesn't even bother to explain more, he just flicks

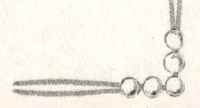

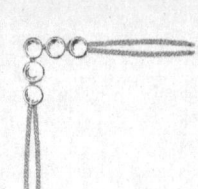

his sword and he's gone in a blink, and I'm left staring at the place where he stood.

If he's right that I must make a decision between Oke's life and his quest, then I know what my husband would want. He would never hold his life as more valuable than his Lighthouse. And if I choose to go against him, then I risk breaking his heart, his spirit, and his body all at once. I clench my fist, thinking hard, but no matter how hard I think, I believe that I know what I must do.

Chapter Thirty-Two

I place my hand in the water, about to shift to the canker in the sea. Instantly, I'm smacked with a torrent of prayers. Prayers to me—the God of the Sea. I'm made breathless by them, bowled over and thrown about. If I were not in a boat, I fear I might be dashed on the rocks by the swell of them.

In my time as a god, I have never been swept away by the power of my people's prayers. They come to me in trickles. One here, one there. But these…these rush over me with the power of a waterfall.

"Help me!" one penitent begs.

"Save your people!" another cries.

"They come in ships. They're everywhere. They've taken the docks." The voices are overlapping, one drowning out another in their wails and sobs and cries.

There are hundreds of prayers. Each more desperate than

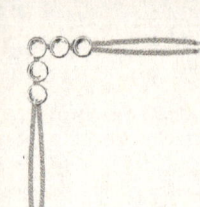

the last, and I am shaking, shuddering, lost in them. This is what had Markanos so rattled. Like him, I was only gone for a couple of nights, and I think I would have heard them if they were praying to me yesterday. This conflict is fresh. The god wars have started, and they have come to my shores. I taste acid in my mouth because I do not doubt the truth or sincerity of these prayers.

I stand up almost unconsciously. I need to go to them.

And yet, I also must discover if my work has freed Okeanos, and I must decide whether to use the five great tasks to restore his life, or restore the Lighthouse. Because if his help is available to me, it could make all the difference to them. My people need that Lighthouse now more than ever. And they need Okeanos, who would know exactly what to do.

I put my hand into the sea, and as the pain of so many prayers descends on me, I twist my hand in the wash of the surf and travel.

When I reach the canker in the sea, all is not right.

I leap from the craft onto the black rocks. Everything looks smaller in the light of day. The island feels claustrophobic, though it is exactly the same—the giant anchor jutting out of the sharp rocks, the chains and loops that hang from it, and the rivets set through the crossbar.

The same, and yet different.

There are no birds. The seaweed has been swept aside. Any remnants of the fire Oke shared with Markanos are washed away. The blood he leaked out over the ground has not even left a stain.

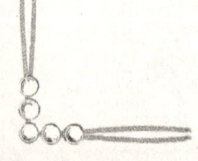

And he is not here.

I stand still for a moment, desolate. Where is my husband? I'm assaulted by a series of imaginings of him drawn under the water and torn apart by sea creatures, or snatched up by an enemy and thrust into a pearl, or sinking in the waves as he tries to swim for safety and drowning under the surf.

I can't quite catch my breath.

I've lost him.

My fingers crawl up and clutch at my own throat, and for a moment I'm lost to shattered thoughts and rough breathing. But no, I am panicking for no reason. There are ways I can verify this.

I trail a hand into the sea, and then wade right into it until it is over my head, close my eyes, and reach out with the part of me that is the sea to sense him.

I reach through the screams and cries, through the quiet pleas and distraught tears. They shred at my mind, scrape across my nerves. I know I need to help them, but I don't know how to answer so many at once. No wonder Markanos was so desperate when I saw him this morning, if he was answering prayers just like this for his own people.

I need Oke to show me what to do. This sudden cataclysmic threat is too big for me alone.

I see my people in tiny glimpses—mothers clinging to little children; tiny ones sobbing, their hands clutching desperately for parents who cannot come. Whoever has attacked our shores has come quickly and brutally.

I didn't expect this yet. I thought there was time.

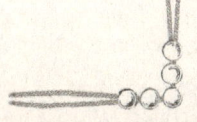

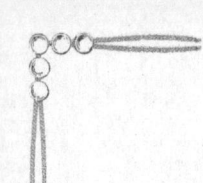

I try to focus. Where are these attacks? Where are these prayers coming from?

It's the shores of the mainland, not my islands. I almost sigh, but then my heart clenches hard, for I am no longer Coralys of the Crocus Isles, I am Coralys, God of the Sea, and that makes all those who pray to me mine. My people on the mainland have been attacked by the armies of these rebel gods who wish to start a war and overthrow their ruler.

I see little bursts of what is happening, a fleet flooding into a harbor, armies roaring as they take to the smaller craft and cross the swell of ocean to reach the shore. My men swept away by waves or floating on the water trailing red for the sharks. My women so cut to pieces that they cannot be recognized. I recoil from it, but I cannot stop the onslaught. The god war has started just as Markanos said it had and my people need me.

They need Okeanos.

I claw through their prayers, looking, searching, sobbing in my frantic scramble.

I do not feel my husband in the sea. It is as if he has ceased to be entirely.

"Oke!" I scream beneath the waves, but he's not there.

"Okeanos!" I call mentally with all my heart as if my prayer—the prayer of a living god—might somehow trump the prayers of the desperate mortals calling out to him and to me.

Something is terribly wrong. Not just with my people,

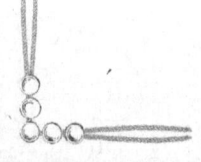

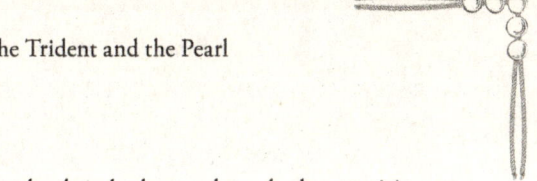

but with the missing dead god who ought to be here waiting for me.

I stumble back up to shore feeling cored and gutted. I don't know what to do. I don't know who to help first.

"Oke!" I call, but the only ones who answer are the gulls and they are far off. I hope that is not because they float somewhere on a corpse. I hope it is only because without him here there is nothing to draw them.

It's no matter. I have Vesuvius's pearl here and he will tell me—for a price. I lift my trident as I remember that Markanos didn't even have to pay a price. Perhaps I, too, can use his method to pry information from the former god.

I draw the pearl from my belt and it's not hard to drop a tear on it. I'm frantic enough that the tears are coming whether I want them to or not.

But the tear does nothing. Or at least—it doesn't draw Vesuvius. There's a moment where I think it draws *someone* out. There's a glimpse of tentacles and an impression of the struggling shape of a man, but then he's gone again. Is it possible that Markanos harmed Vesuvius more than I realized?

I feel cold all over. There will be no help from him, then.

Fine. Markanos will help me. He is, after all, as culpable as I am for whatever befell Oke. I don't know how to get to Markanos's home. I should have asked while I had the opportunity. I grip the trident hard in one hand and stand in the water, twisting my hand and thinking of Markanos, but again, nothing happens.

I try enough times that I feel like a fool.

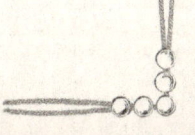

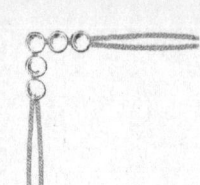

I want to abandon this search for my husband and go and help my people. I want to travel from place to place and beat back their enemies, but I know that a frantic leader loses battles and that if I simply throw myself into the fray, I will be destroyed and my people with me.

For there is only one conclusion I can draw—Okeanos has been taken by his enemies. The magic was broken, he was freed, but dead and tortured, he was easy to snatch up and steal away.

And if they have him, then they have half the sea.

And that alone changes the decision here. Where I might have had to balance his safety with the safety of our people, it is clear that both are tied together. Whoever has him has access to them, and with that access, the ability to conquer them outright.

I must focus all my resources on getting Okeanos back.

I hurry home to gather what resources I can. I must make a plan. For my people. For my husband. I tie up the boat, chewing my lip, deep in thought, trying to formulate a plan.

My eyes drift to where Aurelius stood just months ago taunting us, and there, on the upright he'd leaned against, my husband's fishing spear is jammed into the wood affixing a fluttering piece of vellum to the upright.

That wasn't here when I left. I would have seen it. Markanos would have seen it. Trembling, I clamber out of the boat and over to it. The spear—stained yet by the lifeblood of my husband—quivers in the wood. My hand hovers near the shaft, but then I draw it away. I have no right to take it up again.

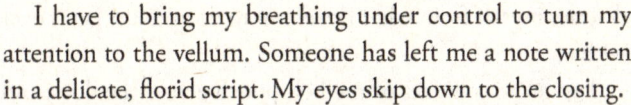

I have to bring my breathing under control to turn my attention to the vellum. Someone has left me a note written in a delicate, florid script. My eyes skip down to the closing.

Aurelius.

I can hardly read, my heart is beating so quickly. My eyes keep trying to dart forward and I have to draw them back to read the note word by word. He has not minced words.

This offer comes but once and if ignored unleashes upon you the hatred of the heavens. It's a dramatic opening. *I have what you desire. Come to me in the way I detailed not long ago upon this very pier. I will await you until dark. Fail and I will consider your rejection of my hospitality a declaration of war and shall take from the flesh of your people an appropriate recompense.*

He's signed it with a dozen titles and then ended it with his name. *Aurelius, God of the Air.*

I stare at the note for a long moment, but there's no ambiguity in what he's said and no doubt in my mind that he can make my people suffer even more than they do already if I do not meet with him as he has laid out. And yet, I hate to go where he has the upper hand and I have only my own desperation and my wits to carry me.

Despite that, I dare not hesitate.

I kneel on the dock and rip the pouch from my belt with trembling hands.

The sea has gone dark, clouds rolling in. I hear a sound like squelching, but I pay it no mind. A sea creature, perhaps, working its way up the beach. I need to stop trying to

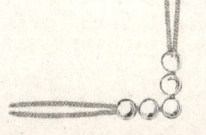

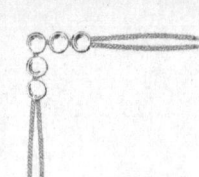

distract myself from what I'm about to do and just get it over with.

I spill the contents of my belt pouch across the dock and fumble past the flint and the black pearl to where the sharp belt knife lies.

I pick it up with trembling hands and look from it to the sea and back again.

I wonder if it matters which finger I pick.

I place the edge of my knife against the joint of my smallest finger on my left hand. I'm sweating, but my mouth is dry.

Behind me, I hear the same slippery sound. This time, nerves frayed, I twist to look.

A familiar figure is hunched over the dock, caught in the act of reaching for the single black pearl lying on the weather-worn boards. It's a man with six tentacles and two stumps where the others ought to be.

We both freeze.

"Going somewhere?" he asks me, eyes wary.

He must know that I know he wasn't in the pearl—that when I tried to draw him out, he didn't appear. He must see that I realize what this means—that when I thought he'd retreated into it, he'd somehow slipped away instead into the shadows of the island and hid there, likely waiting for a moment just like this where he could catch me unawares.

"Stealing something?" I reply.

"It's not stealing if it belongs to you." His words are bold, but he is trembling.

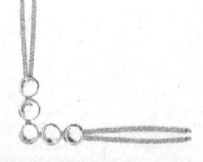

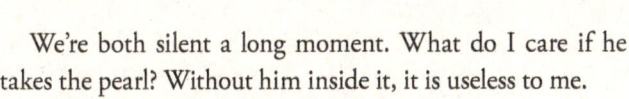

We're both silent a long moment. What do I care if he takes the pearl? Without him inside it, it is useless to me.

"Take it, then," I tell him.

For what use is his ghost to me? He's done nothing but betray me and lie to me and lead me into traps. He's welcome to his pearl and welcome to leave my life forever. He snatches it up and then retreats, and I wait until he has slipped back into the shadows before I turn back to my task, press my left hand firmly to the dock, and with my right hand carve the last finger away and throw it into the sea.

Pain makes me blink and sputter as I fight to control the shaking of my hands. I fumble and manage to wad cloth around the wound as the wind around me whips up, spinning like it means to form a hurricane with me at the center. Back on shore the trees bow down and the ocean at my dock depresses until it nearly touches the land. My little boat bucks and thrashes on the end of its tether and then I'm swept up into the fury of the wind, spun around, and spit out again. It's just like when I move from place to place using the bowl of my hand, but this time I have no control over the movement and no sense of where I'm going.

I crash onto the stone steps of a temple.

It's a temple I know very well—the temple of Okeanos on the island of Talasa, and I know who I will find inside it without having to be told—Aurelius, God of the Air, who by his power, and by the sacrifice of my own flesh to his will, has brought me here.

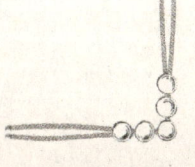

Chapter Thirty-Three

Take your breath for Aurelius,
Drink your drop for Okeanos.

The lines of the song run through my head as the great wind deposits me in a heap on the steps of the temple of Okeanos. Aurelius will be here somewhere.

Hard spikes of pain wash from my hand, leaving me gasping with nausea. But I don't have time for pain.

From my vantage point on the stairs I can see down to the docks and also a great deal of the island. It remains quiet. Few people have returned to it since they abandoned this holy place.

There is no sign of Aurelius below, and why would there be? I know where the God of the Air will be—where he

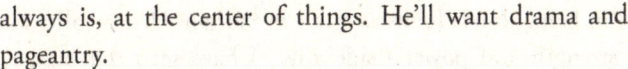

always is, at the center of things. He'll want drama and pageantry.

I mount the steps with trepidation.

I have said before that the temple raised to Okeanos is a beauteous thing, a marvel of white stone carved to delicate peaks and valleys that mimic the caress of the water against the land. It is up the uneven but gloriously wrought steps of the temple that I race, my heart in my throat.

It is nearly the setting of the sun and the white steps are tinted carnation and cantaloupe. The birds are silent, and in the distance, the clouds hang in eerie asymmetry—some are tall and towering, while others are scattered and torn, streaming side to side like a bride's veil in the wind. The sea is just as frenetic, stirring up in troubled waves first one way and then the other. It is an unsettling sight, as if the elements themselves have turned upon us all.

It reminds me—starkly—of a time only months ago when I stood here with my beloved and he pressed his face to mine and smiled into my eyes before he was wrenched away by the very thing I am become—the sea.

I race up the steps, my mouth dry, my mind too full of conjurings that I hope will not prove to be true.

I see no priests. Their braziers are not lit. Their bowls of seawater have not been filled, but in the center of the temple, just as he promised, is Aurelius.

He stands before the statue of Okeanos—the fine, strong marble Okeanos in all his glory. The statue is posed in such a way that every muscle ripples on display and the spear in

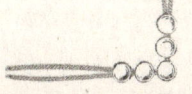

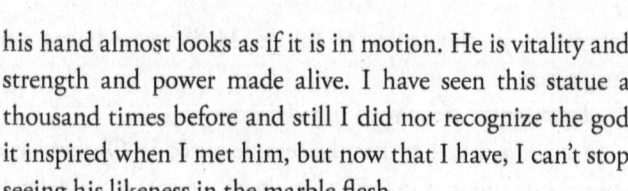

his hand almost looks as if it is in motion. He is vitality and strength and power made alive. I have seen this statue a thousand times before and still I did not recognize the god it inspired when I met him, but now that I have, I can't stop seeing his likeness in the marble flesh.

Aurelius stands before it with his head slightly bowed, facing me.

He looks up suddenly, and a smile dawns on his face like the sun.

"You gave me your flesh after all," he says, and he looks very pleased. "I thought you would eventually."

"Your argument was compelling," I murmur, but I am not listening to him—I can't listen to him because there at the feet of the statue lies the corpse of my dead husband and my heart is hammering so hard in my chest that I can hardly think.

He is draped across the dais as one might drape a cloth or lay a laurel wreath, or spread out a fish to be gutted. The wound in his thigh remains and I clench my jaw at that. We were wrong about Treseano, then. He must not have been the one holding Okeanos's wound price. And yet my dead husband is free of his iron shackles, so perhaps we were correct about that part. Half right and yet half wrong, and if I have not healed the Crown of the Sea, then I haven't completed five tasks, have I?

Panic claws up my throat and I try to press it down. I should have checked the clock before I went looking for Oke.

He still bears the wound in his chest and the fresh wounds

in both wrists from where he was pinned to the anchor. I can see all his broken, mangled body. His beard has grown back to a shadow but someone has sawed the glorious tangled hair from his head, leaving it ragged, and he has been badly beaten. Though he was dead before, it had not truly felt real. Now that he lies here limp and grey and powerless, golden flowers spilled out all around him, I feel the truth of it.

Okeanos's eyes are open, and when he sees me, his lips move thickly as if he is trying to speak. His chest rises very shallowly. He barely breathes at all. And I know without having to be told that he is clinging to the last of his life by the barest thread.

I stumble forward, my hand reaching for him and his name on my lips. "Oke."

But Aurelius shifts two fingers in the slightest of movements and the air in front of me forms a wall that pushes me back a step.

"I don't think so, Wife of Okeanos," he murmurs. "I do not like the pair of you too close together."

"I have come for my husband," I say, but already I can feel that the sands of my life are slipping away with those of Okeanos. "I do not know why you have taken him, but surely he is of no use to you."

Behind Aurelius, Oke wets his lips with a flick of his tongue and one of his fingers twitches. I can hear his gasping words: "Cora. My betrayer." And I think what is left of my heart breaks.

Aurelius flicks a hand indolently. "Let us have this

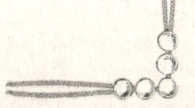

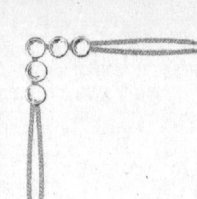

conversation, then. It has been long coming and I must admit that I have been anticipating it with a certain hunger."

"Hunger?" I ask him, careful not to give too much ground at only the opening of our negotiation.

He saunters across the mosaic floor toward Oke's prone form, and though I twitch with my desire to go to my fallen husband, I still cannot move.

I drag my eyes from Oke to study Aurelius and I notice again the slight hitch to his step, the barely discernible intake of breath as he sits on the edge of the dais beside Oke's vulnerable form. The tiniest tremble in his leg. And I know.

I know that beneath his perfectly stitched chlamys and chiton is a secret, and my breath catches in my throat. His sharp gaze follows mine and then his eyes widen slightly.

"Here is a surprise. Coralys, you astonish me. You are the first to divine for yourself my little secret."

His chiton covers his leg and it is wine colored. How very clever of him. And I think back and see that he has been dressed in the color of wine or blood every time I've seen him. Of course he has, for his garments have been working very hard to hide from others what I have just realized—that this is the man who has given Okeanos his godwound, and he has paid the price in his own flesh by bearing an identical wound all this time. Though it cannot be entirely identical since it has not slowed him as Okeanos's has. Perhaps he pays by bearing a smaller wound. Still agonizing, but less inhibiting.

And this means that he has been working against Okeanos since long before Treseano declared war on the King of

Heaven. He is not the lesser member of an alliance who was sent as a messenger to Okeanos on Treseano's behalf at all. He has been the regent uncle, ruling the kingdom behind another's face. I should have realized this when first I saw him walk into the Resurgence with a slight limp.

My eyes narrow as my mind races, but I do not need to speak. My knowledge has freed his tongue.

He hitches his chiton up scandalously, until it barely covers the essentials, and reveals the gaping wound I knew I would see there. It *is* smaller and there are no barnacles in his twin wound, though I think I see a skim of fungus growing pale within the depths of it.

"You wish to ask me why. Why trap him and wound him? Why make it impossible for him to reach his people in time to prevent one queen from making a terrible mistake?"

Here he smirks, but my eyes flick to Okeanos. I see his throat bob as he tries to swallow, his shoulder hitch as he tries to rise, and I can tell by the deep darkness in his green eyes that he is aware of everything being said while he lies immobile. Fury burns in those eyes.

Aurelius does not notice, or if he does, then he does not care.

"If you wish to win a war," he says, "it's usually best to be a step ahead of your enemies. In fact, it's best to take out your strongest foe before he even realizes there is a battle. That is the course I took. I knew well that even taken by surprise the lion of gods would be hard to fell." He pauses as if he's savoring these words. "But he could be sapped. He could be

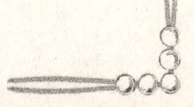

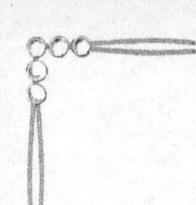

drained of strength. And while he was licking his wounds, I could trap one of his key pieces—a queen he has oft used to exercise his will. It mattered not to me who you married, for anyone could be my pawn. I needed only be sure that it broke your heart so that you turned in his hand—no longer a clever weapon but a double-edged blade."

I feel a little faint at this. For I have been steered as easily as a ship driven before the wind, the merest touch to the tiller enough to divert her. Worse than that, I have come to this confrontation thinking I had five completed tasks in my hand—only to discover I am unarmed. I have only four. I must regain some footing here and quickly, or Okeanos and I will both be dead.

"Then why kill the man you chose to be the face of your rebellion?" I ask him, trying to gain more time to think. "Why slaughter Treseano?"

"What is this you say?" Aurelius looks surprised. Genuinely so.

"You did not know he was dead?" I frown, but before I can elaborate a familiar squelching turns my attention toward the figure sliding out from behind the statue of Okeanos.

Aurelius still seems shaken when he says with false charm, "Ah, and now here is friend Vesuvius come to join us. And just in time, for if we are to have this pleasant discussion, who should be more welcome than he who devised these plans to begin with?"

Vesuvius.

My eyes widen in horror. There is acid in my mouth and

it waters as if I am about to vomit, but that is nothing compared to the scent of death that accompanies the former sea god as he squelches up the stairs. I do not know if it is simply in my mind that I smell it, but decay clogs my nose and makes my mouth water even harder.

He has betrayed me. Not just now, but all along. I should not be surprised.

Vesuvius has found a crown somewhere. He wears it, slightly off-kilter, on his brow, and he bounces on his palm the black pearl that he so recently stole from me.

I am still unable to pass through the wall Aurelius has made, but I can move enough to sidle away from the former sea god as he passes by.

"You," I whisper, shuddering.

"Me," he coos. "It was always me, though of course you never saw it."

I turn to Aurelius, accusing, "This is who you call friend?"

"Did you not call him the same?" Aurelius asks, his lip curling. "Vesuvius is the very dearest of my friends and has been for many centuries, long before Okeanos usurped him in such an underhanded way."

And the look he exchanges with Vesuvius tells me more than any of his words could. There is a devotion here that I have not reckoned with.

Vesuvius keeps speaking, ignoring our byplay. "Did you really think, Coralys, that you would find my prison lying around neglected in your home? Did you ever stop to wonder if it was *meant* to be there?"

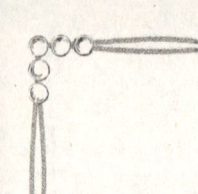

Ice stabs down my spine, and I can hardly make my mouth work to form the words. Behind them, Okeanos lets out a sigh that I think might be a groan if he had the strength. His eyelids flicker.

"But who could go into Okeanos's home except for himself?"

"Ah, but he was married by then," Aurelius says, leaning back and resting a hand on the knee of Okeanos's corpse.

Oke's hand flinches, but he can't move away, and something within me lurches at this violation. Our eyes meet and I shy away from what I see in them. When I look back at Aurelius, he is enjoying watching us both.

"It's always a dread thing to bind yourself to another. For in tying one thing to your breast you may very well tie others with it. Think, Drowned Queen." I do not need his admonishment, my brain is working furiously. "Think on the treaty you signed just a handful of years ago. A treaty with the Spear Coast. Did you not offer them free access to your seas and all the lands they touch, that they may set foot on your land and you on theirs for as long as your life endured?"

I stare at him. It was a simple treaty with a faraway country meant to offer both our populations succor when far from home.

"What of it?" I ask.

His smile is secretive. "The Spear Coast bows its knee to me—or did the day before your dread wedding. I was given the name of king as they became a theocracy. And so I—one of them—could step on the land of Okeanos when he became one with you."

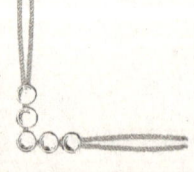

I pale. "But at the docks you made a great show of not being able to enter Okeanos's island."

His smile is as cruel as a drawn bow aimed toward me. "A simple ruse. I had already planted my tiny trap for you by then. Did you ever tell your god-husband about your eight-legged friend?"

"Six-legged," Vesuvius says, and his following laugh is dark with hatred.

The ice in my spine is spreading to my lungs and making it hard to breathe. I never did tell Oke about Vesuvius. Not even after I killed him.

"Why are you telling me all this?" I ask tightly as Vesuvius swarms past me on his six living tentacles.

My gaze catches on the two severed tentacle stumps he bears. I am starting to get a twisting feeling in my stomach regarding those and it gets worse as he slides to stand beside Aurelius, peering down as if he is a gravedigger estimating the correct size for my dead husband's vulnerable form.

Oke's eyes are shut, but his throat bobs again—slower, weaker than before, and his lips part as if he wishes he could speak. That tiny motion is enough to wrench me. I want to throw them both off and stand between him and them. I do not like how Aurelius's hand lingers on Oke's knee or how Vesuvius allows his gaze to sweep over his fallen enemy as if choosing where else he might stick a blade. They violate his person and I want to bite and snap and roar.

The sun is sinking lower, the colors that paint the white marble shifting from subtle to garish as if a gauche hand

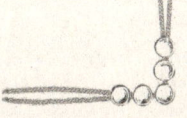

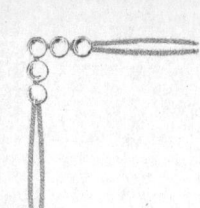

slashed geranium-red brushstrokes all across the world, and under them shadows spread out like spilled blood.

"I think, Coralys," Aurelius says, "that you wish to negotiate for possession of your husband."

"And you guaranteed it would be so by holding my people hostage," I say dryly.

I do not know if I'll be able to pay whatever price they set and I don't want to think about what that will mean.

Aurelius smirks knowingly. "I think that when you've bought him back from us, you plan to no longer build his unattainable sanctuary but to use what he has gathered to return him to the land of the living."

I bite my lip. Of course I'd wanted that. Before I realized the fifth task had not been fulfilled.

He goes on, not knowing my thoughts. "And what a shame that would be after all the work I've done to bring him to his knees. The sea is ever too powerful, too prevalent. It covers three-quarters of the earth and swallows men whole. If I am to gain from the King of Heaven his throne and place, I need the sea on my side. And Okeanos would never agree to that. He's a loyalist through and through. But my old friend Vesuvius." Here they exchange another glance I can't quite read. There's admiration there, but there's wariness in Aurelius's eyes, and I wonder if he's still thinking about how Treseano was dead without him knowing of it. "He will work with me. He will give me the sea if I give it back to him first."

"I don't see how you'll do that," I say frostily. But I am

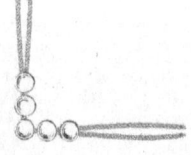

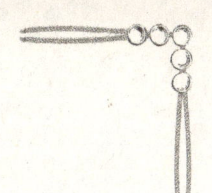

chilled right through. If he means to give Vesuvius the sea, then he means to kill us both.

"Don't you?" His large eyes widen with innocence. Even now he is all boyish beauty. "Did you speak in lies to me, Vesuvius, when you told me of how you poured falsehoods in her ears and tainted her view of her husband until she drove his very own spear through his heart?"

Oke's eyes flutter open again at that, and my heart freezes as they look directly into mine. He knows. He sees. There's no hiding my full treachery from him—that I not only killed him but unknowingly colluded with his enemies to do it.

His lips form a single word: "Betrayer."

It seems fitting that he would spend his last energy to accuse me. And the stricken look in his eyes hurts even more for how very near it is to the look of hunger they held when we kissed.

"I lied about nothing," Vesuvius rumbles, one of his tentacles sliding up to run through his hair as one might run one's fingers.

I shudder, but I channel what strength of spirit I yet maintain into my voice.

"How are you still here, Vesuvius? Shouldn't you be trapped inside that pearl?"

He shrugs just one shoulder, twice, until I realize he is not shrugging to tell me he doesn't know but rather highlighting the barb there.

"It is not fitting that you wield a weapon you are so poorly equipped to possess, Drowned Queen. But what you handle

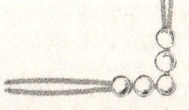

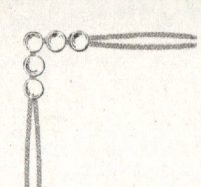

poorly, I was master of, and as a result, I know its capabilities. You, for instance, did not know the danger of letting your chained bull stab me with my own trident. For it carries within it the power to pin a thing into a certain time and place and you pinned me in the land of the living once more. And that allows me to put the question to you."

Aurelius coughs and Vesuvius changes his tune. "It allows *us* to put the question to you." He pauses, and then with a smirk he asks me, "Do you want your husband back?"

I brace myself for a price I cannot possibly pay. "If this is a negotiation for his release, then state your terms."

This is a lot of effort to spend on the wife of a dead god. Even if she is a god herself. Especially when all of us know that each of them could overpower me all by himself and take from me any shred of life I might possess. What price will they ask of me knowing that? They don't think I would betray my people, I hope. I bite my lip so hard that it bleeds.

"This is absolutely a negotiation," Aurelius says smoothly. And his smile grows a little deeper. "With the highest of stakes... for you."

I shoot a glance at my husband and see his green eyes blazing through the slits of his eyelids and how his lips curve to form the name "Cora," and fear twists bitter in my heart. Perhaps what we have is not love, but it is a path that twists very near.

My chest squeezes slightly, and I feel the blood rush to my cheeks as I see his chest flutter and then still. This is taking too long. Every word we speak counts down time that

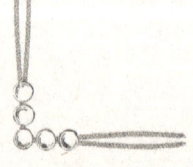

Okeanos clearly does not have. I must bring this to a head somehow and gather my husband up and bear him away to a refuge where we might restore his strength.

I open my mouth to begin with a bid for his freedom, when Vesuvius surprises me.

"I do not refer to *that* husband," he says.

I rip my gaze violently away from Oke's.

"What?" I ask in a gust. I can't even put a name to what my fear is, only that it is there and it is heavy on me.

Vesuvius holds the black pearl in his palm and his smile mocks me as it glitters there. "The pearl is opened by anything precious. For you, that's the grief of a god. For me, it was always the breath of my passion."

He blows gently on the pearl and I gasp.

What pours from the pearl on the end of a smoky tether is the spirit I caught a glimpse of before—the one that shifted and writhed and tangled under the grip of winding tentacles. Only this time, he is perfectly clear and those are not *his* tentacles at all. Rather, someone has brutally tied one severed tentacle in a neat clove hitch around this spirit's mouth and a second tentacle secures his arms to his sides in another tidy hitch. Both tentacles are angry and oozing at the wound site and are an *exact match* to the two missing from Vesuvius's body. I could almost swear they have been chewed off—as if he used his own teeth to gnaw himself into pieces.

Which, of course, he must have.

I barely notice Aurelius speaking in the background. "You bound him with your tentacles? Why?"

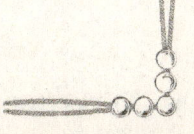

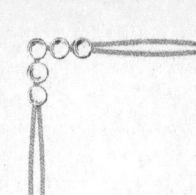

"When you must sleep within a confined space with an enemy who tries day and night to gain the upper hand over you, we shall see how quickly you decide he must be bound in some way," Vesuvius replies. "Besides, it would not have suited me to have him slip free when she opened my gates."

I grimace in disgust, but this terrible binding is not the worst of what I see, for in the grips of the tentacles is the soul I long for.

It's Lieve. Battered and bruised, eyes welling with tears above that terrible winding tentacle, but still mine. My heart lurches. I force myself past the air holding me and take a stumbling step forward only to be stopped by Aurelius's spatha, drawn lightning quick and hovering with the tip just in front of my throat.

"That's far enough, I think." He's on his feet now, still looking relaxed, but because I know to look for it, I see the stiffness in his left leg and the tightness around his eyes. "I think you'll give an answer to our question now."

"Yes, I want him back." The words burst from my lips. "I want Lieve of House Carnelian, husband to Queen Coralys of the Crocus Isles."

Lieve's soul seems to sag a little and his warm eyes meet mine, spilling out love. My breath catches, but the spatha point moves just enough to prick my throat, pinning me in place. Could I slap it away with the trident? Maybe. But also maybe not. Aurelius is insanely quick.

"I never did understand why people assumed you could only put one soul into these pearl prisons," Vesuvius says

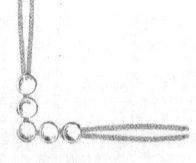

lightly. "Did you find it difficult to scoop up this mortal's soul and house him with mine, God of the Air?"

"You know as well as I, Vesuvius, that any god could do the same," Aurelius says, but he sounds like he doesn't want to keep explaining like Vesuvius does. He wants to get to the point, which I think might be to torture me. After all, that's what he did to Oke until somehow he lost his favorite toy.

Even so, he can't quite keep the look of triumph out of his eyes. This is his moment. All his plans coming to fruition, all his plots tightening into place.

"Treseano would be happy to know that he no longer needs to keep that dreadful creature in his sack to pay for this imprisonment."

I fight hard to school my face. My mind is racing. So Treseano, the God of Death, paid for this? But we killed his monsters. Shouldn't that have set Lieve's soul free? Unless. Something in my chest tightens and I can't quite breathe as I glance over at Vesuvius's tentacles. Perhaps they are what kept Lieve in there after we'd destroyed the monsters. And perhaps my tentacled enemy knew in advance that he was going to need something to keep Lieve in place once the God of Death was murdered.

The tentacles end in round suckers. Just like the impression on Treseano's face.

I think back to how we asked him where to find his old friend and of how we went in after Treseano cautiously. And how a many-tentacled former god had escaped just after he

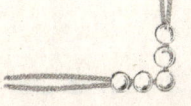

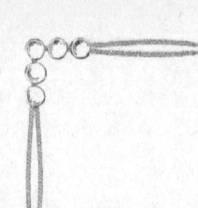

told us where to find the God of Death. He would have had plenty of time to get there first.

"All I had to do was overpower my rival," Vesuvius is saying, ignorant of my sudden revelation, "keep him bound, and be sure it was I who slipped from the pearl every time you called a soul out."

I push aside what he's saying. I push aside my revelations. None of them mean anything compared to what is before me.

My eyes lock onto Lieve's and in his are all the things I wished I could have said. All the "I love yous" we'll never say. All the regrets for the choices we made. All the deep rich feelings that can only be shared between a husband and wife who have been partners for years.

He rips his gaze away to steal a glimpse at Okeanos. I look, too, my gaze flicking from husband to husband, my chest suddenly tight and painful as the breath squeezes out of me.

Lieve's gaze returns to me and that's when I know that he understands. That he knows all that has happened since he died, and when his eyes meet mine, there's a steely acceptance—almost a bleakness in them—and my breath catches. He believes I've moved on without him. He thinks I've forgotten him. But how could I? The sun could burn to dust and still I would love him as the last warmth of the world crept away. Even if my heart also bends to another.

I want to fly to him, wrench those tentacles from his body, and tell him that I love him yet. That there's no chance of me

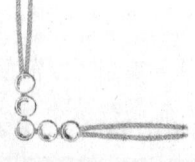

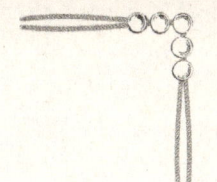

ever choosing someone who isn't Lieve, if there's a Lieve to choose.

His eyes crinkle around the edges like he's trying to smile at me. He's trying to reassure me. I shake my head vehemently.

"You have to let him go," I choke out. "You can't hold his soul this way."

"'Can' is a poor choice of words when you consider the evidence of your eyes." Vesuvius's words are barely louder than a whisper. "And to think—every time you called me, it could have been *him* who came out of the pearl, had he only been strong enough."

If I felt lightheaded before, I feel it even more now. I called Vesuvius out to advise me so many times and I had no idea that the one whispering in my ear kept my husband's soul captive throughout it all. I had no idea that I was opening the door to his tormentor and making him stronger. How different would things be had Lieve spilled out of the pearl to advise me? Would I have killed Okeanos? Would we be here now?

A wrenching gasp rips from my mouth.

"I'm waiting for you to congratulate me, Drowned Queen. For my genius, if you like, or for chewing off my own legs to bind the soul of your beloved. That takes grit, as well you should know. After all, did you not just slice off your own finger to treat with us today? Or if you do not respect me for that, then congratulate me for this—that you can see his soul at all. It ought to be hidden from all but I

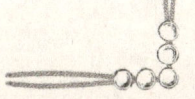

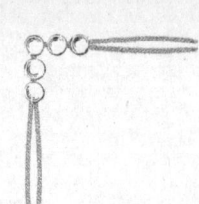

who holds its prison—but those tentacles I have him bound with reveal him to you as long as they are present. That's a clever trick, I think."

"I love you," I mouth in despair to Lieve, for there is no way out now. I am trapped coming and going and I cannot wriggle free. I think his eyes well more in response, but his nod is firm.

"And so we come to the point," Vesuvius says.

"At last," Aurelius says dryly. "You wear our patience thin as cheesecloth with all this talk."

"Will you offer me some bargain, Vesuvius?" I ask. My voice shakes and I no longer care. I have come to the end, I think. Both husbands dead. Both in the power of my enemies. And me, powerless to stop any of it. "What more do I have that I could give to you?"

"Five impossible tasks," Vesuvius says silkily. "Enough to raise the dead. Isn't that what you've been working on for Okeanos? I'm willing to bet that by now you have five complete. Though they need a different name than 'impossible' if you're the one fulfilling them."

"I'm not going to spend them bringing you back to life," I say stonily. But now my heart is beating even faster because I don't have five tasks. I only have four. I have misjudged.

He barks a laugh, but then he stills, growing very serious, and I know we've come to the point because Aurelius's eyes glitter with excitement, too.

"I think you came here tempted to use the power you've stored up for a particular purpose," the God of the Air

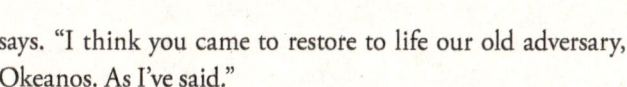

says. "I think you came to restore to life our old adversary, Okeanos. As I've said."

I swallow and glance at the god in question; I do not know if he even hears us. One arm spasms slightly, but he is far gone now, almost fully sunk beneath the Nightwaters. I don't know how a person could be deader than dead, but he seems like he is.

I clear my throat from the lump suddenly there and steal a look back at Lieve. His eyes are so full of understanding that I feel my stomach sink. It is as if he walked in and caught me breaking our vows, as if he's watched me lay my heart out before another, and my cheeks burn with the shame of it.

I muster all my strength to put on a bold face. "If you're planning to kill me, in order to prevent that, I hear it's harder to kill gods than you might think."

Aurelius smirks. "I kill less often than *anyone* might think. No, I don't plan to kill you, Drowned Queen. But I do have an offer for you."

He shifts his grip on his spatha just a little and I clench my teeth as I feel it draw blood and pain from where it nudges my throat.

"You can have the God of the Sea back," he says, and his eyes taunt me. I don't believe him. But he knows that.

"Or you can have something better," Vesuvius adds, and without warning he grabs Lieve and shoves him toward me.

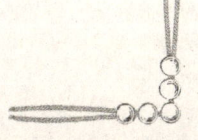

Chapter Thirty-Four

I gasp, arms reaching out instinctually. The trident drops from my grip as I try to catch Lieve, but the rules of the spirit world have not changed and he stumbles right through my arms and falls to the ground.

I'm at his side in a heartbeat, on my hands and knees. Aurelius must be allowing it, because his spatha hasn't plunged through my throat.

My eyes are locked onto Lieve's as he struggles against his bonds and my heart is aching with every flicker in the depths of his brown eyes. He was meant to be safely in the Nightwaters, somewhere far from the cares of this world. That I have been eating and sleeping and plotting revenge while he suffered, trapped with his tormentor, is criminal.

"I'm sorry, I'm so sorry," I gasp out, and my voice is faint with shame.

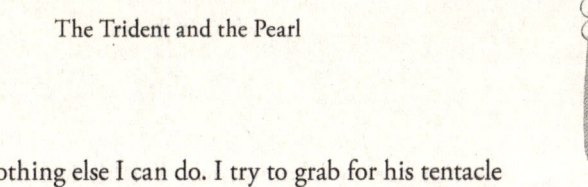

There's nothing else I can do. I try to grab for his tentacle bonds—those, to my horror, I can touch—but I cannot pull them free.

Lieve is shaking his head, his eyebrows drawn low and his eyes filled with a determined passion, but I don't know what he's trying to deny—my help, my affection, or this whole situation.

I wrench my gaze from his and look up at Vesuvius. I am trembling. Never have I felt so much like an animal that might charge and rip out someone's throat. I could lunge at him from here. I could rend him bone from bone with my teeth.

"Release him," I demand. "Release him from these terrible bonds."

Vesuvius's expression is aloof.

"I cannot. For I am pinned to this mortal world in the flesh. If you want to unbind him, then stab *him* with your trident, too, and make him the same living horror that I am—or better yet—much better, bring him back to life. Give him back his mortal body and future with all that power you've been storing up for your sea god husband. Mayhap he'll forgive you yet for the betrayal of marrying another. Mayhap you'll live your days together with joy."

Some instinct of mine is screaming in the back of my head that something is not right. I look from Vesuvius's face to Aurelius's—both incredibly calm. It's as if they're holding their breath. As if they're anticipating. As if far more rides on this decision now than my own happiness or the fates of two good men.

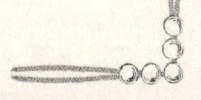

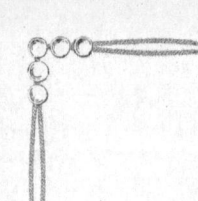

I glance to Okeanos, too, but his face is set, his eyes squeezed shut, and his breath rasps in his lungs in an uneven rhythm.

"Why would you offer me back my husband?" I ask, but I know he won't tell me the truth, I'm simply trying to grasp at strands of time while my mind races to think it through.

I turn my face to Lieve, agonized. He is still shaking his head, his eyes seeming to plead with me. And I know he saw me look to Okeanos first and I hope it doesn't sting for him like it does for me.

"We simply don't want you to bring the sea god back to life with the culmination of your five tasks. We want you to loosen your grip on godhood and his grip with it. Is that so terrible?" Vesuvius says, and there's a dangerous gleam in his eyes as he speaks. "You were, after all, the one who killed him in the first place. Surely you are not so fickle that you have changed your mind?"

Aurelius almost seems bored when he adds, "We are gods. We are not monsters. With one hand we might take, but with the other we give. Let us give you what you want most. Your old life back. Your husband. Your crown. Your mortality. Godhood never suited you in the first place."

And now my heart is thundering, because of course he is right. I never wanted to be a god. I am terrible at it and all I ever wanted is *exactly what they're offering me*. Why would I not take it if I could?

I look long into Lieve's frantic eyes, and if I thought my heart was broken before, it is pounded to dust now. I wish he

could speak to me. I wish even more that I could fall into his arms and he could make everything bad disappear. But he has never had that power.

And even if I could save him, and bring him back to life, what then?

When the two of us are cast living and mortal upon the shores of the Crocus Isles, will the people turn their prayers to Aurelius? They will go unanswered. My folk will be swallowed by storms and sea with no one to save them, plunged into a war that chews them up hundreds at a time, lashed by grim tides and the machinations of gods with no stronghold to which they might flee. But they are nameless, faceless people. Why should I sacrifice everything in my heart for a chance they might be safe? It's too much to ask from a person.

And what would be the result of bringing Lieve into that? Would he not also become nameless and faceless? His mortal life might be spent in a year or a day or an hour in the turmoil of the world in this god war, and I would have thrown aside everything Oke saved up to free his people only to buy Lieve a scant breath of time.

These two enemies of mine have ignored the third option. That I have not the power to save either husband. I can only walk away just as Okeanos pleaded for me to do and finish the tasks somehow. For I have only four: the vow of a god, the marriage of the drowned queen, the dead collected to serve, and the filled thimble. I didn't succeed in healing the Crown of the Sea. No wonder Oke called me betrayer.

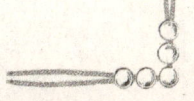

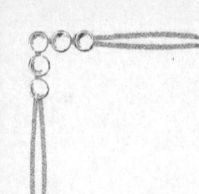

Betrayer. I close my eyes and let the word hurt the way it should.

Wait. My eyes snap open again.

It is as if I have stepped on the trigger of a trap and felt it click. I swallow hard and try to disguise what I have just realized, what he was trying to tell me with his last breath. "Turn the betrayer's heart" is our fifth completed task.

I speak quickly, trying to make them talk while my mind races.

"Why offer me this chance at all? Why not kill me now if the tasks are so great as to threaten you?"

"We are not so cruel," Aurelius says with a benevolent smile, but his smile is brittle and I know I've struck a nerve. Somehow, they do not think it would work simply to kill me. Or there is some nuance I am missing that makes my death unpalatable to them in this moment.

I swallow again and try to think, but my frantic brain can only see one way this can work and I know my time is running short.

I smile at Lieve and pour into my smile all the love of my heart, and I hate how it makes his expression shift from earnestness to something bleak.

Gritting my teeth, I hold out my palm, but I keep my eyes on Lieve, trying with all my might to be his anchor.

"I'll take the pearl, then," I say to Vesuvius. "I can hardly give Lieve back his life without freeing him from captivity. Though I think I'll need to seek instruction on how that's done."

Vesuvius smirks, but I can see the tension going out of his shoulders. I'm making the choice they wanted. I'm following their plan. It's only a matter of the details now. It galls me to bring him joy like this.

"Only the one who put the soul into the pearl can take it out again." Vesuvius hands the pearl to Aurelius. "If you'd do the honors."

Aurelius holds the pearl up between thumb and forefinger, looks me in the eye to be sure he has my attention, and then breathes delicately on the pearl. As he breathes it melts away as if he is blowing away dust.

My breath catches in my lungs and I shift, moving to turn my back to them so that my whole focus can be on my Lieve as we do this part. They have guessed—correctly—that I could never leave him to suffer. That I could never bear to watch him kept from his life. I'm memorizing his dark hair and the lines of his face. It's like I get to make this terrible decision all over again but better this time because this time he doesn't have to go drown beneath the waves far from the arms of the one he loves.

I lean over him and press my forehead to where his should be, but my tears fall right through him and he's fading now that the pearl is gone. I must act quickly before he drifts to the Nightwaters.

"Do it quickly," Vesuvius snaps. "Or he'll fade and it will be too late. Once he's mortal again you'll be able to rip my tentacles from him. Mayhap I'll even be able to reattach them."

"Unlikely," Aurelius opines.

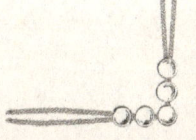

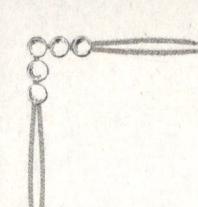

I whisper so quietly that I barely hear the words myself, "I love you forever."

And I can tell by the look in Lieve's eyes that he understands. But what I can't tell is whether or not he forgives me.

I don't look away. I don't dare. Not even when I clench my jaw as hard as I can and turn my heart.

The fifth task.

And as I repent of killing the God of the Sea and make my choice, I also do the one thing that has never come naturally to me at all—I pray. It's a prayer of desperation to a King of Heaven I hardly believe exists. It's a wild entreaty: desperate but doubting, vulnerable but firm. I offer him up the five tasks—complete now—to take and use. And I bid him use them as I ask.

It's so simple—too simple. And I hope that I haven't been misled in this as I have in so many things. I hope that I haven't been made a fool again. I hope these five tasks and all the suffering that went into their completion will culminate in this one vital thing—bringing one man back from death.

Nothing has ever wrenched me as this does. I am light-headed, as if I am watching someone else commit this act. And I steal one last, longing look into the eyes of my Lieve and choke on my sob as he looks beyond me to the Nightwaters. His face is lit with something not unlike the aura of divinity that fell on the gods during the Resurgence—and then he's gone.

The tentacles collapse to the ground as his spirit fades away and I swear he's taken my heart with him.

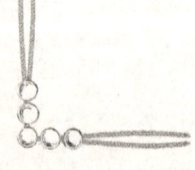

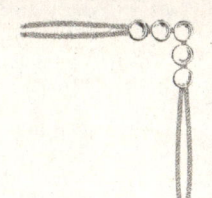

For it is not Lieve I have chosen to restore to life. He's slipped free and I've lost the last sight I'll ever have of him. Again.

Vesuvius lets out a sudden, sharp curse.

By the time I twist toward the noise, my vision is so warped by the welling tears that I don't immediately see that Vesuvius has snatched up my trident from where I dropped it to try to catch Lieve, or that he is rushing toward me with it lifted high in his hands, his many tentacles dragging across the marble.

I fling my hands up, but I'm too late.

The pain hits hard and sudden, overwhelming me before I know what has happened. I'm choking on it, gagging, seeing only black. I can't quite seem to drag in a breath and my heart... my betrayer's heart... it's not quite... my vision finally clears and everything is bursting in sharp violent color.

Vesuvius's face twists as he holds me down with his grip on the trident. I'm choking on my own blood. It's hot and iron-flavored between my lips.

Behind him, the moon is coming up. The garish red sky has bled out into black.

He's stabbed the trident through me by the handle, the weapon reversed, I stare at it as if this tiny detail is of enormous importance. Is he afraid that killing me the normal way will bring him bad luck? There's a story about that, I think, but when I reach for it, my memories are tattered and inaccessible.

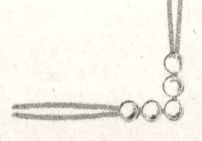

I claw weakly at the shaft of the trident. It gleams in the first glow of moonlight. I'd laugh at the irony, but I feel so very weak. There's blood on my chin. I can taste it with every sucking half breath. Vesuvius's tentacles wrap coldly and far too intimately around me, pinning me down in case the trident isn't enough to hold me, as if I would be as strong as Okeanos to climb back up the shaft stuck through me and strangle him with my bare hands.

I am certainly dying.

Just like Lieve did. Just like my mother and my father did and all those I have failed as both queen and god. My thoughts spiral down that track for a moment before I force them to focus again. Death is a fitting end for me, though I do not desire it and it has a very bitter flavor.

Vesuvius twists the trident and I scream as visceral pain twists through me, clogging all thought so that my whole world is red agony and his shadowed face is swimming before my eyes.

I'm so glad I freed Lieve from this.

So glad.

He can never be touched by these monsters again. If I still had a god, I'd pray I could join him.

"Just finish it. I grow weary of the display." Aurelius's voice is so distant that I barely can make out the disdain in it.

Everything is black. Everything is pain. I drag in one more burning half breath and then even that is gone and my brain panics, screaming as my mouth no longer can, and the scream seems to go on and on and on and on forever.

Forever is a terrible, lingering thing.
There is no relief in forever.
There is no forgiveness in eternity.

I do not know how long I persist through that black fall, but I can count every star, feel each individual nerve of my body and mind as they go out one by one like fires lit and snuffed over the breadth of history.

I do not plead for help. I do not pray at all. I deserve this, I try to remind myself, but it isn't working. I chose this, I try to explain, but in my panic, no explanation sticks. I am small and pitiable, so very insignificant, and yet all my fear and pain and loneliness is of utmost significance to *me* and I am drowned in it. The Drowned Queen.

And now Vesuvius will be God of the Sea again. For, just as in the story Markanos told me, he has come back to life by virtue of the trident barb and he has slain Coralys, who had inherited her godhood from Okeanos, and thus it will revert back to him. My tasks must not have been applied. For if they had worked, Okeanos would have taken his godhood back from me. But they have not worked.

This had to have been their plan all along. Lure me here with the bait of Okeanos or Lieve or both. Trick me into either a mortal existence, giving Vesuvius his godhood and letting Okeanos die since my immortality no longer sustains him, or as a backup, they could kill me, too, if I didn't use the tasks as they liked.

I shudder. Even in this world of darkness and forever, I shudder. I never want Vesuvius's gaze on me again, for I can

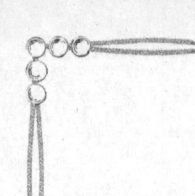

only imagine what other horrors he would visit on me given even half a chance. He has already broken my heart and then speared it through, and that seemed to cost him nothing at all.

But I am not sorry for what I chose, even though I will pay for it forever. Lieve's soul is safe where none can harm him. And I did try to do right by Okeanos.

I drift. The pain fades.

It's over now. I have crossed into the Nightwaters.

And just when I have accepted that this is the end, just when I feel as if I am spooling out like a lure on the end of a line tossed to catch a fish, flying into the unknown, pain hits me again like a blow to the chest and drags me back.

Chapter Thirty-Five

My eyes open suddenly, painfully, and I suck in a long, burning breath.

"...a very convoluted way to get what you wanted," Aurelius is complaining. His back is to me, outlined in silver light. "I mislike that it ended this way."

I try not to choke on the blood in my mouth. I must be silent. I must not draw their wrathful gaze.

Vesuvius's voice drips with bitterness. "Do not scold me when you've benefited just as thoroughly as I. My strength is vital to your plans."

I suck in another breath, shuddering around my broken chest. It feels like I have a gaping hole piercing right through it.

Oh.

Oh.

I do.

I'm shaking violently all over, but my lungs are working, dragging in each breath as if breathing is its own impossible task. The pain has changed. Rather than blurring everything around me, it has made my vision jagged with sharp focus. I can see every edge and sharp line in stark relief.

And that is how I am the first to see Okeanos leap over my body and lunge for them.

It is a dream, of course. I am seeing only what I wish was true.

He's gripping the trident. It is slick with my blood. It must have been when he ripped it from my chest that my consciousness returned.

He's shockingly adept with the weapon, but there's something slightly off. He favors his wounded leg more than ever before and it slows him more than I remember. The wound in his chest is gone, but the ones in his wrists remain, half-healed and crusted over.

He thrusts the trident into Vesuvius's side before that monster knows he's under attack, and while Vesuvius shouts his fury, Okeanos is already landing two more blows in quick succession. The new sea god is flung back, stumbling over his own tentacles and falling to the ground heavily. He thrashes, leaving great crimson arcs smeared across the marble of the floor, and Okeanos lunges forward to take advantage of his triumph.

And it's not a dream. I have lost on every other level, but I succeeded at this one thing. I brought Okeanos back. The fifth task worked.

I'm just beginning to sag with relief when Aurelius flicks a finger and Okeanos flies through the air, hits the marble, skids, and bowls into me.

I see black splotches across my vision and my hands claw in an effort to fight the spasm of agony that washes through me. I blink through it, concentrating on keeping my mind with me, on not giving way to the darkness. I do not want to make that long fall a second time.

I come back to stark reality just in time to see Vesuvius leap toward us. It's me he's aiming for and I can't so much as flinch.

But Okeanos thrusts himself upward, scrabbling across the marble to rise awkwardly, his trident drawn up and angled perfectly just in time to break a second point in Vesuvius's flesh.

Vesuvius roars, his tentacle frill expanding and rippling with the sound. He raises his arm, and in the distance I hear the roar of many waters.

Realization hits me like a punch to the chest. Vesuvius is the sea now and it is a furious, merciless sea.

That means I died. Just as I thought. But while the marriage vow tied me back to Okeanos and revived me with him by the blessing of the King of Heaven, it could not prevent the loss of my godhood or how it reverted back to Vesuvius.

I can feel the wind sweeping into the temple, and on it is the smell of the sea thick with death, and then Aurelius is there, gripping Vesuvius's arm and dragging him backward. Okeanos springs forward after him, but Aurelius flicks up

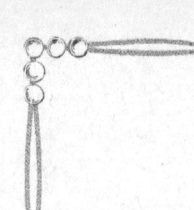

a hand, and just as his wall of air stopped me, so it stops Okeanos.

"Leave them," Aurelius orders, and his small smile is taunting and directed at my husband. "It brings me great pleasure to quit Okeanos in this state. Alive but mortal. Stripped of all power and glory. A faded flower. His dead bride on the floor in a pool of her own blood. What could be better than to watch your enemy die the drawn-out paltry death of a mortal and to know they taste their own frailty, choke on their own dust, and are powerless to save those they love? I might not have planned this, but now that it has arrived, I will have it exactly thus. Though I think I'll leave the wound." He pats his own thigh as a reminder. "It hardly bothers me, but as a mortal, it will certainly be the slow death of him. And this way, I'll know when it has done its job."

Vesuvius tries to shake him off, but Aurelius's grip tightens and in his eyes a warning flashes.

"I'll have it exactly thus, God of the Sea. And you shall gift it to me after all I've given you. Or are you not mindful of how I have brought you vengeance and godhood and a return to power all in one great maneuver?"

I reach for the sea in despair, testing his words. And he is right. I cannot feel the ocean. It is as if an empty void has filled the place in my heart that once sloshed with brine.

I shudder as I draw in a ragged breath. For if Vesuvius is God of the Sea, then Okeanos is not. By my choice... *my* choice... I chose wrong a second time.

And then the God of the Air forms a bowl with his hand, twists it, and they're gone, leaving me to cough a wretched, bruising cough that sprays my lifeblood across the white marble.

I do not know what happens for some minutes as I am consumed in a deadly battle to keep soul and body together. When I emerge, Okeanos's face is there.

I blink up at him, and maybe I am not thinking well, because his face is sweet to me, as if it is what I was searching for all along. His *life* is painfully sweet to me.

"You stupid, stupid girl," he's saying between clenched teeth. His shorn hair is as wild as the look in his eye, and I flinch away from something hot that falls from his cheeks and lands on mine. It tastes of salt and it stings. "Stupid, stupid, stupid."

It's a mantra: calming, detaching, a sweet rhythm to die to. He's trembling with it, too.

"Do not think you have my leave to die, Coralys." His voice comes out in a growl. "Do not believe I'll ever allow it now."

He's dragging me up into his arms and I choke on the moan trying to escape my chest. It's no matter. He's very warm. I think I'd like to die warm.

But why are his eyes swimming with tears and why is his expression so black?

"What have you done, Cora? What have you done?" he mourns.

I'm swaying ominously as he rises and stumbles, holding

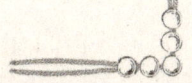

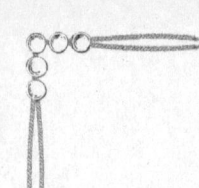

me in a sliding, lurching carry across the floor. He's so terribly gentle with me.

I want to tell him not to spend himself so, that I did not purchase his future so he could waste it in a futile attempt to save mine. But my life is leaking away like the tide washing out of the bay. I use my last breaths as best I can.

"I chose you," I murmur. I want to explain why, but the words cannot be grasped.

There's a hitch in his voice. "You should not have chosen me. And I curse you forever for choosing wrong."

But his hot tears spilling over me feel more like a baptism than a curse and the tender way he cradles my limp body to his chest feels more like guarding than damning. And I feel the hot press of his lips against my forehead as if he can restore life to me with nothing but a kiss.

He's whispering something fervently, but it sounds more like he is rendering a judgment than speaking to a dying woman. I think it is part of his wedding vow to me.

"Wherever your soul lingers, there will mine be, and if it slips into the Nightwaters, even there will I join you."

I am not comforted by the idea of him sailing off with me into the seas beyond this life. I gave too much to prevent that fate, though he murmurs it so sweetly.

He carries me out to the edge of the open-walled temple where I can see the wide sky. Though my neck will not support my head, the darkness of the ocean spreads out before me. On it bob the lights of ships far away, caught in the roar of the breakers. I feel again the terrible ache that I am exiled

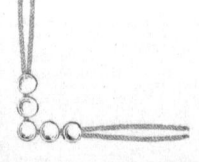

from the sea, for though I might sail upon her again, though I might dive into her waters and even drown in her depths, she is no longer me, she is no longer Oke, she is lost to us forever.

As if he hears my thoughts, Oke is whispering to me as he lays me down on the cold marble.

"Hold on, Drowned Queen, this is not the end. Hold on."

And then he's gone for a moment. Or maybe many moments. It's hard to be sure when every breath is agony and pain.

When he returns, he kneels down beside me and his hands are full of golden flowers, bloody around the edges. His wounds, I remember, were full of them, and some had fallen from where he'd been draped and had scattered across the marble floor. They smell of honey and frankincense—and no wonder when they are sprouted from the lifeblood of a god.

Perhaps they are like the flowers you lay upon the dead.

His face hovers over mine, lined with worry and so terribly beautiful. I had not expected that. I thought the beauty was because he was a god, but all the glory is faded and still he drags at the anchor line of my heart. There's a vulnerability to his face that wasn't there before, a deep sadness that makes him seem—for the first time yet—older than I am.

"Let's pray this works," he says, and he's mouthing some kind of prayer as—to my horror—he jams the flowers into the wound on my chest, packing them in like one might tamp a crack between cobbles.

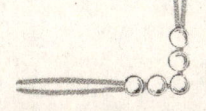

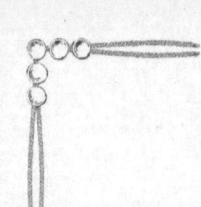

I would scream with the pain of it, but I can't quite catch my breath. I'm choking, gasping, caught in the grip of death and shaken hard.

My gaze is stuck on him, and I see when his face twists with despair and a single tear rolls down his cheek and lands in his messy handiwork.

I'm warm. Hot, even. As if my heart is the sun. It burns me up and flushes every inch of my skin, and I'm lost in the heat, the pain suddenly evaporating as if even it cannot stand against the inferno. I think I will live.

I have lost all sense of time and space, but I feel it as he binds up my ruined chest, packed with the remnants of his second death. And as he works, he makes me outrageous promises of revenge and a hope not yet entirely lost, though his eyes are as haunted as I'm sure mine must be. And the kisses this cold fisherman sets on the skin of my brow and my cheek feel as molten as hot gold. We are a matched set, we two contradictions—the Drowned Queen and her Fisher King.

The story continues in...

Book Two of the Fisher King

Acknowledgments

I would like to start by thanking my agent, Whitney Ross, who I have said many times ought to be credited as a co-author for how much of a partner she has been with me in the shaping of this story. Thank you for your passion, enthusiasm, and expertise! Without you, this story would not exist.

I'd also like to thank Brit Hvide and the whole Orbit team. Without Brit, half the romance would be missing from this novel, the hero wouldn't have been nearly as attractive, and we would all be missing out. Thank you for taking a chance on my work and believing in this book, Brit!

At the writing of this note, I don't know many of the hands through which this book will pass, but I trust I will wish I had thanked them by name before this process is complete. Thanks to Nick Burnham and Bryn A. McDonald and all the others at Orbit who will work on this project as it publishes.

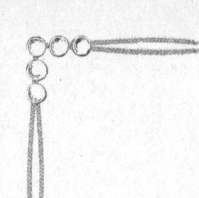

Acknowledgments

I owe a debt of gratitude to Melissa Frain and to her cat. You know what you did to get me here. Thank you.

I'd like to thank my friends in the Noble Order of Female Fantasy Authors for their advice and support, and especially Barbara, Janice, and Danielle, who made special efforts for this story.

Every line you have read here was heard first by my friend Melissa Wright, who frequently reminds me to please refrain from killing or maiming the characters you have come to love. If I have written something unforgivable, it is not her fault. She did all she could. Thank you, Melissa, for not dying three years ago and for being the only person other than my husband willing to let me bother them with my bookish rants and "discoveries" at any time of the day or night.

Thank you to my mom, who taught me to read and write when I was very small. Without you, I would not have fallen in love with books.

Thanks to my patient husband and the love of my life (to be clear, they're the same person), Cale, and to my sons, Neville and Leif, who are asked to look at fantasy art and listen to me talk at them about all things bookish while they are trying to work in the shop. I am responsible for at least two oil spills and multiple lost bolts in engine compartments. But without them, I would not be even a little bit grounded, and I owe them everything. Words are not enough for all you are to me.

And thanks be to God for not being anything like the

Acknowledgments

gods I have created and for permitting me this artistic latitude and a great deal of mercy besides.

Thank you, finally, to my readers. I hope you will feel that I have given you a book worth treasuring and that I upheld your trust. Stick with me, and there will be much more to come.

Sarah
Kakabeka Falls, February 2025

About the Author

Sarah K. L. Wilson loves writing because it is the only way to make a living and give back to the world when your primary skill is an overactive imagination and a tendency toward anxiety-fueled daydreams. She can be found in the outdoors of northern Ontario with her young boys and beloved husband, reading a book or fending off her husband's pet turkeys with a straw broom.

Find out more about Sarah K. L. Wilson and other Orbit authors by registering for the free monthly newsletter at orbit-books.co.uk.

RAISING READERS
Books Build Bright Futures

Dear Reader,

We'd love your attention for one more page to tell you about the crisis in children's reading, and what we can all do.

Studies have shown that reading for fun is the **single biggest predictor of a child's future life chances** – more than family circumstance, parents' educational background or income. It improves academic results, mental health, wealth, communication skills, ambition and happiness.[1]

The number of children reading for fun is in rapid decline. Young people have a lot of competition for their time. In 2024, 1 in 10 children and young people in the UK aged 5 to 18 did not own a single book at home.[2]

Hachette works extensively with schools, libraries and literacy charities, but here are some ways we can all raise more readers:

- Reading to children for just 10 minutes a day makes a difference
- Don't give up if children aren't regular readers – there will be books for them!
- Visit bookshops and libraries to get recommendations
- Encourage them to listen to audiobooks
- Support school libraries
- Give books as gifts

There's a lot more information about how to encourage children to read on our website: **www.RaisingReaders.co.uk**

Thank you for reading.

hachette UK

---

[1] OECD, '21st-Century Readers: Developing Literacy Skills in a Digital World', 2021, https://www.oecd.org/en/publications/21st-century-readers_a83d84cb-en.html

[2] National Literacy Trust, 'Book Ownership in 2024', November 2024, https://literacytrust.org.uk/research-services/research-reports/book-ownership-in-2024

Enter the monthly Orbit sweepstakes at www.orbitloot.com

With a different prize every month,
from advance copies of books by
your favourite authors to exclusive
merchandise packs,
**we think you'll find something
you love.**

facebook.com/OrbitBooksUK
@orbitbooks_uk
@OrbitBooks
orbit-books.co.uk